Stoney Beck

STONEY BECK

A Novel

by

Jean Houghton-Beatty

BOSON BOOKS
Raleigh

Published by
Boson Books, a division of C&M Online Media Inc.
3905 Meadow Field Lane
Raleigh, NC 27606-4470
cm@cmonline.com
Tel: 919-233-8164

ISBN: (ebook) 978-0-917990-47-2
ISBN: (print) 978-0-917990-84-7

http://www.bosonbooks.com

Cover art by Joel Barr
Designed by Amanda Faber

Dedication

To my brother Jack, who suggested the title for this book.

Acknowledgements

Special thanks to my wonderful critique group for their encouragement and friendship—Ann, Carolyn, Judy, Lisa, Nancy, Maggie and Ruth Ann.

Chapter One

Jenny Robinson bent over the casket and kissed her father's cheek. It felt cold and hard as stone. "It's all over, Dad," she whispered. "Over at last. You can rest now."

Dry-eyed, all the tears wrung out of her ages ago, she took one long, last look, then turned and joined her mother on the front row of Delshire Methodist. Her mother's brother slipped into the pew beside them and for the first time that day, Jenny's eyes grew misty. Uncle Tim had been a rock during these final days. She reached for her mother's hand, tightening her grip as the undertakers closed the coffin lid over Michael Robinson's face.

After the service and burial in Sharon Memorial Park, they came back to the house. Jenny lagged behind Mother and Uncle Tim as they walked up the path. She climbed the steps and stood on the wide columned veranda, staring down at the front yard, then across the street to the other houses. It was the middle of April and the huge willow oaks, planted over fifty years ago on both sides of the road were coming into full leaf. She had lived on this street nearly all her life, gone to Myers Park High School, gotten her degree from Queens College, which was no more than three miles from her house. Before he had become sick, her dad had said there was no place in the world any prettier than Charlotte in April, all decked out in her best spring dress. And he was right. Two days before he'd died, she and Uncle Tim had pushed her father's bed up close to the window so he could see for the last time the dogwoods and azaleas in bloom. When Jenny pointed out the cardinal perched on the dogwood tree, her father smiled but it was hard to know if he had been aware.

As cars began pulling into the driveway or parking on the street, Jenny pushed open the door and went inside. She was in time to see her mother climbing the stairs, and knew she wouldn't come back down until everybody had gone. Earlier she'd said no way could she handle the hoards of people expected to fill the house. She'd take a tranquilizer and spend a couple of hours in her room. Jenny sent up a fast prayer that her mother could somehow make it through the next few weeks without falling apart. The long agony of her father's sickness had taken its toll on her mother, who'd been suffering on and off for the last couple of years with clinical depression. Jenny could hardly remember the way things used to be.

Neighbors had brought most of the food, and now casseroles, ham, fried chicken and cakes covered every inch of the dining room table. People began straggling into the house, fixing a plate of food before settling themselves in the living room. Between slicing ham and serving plates, Jenny heard the whispers.

"Terrible way to go," old Mrs. Newsome said, her mouth full of lemon pound cake. "I'd never heard of Huntington's disease until it hit the Robinsons."

Bertha Trumble, a member of the church choir, sipped her coffee. "If you ask me, it's a blessing the poor soul's gone. The funeral parlor did a good job on him though. Did you see him? He looked almost normal."

Mr. Feldman from across the road bit into a ham sandwich. "It's Jenny I feel sorry for. I wouldn't want that hanging over my head. It's like facing a firing squad."

"Oh, wow," said sixteen-year-old Wesley Pratt from the house next door.

Jenny shivered as the boy sank his teeth into a drumstick, then she walked out of earshot.

For the next hour, she busied herself making sure everything went smoothly, at the same time longing for the time when everybody would be gone.

After a while, Uncle Tim gathered some friends from the old days around the piano for a sing-a-long. There was "Abide with Me," and "Amazing Grace," then songs like "Michael Row the Boat Ashore," and even her Dad's favorite, "Peggy Sue."

Mrs. Newsome brushed the crumbs off her skirt onto the carpet, and got to her feet. She reached for another piece of cake, black forest this time, and wrapped it in a paper napkin. She rolled her eyes at Bertha, who also stood up. "Strange carryings on for a funeral if you ask me," she said, loud enough for Jenny to hear. "The hymns were all right but these songs are a mockery. That brother of Beverly's has got some nerve."

Jenny forced a smile as she walked over to the women. "Hasn't he though," she said, smiling and deliberately misunderstanding. "Uncle Tim wanted to do this for Dad. It's a celebration of his life, you see. And Dad, well he just loved Buddy Holly singing 'Peggy Sue.'"

Before they saw the tears, Jenny turned away and went to stand by Uncle Tim. She put her hand on his shoulder, and looked at her father's picture on top of the piano, taken years ago when he was well. He laughed right at her, from the golf course the day he bagged the fluke of his life, a hole in one. Maybe if she listened really hard, she might still hear him laugh. Nobody had a laugh as warm as his. Nobody. Uncle Tim looked up from banging out "Old Man River" and winked at her. *You're doing great*, the wink said, *hang in there*. Jenny winked back and smiled. Maybe the good times would come back now. Life did still have to go on.

By six o'clock, everybody had gone except Uncle Tim who stayed for a final cup of coffee. Jenny walked with him to the door, her arm through his, hanging on, hating to see him go.

"Thanks, Uncle Tim. For everything."

"I wish I could have done more. I was out of town half the time. Most of it fell on you. God knows, your mother hasn't been much help."

"Ah, Mom did try," Jenny said, "Thank the lord for Hospice, though. Her nerves are acting up again and she's popping pills like crazy. I'd hate for her to have to go back to that clinic."

"Let's give her a week or two," her uncle said. "Maybe she'll snap out of it. It's time for us to pick up the pieces. That's what your dad would want."

Jenny snapped her fingers. "Hang on while I fix you a doggy bag. You hardly ate a bite all afternoon. I watched you. There's enough food left to feed an army and it'd be a crying shame to waste it."

Tim watched his niece walk to the kitchen, shoulders slumped now that the need to be strong was behind her. The lump in his throat was a stone he couldn't swallow. All through last night's receiving of friends and today's funeral and long afternoon, Jenny had taken charge, that brave smile of hers glued on. She had chatted with neighbors and friends, thanked everyone for coming. From where he stood, Tim could see his sister Beverly in the room across the hall, hunched on the sofa, eyes downcast, as though counting the filaments per square inch in the carpet. He stepped inside and kissed her cheek. "Jenny's all you've got now, Bev. Please, for her sake, try to hold on. She's grieving too." Gently he shook his sister's shoulder. "Beverly, are you listening?"

"I heard you," his sister said without looking up. "All those people in the house. I just wasn't up to it. Jenny's not so sensitive. She's tough. Can handle anything."

"She's a daughter in a million and missing Michael just as much as you are. Not only that, she's frightened. How about trying to put yourself in her shoes."

He straightened up as Jenny returned from the kitchen, carrying a cardboard box. "There's a plate for when you get home, and a couple of containers for your freezer."

"Were there any deviled eggs left?" he asked as they walked toward his car.

"Six. They're all in there."

He put the food on the back seat then held his niece at arms length while he examined her pale, tired face. "OK. Now remember, I'll be at the Hyatt in San Francisco for the next ten days. I've put the number on the pad by the phone. Get some rest. And I want to see some color in those cheeks by the time I come back."

"Will you quit worrying about me," Jenny said. "And try to have some fun yourself. Don't let one lousy marriage turn you off women forever. A good-looking man like you. What a waste." She pushed the hair out of her eyes and looked at her watch. "It's rush hour, Uncle Tim, and the traffic's crazy. Keep your mind on the road and call when you get home."

He got in the car, rolled down the window. "When I get back we'll go on up to the lake. We'll get the boat out and see if you can still ski. Bring some of your friends." After he backed into the road, he gave her a thumbs up then headed home.

Jenny watched until her uncle's car had turned the corner, and then went inside. In her father's bedroom, the tears she had held back filled her eyes. She blinked and they rolled down her cheeks. She sat on his bed and ran a hand over the spread, remembering the good times before her father's illness. Her last happy memory of him was when she received her high school diploma. He and her mother had been so proud. Even now Jenny could see their laughing, happy faces. They had made her close her eyes, while Uncle Tim drove into the driveway with her graduation present, a brand new Honda. A week from that very day, the first sign of Huntington's disease showed itself. From then on, nothing was ever the same.

***

Ten days after the funeral, Jenny placed a small stack of sympathy cards on the kitchen table, set a mug of coffee in front of her mother and a can of Diet Pepsi at her own place. As she pulled up a chair, her mother asked the question for at least the hundredth time.

"When are you going to get tested?"

"I don't know. Soon maybe."

"You've been saying that for years."

"I might not ever do it. This way, I've still got that little ray of hope. But if they tell me for sure.... First Grandma, then Aunt Mary and Uncle Bob. Now Dad. Think of it, Mom. All of them gone. My genes must be crawling with it." She snapped the tab on the can and wiped the top with a tissue. "Still, I'm only twenty-three. It'll be years before anything shows up. And now you won't be needing me at home, I'll get a job. I'd like something to do with travel, maybe a flight attendant." Her voice became softer, as if talking only to herself. "But marriage is out for me. I'd never saddle a husband with what you've had to go through."

Beverly backed away from those eyes. Distant now, remote, they looked through her and beyond, to a barren lonely place she couldn't go. Her breath caught in her throat as the strangled words came out. "What if I told you your dad wasn't your real father."

The can stopped halfway to Jenny's mouth. "What's that supposed to mean?"

"You were never told the truth about your birth."

There, she'd said it at last. The rest would be easy.

"What truth? What are you talking about?"

Beverly picked up a sympathy card. She glanced at it and let it fall. "Michael Robinson was not your father, Jenny. Not your real one. I mean he wasn't your biological one."

"Of course he was." Jenny's voice was taut, barely above a whisper. "Why are you saying this? Don't you think I'd know if he wasn't?"

"Would you? Haven't you ever wondered why you didn't favor him? Him with his red hair and freckles. You tall, him short."

It was the way her mother said it. Her face had turned white as though the words had drained the very life out of her. "I thought I favored your side of the family," Jenny said. "My hair's lighter than yours, but we've both got grey eyes."

"Yes, I know, but still—" Her mother looked down at her nails, began to pick at the rough edges.

"Why are you saying this?" Jenny said, even as goose bumps popped out on her arms. "Dad would have told me. He wouldn't let me think—"

"He didn't know. Nobody did."

Jenny pushed back her chair and got up, did a turn about the room, then plopped back down. "What are you saying? Are you trying to tell me Dad didn't know? That he didn't know whether or not I was his little girl?"

Her mother reached across the table and gripped her daughter's arm. "I lied to him, Jenny. I lied to Tim as well. I had to. I lied to everyone. It was for your sake as well as my own."

Jenny pressed the can of Pepsi against her face as the temperature in the room suddenly shot up about five degrees. "For God's sake. Who is my father then? Where is he?"

Her mother shook her head. "I don't know."

"You mean——"

"I mean apart from being born in that English village I told you about, it's all been one big lie after another."

"Hold it." Jenny raised a hand as her mother opened her mouth to say more. "How about if you give it to me all at once. Let's get it over with."

Beverly ran a finger round the rim of her coffee mug. Then, in short disjointed sentences, told Jenny that she and her boyfriend Michael Robinson had made love the night before she left home for a summer student exchange course at the University of Edinburgh. On her way to Scotland, she'd broken her journey in the Lake District, renting a cottage at the Hare and Hounds Inn in Stoney Beck. But the village was a cold Godforsaken place, with the weather more like February than July. She hated the Lake District, hated England and everything in it. That was until the third day, when the sun came out. Then this dream of a guy materialized from out of nowhere and sat beside her on a bench outside the inn. Even though Charles Woodleigh was older than Beverly by about three or four years, he was also a student, and had a room in a farmhouse just outside the village. He was easy to talk to and made her laugh. Suddenly, things weren't so bad.

Jenny gulped a mouthful of Pepsi and leaned against the chair back. "Are you trying to tell me I'm the prize you got for a quickie? A one-night stand?"

Beverly raised a hand to her cheek as if Jenny had struck her. "It wasn't like that. I was in the Lake District for almost a month. We fell in love and it wasn't until the second week...the cottage was hidden a bit by trees and we were very careful. You were conceived there." Beverly reached for her purse propped against the breadbox and pulled out a slim hardback book that she handed to Jenny. "I've kept this at the back of my closet all these years. It's all I have to remember him by."

Jenny stared at the title: *Sonnets from the Portuguese.* Inside, a forget-me-not and four-leaf clover were pressed between the pages and on the same page as "How Do I Love Thee?" was a snapshot of her mother as a young girl. Her long, wavy brown hair blew about in the wind. The tall young man beside her had a cap of blonde curls and a movie star face. His arm was around her waist and they laughed into the camera. Jenny stared at the picture for a long time then continued to leaf through the pages. On the back cover he had written, *I'll love you always, Charles.*

While Beverly's restless hands picked at her nails, she told Jenny that Charles had said it was love at first sight for him. She thought she loved him too, but when she realized he was serious, she had second thoughts. How could she, a girl who had been brought up on Carolina sunshine and an oh-so-different way of life, ever be happy with this suddenly very serious man. England was a bleak, alien place, where it hardly ever stopped raining. Beverly had tried to let him down gently, but in the end she had laughed and said she hadn't meant for things to get out of hand. The very next day she was on the first train out of there.

Beverly took the poetry book from Jenny and held it against her chest. "When I didn't get my period, I wasn't worried. I'd never been all that regular. But by the second month, I was a basket case. I packed my things and went back to Stoney Beck to tell Charles."

Jenny was by now on the edge of her chair, back rigid, hands clenched together. "What did he say?" she whispered to her mother.

"He wasn't there. Folks at the farm said he'd left two weeks before. Something about being needed at home." Beverly picked the pilling from the sleeve of her old black sweater as she told Jenny that Charles Woodleigh had left no forwarding address. He was from London, but had never said what part, or if he did, Beverly wasn't listening. She called every Woodleigh in the phone books, but none had a Charles in the family. Making a last ditch effort, she placed an ad in the local paper, then another in one of the nationals.

"I never found him. Don't know whether he's alive or dead." She picked up one of the envelopes, and while she tore it into strips, told Jenny it wasn't until she lost Charles that she realized she did love him after all. She checked in with the village doctor who was very kind, even arranging for a midwife to visit her. By then it was fall and with business at the inn slow, the owners let her rent the cottage for a song. Socialized medicine had covered her hospital bills. She had always thought foreigners had to pay at least something toward their medical expenses, but she didn't. Nothing to worry about, the doctor had told her. It hadn't cost a penny. Beverly had told the doctor and a few others she knew in the village that Michael, her American boyfriend, was the baby's father. They had both gotten carried away the night before she left home. When the doctor had advised her to let the baby's father know, Beverly replied she didn't want to force Michael into marriage. She would tell him when she finally returned home.

Beverly gave a deep sigh. "But of course you weren't his," she said without looking at Jenny. "I did write to him, but didn't tell him I was pregnant. I just said it was over between us. By then, you see, I was praying for Charles to come back."

She pulled at the rough spot on the nail she'd been toying with since she'd sat at the table. It came off right down to the quick. She winced and stared at the nail as blood oozed from the painful spot. "I never forgot that doctor," she said. "Just last year, I got up enough nerve to send him your picture. Silly maybe, but he'd been so kind and I wanted to show you off. I still didn't want to tell him where we lived so I didn't put a return address. I asked Tim to mail it on one of his trips out west. Thought he might ask me why, but he didn't. Guess he had his mind on his divorce." She spread her arms on the table, palms upward. "So you see, you don't need to worry about getting Huntington's disease. There isn't a drop of Robinson blood in your veins."

Jenny gathered up the thank you notes, trying to stop her hands from trembling, but it all became too much. She flung the notes across the room. "I honest to God don't know how you could have put me through this." She drank the rest of her Pepsi, slaking her parched dry throat, and crushed the empty can between her hands. "For years I've been terrified I'd end up like Dad."

"I know, I know. I kept hoping you'd get tested. Then I was afraid. I thought I'd let it go too long. That if I told you, you might hate me."

"Is this why you never took me to see Gramps and Grandma?"

Beverly nodded. She'd lied to them too, said she loved England and had taken a job in a bookshop. The last part was true. It helped to pay the rent and get her through. When she finally did come home, her strict high-and-mighty parents said they were ashamed of her. Thank God for Tim, who not only sent her money to come home but also even found Michael Robinson.

Beverly's eyes were huge in her ashen face. "Michael thought you were his, so I just went along. I couldn't believe it when he asked me to marry him. We went to London on our honeymoon and applied to have your birth re-registered. Then when we got back to North Carolina, we moved from Asheville to the beach in Wilmington and then to Charlotte where nobody knew us."

Beverly stretched out her hand to Jenny but let it fall when Jenny kept her own hands in her lap. "Please, Jenny, try to understand for my sake. In my own way, I loved Michael dearly. I owe him my life, my very sanity. I couldn't take a chance on him finding out. But most of all there was the—"

The grandfather clock in the hall sounded out the hour. Jenny's mother jumped, her hand covered her mouth. It was as if the chime sent a warning.

"What is it? Why did you stop?"

"There's nothing else to tell. It's just that—" There was an edge of something in Beverly's voice that wasn't there before.

Jenny pushed back her chair and got to her feet. It was getting dark and she switched on the lights. She studied her mother's face, saw the lipstick bleeding into the furrowed skin around her mouth. There were bags under her eyes and her hair, mostly gray now, was wild and unkempt. She was only forty-seven yet had the face of a woman in her late fifties, sixties even. Jenny compared her with the picture on the dresser behind her: a slender laughing girl in shorts and blouse, hamming it up for the camera, tennis racquet poised over her head. Jenny remembered happier times when her pretty mother laughed a lot, had friends. But the years of missing her first love, guilt over deceiving her daughter and husband, then the final strain of caring for him, had all taken their toll.

Beverly sat very still, cradling her sore finger, her face wet with tears. "Please, Jenny, say something. I know I should have told you and I'm so sorry I didn't. But I've always loved you. At least tell me you don't hate me."

Jenny stared at her mother. "How could you do this to me. I've been haunted by this worry for years and all you can do is sit there and tell me you're sorry." She pushed her chair back and got to her feet. "I need time to think. I'm going out."

She went into the utility room and changed out of her ordinary shoes into her Reeboks. For a couple of minutes, she stood on the stoop, then went back into the kitchen. Her mother was still in the chair, her head in her hands. "You'd better put some salve on that finger. It could get infected."

As Jenny jogged past the local deli, she saw a couple of friends sitting by the window so went inside. She joined them for coffee but didn't stay long. Even though they tried to hide it, Jenny saw the looks, felt the distance between them widen. It was all she could do not to scream. She didn't need their pity. She was no more at risk than they were. But explaining what she'd just found out would take all night, and did it really matter any more?

Two hours later she climbed the stairs to her mother's room. The light shone under the closed door and Jenny could hear the TV. She had her hand on the knob then changed her mind and went back downstairs to her own room. That night, she lay in bed, hands behind her head and stared at the ceiling. All these years she'd had a death sentence hanging over her head. And now, even though she'd loved her father dearly, her heart began to dance. She couldn't help it. She was free, free. Life was wonderful, fantastic, and with a bit of luck she could maybe live to be a hundred.

Her thoughts drifted now across the Atlantic. If her real father was alive, he was probably married and had forgotten all about his American love. It was all a long time ago. Jenny could never be one of those kids who couldn't rest until they'd found their biological parents. And besides, what proof did she have? She believed every word of her mother's story, but Charles Woodleigh could very easily slam the door in her face. She sat up in bed and hugged her knees as one scenario after another trekked through her mind. What if he wasn't married? What if he were a bachelor, or widowed even? What harm could there be in at least finding out that much?

Earlier, Jenny had wanted to pay her mother back for all the hurt. Now, though, in the dark of her room, all Jenny saw was the anguish and hopelessness etched in every line of her mother's tormented, weary face. She pushed back the covers to get out of bed and go to her, then hesitated. Surely her mother was asleep by now. Jenny lay back down. First thing tomorrow, she would tell her mother she still loved her.

***

Beverly sat on the side of her bed and applied ointment to her finger, then wrapped it with a Band-Aid. After all these years, she still thought of Charles Woodleigh. And tonight, even with Michael just gone, the memory sneaked in. She still remembered the color of Charles's sweater. Loden green. When he had said he loved her, how insensitive she must have seemed when she'd laughed, patted his cheek, and then closed the cottage door for the last time. For the thousandth time Beverly speculated. Had Charles left the Lake District because he couldn't bear it without her? Or, more likely, had he been afraid she would come back pregnant? Was this the reason he had vanished? And now, Michael, the second man Beverly had loved, had gone away. Dying was a form of desertion, wasn't it? She had at last told Jenny everything, she would be the next to leave. They all did in the end. Since the onset of Michael's illness, Beverly had been hospitalized twice with clinical depression. Now she felt the onset of another one. Sleep was almost impossible, even with the medicine. If she did somehow fall into a jerky sleep, she woke early, anxious, and jittery. Concentration was impossible. Combing her hair or even putting on lipstick was turning into a monumental task. Once again she was sinking into the mire and just too sick of it all to pull herself out.

Out of habit, Beverly switched on TV. With the volume turned down low, she watched a few minutes of the movie *Casablanca*, at the same time thinking of her confession to Jenny. She was sorry now she had mentioned the Lake District, even told Jenny the name of the village. If her daughter ever decided to search, she now knew where to start and there was more than a slim chance she would discover the one secret Beverly had still not been able to tell. Still, Jenny had been freed at last from the Robinson curse. She could now marry, have a husband and family. Surely this was something, some sort of restitution.

Beverly bit her lip. Wouldn't it be better to tell Jenny the rest of the story, rather than risk her daughter finding out for herself? Beverly had sworn to herself that she would never tell anyone this side of the Atlantic. She would carry her secret with her into the hereafter. Her palms began to sweat. Maybe there wouldn't be a hereafter if she didn't tell Jenny everything.

Even though she drank hardly at all, tonight Beverly brought a bottle of wine up to her room. The sleeping pills hadn't worked for the last couple of nights and if she didn't get some sleep tonight, she would be a basket case by tomorrow. She went into the bathroom and opened the medicine cabinet. Her brand new bottle of fifty Xanax pills as well as her last four sleeping pills stood on the shelf. She filled a glass to the brim with wine and swallowed two of the sleeping pills along with five or six Xanax. With her hand on the light switch, she turned back and picked up the last of the sleeping pills. Surely this would be enough to give her a good night's sleep. She gulped the glass of wine; then filled the glass again just to make sure.

Beverly opened the drawer in the nightstand and took out her notepad and pen. She would explain everything in a note and perhaps sometime tomorrow she would put the note on Jenny's pillow. *Dear Jenny*, she began, and hummed along while Sam played "As Time Goes By," for Ilsa in Rick's Café.

***

There was no elaborate funeral for Beverly Robinson. A graveside service, family only. Jenny felt the warm Southern sun on her arms and held on tight to Uncle Tim's hand. While Reverend Lancing intoned *let not your heart be troubled*, a wren sang at full throat in the ligustrum bushes nearby. Afterwards, she and Uncle Tim went back to the house and sat on the back porch, drinking cup after cup of coffee.

Jenny rubbed her burning dry eyes, then brought her fist down hard on the arm of the Adirondack chair. "This is all my fault. Why couldn't I see how desperate she was."

Tim Pender leaned forward, elbows on his knees. "Jenny, for God's sake. You'd just had one hell of a shock yourself. Your mother understood. She probably expected a lot worse. And we've gone over this a hundred times. What about that salve she'd put on her finger? She even bandaged it? You don't do that if you plan on killing yourself. And you swallow all the pills, not just a few. It was an accident, the combination of wine and pills."

Jenny looked up at the ceiling, saw the huge cobweb in the corner, the spider waiting while the little bug struggled in vain to escape. She had this insane urge to get on a chair and sweep the cobweb away, letting the bug loose. That very morning she had made a halfhearted attempt to dust the furniture. There was dust on everything. Ashes to ashes, dust to dust.

She took the sheet of folded notepaper she'd found on her mother's bed and handed it to her uncle. The writing was shaky, uncertain, as if written by a very old person.

> *My Dearest Jenny,*
> *Even though I've freed you from the Robinson curse, I haven't told you everything about your birth. For years I've wanted to tell you the whole story but it was too hard. After you've read this letter, I pray you won't hate me. But you have a right to know and I'd give the world—*

The unfinished sentence trailed away down the center of the page. Tim's brows drew together as he read the note, then he stared out the window at the cluster of red and white azaleas in the far corner of the yard. "I don't have any idea what she was trying to say. Don't guess we'll ever know now."

He turned back to his niece, her eyes wide in her pale, anxious face. "Just remember, Jen, in spite of everything, your mother loved you. She didn't mean to kill herself. All she was trying to do was get a good night's sleep. So for God's sake get yourself off this guilt trip."

At the inquest ten days later, a verdict of accidental death was recorded.

Chapter Two

Two months after her mother's funeral, Jenny stood with her Uncle Tim, waiting her turn at the ticket counter of Charlotte International Airport. After she had sold the house for more than expected, she placed the furniture she wanted to keep in storage, and sold the rest in a yard sale. Her mother's one hundred thousand dollar life insurance policy came as a surprise. After Jenny had paid off all the family debts there was enough left over to buy a decent condo when she returned from Europe.

"Promise you'll call often," Uncle Tim said, his hands stuck in his pockets. "I don't like the idea of you traipsing around England alone. It's too soon after all you've been through."

Jenny stuck her arm through his. "I've got to get away, Uncle Tim. Can't you see that?"

"Yes, but do you have to go so far and especially there? Why couldn't you have picked somewhere closer? Myrtle Beach or Charleston."

"It was Dr. Bissell's idea. And you're the one who said he was the best shrink in town."

Uncle Tim rolled his eyes. "I must have been out of my mind."

"No, you were right. He's been good for me. He said this trip might help to come to terms with Mom's—with Mom doing what she did. He said to keep telling myself over and over that it wasn't my fault. Guilt can kill you if you let it, he said. It'll give you phobias or make you depressed."

Uncle Tim moved forward a couple of steps. "He's exaggerating. These guys all do this. It's their way of keeping you coming back."

"Maybe, but I think I've already got a phobia."

Her uncle turned to look at her. "What do you mean? You're not afraid to fly are you?"

Jenny gave a brittle laugh. "No, I love flying. But all of a sudden I've got this awful weird fear of hospitals. A friend from college was having her appendix out in Presbyterian. It was just the other week. I went to see her, or at least I tried to. I know you'll think this is nuts, but I couldn't even drive into the parking lot. I even drove down Elizabeth Avenue and back up to the hospital, trying to get myself together. In the end, though, I just drove off. It was real strange and I can't explain it. Now I can't even drive past the place without being afraid I'll get sucked in. And it's not just Presbyterian. I feel just as bad when I pass any hospital."

Uncle Tim pushed her suitcase along with his foot as they moved closer to the counter. "This has come on with you spending so much time in places like that. All the time Michael was sick, your mom's been in and out of clinics. But what you've got isn't a real phobia. Nobody likes visiting hospitals, Jen. Maybe Bissell's right. Three or four weeks away from everything should do you good."

"I'll be safe enough with the tour group in London. Then it's on to the Lake District. Stoney Beck sounds nice, a quiet little place." She gave him a playful tap on the shoulder. "Now don't you be worrying about me. I'll call you soon as I get there."

"You'd better. And be careful, for God's sake. Stay in good safe places. You can afford it."

"Next please," the man behind the counter said. Uncle Tim lugged Jenny's suitcase onto the scale, while she handed over her passport and ticket.

As they walked toward security, she linked her arm through his. "You think I'll be searching for my real father, don't you, but you're wrong. Oh, I might look for his name in phone books here and there, but that's as far as I'd go." She hitched her carry-on luggage higher on her shoulder. "Still, I have a right to see where I was born. Ever since Mom told me, I've felt this tug. And we both know she didn't tell either of us everything."

"You're thinking about that note aren't you?"

Jenny reached up to kiss him. "You'd better be giving me my hug. I need to go on through to the gate and for cryin' out loud, will you quit worrying about me."

"What. Me worry? Are you crazy?"

His face suddenly cracked into a smile. "Watch out for the English, Jen. They've got no sense of humor, none at all. They drink warm beer for God's sake, and they're the world's worst cooks. They eat kidneys, and there's this blood sausage as well as some sort of smoked fish they call a kipper. And you can forget about grits or cornbread. On top of that, it never stops raining. If the sun does come out, all the English raise their faces toward it trying to get a suntan."

Jenny laughed her first good laugh in ages. "You're just an old tease and I'm really going to miss you."

Her uncle wrapped his arms around her. "Goodbye, honey. Forget what I said. It's just that you're all I've got and I worry, you know? Call me when you get settled and have yourself a real good time. You deserve it."

Chapter Three

Jenny watched the English countryside whiz by as the train raced north. The week in London had worked wonders. The tour group was made up of people from several European countries and she had met two or three other women traveling alone. As usual, she'd put on her happy face until finally it wasn't just for show. There'd been no time for grieving. After a sightseeing trip every day and a show every night, she had fallen exhausted into bed. London was a wonderful city. She could have stayed six months without getting bored.

Eventually the train slowed at her stop and with the help of a couple of uniformed schoolboys, she yanked her brand new suitcase onto the platform. The boys tipped their school caps and stepped back inside the train. She dusted off her jacket and slacks then looked about her. Climbing red roses grew in patches along the stonewall which ran the length of the platform, and the ancient little building looked more like a medieval house than a railway station.

A young man in soiled white overalls strolled toward her. His name, Andy Ferguson, was stitched in red thread on his breast pocket. Dark blue eyes gazed into hers, and unruly brown hair flopped across his forehead.

"Can I help you?"

"I hope so. Is there anywhere around here I can get a taxi?"

"Yes but you'll have to ring for one. Where are you going?"

"Stoney Beck. The Hare and Hounds Inn. Is it far?"

"About twenty minutes. If you don't mind riding in my old van, I'll be glad to give you a lift. I live there."

Jenny pretended to check the lock on her suitcase, then opened and closed her handbag as she tried to appear nonchalant, well traveled, as though she got on and off trains in a different country every week. She didn't want this stranger knowing she'd hardly set foot out of the Carolinas, but neither was she about to take a chance on being abducted. One heard such tales.

"Thanks all the same, but guess I'll call a cab."

"That's my van over there," he said, "the tan one with the dog hanging out the window. He doesn't bite and neither do I."

His amused shrug irritated her. Was she that easy to read? "I didn't mean to imply—it's just that—"

"I know," he said with a grin. "Who can you trust these days?"

She felt her face turn crimson. He was taunting her. They both turned as a guard blew his whistle and the train started up.

"Was your package on the train, Andy?" he shouted.

"No, but that's nothing new. I'll ring them later. Thanks, Jim."

After the man had gone inside, Andy turned back to Jenny. "See, even the station master knows me. Still, if you'd rather get a taxi, my mobile phone's in the car."

"No, please. I'd appreciate the lift." She extended her hand and smiled. "I'm Jenny. Jenny Robinson from North Carolina."

Andy Ferguson picked up the suitcase as easily as if it was filled with down, and then placed it in the back of the van next to a stack of used tires. Beside them, nestled in a huge nest of old pillows, was a grandfather clock.

"Move over, boy," he said to his dog as he opened the door, then picked up a rag from under the dashboard, and wiped off the seat. "This is Pete," he said to Jenny. "Pete, meet Jenny Robinson from America."

The dog, a border collie with large intelligent eyes, gave a little happy woof and held out his paw. Jenny laughed as her fear of Andy Ferguson faded. He drove slowly as if giving her time to take in the scenery, all the time talking as if he were a guide. There were almost two hundred fells in the Lakes, he said, with eight of them over three thousand feet, high enough to be classified as mountains. There were about fifteen lakes and at least twenty mountain passes.

Jenny stared out the window. "I didn't know it was this wild, or this undeveloped. I'd always thought it would be more touristy."

"Some parts are," he said, "but not so much in this area. The Lake District is a national park and you almost have to have a permit from God to build up here." He glanced at her. "Why, are you disappointed?"

"No. I like this better. It's beautiful."

Pete rested his head on his master's shoulder, Andy's hand sneaking up every now and then to rub the dog's ears.

"That's Stoney Beck down there," he said, as they came over the last rise. He slowed the car almost to a stop, as if giving Jenny time to take in the view.

She took a long deep breath, unprepared for the postcard scene spread out before her. Her mother hadn't told her the village was in the center of an emerald green valley or that it bordered a lake. She hadn't said a word either about the meadows, most of them dotted with sheep, or the heather-covered hills. It was June, a few weeks past lambing season, Andy said. Jenny watched the lambs chase after their mothers.

"Oh, man," was all she could manage.

"That's my garage up the brow to the left there," Andy said while they waited at the stop sign leading onto the main street. "I live in the house next to it." The grey stone house was trimmed in white with a green door and shutters. Gas pumps and what looked like a body shop in the same grey stone was next door. Five or six cars were parked outside.

"Everything's so quaint," Jenny said. "Is that the village green in front of your place?"

"You could say that. It used to be the old market square but it's Hallveck Common now."

On the far side, the common was bordered by stores. There was Malone's Corner Shop with the Bookworm next door, then the Lake Boutique and The Cup and Saucer Tea Shop. Jenny leaned forward holding tight to her seat belt. Her mother had said she worked in a bookshop until Jenny was born. Was this the one and was it likely anyone there or anywhere else in the village would remember her after all these years?

They turned right at the post office onto cobble-stoned Market Street and crawled past a yarn shop next door called The Knitting Needles. Then followed a string of whitewashed houses huddled together as if for warmth against the cold her mother had told her about. Each house had a handkerchief size lawn with a border of flowers. Jenny had never seen the like of the flower boxes, not only on windowsills or hanging over the front door, but nailed into the walls of the houses. Even the street's lampposts had baskets dripping with blossoms hanging from the post arms.

Just when it seemed they'd leave the village behind, Andy pulled into the parking lot of the rambling three-story Hare and Hounds Inn. The road continued on, snaking its way into the hills beyond. Jenny stepped out and shaded her eyes as she looked about. The sun was warm on her face. There were tables and chairs on the terrace in front of the inn, and more hanging baskets overflowing with flowers hung at intervals on brackets along the wall. On the lawn outside the inn sat two of the sun worshipers Uncle Tim had joked about. A man and women, probably in their seventies, sat in lawn chairs, eyes closed, faces raised to the sun.

She turned back to the van. "Bye, Pete," she said as she shook the dog's paw, then followed Andy past tubs of geraniums into the inn.

He set her suitcase on the worn stone-flagged floor, at the edge of the bar. "If you need to hire a car while you're here, I'll be glad to rent you one of mine. I'm even cheaper than Hertz."

"Oh Lord, I don't know if I'm brave enough to drive. I'll have to think about it,"

One of the men playing darts across the bar walked toward them. "Can I drop my clock off at your place this week?" he said to Andy, at the same time giving Jenny a friendly nod. "The minute hand fell off. I'm afraid to tinker with it."

"Drop it off any time. No problem."

"Is my car ready yet?" shouted another man from the corner.

"I think so, George. Let me get on back and I'll give you a ring."

Andy grinned at Jenny as he ran a hand through his hair, pushing it back from his forehead. "See how popular I am. Everybody knows me."

"Yes, I can see that," Jenny said, grinning back. "And thanks for the lift."

She watched him walk away, and when he looked back over his shoulder and caught her looking, she felt her face burn. He threw up his hand and winked before disappearing out the door.

A short round man, fiftyish, came from behind the bar toward her. He had twinkling green eyes and a full head of curly red hair, turning grey now. There were curls too in his neatly trimmed beard and he was the nearest thing to a real live leprechaun she'd ever seen. He smiled and extended his hand. "Miss Jenny Robinson from America? Welcome to Stoney Beck. I'm Walter Pudsley, the man you spoke to on the phone."

She returned his smile and shook his hand. "How did you know who I was?"

He rubbed his hands in a delighted sort of way and pointed to her suitcase. "Well, for starters, you've got those airline labels on your luggage. Besides all our other reservations were for people we already know. On the phone you said someone recommended the cottage. Were they here recently?"

"No, it's been about twenty-four years. It was a friend of the family. She stayed in the cottage. Said for me to get it if I could."

"That was before my time. I was born in the village but joined the merchant navy at seventeen. Bought the inn fifteen years ago."

"Ah."

He pulled out the handle of her suitcase. "Come on; let's get you settled in the cottage. You'll be tired after your journey."

She walked behind him as he wheeled her suitcase through the bar, along a passage and out the back door. The late spring afternoon was heavy with scents. Honeysuckle, blended with roses, and from the inn's open kitchen windows came the mixed fragrances of hot bread and smoked salmon.

Walter Pudsley took the key out of his pocket and unlocked the cottage door. As Jenny stepped inside, there was a feeling of going back in time, to another century. The warmth of the little bungalow reached out to her, with its wide plank floors, rosewood furniture, and chintz curtains that matched the wallpaper. A bedroom with the same warm country feel led off to the left, and through an open door, she glimpsed the claw-footed bathtub, with a shower curtain over it. The kitchen was nothing more than a tiny fridge, stove, a little sink, and two feet of counter.

"The telly's brand new." Mr. Pudsley gave the top a quick dust with the sleeve of his jacket, then opened the window and stood back. "Well, what do you think?" His face was suddenly serious, anxious to please.

"It's very lovely," Jenny said, turning away, pretending to study the room, so he wouldn't see the emotion working in her face. What would be his reaction if she told him she'd been conceived in this very cottage?

He straightened the curtains and fussed around the vase of wild flowers on the windowsill. "Do you have any plans? I mean do you know how long you'll be staying?"

"Not really. My time's my own. Will this be a problem with renting the cottage?"

He shook his head. "To tell you the truth, it's stood empty for years. Just been refurbished. It wasn't quite ready when you rang but because it seemed to mean a lot to you to have it, we buckled down. Finished it a couple of days ago. Nobody else asked for it especially, so consider it yours for as long as you like."

Jenny, her emotions now under control, gave him a big appreciative smile. "That was very kind. Thanks a lot."

"I've booked you in for bed and breakfast like you said. We serve a nice afternoon tea at four in the tearoom and there's the usual pub food in the bar every day from twelve noon."

Jenny looked at her watch. Three o'clock. "I really could eat a bite. I'll freshen up, then come over for tea."

He beamed as he handed her the key. "You be sure to let us know if you need anything. Press nine twice on the phone there. Someone will pick up."

After he'd gone, she walked round the cottage, ran her hand along the wainscoting, touched chairs, the chest of drawers in the bedroom, straightened the cushion on the chair, and then sat on the bed. She stared into the mirror over the dresser, half expecting, even longing to see her mother staring back at her. She gripped the bed's headboard and closed her eyes, imagining how it was, them holding hands across the tiny kitchen table, sitting by the fire, in the bed making love, making her.

She telephoned Uncle Tim but heard only his voice on the answering machine. She told him she'd arrived safely. Stoney Beck and the Hare and Hounds were straight out of an English novel. And guess what, it was a fine warm day. She gave him the phone number then hung up and ran water for a bath.

***

The tearoom was crowded and Jenny felt lucky to be shown to a small table set in one of the bay windows. Afternoon tea at the Hare and Hounds was better than anything she'd had in London. As well as the usual cucumber and watercress sandwiches, there was a plate of crackers and three kinds of cheeses, along with a delicious pâté the waitress said was wild boar. There was clotted cream for the scones, still warm from the oven, and a tray with miniature jars of assorted jams. The sun glinted off the small brass vase of pansies in the center of the table.

A woman stared at her from across the aisle. Jenny smiled and nodded but when the woman didn't respond, except to continue to stare, Jenny turned away.

A group of people in their twenties or thirties, in khaki shorts or blue jeans, probably hikers or mountain climbers, sat at a large table in the center of the room. She listened in on their conversation, and when they laughed at some joke, she smiled at one of the girls who looked her way. The girl, still laughing, gave a casual nod, then turned back to her friends.

Jenny looked out the window and played the game she'd played since she'd stepped off the plane at Gatwick Airport, searching the faces of most middle-aged men, looking for a match or any resemblance at all to the Charles Woodleigh in the picture she now had in her purse.

"You here on holiday?"

Jenny spun around. The woman who had stared at her made a loud scraping sound as she pulled out the chair across from Jenny and sat on it. She leaned forward, her thin, pointed face now no more than two feet away. The thick lenses in her glasses magnified her eyes and the smile that wasn't a smile displayed a mouthful of loose-fitting false teeth. Her hair had alternating streaks of grey and brown and was snatched back into a bun. A badger in glasses.

As the woman leaned across the table, her face up close, Jenny pressed her shoulder into the wall. "Why, yes. Yes I am. I've wanted to come to England ever since high school. I can't believe I'm really here." She picked up a tiny three-cornered sandwich and took a bite while the badger continued to stare.

"I knew you'd come one day," she said. "I knew you'd find out and come."

The sandwich slipped out of Jenny's hand and landed on her plate. "Find out what?"

"Come on. You don't have to play coy with me." The grainy, heavy smoker's voice emphasized every word.

"I think you've got me mixed up with somebody else."

"Oh, there's no mix-up. It's you all right. I've seen your photograph."

"My photograph?"

"The one your mother sent to the doctor. I was in his office when it came. He pulled it out of the envelope and showed it to me. I'd have known you anywhere."

"I think probably—"

"Staying at the inn are you? In the cottage?"

The false teeth clacked, watercress from the sandwiches lodged between them. "Thought so," she said when Jenny nodded. "Only natural you'd stay there."

Jenny gripped her cup with both hands as she tried doing something normal like sipping her tea.

"You've come snooping around haven't you?"

Jenny lowered her cup with a clatter, slopping tea onto the tablecloth. "I don't know what you're talking about. Snooping around for what?"

The woman got to her feet. "Don't you play little miss innocent with me. It'll get you nowhere." Her harsh raised voice carried round the room causing heads to turn.

Jenny also stood up and at five feet nine inches, towered over the woman. "Hang on a minute. What do you mean by—" But the woman was already heading for the entrance.

Jenny snatched up her purse and turned to hurry after her. Her face burned as she grazed the arm of a man in the seat behind her causing him to drop his fork. She stopped to pick it up and after apologizing, threaded her way around crowded tables, filled with people all turned to look at her.

Mr. Pudsley stood in the doorway, his face anxious as Jenny strode toward him.

"Did you see that woman?" she asked, amazed at her strong steady voice. "She sat at my table and started talking as if she knew me. Then she just got up and took off. She was real strange."

"That's old Biddy Biggerstaff," Mr. Pudsley said. "And you're right, she is strange. She's always been a bit odd, but lately it's as if—still, it's not like her to talk to strangers. She doesn't leave the big house much any more. There's just her and a girl. I'm sorry if she bothered you."

The worried frown on Mr. Pudsley's face and the way he bit his lip made Jenny wish she hadn't said anything.

"It was nothing. We've got someone just like her back home." Jenny couldn't think of anyone in her neighborhood quite like Biddy Biggerstaff but at least the remark brought a ghost of a smile to Mr. Pudsley's face.

"Maybe she was interested because you're an American. You know, different."

Jenny looked down at her clothes. White slacks, blue denim shirt, tennis shoes and white socks. As far as she could see no different from other young people in the inn or roaming around outside. Her clothes of course had nothing to do with it or even that she was an American. It all had something to do with the photograph. What had the woman said? "It's you all right and I know why you're here." She'd accused Jenny of snooping around. Snooping around for what? Could this have anything to do with what her mother had so desperately wanted Jenny to know? She took a long breath. In spite of the shaky feeling, she began to feel a little satisfied. After no more than a couple of hours in Stoney Beck, already she was getting somewhere. Even though the woman had unnerved her, the confrontation had given Jenny a lead, something to go on.

"I left the table in a hurry," she said to Mr. Pudsley. "I didn't even wait for my check. Perhaps I—"

Mr. Pudsley waved his hand. "Don't worry about it. They'll just add it to your bill, but I want this first one to be on me."

"You don't have to do that. It was really nothing."

"This has nothing to do with Biddy. I just happen to like Americans."

The bar was almost deserted now, obviously a quiet time between afternoon and evening. A shaft of sunlight streamed through the open door onto the ancient stone flags and burnished mahogany counter with its brass fittings. The smell of flowers from outside mingled with the smell of beer.

Without even planning to ask, and more to get her mind off the strange woman, Jenny blurted out the words. "Have you ever heard of a man called Charles Woodleigh?" She watched Mr. Pudsley's face for any sign of surprise, but saw none. "A friend of the family came through here years ago. Said if I met him, to say hello."

The question was a long shot because her mother had said Charles was from London. Still, there was always the chance he'd come back, maybe just to see the place. And if he had, wouldn't it be the most natural thing in the world for him to stop at the Hare and Hounds for a glass of beer, or a meal even?

Mr. Pudsley scratched his beard and stared upwards at the ceiling. Then, as if he'd seen the answer written there, he turned back to Jenny. "There's a priest at St. Mary's Church in Daytonwater goes by the name of Woodleigh. It's the next village over, nine or ten miles to the east of here. Don't know his first name though. Never been inside his church. I'm Church of England y'see. Not that I go much. Running a place like this doesn't give you much time to yourself."

"I understand. Anyway, I doubt it's the same Woodleigh. Thanks again for the tea. It was delicious."

She ran her finger under the collar of her blouse as she headed for the door and out of the inn, then undid the top button to relieve the sudden tightness. A priest, for heaven's sake. The words swished around in her brain making a rhyme. A priest, a priest, nine or ten miles to the east.

She crossed the road and leaned against a tree, then reached in her shoulder bag and pulled out the slim volume of poems. She flipped through the pages to "How Do I Love Thee?" where the picture was lodged. It was easy to see why her mother had fallen for this guy. He had a sexy smile and bedroom eyes, and looked no more like a priest than Jenny did a nun. Her mother, sheltered minister's daughter that she was, maybe wouldn't have recognized good-time Charlie as a smooth talker, and perhaps wouldn't have understood the line he'd use on innocent girls, especially pretty young American college students, thousands of miles away from home. Jenny remembered her mother telling her he was older than she was by three or four years but still a student. Yeah, in a pig's eye. Charles Woodleigh was already a priest, Jenny would bet a thousand dollars. Wouldn't that be the very reason he'd disappeared, without even a forwarding address? He'd probably taken the next train out of there, back to his parish, worried sick she'd come back to tell him she was pregnant.

Jenny stuffed the book back in her purse and as she headed down Market Street tried to turn her stiff, tense stride into something resembling a stroll. She stopped to stare at the shingle outside the large house. Dr. Jonathon T. Hall, General Practitioner, the sign said. Was this the doctor who had delivered her? She traced her fingers over the latticed grillwork of the iron gate as she pictured her mother, alone and frightened opening the gate and trudging up the path to the door. Jenny's own trembling hand was on the latch, ready to open the gate, when she saw the sign in the bay window. *Surgery - 9:30 - 11:00 a.m. and 5:30 - 7:00 p.m. weekdays. 9:30 - 11:00 a.m. Saturday only.* No surgery on Sunday. There was a number to call for emergencies. She pondered over the word *surgery* until she remembered an English movie she'd seen ages ago. Surgery in England didn't necessarily mean an operation. It was also the name of the doctor's office. She looked at her watch. Twenty after five. She would come another time.

On down the street, she sauntered past the row of houses, all with names as well as numbers. There was Rose Cottage, The Hollies, Squirrel Lodge, Hawthorne House, even Molly and Me. While she debated whether to go inside The Knitting Needles yarn shop to let them know their cat was in the window playing with a ball of yarn, a woman thrust her hand through the curtain and yanked the cat out. She smiled at Jenny then disappeared.

At the post office on the corner of Vallhellyn Lane, she crossed Market Street to Hallveck Common, and slowly walked up one of the four pink gravel paths that led from each corner of the common to the obelisk in the center. *In memory of those who died on foreign soil during the two Great Wars, 1914-1918 and 1939-1945* the inscription read. Three Japanese tourists posed in front of the memorial while a fourth was about to take their picture.

"Please, please," one of the three called to her, pointing to the camera, and gesturing to their friend.

"Why sure," Jenny said, as the young man handed her the camera. After explaining how it worked, he joined the other three and Jenny clicked the shutter.

She smiled as she returned their camera, then climbed the steep hill called Coppers Brow to Ferguson's Garage. Pete, sentinel like, sat upright beside the desk.

"Hi Pete," she said, giving him a rub behind his ears.

Pete's tail began to swish slowly from side to side.

"You're taking a chance with that dog," Andy Ferguson said as he strolled toward her. "He's vicious when he's on guard. Any second now and he'll go for your throat. Come on boy, show her your teeth."

Pete's tail picked up speed as he laughed up at his master.

Andy wiped his hands on an oily rag. "How do you like the inn?"

"It's all I hoped for and then some. And now, if you'll show me your rental cars."

"Ah yes, the cars. You know, I should have asked you when we drove in, but didn't think about it. Have you driven in England before?"

"Never. Don't forget I only arrived in London a week ago. This is my first visit to England." She studied her shoes as she mulled over her response. It hadn't occurred to her before but this wasn't her first visit. She'd been born here.

Andy looked from the car back to her. "Well, it'll be tricky. Opposite side of the road, steering wheel on the right, and—"

"Ah, that won't bother me," she interrupted. "I've been driving all over North and South Carolina since I was sixteen. Never even put a dent in a car."

"Can you handle gears or did you drive an automatic?"

"Automatic, but the first car I ever had was stick."

He looked to the left where his cars were parked. "There's a Ford Escort over there you can use, the blue one on the end."

"Great." She pulled her credit card from her wallet and handed it to him. "Would it be too much of an imposition to ask you to come for a ten-minute drive? It isn't just that y'all drive on the wrong side, it's—"

"We don't drive on the wrong side. We drive on the opposite side, the left."

"Yes, well, whatever. I think I can handle that. It's these crazy roundabouts that scare me. My uncle warned me about them."

"Oh, they're not too bad. After you've gone around them ten or twenty times, you'll get the hang of it." He smiled. He had white even teeth and a half-inch scar above the left side of his lip.

"I may drive to Daytonwater tomorrow," Jenny said, "to St. Mary's church. I want to get the hang of this driving on the left."

He lifted some keys off a nail on the wall behind them. "Give me a minute to let Alf know where I'm going. He's my right-hand man."

After a few minutes spent fastening seat belts and explanations about where the lights and windshield wipers were located, they headed out of Stoney Beck.

"You'll like Daytonwater," Andy said. "It's very old and St. Mary's is pure Gothic."

"Uh, huh." Jenny focused on the road ahead, drove a steady thirty miles an hour, and tried to remember to step on the clutch every time she changed gears.

"Take the first road on your left beyond the next farm," he said after they'd gone about five miles. "We'll circle back through the village. You're good enough on the country roads."

Andy Ferguson watched her out of the corner of his eye. She reminded him of those American prom queens he'd seen on TV or those cheerleaders twirling their batons and flouncing around all over the place. They were all knockouts, if you liked that sort of look, always smiling and flashing their gleaming all-American teeth. Gradually, though, while Jenny concentrated on the road, Andy noticed the determined jut of her chin, the way she bit her lip as she maneuvered the car round each curve of the winding country lane. She looked strong and fragile at the same time. There was something in her air, a hint of hard times. Even when she smiled he could tell. It showed in her eyes.

"Give yourself plenty of time tomorrow," he said. "The road's narrow and snakes around the fells so be careful. And don't let this warm weather fool you. It can change up here in a heartbeat. Especially watch out for the mist. It comes from out of nowhere and if you're not used to it, you can find yourself in trouble. If it happens, park your car as soon as you can and wait it out. It's the only safe way."

Jenny only nodded, as she steered the car into the parking lot of the garage. She came to an easy stop and turned off the ignition.

Andy opened the door and got out. "Hang on a minute. I'll be right back." He opened his van and picked up the cellular phone. "Better keep this with you. You can recharge it in the cigarette lighter. And here's my card in case you run into trouble."

As Jenny drove back to the Hare and Hounds, she thought about Andy Ferguson. He was one of those rare men, a gentle man who wasn't afraid to show it, yet at the same time losing none of his masculinity. She pushed thoughts of him aside, not about to follow in her mother's footsteps and get tangled up with some guy who lived an ocean away. She had enough problems.

Chapter Four

On her way home from the Hare and Hounds, Biddy Biggerstaff stopped at Braddocks Apothecary for medicine to quell a fever and some aspirin which helped anything. She climbed back in her dark green Toyota and headed out of the village. Her mind was riveted on that girl in the tearoom, the last person in the world Biddy had expected to see. Until the arrival of the photograph, the doctor had not received so much as a line from Beverly. Even when the photograph arrived, there was no return address on the envelope, with the postmark no more than a smudge. After all these years, she still didn't want anyone in England to know her American address. And now, with just six weeks left to go, Biddy was almost home free, at least she'd thought so until today.

When she'd spotted that girl in the Hare and Hounds, sitting there, bold as brass, red and black dots had danced in front of Biddy's eyes. Now, though, as she drove slowly up Vallhellyn Lane and thought about the encounter, she began to see it differently. When she'd accused the girl of snooping around, it was obvious Biddy had startled her. She acted puzzled as if not understanding anything Biddy was saying. Was it possible Beverly hadn't told her daughter everything, except perhaps to say she was born in Stoney Beck? That couldn't be avoided because it would be on her birth certificate. Was that all she knew? Had Beverly fabricated lies to avoid telling her daughter the truth? Had this Jenny come innocently to Stoney Beck for a holiday like she said? And was it just coincidence she had come at this crucial time? The more Biddy thought about it, the more feasible it sounded, and the better she felt. Still, on the other hand—But Biddy couldn't bear to think of that now.

As she drove up Glen Ellen's gravel drive, she gave a guarded look at the dead oak tree in the center of the front lawn. It was enormous, with a trunk at least eight feet around and half again as tall as the two-story house with its steep gabled roof. Even though the tree had been dead two years, Biddy swore it was growing still, its naked, bleached branches reaching out, stretching toward the house, toward her.

The back door was on the side of the house and in a spot where Biddy was hidden from the tree. She parked as close to the door as she could, stepped out of the car and went inside. The house was nowhere near as clean as it used to be. Dust coated everything and cobwebs were all over the place, even hanging from the chandelier in the hallway. But Biddy didn't care. These days visitors were almost non-existent and those who did come stayed in the kitchen.

As gloomy and run-down as the house was, the upstairs bedroom Biddy now entered was bright and airy. A young woman sat at a card table doing a jigsaw puzzle. She had sparse straight hair, cut short, just below her ears. Her eyes behind the wire-rimmed glasses were cautious as Biddy walked toward her and held out the bottle.

"Here's your medicine, so you don't need to be telephoning the doctor. I still think you're imagining things. You've been like this all your life."

"No, this is different." The girl had a breathless sort of voice, but that was part of her condition. Biddy was used to it. She put her hand under the girl's chin, looked closely at the round, flat face, examined the sallow splotchy skin. "It's just a flare up of your eczema. Nothing to worry about."

The girl's lip trembled. "Ever since I had that sore throat, I've felt poorly. And I'm always tired." She dropped one of the jigsaw pieces but left it where it fell. "I miss Mummy and Daddy so much. You do too, don't you, Biddy," she lisped, her tone pleading.

"Oh, I miss them all right," Biddy ground out. "I miss them because there's only you and me now. You and me twenty-four hours a day, Sarah. I gave up a good job to take care of you and now look where it's got me."

Sarah picked at her nails, cringing at the look on Biddy's face, all twisted as though she hated her. Back in the old days, when Mummy and Daddy were alive, Biddy had been nicer. Oh, not loving, not anything that special, but not mean like she was now. This last year she had started changing. She had begun talking nasty and drinking a lot. Sarah couldn't pin down the very day she had first noticed. Maybe it was the day Biddy had talked about the tree. She had started saying the strangest things, like had Sarah noticed how it was growing still, even though it was supposed to be dead. Sarah had tried to tell Biddy that dead trees didn't grow, but she wouldn't listen. Then one day she had closed all the curtains on the front of the house and told Sarah not to open them ever again. These last few weeks Biddy had grown meaner than ever and Sarah didn't know what she was going to do.

"You're a great big fibber, Biddy," Sarah blurted out, wagging an accusing finger. "I heard you tell Mummy you hated that other job."

"Yes, well. Times have changed. I never dreamed I'd be stuck here with you twenty-four hours a day, seven days a week."

Sarah's throat tightened. Her parents had been good to Biddy and would have been very hurt to hear her talk like this. Sarah spread her arms wide. "You've got me and this nice big house. You can stay here all safe and warm for the rest of your life."

Biddy glared at her. "I've got you and this nice big house," she said, mimicking Sarah's lisp. "You're too stupid to understand I might not want you for the rest of my life. Still, you never know. I might get lucky yet. Everyone knows mongoloids don't live as long as normal people."

"Please, Biddy, don't say mongoloid. You know how Mummy hated that word. It's Down syndrome. She was so proud of me. So was Daddy. Remember what he called me? His little Angel?"

"Ha! Some angel. There's nothing little about you. But you'll die young, Sarah Fitzgerald. Then the house will be mine. All mine."

Sarah's stomach churned. She put a hand over her mouth and stumbled through the door to the bathroom.

Biddy stood, arms folded and watched her go and thought about the night she had listened outside Fred and Edna Fitzgerald's bedroom door and heard them making plans for the unexpected. But who could have foretold then that two healthy people in their early fifties would get killed trying to avoid a goat on a lonely mountain road in the Pyrenees. They had gone to Lourdes every year to try to get the Virgin Mary to perform a miracle on Sarah. The only miracle that had come out of the whole thing was a dubious one as far as Biddy was concerned. Sarah hadn't been killed with them. She had survived without a scratch.

Edna and Fred had been dead for almost two years. The long wait was almost over, and if Biddy played her cards right, in a few short weeks she would be a rich woman. Sarah was the snag of course. Thanks to the marvels of modern medicine, her kind were living longer than ever. Still, Biddy was not too worried. After everything was finally settled, she could easily get rid of Sarah. With a little diplomacy, it should be easy enough to convince the Social Services that the girl would be better off in a home, a place for those with special needs. If that didn't work, well, there were other ways. Once Sarah was out of the way, Biddy would get it all. After she'd sold the house, Stoney Beck and everyone in it wouldn't see her for dust.

A sudden vision of the American girl in the tearoom flashed in front of Biddy. Was it possible the girl somehow had found out about the clause in the will? Was this why she had suddenly materialized? Biddy shook her head, remembering again the girl's puzzled, confused look. There was no way she could have found out. Even Beverly herself couldn't have known. Just weeks after the birth, she and her baby had disappeared off the face of the earth. The Fitzgeralds had tried everything to find them but the search had been futile. That was almost a quarter of a century ago. That girl coming to Stoney Beck at this critical time was nothing more than a coincidence. Biddy told herself her jitters were understandable because in just a few weeks everything she had waited for these long years through would at last be hers. It had all been worth it. And yet, she would feel a lot easier when that girl left the village, and the sooner, the better.

The sound of the flushing toilet jerked Biddy back to the present. She had to be careful, keep her wits about her. If Dr. Hall asked Sarah how Biddy treated her, the stupid girl would tell. It wouldn't occur to her to lie and Biddy had waited too long to bugger it up now. She dredged up a caring smile and limped into the bathroom.

"Come on, Sarah, Biddy was only kidding. When my arthritics are acting up, I get cranky. You know I didn't mean it." She leaned against the bathroom wall while Sarah rinsed her mouth and brushed her teeth. "The only reason I stay is to take care of you. Do you remember what I said would happen if I left?"

Sarah's round eyes grew wider more frightened. "The men in the white coats would come for me with their paddy wagon and carry me off."

"That's right. So don't you go saying anything bad about old Biddy will you?'

"I wouldn't do that. You know I wouldn't."

"That's a good girl because those men in the white coats are mean as snakes. They'd lock you in a big dark room with bars on the windows and never let you out."

Sarah grabbed hold of Biddy's arm. "I'm not that bad am I, Biddy? I know I'm slow, but don't I help you clean the house? I can read and write, and I've even got a job. I can do nearly everything anybody else can do."

"Not in the eyes of the Social Services you can't. They don't let people like you live alone. Not in a house the size of this, anyway." She put her arm round Sarah and pulled her close. "But you know Biddy loves you. I was just kidding when I said you wouldn't live long. You'll probably outlive the whole village."

Sarah wanted to pull away from the suffocating embrace but didn't dare risk upsetting Biddy again. Her bad breath and the smell of tobacco which always clung to her made Sarah feel sick all over again. She did her best at a big smile and tried hard to look well and strong. She didn't want the paddy wagon men carting her off to the home for mongoloids. She hated that word and Biddy knew it. She only said it to be mean and spiteful. Almost everybody knew to say Down syndrome. Sarah remembered Mummy and Daddy telling her to think always of the things she could do and not to dwell on the hard things. She could read and write and even play the piano. Daddy had made her and Mummy laugh when he'd said that doctor's name should have been Dr. Up instead of Dr. Down, because then Sarah would have had the Up Syndrome.

"Ada rang," she said to Biddy. "I told her I'm nearly well and begged her not to give my job to anyone else. She promised she wouldn't. Oh, and Andy rang too. He said he's some new CD's for me."

Sarah liked Andy Ferguson. He'd put in a good word for her at the shop when Ada needed more help with the cards and sweets and had spent ages showing her how to group the greeting cards for different occasions as well as arrange the picture postcards for the tourists. And best of all, he or Alf came by the house every day to pick her up and drive her to and from work.

Sarah had started work at the shop over two years ago, six weeks before her parents had been killed. They'd been so proud of her, so pleased she'd been clever enough to get her very own job and a wage packet every Friday. And they'd have been prouder still if only they could have heard Ada tell her just last month she didn't know what she'd do without her.

Biddy examined Sarah's pale sallow face. The girl wasn't any better. Any fool could see that. Still, if she wanted to go back to the shop, Biddy wasn't about to stop her. Having the house to herself for a few hours a day was better than nothing.

"How's about if I heat us up a frozen chicken pie in the microwave," she said. "If you want to get back to work, you'll need to put some food in your stomach. I'll give you a shout when it's ready."

The tension drifted away and Sarah did feel a little hungry. Maybe she could eat something this time without losing it.

"Yes, OK. I'll sit in here and watch the telly till you call me."

Chapter Five

On Sunday morning, Jenny sat straight and stiff in the car as she drove toward Daytonwater and St. Mary's church. She kept to the left, sometimes no more than a foot or so from the miles of dry stonewall which skirted the fields. She held her breath as she inched ever closer to the wall every time a car coming from the opposite direction hurtled past. Her arms ached from the strain of gripping the steering wheel, while she waited for the tearing scrape, the sound of metal against stone. Nobody had warned her the English drove like maniacs.

She stopped and watched while a couple of border collies, on their own, with their master nowhere in sight, herded about ten sheep wandering in the middle of the road. The dogs guided the sheep toward an open gate then into the pasture to join the rest of the flock. As she eased the car forward, she saw a boy of about twelve tear across the field to close the gate and follow after the dogs.

Up ahead she saw the sign: *Daytonwater, one mile.* Andy had said she couldn't miss St. Mary's because it had a clock tower and she could see it even now. She crossed the bridge over a stream then guided the car into a small parking lot between the church and a school next door.

She walked up to the gate and stopped to stare at the notice board. *Reverend Father - Charles R. Woodleigh,* the sign said in large gold letters. *Charles.* The priest's first name was Charles, the same as her mother's lover. Jenny stumbled a bit as she walked on ancient stone flags beside tombstones centuries old, and then climbed the steps to the entrance.

Inside she sat against one of the pillars, hoping this would make her less conspicuous. By the time the organ started up, the church was no more than one quarter full. Jenny thought of Reverend Lancing back home who would have been mighty ashamed of a congregation as small as this. She didn't have many Catholic friends and couldn't remember attending a Mass. She remembered movies she'd seen, where a procession came slowly down the aisle, altar boys first, followed by the priest swinging his incense ball and chanting something in Latin. But she'd read about how the Catholic church had given up the Latin years ago and also changed the Mass format. She kept her gaze on the stained glass window behind the altar while she felt in her bag for the book of sonnets. She took out the picture and held it between her fingers, when

Father Woodleigh suddenly appeared from a door beside the lectern, just like Reverend Lancing back home.

She looked from him to the picture and back again. There were streaks of silver in the priest's blonde hair, but it was still thick and wavy. His face was tanned, or weather beaten, as if he spent a lot of time outdoors. It was him all right. Some people as they aged changed beyond all recognition, but not this man. As soon as he smiled, Jenny knew for sure. Even in his priest's robes, she'd have known him anywhere. She pressed a hand against her chest as she stared at an older version of the man in the photograph who laughed into the camera and had his arm around her mother.

She leaned her back against the pew and watched his every move, listened to his every word. When the congregation stood to sing, he sang along with them, his open hymnbook against his chest, without once looking down at the words. Jenny could hear him over everybody else, a good strong baritone. His eyes inspected the congregation as he sang. When his gaze lingered for a second on her face, her heart bounced up near her throat. Surely he'd recognized her. When his roving eyes moved on, she let her breath out in a rush. The congregation remained seated while the choir of young boys gave a beautiful rendition of Ave Maria. The priest turned to them and, as if unable to help himself, conducted with an invisible baton.

His sermon was tailor-made for Jenny. He spoke of loss of a loved one, of battling on against overwhelming odds. How, after coping with the initial hurt, you learn to endure, discover that sorrow has made you stronger, you've become more compassionate. Jenny tucked her arms in at her sides and dug her nails into her palms. He could easily have been speaking directly to her, especially when a couple of times, he turned her way. It was unreal, as if he knew her and why she'd come. Deliberately she turned away from him and fixed her gaze on one of the stained glass windows. Her imagination was playing games with her.

She stayed in her pew while the others took Communion, not knowing if it would be proper for a Methodist to take Communion at a Catholic Mass. When the organist began the opening bars of the final hymn, the congregation got to its feet and while they belted out "This Little Heart of Mine," Jenny stood mesmerized. As the floor moved under her feet, she grabbed the pew in front. That priest up there in the pulpit was her father. She'd never laid eyes on him until less than an hour ago, and even though it was impossible to explain, there was a stirring inside her, something beyond explanation.

When everybody rose from their seats and gathered their things, she sat motionless in the pew until the last person had gone. Eventually, she reached for the back of the pew in front and pulled herself to her feet in the way of an old person stiff from sitting, then took out her sunglasses and put them on. Everybody said she had her mother's eyes and a lover would remember eyes.

She was the last in line and as she approached him, the priest extended his hand and beamed at her. "Welcome to St. Mary's. I saw you in the congregation. Are you here on holiday?"

She nodded as he enclosed her trembling fingers with his own. "I'm staying in Stoney Beck at the Hare and Hounds," she said in a hoarse voice.

A flicker of something, a shadow maybe, touched his face and just as quickly was gone. "And you're an American. We have many who come to St. Mary's. You're from the South aren't you?"

She cleared her throat. "Yes, Father. I'm Jenny Robinson from Charlotte, North Carolina."

"Ah, North Carolina. Well, we must make you welcome." He looked toward the small group gathered over to the side, then turned back to her. "A few always stop back for a spot of tea and a chat. We usually go into the rectory but with this warm spell, today we're having it on the terrace. Will you join us? It would be our pleasure."

"Yes," she whispered, barely able to believe her luck, "I'd like that."

Did she imagine his quizzical look? Did he know? Had he guessed? She held her breath, waiting for him to blurt out the words. *My God, you're my daughter.* But he only smiled, the very same smile as the one in the snapshot, then walked beside her to join the others. He presented her to the group who sat around on white wicker chairs.

A plump woman carrying a tray appeared almost immediately. The priest introduced her as Mrs. Thwaites, his housekeeper. "I always bring a few extra cups," the woman whispered to Jenny. "It saves steps, y'see. It's seldom the Father doesn't have a few stay back for a chat." She shot the priest a motherly look as she placed the tray on the wicker table, then ambled back to the house.

"Do you take sugar? Milk?" the woman beside her asked.

"Yes, a little of each, please."

Jenny always drank it with lemon but knew already to an Englishman this was the same as asking an American did he take lemon in his coffee.

"Care for a biscuit?" a man asked as he passed a plate of cookies around.

She took one and thanked him.

For a few minutes they made polite small talk, before she became the center of attention. No, she'd never been to England before but had always wanted to come. Yes, London was a fantastic city all right. She'd done all the tourist stuff, seen at least four shows. The conversation was easy, relaxed, and she began to unwind.

Was it true, one of them asked, that there were more murders in America in one week than in a year in all of Western Europe? Well, yes, she'd heard that one too but you'd never know it from where she lived. Oh, Charlotte was a high crime area all right but her neighborhood was quiet, seemed safe enough.

"What do you think of England?" another wanted to know.

"I like it," she said. "I'm here mainly for the architecture. You know, fine old churches like St. Mary's." She didn't know why she said this unless to give credence as to why she, a Methodist, was attending a Catholic Mass.

The man who'd passed around the cookies tossed his thumb towards the priest. "Get Father Woodleigh to give you the grand tour. He loves to show off his church. Isn't that right Father?"

The priest laughed. "I suppose it is. And yes, if Jenny has time, I'd be pleased to show her around."

"Thank you; that would be nice."

While the conversation turned to other things, she nibbled on her cookie, her gaze on the bumblebee buzzing among the roses, yet all the while thinking about the love affair between her mother and this priest. Jenny had expected to dislike him on sight, even hate him. But it was impossible not to like this man. The thought had crossed her mind that maybe he wasn't a priest when he had the affair with her mother, perhaps still in the seminary or whatever it was called. Even that was wrong of course for a man with his leanings, and it didn't explain his disappearing. Still, her mother had been the first to leave with at least six weeks passing before she returned to the village to look for him. Wouldn't it be reasonable for him to think she didn't want him? When he had finally left the Lakes and returned to London, why would he feel the need to tell anybody? Why hadn't Jenny thought this through before? Perhaps it was her grief, or guilt, anxious to take her mother's side. What would he say if she told him her mother had come back to Stoney Beck to tell him she was pregnant, then alone and desperate she had gotten a job in the village bookshop and stayed to have their baby? What would he say about the price she had paid?

When he took Jenny on a tour of the church, she pushed her sunglasses to the top of her head, but avoided looking at him. She continued her pretense of being interested in Gothic buildings and asked about the history of the really old part of St. Mary's, consisting of a round tower which he said dated back to the Middle Ages.

As the tour ended and they came out into bright sunlight she put her glasses back on and thanked him. "I'm glad I came and I'll try to come back. I've got to hear that choir once more before I leave the Lakes. How did you find so many good voices in such a small place?"

"Seven of them are from a boys' boarding school nearby and the other three are local boys. We're lucky to have them."

"You sure are. When they sang 'Ave Maria,' it took my breath away. It was so beautiful. Is that your favorite?"

He nodded. "One of them. Still, priests are only human you know, and most of us listen to all kinds of music. I play the radio all the time, especially in the car, and if I tell you my favorite song, well, I'm sure you won't believe it."

"What is it?"

"Knock three times on the ceiling if you want me—"

Jenny laughed out loud as a sheepish smile flickered on the priest's face.

"You're right. I don't believe it." She gazed across the fells, heard the gulls laughing with them overhead.

When the church clock tolled out the hour, the look on the priest's face told Jenny he was running late with his church work and it was time for her to go. She hesitated, trying to get the words out but couldn't. Perhaps she'd try another day, or maybe she'd never tell him. There was something so nice, so decent about this man. It was almost impossible to think of him as lecherous, and Jenny had always considered herself a good judge of people.

"I need to be getting back," she said, as she hitched her shoulder bag higher. "Thanks for the tea and cookies, Father, and for showing me around."

He held out his hand. "It's been my pleasure."

***

Charles Woodleigh shaded his eyes with his hand as he watched the American girl drive away. She had worn those dark glasses and so he couldn't see her eyes, but when she'd laughed in that certain way, with that little tilt of her chin, it was as though he knew her, as though— He had come within a hair of asking her mother's name but what reason could he have given for wanting to know? He shook his head, impatient with himself. Why, in the name of all that was holy, did he still remember? Why couldn't he stop searching every American face for a resemblance to Beverly, or even for Beverly herself. He watched as the car grew ever smaller then disappeared over the crest of Badger Hill. He looked away from the road, picked up the tray and strode toward the rectory.

***

The day had turned warm and Jenny opened the windows for the drive back to Stoney Beck. Funny how she'd seen only the grey stone walls on her way to St. Mary's and hadn't noticed the long stretches of hawthorn. The hedgerows were in full flower and smelled of summer, a white frothy border to the greenest fields she'd ever seen. And curious how the road wasn't nearly as narrow as she'd at first thought. She tapped her fingers on the steering wheel and hurtled along as fast as the other cars as she sang *"Knock three times on the ceiling if you want me, twice on the pipes if you ain't gonna show—"*

Once inside the cottage, she leaned her back against the door and closed her eyes, still hardly able to believe she had found her father within only days of arriving in the Lakes. "He's a priest, Mom," she confided to the empty room. "My father's a priest. Can you believe it? You fell in love with a priest."

She pulled out the book of poems and held it against her cheek as she walked to the window, then thumbed through until she came across her mother's unfinished note. What had she meant by writing she hadn't told Jenny the whole truth? Uncle Tim had been close to his sister but he was as puzzled as Jenny. She fingered the note, that last hardly legible sentence standing out more than the rest. *You have a right to know and I'd give the world—*

Jenny looked out the window and watched a low cloud climb up one side of the mountain and roll down the other. "The answer's here somewhere," she said out loud, her breath fogging the windowpane. "It's here in this place." She pressed her forehead against the cool of the glass and looked down at her watch. It was early, only one o'clock. She'd start with Biddy Biggerstaff and get to the doctor later. Eager now to be gone, she slipped out of the dress she'd worn to church, pulled on a pair of white slacks, and topped them with a red cotton T-shirt.

While Jenny ate a baked potato, or jacket potato as the English called it, and drank a glass of bitter lemon, she tried to think of a plausible reason for visiting Biddy Biggerstaff. The woman was weird and Jenny would have to tread lightly if she was going to get anywhere. A visit such as this called for more than a touch of finesse.

The inn's bar was less formal than the tearoom and people who ate a pub lunch paid for it at the counter. Mr. Pudsley looked up from the cash register as Jenny approached. "How did it go this morning?" he asked while she fished in her purse for the money. "Was the priest the man you were looking for?"

She faked a smile and shook her head. "'Fraid not," she lied. "I'm glad I went, though. I'd never been to a Catholic Mass and Father Woodleigh was real nice." She told Mr. Pudsley she had been invited to stay for tea and cookies, followed by the priest taking her on a tour of his church.

Mr. Pudsley beamed as he counted out her change. "Well now, wasn't that nice. St. Mary's is on the list of historic places." He pulled a brochure from a stack in the corner. "You might want to browse through this. It's choc-a-bloc with interesting places to see."

Jenny glanced through the pages. "Thank you. This will come in handy. I thought this afternoon that I'd drive out to Miss Biggerstaff's house. I hate what happened in the tearoom. She thought she knew me is all, and I certainly didn't mean to come across as rude. I was tactless and I'm sorry about the whole thing."

Mr. Pudsley's right eyebrow went up about half an inch. "If I were you, I'd just forget it. Biddy meant it all right. She's like that with everyone."

Jenny put the change in her purse. "Still, I can't stand mixed signals. It'll drive me nuts until I've apologized. And I'd hate to give Americans a bad name." She stuck her purse back in her shoulder bag. "Is her place hard to find?"

"No, take a left out of here, up Market Street." He gestured with his hand. "Then another left at the post office onto Vallhellyn Lane. Go about three miles and you'll come to Glen Ellen on the right. Big Tudor-style house, sits back off the road. That's where Biddy lives. There's a massive dead tree in the middle of the front lawn. You can't miss it." He polished a glass and held it up to the light. "It's the biggest house for miles around. It used to be a showplace when the Fitzgeralds were alive but all that's changed. Now you can hardly see the place for the weeds."

Ten minutes later Jenny drove through the open gates of Glen Ellen. The drive was littered with last year's dead leaves and the roses bordering the overgrown lawn fought with weeds for a bit of sun. A couple of squirrels chattered and scampered along the naked limbs of the dead tree, while another sat in a hole halfway up the trunk, a nut between its paws. There was a fishpond covered with water lilies near the tree and a huge black cat crouched at the edge hoping for the odd goldfish that swam too close. Jenny jumped at the grating sound of a shutter as it swung loose from the huge front window. She counted the windows, six downstairs and six on the floor above, all with drapes tightly closed except for the upstairs window closest to her. It all looked so sad and neglected. Still, if she squinted her eyes to soften the edges, it wasn't hard to imagine the showplace Mr. Pudsley had said it once was, to see the manicured lawn with the roses in full bloom, and a strong healthy tree offering shade.

She parked next to the green Toyota which she guessed was Biddy's, then walked around to the front entrance. She pressed the bell and waited, her mouth poised to give a big friendly smile when Biddy came to the door. But when the door opened, Jenny found herself staring into the face of a girl who could have been any age from eighteen to thirty. Sometimes it was hard to tell with Down syndrome.

Jenny gave her biggest smile. "Is Miss Biggerstaff at home?"

The girl nodded and put a finger to her lips. "She's asleep," she lisped in a soft wheezy voice. Her face was pale, anxious. "I can't let you in. Biddy said strangers are dangerous."

"Yes, well, she's right of course. There's no way I'd ever let a stranger in my house."

The girl stepped outside and plopped down on the dusty bench placed against the wall. She patted the place beside her and looked up at Jenny. "Can you sit with me for a bit? My name's Sarah and when Biddy wakes up, you can come in. I mean we won't be strangers any more and then I'll make you a nice cup of tea. What's your name?"

"Jenny, Jenny Robinson. If Biddy's taking a nap, she might sleep for ages. Maybe I'll come back another time."

"Are you from America?" Sarah asked shyly. "You talk like some of those women on the telly."

Jenny smiled, at the same time warming toward Sarah. "Yes, I'm American but I've never been on the telly. I'm just plain old Jenny Robinson from Charlotte, North Carolina."

"You're not old." Sarah patted harder on the bench. "Please sit with me. I've never spoken to an American lady before. You're so pretty. Bet you could be on telly if you wanted to."

"Thanks, Sarah," Jenny said, sitting beside her, "and you can be my press agent."

They both turned at the sound of a car coming up the gravel drive, then Sarah let out a little whoop.

"It's Andy." She stood up and almost knocked Jenny off the seat as she lurched past. She held fast to the rail as she took the steps one at a time, then shambled across the gravel toward Andy Ferguson who had just stepped out of his car.

A huge grin split his face as he strolled toward her. "How's my best girl?" he asked as he pulled a small plastic bag out of his pocket. "Here's your Elton John CD and his 'Candle in the Wind.' Took me ages to find it. Finally got it in Grasmere. Got this Chris de Burgh one too. It's got 'The Lady in Red' on it."

Sarah took the CD's then reached up and plopped a big wet kiss on his cheek. "Oh Andy, I love you. Thank-you, thank-you."

Andy looked across at Jenny, still sitting on the bench at the top of the steps. He walked toward her, Sarah at his side. "What's Miss America doing at Sarah's house?"

Jenny smiled, focusing on an oil stain on his collar. "I met Miss Biggerstaff in the Hare and Hounds on my first day. We talked, and well—"

"Why don't you call her Biddy," Sarah interrupted. "Everybody else does." She rocked on the balls of her feet. "You can come in now. Andy's my friend, and you're his friend, so that makes us all friends. Come on in. I'll put the kettle on."

Jenny turned to Andy. "I hate to just barge in. Biddy's asleep but what if she wakes up and finds me sitting in her house?"

Andy shrugged. "What if she does? This isn't her house, anyway. It belongs to Sarah. Biddy's the housekeeper. Sarah isn't able to live alone. Still, she has a right to invite friends in. God knows, she doesn't get much company up here."

Sarah came to the door. "Come on, come on. I've got the kettle on and I've already got out the biscuits. They're your favorites, Andy, the chocolate-on-one-side ones."

Andy stood aside while Jenny stepped into the wide hall. There was a mustiness about the place, as if no windows were ever opened to let in the fresh air. Most of the doors were closed and the dark paneling only added to the gloom. A crystal chandelier hung over the wide staircase, its obvious beauty marred by a patina of grime on its myriad prisms and by the cobwebs strung between the arms. Sarah led them through the hall and took a right into the kitchen. This room was cleaner and brighter than the rest of the house. Sarah pulled back the curtains and raised the window.

"Biddy doesn't like the curtains pulled back like this," Sarah said. "She won't let me open the window either, so if she comes down I'll shut it." She closed her eyes, tilted back her head, and took a deep breath. "Don't you just love that fresh air coming in."

She motioned for them to sit at the big refectory table while she filled their cups, placed a cookie in each of their saucers, then sat beside Jenny with Andy in the chair opposite. "Isn't this nice," she said in her wheezy voice. "Friends coming to visit and us having tea together."

Jenny took a sip of the tea. "It sure is. This tea's the best I've ever tasted."

"Jenny's an American lady," Sarah said to Andy. "Isn't she beautiful?"

Andy had his elbow on the table, chin resting on his hand, his blue-eyed gaze full on Jenny. "Yeah, she's a smasher all right. Definitely not the type you see every day."

Sarah giggled in her funny way. "Are you in love with her?"

"Almost," he said with a grin. "Just give me a couple of minutes."

Jenny laughed and rolled her eyes. "Hey, come on, you guys. Give me a break."

Sarah poked her in the side. "I'm not a guy. I'm a girl. Guys are boys like Andy."

"Americans call everyone guy," Andy said, his gaze still on Jenny. "It's a sort of unisex thing."

He gave Sarah a teasing look. "But see, your guest is embarrassed, so why don't we change the subject. You said on the phone you felt better. Are you sure you're up to working tomorrow?"

"Yes. Please come and get me, Andy." Sarah twirled the spoon round in her cup creating a mini-maelstrom. "I'm nearly better and it's so lonely here with just Biddy."

"If she thinks it's OK, I'll pick you up at eight thirty. Someone can always bring you home if you don't feel well."

He bit into his biscuit and turned to Jenny. "Sarah works in Malone's Corner Shop, but she's been under the weather lately."

Jenny smiled to hide her surprise. Sarah didn't look capable of holding a job.

"I'm a good worker, even if I am a bit slow," Sarah said as if she'd read Jenny's thoughts. "Ada said I'm the best help she's ever had. You tell her Andy."

Andy nodded. "It's true. Ada did say that and she also told me she didn't know what she'd do without you."

"You got me the job, didn't you, Andy. I'm in charge of the magazines and newspapers. Oh, and all the cards, as well as the sweets and chocolates. Things like that. It's a very 'sponsible job. Pretty soon I'll be able to run the whole shop." She looked fondly at Andy then turned back to Jenny. "Andy's my very best friend in the whole wide world."

Andy winked at Jenny. "Sarah's a big con artist. Last week she told Ada Malone she was her very best friend."

Sarah giggled. "She is. You both are."

When they heard the heavy tread on the stairs, Jenny and Andy looked toward the hallway, while Sarah got to her feet and scuttled as fast as she could to the window. She closed it, yanked the curtains back in place, then flopped back in her chair just as Biddy turned the corner and came into the kitchen. Her gaze swept the table, and settled on Jenny. Her question though was directed at Sarah.

"I thought I told you not to let strangers into the house."

Sarah rolled her eyes, her third biscuit halfway to her mouth. "Biddy, honestly."

Biddy's eyes bored into Jenny's. "Well, you didn't waste any time. You acted so insulted when I said I knew you'd come snooping around, yet here you are. Proves I was right."

Biddy could have bitten out her own tongue. Hadn't she promised herself if she ever laid eyes on the girl again, she'd apologize for her outburst, explain it away as a case of mistaken identity. She sneaked a glance at Andy Ferguson. The stunned look on his face irked her, him with his raised eyebrows and superior ways. Still, she couldn't afford to let him, of all people, see her lose her temper. The last thing she needed was him reporting her to the Social Services, or saying something to his friend Dr. Hall. More than anything though, she didn't want Andy Ferguson's uncle to know any of this. Thank God the man was away for the summer. Surely the girl would be gone before he got back from France.

Jenny pushed back her chair and got to her feet. "You keep insisting you know me, but how could you? I've only been in the country a couple of weeks. Never been here before in my life. I must look like someone you knew and I don't have the least idea what you're talking about."

Biddy pretended to peer at her more closely, even took off her glasses, blew on them, and wiped them on the dishtowel. She put them back on as she got right up into the girl's face. She gave a little fake laugh of embarrassment, and even managed a shame-faced shake of the head. "I've changed my mind. Now that I look at you closely, I don't think you're that girl in the photo after all. Can you overlook the faults of an old woman with bad eyesight?"

Jenny almost clapped. The woman's sudden about-face was good enough to win her an Oscar. Still, it was to Jenny's own advantage to play along. Biddy smiled her toothy non-smile, but at the same time looked unsure, as if she didn't know whether she was the cat or the mouse. "Let's forget it," Jenny said. "Stoney Beck was on my list of places to see and I'll be gone soon. Besides, I don't want to come across as an ugly American."

Sarah grabbed Jenny's arm. "You're not ugly. Andy's nearly in love with you and we both think you're gorgeous." She turned to Biddy. "Isn't she gorgeous, Biddy?"

Biddy's smile was locked on her face "It's plain to see she's made a hit with you."

Jenny stuck out her hand. "Friends?" She tried not to stare at the nails of the hand grasping hers. They were bitten down to the quick, while the nails on the woman's other hand were long and curved, reminding Jenny of a claw. She glanced beyond Biddy at Andy, who was leaning back in his chair, arms folded, a cynical smile on his face and rolling his eyes for Jenny's benefit. She wasn't the only one who had a handle on this strange woman. She picked up her purse and edged closer to the door. "Guess I'll be going. Thanks for the tea and cookies, Sarah. They were real nice."

Andy was already on his feet. "I need to go too. I'll be here tomorrow, Sarah. Eight thirty sharp."

"Are you going back to the Hare?" he asked as he and Jenny walked toward their cars. "If you are, would you join me for a drink in the bar?"

She concentrated on that tiny scar on his upper lip. Andy Ferguson was a deal all right and she almost said yes, but too much was happening too fast. Out of nowhere came a vision of the cottage's oversized easy chair. She wanted to snuggle down in it and re-live her visit to St. Mary's, savor her time with the priest minute by precious minute. She pulled out her car keys. "Can I take a rain check? I've hardly had a minute to myself since I left home. Think I'll go back to the cottage and read some, and maybe take a nap. If I take it easy today I should feel like a million dollars by tomorrow."

Andy leaned against his car door and folded his arms. "If I said you already look like a million, you'd consider it a line, so I won't say it. Anyway, you're probably sick of hearing it."

"I sure am. I'm so sick of guys lining up for miles, falling all over themselves to tell me."

He grinned. "Yes, well, I might just have to jump the queue."

She almost told him she didn't mind if he went right to the head of the queue, but instead she gave a casual wave and headed for her car. Because of the presence of him and Sarah, her visit to Glen Ellen had gotten her nowhere. There'd been no chance to ask Biddy a single question and now she needed time alone to plan her next move. Intuition told her unless she trod lightly, this uneasy peace with the woman wouldn't last long.

Chapter Six

Jenny woke early, before six, shaking and sweating. She hadn't slept well, her night full of disjointed dreams about the priest. In one dream she told him she was his daughter. He smiled and when he opened his arms wide, Jenny walked into them. She danced from him to the boys' choir and they all sang "Ave Maria." But then the dream changed. This time Jenny stood before the lectern and told the congregation that this God-fearing priest of theirs was a phony. Father Woodleigh had talked Beverly Pender into sex. Jenny had thumped on the lectern and said she could prove it because she was the priest's daughter. Father Woodleigh had sprung to his feet and screamed at her *liar, liar*. The congregation got to its feet, pointed at her and chanted *liar, liar*. The priest had finally told her to get out of St. Mary's and if she ever set foot in the church again, he would have her thrown into the tower.

Now though, after a shower and a full English breakfast, and with the sun already warm on her bare arms, only fragments of the dreams remained. As she headed up Market Street, her mind was a beehive. Questions whirred around in there like drones, questions for which she had no answers. She had told the priest she wanted to return especially to listen to the choir. But where would that lead? It was all too hard. Seeing him, liking him, yet unable to let him know she was his daughter. And if she ever did decide to tell him, what would be his reaction? How could she ever expect him to feel anything but resentment at her turning up like this? Hadn't she noticed? He was a priest and the scandal would ruin him. What would it benefit if she went back to St. Mary's? The memory of two visits instead of one?

Once again she stood outside Dr. Hall's surgery. The light was on in the front room, and through the net curtains she saw the fuzzy shapes of five or six people in chairs lining the walls. Obviously the waiting room. Maybe this evening she would stop and see if Dr. Hall was the doctor who had her photograph.

Further along Market Street, she smiled and nodded at the woman weeding her garden and said good morning to an old couple coming out of the post office. She crossed Hallveck Common, and after she checked out the pink and white pants suit in the window of The Lake Boutique, she went inside The Bookworm. A man in his early twenties with a gold ring in his left ear stood behind the counter. He leaned his back against a shelf of books while he watched a tiny television placed beside the cash register. When Jenny gave a loud attention-getting cough, he turned round, still laughing at some joke from the set.

"Yes?" His tone was brusque, as if she'd interrupted him.

She fumbled in her bag for her pen and small pad to give the impression she was a woman with a purpose. "This may sound like a crazy question, but has this bookshop been here long?"

"What do you mean by long?"

"Twenty-six years maybe?"

"At least that." He gave the television another quick look and turned back to her. "Are you making a survey or something?"

"I guess you could say that. Some friends back home told me about a bookshop they visited when they came here on their honeymoon twenty-five years ago. They couldn't remember the name and I wondered if this could be it."

"This is it, all right" he said. "The only bookshop as far as I know that's ever been in Stoney Beck."

"Guess it's changed hands a couple of times since then though?"

"My partner and I, own it now. Bought it a couple of years ago from an old woman. She died last year."

"Ah."

"Can I show you some books?"

"Thanks but I guess I'll just browse."

He nodded before turning back to his TV.

She wandered down the aisles, ran her hand along the books, and pictured her pregnant mother lugging armloads of them around the shop, bending and stretching her swollen body as she placed them on the shelves. What an act she must have put on to appear carefree as well as strong and healthy so she wouldn't lose her job.

The man looked up from his TV as she headed for the door. "Couldn't find anything?"

She shook her head. "Just browsing, really."

She gave the shop one last look from the outside, and then went next door to Malone's Corner Shop. There were fresh vegetables in wooden crates out front under the windows. A woman tore a couple of small paper bags from a nail hammered into the wall and filled them with Brussels sprouts and tomatoes. She put them into her basket and went into the shop.

The inside of Malone's was almost the English equivalent of the American General Store. It was larger than it looked from the outside, about thirty feet wide but twice that distance in length. Shelves stretched from floor to ceiling, stacked with everything from a screwdriver to a box of After Eight chocolates. Jenny savored the mixed smells of cured bacon and aged cheeses, mingled with fresh crusty bread and pastries, as well as furniture polish, leather, scented soaps, candies. She walked over to the stand of picture postcards and turned it slowly, studying the different scenes. She picked out one of Lake Windermere and another of Buttermere, as well as a winter scene of the mountains covered with snow. She chose a few cards of Stoney Beck: a couple of Market Street and one of the Hare and Hounds. She smiled to herself. She'd send one of these to Uncle Tim with a big cross over the cottage, barely visible through the trees.

"Is Sarah Fitzgerald here?" she asked the woman behind the counter as she paid for the cards. "She said she'd try to come to work today."

The woman inclined her head toward the back of the store. "She's lying down in the living room. She came in this morning but should have stayed at home. She just isn't well enough."

"I sure am sorry," Jenny said. "She was excited about coming back."

The woman smiled as she handed Jenny her change. "I'm Ada Malone and you must be Jenny, Sarah's beautiful American lady. She's done nothing but talk about you all morning. At least she did until she ate a sandwich and couldn't keep it down." The woman hesitated. "Would you like to see her?"

"If it's not a problem."

Mrs. Malone looked at the four or five people wandering through the store. "I need to keep an eye on the shop. The tourist buses are coming in. We're a summer place and have to make hay while the sun shines." She pushed the graying hair away from her harried face. "You go on through. The living room's through that door at the back."

Jenny stopped in the doorway of the comfortably shabby room. Sarah sat on the sofa opposite and stared bleakly into the empty fireplace, absently picking at the flaking skin on her face. When Jenny rapped her knuckles gently on the door, Sarah looked up and half got to her feet, a smile hovering around her mouth. However, the effort was too great. She put her hand over her mouth and ran through the kitchen beyond and out the back door.

Jenny followed her as far as the kitchen, then stood listening to Sarah's retching. Steeling herself, she pulled a couple of feet of paper towel from the rack, wet it under the tap, and went outside. Sarah eventually raised her head from the grid that covered the outside drain and leaned against the wall, breathing hard, her face covered in perspiration. She took off her glasses and wiped her eyes with the back of her hand. Jenny felt a stab of pity so strong it overcame her distaste of the smell of vomit. She took Sarah's glasses, then gently wiped her face with the wet paper towel, and patted it dry with a tissue.

"You feel real bad don't you?" Jenny said as she took Sarah by the hand and led her inside. She rinsed the glasses under the tap and after she'd wiped them, replaced them on Sarah's nose. "How long have you been like this?"

"Donkey's years," Sarah said breathlessly as she leaned against the kitchen wall.

"You're too sick to be at work, Sarah. Why don't you let me run you home?"

Sarah's grabbed hold of Jenny's wrist. "I can't go home. Biddy'll kill me."

Jenny stared into the round frightened eyes. "What do you mean she'll kill you?"

"I've just wet my knickers. I never do that, never, but I couldn't help it this time. She'll murder me."

"No, no, it's all right." Jenny put an arm across Sarah's shoulders. "You couldn't help it. Anybody can have an accident when they're sick, anybody." She handed her a plastic bag from a stack in the corner. "If you take them off and put them in here, you'll feel more comfortable."

Sarah slipped out of her panties and stuffed them in the bag. "Biddy said she'd take me to the doctor but I know she's fibbing. She's turned mean and funny and doesn't like me any more."

"You're only saying that because you don't feel good," Jenny said as she led Sarah to the sofa.

"No, honest, she hates me. She said if I'm naughty these men in white coats will come after me and carry me off in their paddy wagon. It's special made for people like me."

Jenny wanted to tell her that was pure bullshit. "She's teasing you, Sarah," she said instead. "There is no such thing as men in white coats pulling a paddy wagon."

"Oh yes there are. If I'm bad, they'll nab me. Their place is miles away and it's got bars on the windows. And once they get me, I'll never get out." A sob sent a shudder through her as she grabbed Jenny's arm. "Don't tell Biddy I told you. She'll tear me to pieces."

"I won't breathe a word, honest. You can trust me."

"Spit on your hand, cross your heart and say hope to die."

Jenny did as she was told; then put her hands on Sarah's shoulders and studied the pale, frightened face. "I don't know why Biddy's telling you these things, but they're not true. Don't listen to her."

Ada stuck her head inside the room. "How's it going, Sarah? Are you feeling better now Jenny's here?"

"A little bit."

Ada crossed the room and put a hand on Sarah's forehead. "You're hot and clammy. You rest here a minute while I have a word with Jenny. We won't be long." She motioned for Jenny to follow her into the shop.

"Dr. Hall's outside talking to Andy. I think we should call him in." She took cans of beans out of a box and banged them onto the shelf as she talked. "Someone ought to horsewhip that Biddy for not doing something about this."

"How long has Sarah been like this?" Jenny asked.

"At least a month, maybe longer. It started out with a sore throat, something like the flu, but she should be over that by now."

The bell over the door jangled and two women entered.

"I'll go get the doctor," Jenny said. "You're needed here in the shop."

Dr. Hall looked about the same age as Andy so plainly was not the village doctor who had delivered Jenny twenty-three years ago. After Andy introduced them, she told the doctor about Sarah, then watched as he opened his car door and lifted out the familiar emblem of doctors the world over, the black leather bag. It was as though she'd drifted back in time to an old black and white movie. In Charlotte and other big cities in America, the huge sterile clinics had years ago replaced the family doctor who made house calls. Apparently though the practice was still very much alive here in England.

"I'll wait here," Andy said.

At Dr. Hall's request, Jenny sat on a chair in the corner of the room while he held a stethoscope against Sarah's chest and then her back, shone a light in her eyes, pressed her stomach. All the while he talked to her, asked questions, and reassured her at least twice that wetting your knickers when you vomited was nothing to be ashamed of. Yes, he'd be sure to let Biddy know this and would Sarah please stop worrying about it. Every now and then he turned to Jenny, making the odd comment in an effort to include her in the conversation.

"Am I going to die?" Sarah asked in a shaky voice.

He put his stethoscope away. "Of course not. I do think you should get on home, though. I'll ring Biddy and ask her to bring you into the surgery for a checkup."

Sarah's already swollen eyes looked ready to spill over again. "What'll Ada do without me? She said I'm the best worker she's ever had"

"Nobody's putting you out to grass, Sarah," Dr. Hall said, with a comforting hand on her shoulder. "We all get a little under the weather every now and then. Ada will manage somehow. You're right though, she's bound to miss you."

Sarah turned to Jenny. "Will you fill in for me, Jenny? You'd do almost as good a job as me, I just know you would."

Jenny looked from Sarah to Dr. Hall who gave an almost imperceptible nod on Sarah's behalf. "We'll see. I'll have a word with Mrs. Malone, and then drive you home."

When Jenny went into the shop, Mrs. Malone was weighing a string of sausages on old-fashioned scales. She added one more sausage to make up two pounds, then wrapped them in wax proof paper and placed them on the counter.

"That'll be two pounds, ten pence, Betty," she said to the old woman facing her.

Betty took them and placed them in her string bag. "That's five pence more than they cost me last week."

"And it's four pence more than they cost me." Mrs. Malone said. "I'm still only making the same profit."

Jenny waited until the woman had waddled out of the shop, and then she told Mrs. Malone the doctor said Sarah should go home.

"You're busy here in the shop. I'll be glad to take her."

"I'd be ever so grateful if you would. To tell you the truth, I can't stand that Biddy. Still, I'm sorry about Sarah. She should be on the mend by now. I hate to say it but I think she's got something serious."

"She's worried about leaving you to handle the shop by yourself, said you'll miss her."

"Well, she's right about that. I will miss her. Especially this week. One of my girls is gallivanting all over Paris with some boy she hardly knows, and the other is home in bed with the cramps." Mrs. Malone replaced the remaining sausages in the refrigerated glass case. "Anyway, Jenny, it's not your problem. I'll muddle through somehow."

Jenny ran her fingers along the counter. "Sarah asked me if I'd fill in for her until she's well. If you want me, I'll be glad to help out. I worked in a gourmet food store in our local mall when I was in college, so it isn't as though I don't know anything about the business." She didn't say that after only three weeks on the job she'd been forced to quit. Every evening she'd sprinted the ten blocks from Queens College to her home to relieve her mother, worn out and haggard from long days tending her sick, almost helpless husband.

Mrs. Malone wiped the already spotless glass. "For goodness sake. I can't let you do that. You, an American tourist, over here on holiday, having to stop all your fun to help me in this little shop. I—well, it's just unheard of."

"I don't mind, honest. Your girl with the cramps is bound to be back in a couple of days. And anyway, Sarah's convinced you'll go bankrupt if you don't let me help."

"Well, perhaps just for a few days. Anyway, I'm not sure you can work in this country without a permit. It might be against the law."

"Ah, let her do it, Ada."

Andy Ferguson came from behind the magazine rack, a copy of *Popular Mechanics* in his hand. "It'll be something to tell the folks when she gets back home. You can dance around the working-without-a-permit thing. Pay her in cash. All the countries do it on a small scale."

Jenny grinned, suddenly looking forward to the challenge. "Andy's right," she said to Ada. "My friend worked in Switzerland for a few months and they paid her in cash. If you'll take a chance, so will I. Give me half an hour to run Sarah home, and I'll come right back."

Andy stood beside his friend as they watched the Ford turn right at the post office. "What do you think Sarah's got?"

Jonathon Hall stroked the day old stubble on his chin. "Don't know right off. Judging from the color of her skin it could be any one of a number of things. I'll know more after I've examined her. Might need to check her into hospital for tests."

He gave Andy a sly smile. "You fancy that Jenny, don't you? I saw the way you looked at her."

Andy shrugged, knowing from experience he could never hide his feelings from his friend. Moreover, it was true. He did fancy her. "You don't miss much, do you Jon," he said. "But she's an American. I'm not about to get tangled up with somebody who lives three thousand miles away."

He stuck his hands deep in the pockets of his coveralls, remembering the strange conversation between Jenny and Biddy Biggerstaff. "There's something about her I can't fathom, mysterious one minute as if she's working for Interpol or the CIA, then suddenly she's all dewy-eyed like some American prom queen. But if you catch her off guard, she'd got this other look, strange and sad. Something's on her mind. I can tell."

Jonathon Hall gave him a quizzical look. "What the bloody hell are you rambling on about?"

"She's no ordinary tourist, Jon. I'd bet the garage on it." Andy looked the length of Market Street. "Now what secrets do you suppose a little out-of-the-way place like this could hold for a girl from Charlotte, North Carolina who's never set foot in England before in her life?"

Jonathon smiled and clapped his friend on the back. "The trouble with you is you read too many mysteries. Come on, I'm famished. Tell Alf you're knocking off for lunch. We'll get a beer and sandwich at the Hare."

After Andy had a quick word with Alf, he got into the car beside his friend. He had acted casual enough in the shop, flipping through the pages of that magazine as if it didn't matter at all that Jenny would be in the shop just across the common from his garage, working behind the counter of Malone's. It was almost as though she lived in the town. He grinned at Jonathon. "Lunch is on me today."

Chapter Seven

On the way home, Sarah held on to the plastic bag containing her knickers. She sneaked a look at Jenny. Her dark blonde hair was thick and shiny, with the prettiest way of turning under at the ends as it rested on her shoulders. She had little gold rings in her pierced ears and a thin gold chain around her neck. Sarah raised a pudgy hand to her own short, straight hair and wondered how it felt to be beautiful and normal like Jenny. She had come all the way from America on her own. She didn't know a soul in Stoney Beck and was staying in the Hare and Hounds cottage all by herself and driving one of Andy's cars all over the place. She could drive a car and do things Sarah only dreamed of. She felt a little puff of pride. Jenny was like a real fairy princess. And just look at the two of them, driving along together like they were very best friends. Sarah wished the other girls from the shop had been there when she asked Jenny to take her place in the shop and Jenny had said yes. Oh, the girls weren't nasty or anything. Still, they giggled and talked to each other all day long and didn't say much to Sarah unless it was to do with the shop. Even Ada did that sometimes but she was nicer than most and Sarah could tell Ada really liked her. Even so, none of them would have been as kind to her as Jenny when Sarah had wet her knickers. They would have nudged each other, sniggered, and rolled their eyes like they did lots of times when Sarah got things wrong. If Jenny had not come home with Sarah, she would have been terrified to tell Biddy she had wet herself. Now she didn't have to because Jenny had promised to explain. And hadn't Dr. Hall promised to tell Biddy she must bring Sarah to his surgery for a checkup.

Every now and then, Jenny turned to Sarah and smiled. She had lovely white even teeth, not little dingy ones like Sarah's. Best of all, when Jenny pulled up outside Glen Ellen, she took hold of Sarah's hand and gave it a little encouraging squeeze, just like Mummy used to do.

***

When Biddy looked through the window and saw the blue Ford coming up the drive, she scuttled to the downstairs bathroom and put her teeth in, then opened the door. She stood with arms folded, feet apart as Sarah and the girl came up the steps holding hands, and went into the kitchen.

"Didn't I warn you this would happen?" she said to Sarah. "But as usual you wouldn't listen. You can be so stubborn if you don't get your own way."

Out of the corner of her eye, Biddy saw the half-empty bottle of gin on the counter. She grabbed it and shoved it in the cupboard under the sink, then pressed her hand against her lower back as she straightened up. "It's for the arthritics, strictly medicinal," she said. Then turned away from the American girl's knowing eyes.

"Go up to your room and lie down," she said to Sarah. "I'll bring up a glass of ginger ale later."

Jenny took the plastic bag from Sarah, then more to irritate the woman than anything else, she put her arms round Sarah and gave her a hug. "It's all right, honey," she said softly, "I'll explain everything."

She waited while Sarah mounted the stairs, then placed the bag on the table. "Sarah vomited and strained so hard, she wet herself. Dr. Hall told her it was nothing to be ashamed of. It could have happened to anybody."

Biddy's owl-like eyes narrowed into slits. "Are you telling me you took it upon yourself to take her to the doctor?"

Jenny shook her head. "He was outside the shop. It was Ada's idea to call him in. Sarah asked me to explain about her panties."

"Why couldn't she tell me herself. That's so typical of her, trying to give the impression I'm a witch. The arthritics are creeping into every joint I've got, but still I cook and keep this house clean, big as it is. It's a thankless job, I can tell you."

Jenny bit her lip, holding back the questions. What about scaring Sarah half to death with stories of paddy wagon men in white coats coming to cart her off to a home. "I'm filling in for Sarah at the shop for a few days and need to get back," she said instead. "Ada's there by herself and it's a busy day. Oh yes, one more thing. Dr. Hall asked me to tell you he'll be calling you after lunch. He wants Sarah in for a checkup."

Biddy leaned her back against the counter and glared at Jenny. "First you tell me I've got you mixed up with someone else, then here you are, fawning all over Sarah. Now you tell me you're working in Malone's, already on a first-name basis with Ada Malone. You're worming your way in everywhere aren't you?"

Jenny slapped her hand on the counter. "What are you talking about, for God's sake? Why are you so suspicious of me and what's this great big secret you're scared to death I'll find out?"

Biddy's already pale face turn paler and there was a wildness about her eyes. But her voice was steady. "Why wouldn't I be suspicious? Anyone can see you're not the type to make friends with the likes of her."

Jenny pulled out her car keys. Getting mad would get her nowhere, especially since Biddy's words hit home. If Sarah had not been the best excuse in the world to find out what was nettling this woman, would Jenny honestly have gone to Malone's this morning? Or would she have offered to take Sarah's place in the shop, or even brought her home when she was sick? Biddy Biggerstaff was Jenny's best lead to finding answers to her mother's note. Why was this woman so hostile? Jenny had no idea. But it made her all the more determined to find out.

"I have to go," she said, glancing at her watch. "I told Ada I wouldn't be long."

As she walked out the door, Biddy's eyes burned into her back.

An hour later, when Biddy answered the phone, Sarah was fast asleep in her room. Dr. Hall said he wanted to see her in his surgery at ten on Thursday for a physical exam. If, in the meantime, there was any change in her condition, Biddy should ring him immediately. When Biddy asked if he knew what was ailing the girl, he said it was too early to say.

After she hung up, she reached in the cupboard under the sink for the bottle of gin and poured herself a double. What if Sarah had something life threatening? God knows, things were bad enough with her reasonably healthy. Biddy still couldn't get over what that old bugger of a doctor had the nerve to say before he had gone to France. "You're not yourself, Biddy. You need a medical checkup, mental as well as physical." He had said it casually enough, but it had alarmed Biddy. Had he noticed anything strange about her? Sometimes, lately, even Biddy herself had wondered, like the day she'd seen those worms on the kitchen table. There must have been at least twenty of them, and some as much as ten inches long. They'd crawled all over the cheese and sliced bread. The largest one of all had hung from the side of Sarah's cup and when she raised it to her mouth, Biddy had screamed. Sarah was so startled, she'd dropped the cup, breaking it and spilling tea all over the table. At that instant the worms disappeared.

Biddy had glossed over the whole thing, saying she'd seen a mouse peeking out the pantry door. But the awful doubt lingered. If there had been worms, Sarah would have said so. Just thinking about it set Biddy to trembling all over again but she shook herself and gave a little laugh that turned into a croak. Living alone with the likes of Sarah Fitzgerald was enough to drive anyone round the bend.

Now, on top of everything else, there was this added worry of Jenny Robinson. Biddy gulped half the contents of the glass. She had changed her mind. The American girl was not innocently passing through. It was too much of a coincidence. She had deliberately waited until this late date to make her move. Biddy thanked God that she had seen the girl's photograph. Otherwise, she would never have recognized her. She didn't resemble Beverly all that much. It was only when you knew and looked at her up close. Then you could see.

Biddy poured another strong one, then took her teeth out and put them in a glass on the counter. After she'd downed the gin in two swallows, she headed for the sofa in the study to sleep it off and think of some way she could force that girl to leave Stoney Beck before it was too late. Sarah's ginger ale could wait. Biddy had to think about herself. If she didn't do it, who would? Before she settled down, she made sure the curtains were closed so she couldn't see the tree, or more to the point, so the tree couldn't see her.

The night of the big storm would stay with Biddy forever. She had been staring out her bedroom window when a bolt of lightning hit the tree with a window-rattling crack, lighting her room as if a thousand roman candles had gone off at once. It had knocked out the electricity in the house and Biddy had cowered on the floor at the foot of the bed, too petrified to move until daylight. The three electric clocks in the house had stopped at eleven o'clock. Later in the day, when the report came from France about the accident, she learned that Edna and Fred Fitzgerald had been killed at midnight the night before. If you allowed for the one-hour time difference, this was the selfsame time that lightning had struck the tree. Most people would probably say all this was nothing more than a coincidence. But Biddy knew better. The spirits of Edna and Fred had somehow jumped from the wreck site in the Pyrenees into the tree right here on the front lawn. Biddy would have had the tree chopped down ages ago, but Sarah wouldn't hear of it. Over almost anything else, Biddy had her way but she was too afraid of the tree to go against Sarah this time.

Chapter Eight

Jenny looked upon her job at Malone's as a godsend, a good vantage point to continue her search for clues, while at the same time earn some extra money. Ada told her Sarah had been diagnosed with a kidney infection, was on medication and under Dr. Hall's care. She wouldn't be back in the shop for at least three or four weeks. On top of that, the girl who'd stayed out a couple of days with cramps had gone to work in a hotel in Windermere. When Jenny offered to stay on at the shop, Ada was only too willing. Not only did this give Jenny an excuse to hang around the village, without people asking questions, but also she liked the job. Rather than bulk buy like Americans, most people in the village came into the shop every day and before the first two weeks were gone, Jenny was on a first name basis with most of them. She and Ada had made a deal that Jenny would receive no pay until her last day in the shop which surely couldn't be far off because hadn't they put that sign in the window.

Wearing the apron with the big pockets Ada had given her, Jenny walked up and down the rows, scribbling notes as she went, until she was as familiar with the shop's layout as Ada herself. Jenny wondered how many of the customers, especially those over forty, who had lived in Stoney Beck all their lives, remembered her mother. Surely there were some, probably Ada herself. She was born here and was about her mother's age. Every day Jenny planned to ask Ada if she had ever known a Beverly Pender, and, by the way, what was the name of the village doctor about twenty-three years ago. But somehow the words wouldn't come. Jenny couldn't shake the feeling there was something dark about her mother's secret, something even worse than having a priest for a father, a priest who didn't even know he had a daughter.

Most days, Andy exercised his dog on the common and two or three times, when business was slow, Jenny joined them. He shopped in Malone's and sometimes, when there was time, Ada made a pot of tea and the three of them sat swapping stories. One day, after Andy had gone back to the garage, Ada told Jenny that he had been jilted by some star struck girl who didn't know her arse from her elbow. It had been just weeks before their wedding with the invitations already sent out, and even the wedding cake ordered. As far as Ada knew, Andy had formed no serious relationship since. Jenny knew then the reason he hadn't asked her for a date, even though it was obvious he liked her. He was afraid of being burned again.

At the end of her second week, Jenny said goodnight to Ada and headed back to the cottage. She washed and dried her hair, then picked up the phone and dialed Uncle Tim's number. As much as she loved him, she'd kept him in the dark about most of what had happened since her arrival in Stoney Beck. Was there any way to break it to him gently that her father was a Roman Catholic priest? She hadn't mentioned either that she was working in Malone's while she tried to find out what the weird Biddy Biggerstaff knew about her yet wouldn't tell. After the sixth ring, the recorder came on. "Hi, Uncle Tim," Jenny said. "Wish you could have been here this morning. The lake was covered with a white mist and the tiny island in the center looked as if it was floating in the clouds. Weather warm. Talk to you soon. Love you."

After she hung up, she strolled down to the lake. There was a fog at the far end, slinking nearer, veiling the hills and meadows in an almost purple mist. Restless, she walked to the front of the inn and sat on a bench outside. She looked down at the slats and ran her fingers through the gaps. Was this where her mother had sat when she met Charles Woodleigh? Could it be the very bench? The hikers or mountain climbers, or whatever they were, sat at a nearby table, laughing and talking among themselves. Jenny watched and smiled if one of them looked her way, almost wishing she were sitting among them. Suddenly, the pretty blonde girl on the end flashed her a smile and beckoned her over. Jenny gave an answering wave, and was half out of her seat when a young couple rushed past her and laughingly joined the others at the table. The blonde girl moved her chair to make room for the couple and looked straight through Jenny as though she wasn't there.

Jenny felt the heat rush to her face as she quickly looked away and plopped back on the bench. Even Mr. Pudsley, who'd obviously seen it all from the doorway, and who now came over to chat, couldn't budge the awful lonely feeling that suddenly cloaked her. The group weren't hikers or mountain climbers at all, he said, but archeologists who stayed at the inn for months at a time while they dug for Viking remains. They were working on a dig up in the fells and were nice once you got to know them.

After Mr. Pudsley had gone back inside, Jenny stayed, lost in her memories. It was as if her mother were nearby, watching. And why shouldn't she be here? This was the very place it had all began. Didn't some people believe the soul hung around the earth for a while before going on to heaven? Jenny tried to imagine the young Charles Woodleigh walking shyly up to the lonely American student.

"Is this seat taken?" he could very well have said.

"No," her mother had probably answered, or perhaps just shook her head. She'd have given a bashful smile, and moved over a little to make room for him.

Market Street sailed away and Jenny was home now, in Charlotte, in the kitchen sitting across the table from her mother, a stack of sympathy cards between them. She listened again while her mother told her she didn't have to worry any more about getting Huntington's disease because Michael Robinson wasn't her father after all. Her real father was some Englishman who had disappeared off the face of the earth. Jenny had flung the cards across the table, and lashed out with those vicious words. Now, all too late, she could see. She went over it all again for the hundredth time. Her mother's stricken face, the desperation in her eyes, and surely her hands had been shaking if Jenny had only taken the trouble to look. Why hadn't she at least uttered words of encouragement, placed a hand on the drooping shoulders? If she had, would it have made a difference? Would her mother be alive today?

"Jenny?" Andy Ferguson said. "You OK?"

She looked up, startled, hardly seeing him through eyes blurred with tears. She blinked and the tears rolled down her cheeks. He reached for her hand and she let him pull her to her feet, let him put his arm around her waist and lead her to his car. He drove without saying a word. Minutes later, he parked outside the Prince of Wales, a restaurant on the lake's opposite shore.

He came round to her side to help her out, as if she were incapable of doing it herself.

She sniveled. "Oh man, I'll bet you think I'm some kind of clown."

"No, I don't." He took her hand and led her away from the parking lot, to a secluded grove of trees. "Do you feel like talking about it?"

"I don't know. I hardly ever let my guard down like that. Even when my dad was real sick, I held up until the very end."

"I'm sorry. I didn't know. How long has it been?"

"Just three months. He'd been sick a long time. I couldn't help but be glad for him when he went. It was real hard to watch him suffer. I did the best I could to help my mom. She—"

"You should have brought her with you," Andy interrupted. "Maybe a change of scene would have been good for her."

"No, no, you don't understand—"

"It's all right, it's all right," he said, alarm stealing into his voice. "You don't have to tell me. Just cry if you want to. You're still grieving for your father. You need time to heal."

"It isn't just him. A couple of weeks later, my mother, she didn't mean to, but the pills and wine, the combination, she—"

Jenny let Andy push the hair away from her face and take her in his arms, let him rub his hands up and down her back. He leaned his back against a tree and held her while she sobbed on his shoulder until only the odd shudder was left. She could feel the wetness of his shirt where all her tears had fallen and even though the crying had stopped, she didn't want to move. The agony of it all had turned into a quiet peace. There was some of the smell of his garage left on him. Leather, oil, the scent of a man.

He took the wad of tissues out of her hand and wiped away the rest of her tears. "You'll feel better now." He put his hands on her shoulders while he studied her face, then pulled her to him again and stroked her hair, patted her as if she were a child.

She pulled more tissues out of her purse and blew her nose. "I've been fine until tonight. Don't know what came over me. I'm real sorry to dump on you like this."

"Have you had dinner?" he asked, tracing his finger gently along her jaw line.

She shook her head. "I'm not hungry."

"Well I am," he said with a little laugh. "Let's go on in. We can get a glass of wine and if you change your mind, this place has the best salmon and trout in the Lake District. Why don't you go to the ladies room and freshen up a bit while I try to get us a table at the window."

Ten minutes later, after she'd wiped the running mascara from her puffy eyes and applied new lipstick, she and Andy stared out the huge plate-glass window and watched a wide ribbon of gold stretch across the water toward them. Then the huge orange ball of the sun slipped between the fells. Lights blinked on in Stoney Beck across the lake. She reached across the table and took hold of Andy's hand. It was rough, calloused. He turned toward her, eyebrows raised a notch or two, but he only smiled and held on tight. While they drank the wine, he talked her into eating something and ordered for them both. The poached salmon was served with tiny new potatoes and spinach soufflé. There was a thick white sauce with bits of egg and parsley to go over the potatoes.

"Why did you travel so far from home by yourself?" he asked after the waiter had gone. "And why here? You didn't know a soul when you got off that train. People come here from all over, but not when they're alone and grieving over their parents."

She almost smiled. "You sound like my Uncle Tim. You should have heard him when I said I wanted to come to England. But I'm OK, honest I am."

She spread her napkin on her lap. "Can't we change the subject. How about telling me something about yourself."

"What do you want to know?"

"Well, how come you're such good friends with Sarah? You got her the job at Malone's, pick her up, take her to work, and bring her golden oldie CD's."

He passed Jenny the salt and pepper. "Sarah's parents and mine were friends. When Ada needed more help in the shop, I talked her into giving Sarah a try. Now Ada thinks the world of her. Sarah may be slow but there's something so special about her. You must have seen it. She knows she's limited and yet tries so damn hard."

He twirled the stem of his wine glass. "When her parents were killed in that wreck, we all thought she'd go to pieces. But she didn't. Soon as the funeral was over, she went right back to work."

Jenny sipped her wine. "I guess anything was better than staying at home with Biddy. She's weird as hell, Andy, and the whole setup seems strange to me. It's Sarah's house, but Biddy calls the shots. What gives?"

Andy told her that in the beginning Biddy was hired as a nanny for Sarah; later she became the Fitzgeralds' housekeeper. It was village gossip that the Fitzgeralds had included Biddy in their will as long as she stayed with Sarah who was considered mentally handicapped. If there'd been no responsible person living with her, her fate would have been in the hands of the Social Services. Oh, they would probably try to find somebody to live with her, perhaps a couple, but if nobody was available, Sarah was in danger of being whisked to some home miles away. Once in one of those places, she may never get out.

"Biddy's always been strange," Andy said. "It didn't matter so much when Sarah's parents were alive. Fred Fitzgerald was an artist, a painter, did some pretty good work too. They traveled a lot and Sarah always went with them. Still, they had this blind spot where Biddy was concerned which is probably why the will was written up the way it was."

He looked up from spreading butter on his roll and gave Jenny a guarded look. "I'm not implying Sarah isn't safe with Biddy, you understand, but things are a lot dicier than they used to be."

"Where did the Fitzgeralds get her from?"

"She used to be the town's midwife."

Midwife.

The word echoed in Jenny's ears as though she were in a cave. Biddy had been the village midwife and Jenny would bet every penny she had that this woman had been the midwife who had delivered her. Why hadn't the woman said something? That day in the tearoom, when she told Jenny she'd seen her photograph, wouldn't it have been the most natural thing in the world just to say so?

Andy reached across the table and took the wineglass out of her trembling hand. "Jenny, for God's sake, what is it? You've turned grey. You're not going to break down again are you?"

She shook her head. The air in the restaurant had become stifling and she wiped the perspiration from her hands with her napkin. "Can we walk by the lake? There's a full moon tonight."

Andy signaled to the waiter standing near the dessert cart. "Check please," he mouthed.

They took off their shoes and trudged along by the water's edge. Andy glanced at Jenny as she strode along beside him, her long dark blonde hair blowing behind her. He longed to put an arm around her and pull her to him, but didn't dare. One wrong move on his part and she would be gone. This was no ordinary girl from the village or anywhere else. There was nothing ordinary about her. Oh, she'd cried on his shoulder and grasped his hand in the restaurant, but he'd recognized those acts for what they were. She was grieving over the loss of her parents and had perhaps come to the Lakes to get away from the sadness, then realized too late she'd brought it all with her. In a weak moment, she had reached for him. Still, he couldn't shake the feeling that something else was worrying her.

When they came to a stream that emptied into the lake, they sat on a rock facing the water.

"You're a hard one to figure out, Jenny," he said. "I've got this strange feeling about you. It's as if you're looking for something. Then there's this thing with Biddy." He leaned back against the rock but didn't take his gaze away from her face. "Something was going on between you two the other day. She was abrupt and rude, even acted as if she knew you, or at least knew of you. And what was all that talk about a photograph? Was it you or wasn't it? And why would you care that she used to be a midwife?"

He gave her a lopsided grin, taking any bite out of the words. "You're not working for the CIA are you?"

"No, and I'm not working for the FBI either." She tried to put a smile in her voice. "I couldn't care less that Biddy was a midwife. Just surprised that's all. And I wish she'd stop thinking I'm somebody I'm not."

They sat quietly for a few minutes, then when Jenny got to her feet and stared out across the lake, she reminded Andy of a figurehead on the prow of some ancient sailing ship.

"What are you thinking about?" he asked.

She looked down at him. "You. You're very nice, you know."

She reached for his hand to pull him up. "Come on, it's chilly. Let's go home."

***

Something woke her in the night, the wind perhaps or the rain pelting against the cottage windows. She put her hands behind her head and stared into the blackness, trying to get her thoughts in some sort of order. Finally, she got up and made a pot of tea on the little stove, then sat in front of the window and stared out at the sleeping English street, while she concentrated on her mother and Charles Woodleigh. Surely they had sat at this very window and looked out at this exact same scene. The feeling came from out of nowhere, the strange sensation the cottage was bewitched, that it was trying to ensnare her in the same web it had trapped her mother with all those years ago. Jenny's skin prickled as she turned to look over her shoulder into the room. Of course there was nothing there. She sipped the tea as her thoughts turned to Biddy. She was over the shock of finding out the woman had been a midwife, the only one in Stoney Beck when Jenny was born. In a way it helped to know, somehow inching her closer to solving the mystery.

But Jenny hadn't bargained on meeting Andy Ferguson. When her father had been diagnosed with Huntington's disease, she'd steered clear of romance, never even had a steady boyfriend. Now that she'd been freed of her fear, Andy had come along. But he was causing problems. As Jenny felt sleep overtake her, she made up her mind to cool it with him before it was too late. He was already suspicious of Jenny's explanation of why she had come to Stoney Beck and was asking too many questions. The last thing she needed was to make the same mistake as her mother and fall in love with an Englishman.

***

The next day Jenny watched through Malone's window as Andy threw Pete's Frisbee high into the air on Hallveck Common. After a dozen throws and a dozen perfect catches by Pete, Andy did no more than raise a finger, and his dog changed into his other self, walking sedately beside his master toward the garage. When Andy looked across at Malone's and saw her, he headed for the shop.

"I'm driving to my brother's tonight in Kendall," he said, as he picked up the *Daily Telegraph* from the rack. "I've got a clock he's interested in, then staying for supper. His wife's Indian and cooks the best curried lamb you ever put in your mouth. Will you come with me?" His voice was confident, probably still thinking of last night.

"I'm sorry, Andy, can't make it tonight. Can I take a rain check?"

A shadow crossed his face. "Is everything OK? You sound different. Last night, you were—"

"Yes, I know, and thanks for your shoulder. Still, I wouldn't read too much into that if I were you."

He dropped forty-five pence on the counter and folded his newspaper into a tube. "I wouldn't dream of it. Maybe some other time."

A timid cough came from a customer at the back of the shop. "Excuse me, love, can you give me a hand. I've told Ada to put the prunes down lower, but she never listens. We're not all six feet tall like she is."

As Jenny handed the cans to the old woman, she heard the lonely jingle of the bell as Andy went out the door.

An hour later, over their third cup of tea that day, Jenny told Ada how surprised she'd been to learn Biddy used to be a midwife.

"Aye, but that was a long time ago," Ada said. "Biddy was different then. Oh, never very friendly or anything, you understand. Still, Angus Thorne, who was our doctor back then, said she was good at her job."

Jenny kept a politely indifferent look on her face as she pulled an order pad out of her pocket, and pretended to check the assorted brands of tea on the shelf while Ada prattled on about Angus and Gladys Thorne's stone cottage in the south of France.

"That's where they are now," she said, "at least they were until this morning. They've gone on a fortnight's cruise round the Med." She smiled at Jenny. "Nice work if you can get it."

"Do they come home much?" Jenny asked.

"They spend about half the year here and the rest in Provence. They're coming home in about six weeks." Ada walked to the window and pointed up the brow. "They live in that big white house opposite Andy's, the one with the weathervane on the roof. Dr. Thorne is Andy's great uncle."

"*Andy's great uncle*," Jenny blurted out. "But he never said." She bit her lip when Ada swung round, eyebrows raised to her hairline.

"Why would he? Does it matter?"

"No. I guess I'm just surprised, that's all."

The phone rang and Ada went to answer it. Talk about being saved by the bell. Jenny stood at the window and stared at Dr. Thorne's house. She felt like a marathon runner with only those last three hundred odd yards to go. This had to be the doctor who had her picture. Ada had said he would be back in the village in six weeks, but that was a long time to wait. Perhaps Jenny could get the phone number for his place in France, or if he had a computer, maybe she could even e-mail him. She had seen a laptop in Andy's garage, and there was another one in the Hare. She shoved the scratch pad into her apron pocket and stuck the pencil behind her ear. She didn't need Biddy after all.

By the next evening, Jenny had changed her mind. Dr. Thorne was a thousand miles away on some ship in the middle of the Mediterranean and even ten days seemed a long time. After work she put on her running shoes and jogged toward Glen Ellen. She raised her hand to knock on the kitchen door, and jumped when it was yanked open by Biddy as if she had seen Jenny coming. Jenny forced a friendly smile. "I told Ada I would be jogging up this way and she asked me if I'd check on Sarah. Is it OK if I come in for a few minutes?"

Biddy folded her arms and stood in the center of the doorway. "No it isn't. And it's strange Ada didn't mention you coming. She rang me herself just a couple of minutes ago."

Jenny stared down at her Reeboks. "I guess she forgot."

"If that's all you came for, I'm going back inside." Biddy made to close the door. "It's chilly standing here."

"So, how is Sarah?" Jenny said, stopping short of sticking her foot in the door. "She doing OK?"

"What do you think? She's not as daft as she looks. It's the attention she's after. Anyway, I'm taking her to Dr. Hall tomorrow for a checkup."

Biddy lit a cigarette and squinted at Jenny through a swirl of smoke. "Looks as if you've trekked all the way up here for nothing."

"Not for nothing," Jenny said. "There is something about my being here that's really bothering you. I don't understand. You don't even know me."

Biddy took a deep drag on her cigarette and blew the smoke out of the side of her mouth. "So, now it comes, the real reason you're here. You're no more concerned about Sarah Fitzgerald than I am. She's just an excuse for you to stop and nose around here isn't she?"

"Nose around for what? What's this big secret you're hiding from me? I'm totally in the dark. I didn't even know my mother had sent the doctor my picture until the night she—"

"Until the night she what?"

"It doesn't matter."

"It does to me. Is she dead?"

Jenny stared at the vein throbbing in the woman's neck. "Yes."

When Biddy let out a long, satisfied sigh, Jenny turned to look at the tree, pretending to be interested in a huge crow perched on one of the dead limbs.

"What are you looking at?" Biddy's voice was suddenly shrill.

Jenny swung round to face her. "Excuse me?"

"Why were you staring at the tree?" Biddy leaned on every shaky word.

"I wasn't. Just looking at that crow. Why?"

"None of your business.

Jenny felt a sudden chill at the woman's bizarre dialogue. "I know you used to be a midwife," she said, trying to get the conversation back on track. "You tended to my mother didn't you? Was there some mystery about my birth?"

Without a word, Biddy dropped the cigarette end and ground it into the kitchen tile with her foot.

"Don't underestimate me," Jenny said. "I'll find out and I'm not leaving Stoney Beck until I do."

"If you hang around here, you'll be sorry," Biddy said before she slammed the door in Jenny's face.

Chapter Nine

Sarah had her cup of tea and two pieces of toast ages ago and was dressed and ready to go. She lifted up the tea cozy and felt the pot. Still warm but it wouldn't be much longer if Biddy didn't soon wake up.

The big red and brown bird, its wooden wings flapping, hurled himself out of the clock on the wall and cuckooed ten times before he was yanked back in and the door slammed in his face.

Sarah's Daddy had bought the clock the last time they'd gone to the Black Forest. It had been her favorite thing in the entire house when Mummy and Daddy had been alive and even now she'd laugh sometimes when the doors flew open and the bird shot out. She sat on the edge of the chair and drummed her fingers on the kitchen table. Dr. Hall was in his surgery for only a couple of hours and if she and Biddy didn't leave soon, it would be too late. He opened again in the evening, but that was too late for Biddy who never went anywhere after five. She'd been dipping into the mother's milk again. There'd been all the usual signs last night. At first she'd put the bottle back under the sink after each drink, but later hadn't seemed to care whether Sarah saw her or not. When Sarah begged her to put the bottle away, Biddy had laughed right in her face then staggered up the stairs, swinging the bottle as she went. Sarah remembered Mummy scolding Biddy for drinking the mother's milk and for a while she'd been more careful. Lately though, she'd gone back to the old ways and drank it any time she felt like it.

Sarah heaved herself out of the chair and held on to the banister as she climbed the stairs. She knocked softly on Biddy's bedroom door then opened it. The mixed smells of stale cigarettes and mother's milk filled the room. There lay Biddy sprawled across the bed, the empty bottle on its side on the nightstand, next to her false teeth. A glass lay shattered beside the bed on the hardwood floor. Sarah got the dustpan and brush from under the sink in the bathroom and swept up the glass so Biddy wouldn't cut her feet. She emptied the overflowing ashtray into the dustpan and blew away the loose ash coating the bedside table.

Gently, she shook Biddy's shoulder with her free hand. "Wake up, Biddy, wake up. You've got to take me to Dr. Hall's. You promised."

Biddy grunted and shifted position.

Sarah carried the dustpan downstairs and emptied it in the pedal bin by the sink, then sat at the kitchen table while she wrote a note to Biddy. She used her red pencil and wrote it extra big so Biddy would be sure to see.

Could not wake you so I am going to the doctor's by myself. I will be back soon. Sarah.

She read it three times to be sure she'd got it right, then after adding two crosses for kisses, she propped it between the salt and pepper shakers. She picked up the beige leather bag that had been her mother's favorite, and after one last look around, walked out the kitchen door.

She crossed the lawn to the tree, seeing it as it once was, full of leaves, and remembering the summer days she'd sat with Mummy and Daddy in its shade, drinking lemonade and eating sandwiches. The white bench that encircled the trunk was still there, even though the paint was peeling now and some of the slats were gone. She looked up through the branches thinking of the Christmas Daddy had climbed the ladder for the mistletoe way up at the top, and Mummy had begged him to come down before he got himself killed. He'd hung the mistletoe over the dining room door and surprised Mummy when he'd come from behind. When he'd grabbed her, she'd squealed, until he put his arms round her and gave her a great big kiss. Sarah had laughed so hard she'd almost wet her knickers.

Biddy was afraid of the tree and kept the curtains on the front of the house closed so she couldn't see it. She never looked at it when she went out. One day when Sarah asked why she did this, Biddy had said the silliest thing. She kept them closed because Sarah's parents were up in the tree. Sarah said how could they be in the tree when they'd been killed in a wreck in Spain. Biddy wouldn't listen though and told her she was too stupid to understand.

Sarah gently pushed the swing that still hung from the lowest limb as it had since she was a little girl, then patted the tree one last time before she headed down the drive. When she reached the lane, she stood by the hedge, suddenly unsure. She had never walked all the way to the village alone, never in her whole life. But Dr. Hall had said he wanted to see her and what would he think if she didn't come. She took a great big breath, looked back at the house just once then set off down Vallhellyn Lane. She swung her arms and sang a little song. "*Up the airy mountain, Down the rushy glen, We daren't go a hunting for fear of little men—*" She stopped singing, suddenly seeing the little men tearing after her. They all wore white coats, and screamed with laughter as they pulled that paddy wagon of theirs behind them. She sang another song her daddy had taught her. *"Roll out the barrel, we'll have a barrel of fun—"* The song cheered her and made her sad at the same time. She saw again her daddy walking along beside her, laughing down at her in that way he'd had, delighted she'd remembered the words.

Walking and singing at the same time made Sarah breathless and she slowed her pace still more. She knew from the signpost by her house it was three miles to the village and even though it sounded a long way and she'd never done it before, it wasn't all that far. Not by a normal person's standards, and hadn't Jenny done it just yesterday. Sarah would not have known about this because Biddy had not said a word about it, but Sarah had heard the door slam and when she looked out the window, saw Jenny jogging back toward the village.

Sarah leaned against a stile to catch her breath. Almost there now, almost there. She could see the village church just up ahead, and once she reached the Post Office and turned the corner, Dr. Hall's surgery was just on down Market Street. The day was warm and she felt a slick of sweat trickle down between her breasts. She reached for the hem of her skirt to wipe her sweating face. At the same time she prayed the nausea rising in her throat would go away as it sometimes did and she wouldn't have to throw up on the side of the road. She stopped in mid-stride and her mouth went dry when she saw four or five village boys walking toward her. They were laughing and nudging each other as they came and she prayed they would keep going and leave her alone.

"What's daft old Sarah doing out by herself?" one of them wanted to know.

"Does Biddy know you're out, Sarah?" asked another.

"How'd you like to come in the field and fuck?" asked the biggest boy of all.

Sarah wrapped her arms across her chest. "You shouldn't say that," she sputtered. "It's a very bad word."

"Aw, don't be like that, Sarah. C'mon and try it. You might like it."

They all laughed.

"You're very naughty boys." She wagged her finger at them so they wouldn't see she was frightened. "I'll tell your mothers, just you see if I don't." She tried to raise her voice but the effort made her cough.

The biggest boy pushed her. "Tell your own mother, dopey," he said, index finger pointed in the direction of the cemetery. "She's over there in the bone yard. See if she cares now."

The other boys had become uneasy, Sarah could tell, and one dragged the really naughty boy along with him. "Come on, let's leave her alone," another one said. "Can't you see she's sick."

Sarah watched them go until they disappeared round the bend, then she turned and plodded on until she finally reached the Post Office. She leaned hard against the lamppost on the corner. The cool metal against her face eased the ache in her head. On down Market Street she could see Dr. Hall's shingle hanging outside his house. She walked very slowly now, from garden gate to garden gate, leaning on each one before moving on.

Even though all of Market Street had become blurred, Sarah recognized that nice Mr. Pudsley from the Hare and Hounds running toward her. He must have thought she couldn't make it but she'd show him. She was nearly there. If she hadn't felt so awful and Mr. Pudsley hadn't looked so serious, she would have laughed. She used to go with Mummy and Daddy to the Hare and Hounds every Sunday for lunch and remembered Mr. Pudsley smiling a lot and always rubbing his hands together. He was kind to her and didn't ignore her like a lot of people did. But he wasn't smiling now, even though she raised her hand so he wouldn't worry. She reached the surgery at last and because she couldn't muster enough breath to speak, and felt horrible, she pointed to the house to let Mr. Pudsley know where she was going.

"It's all right, Sarah," she heard him say. "I've got you, love."

She vomited all over his nice clean shoes and didn't remember anything else except he had tight hold of her so she wouldn't fall.

Chapter Ten

Ada Malone watched through the shop window as the ambulance pulled up outside the doctor's surgery. As the trolley was eased out of the house, she saw Walter Pudsley lean over it, then tear up the street toward the shop. He bounced along like a wound-up rubber ball in a red and grey cardigan. The bell over the door jingled madly as he plunged inside.

"Dear God in heaven, Walter, are you trying to give yourself a heart attack?"

"It's Sarah," Walter said between gasps. "Sarah Fitzgerald. That's her on that stretcher. They're taking her to the hospital."

Ada was torn between watching events down at the doctor's place and getting a glass of water for the man she'd had her eye on for years. "You'll be in there with her if you don't watch out," she said, concern for him as well as for Sarah making her voice unusually gruff. "Sit yourself down on that barrel and catch your breath. Honestly Walter, sometimes I think your brains are in your feet."

Obediently, Walter sat on the barrel and took deep breaths, then sipped some water out of the Styrofoam cup Ada gave him. "I'm out in front of the pub watering the flowers when I look up and see her. There she is, weaving along the pavement. For once, the street was almost deserted. I tell you, Ada, I've never run so hard in all my life. Just as Sarah keels over, I catch her. She collapses in my arms." He held out his arms to stress the point. "Now, I ask you, what was Sarah doing going to the doctor's on her own. Practically dead on her feet she was. And where in God's name was Biddy?"

Jenny came out of the storeroom in time to hear the tail end of Walter's remarks. She placed the box of Mars Bars and Milky Ways on top of the newspapers and moved to join them at the window. They both began talking at once, each wanting to be the first to tell her the news. She screwed up her eyes as she stared down Market Street. "You mean Sarah's in that ambulance?"

"That's right," Walter said. "And she's on her own. Not a soul with her."

Ada grabbed hold of Jenny's arm. "Would you be a love and go with her? Just for the company?"

"You mean to a hospital? In that ambulance? I couldn't do that—
Sarah hardly knows me. Don't you think—"

"No, no, it'll be all right. I'd go myself but the solicitor's coming to go
over the books. She'll be scared to death by herself. You know how she
is."

"No, I don't," Jenny said, "I don't know much about her at all."

"But she needs someone with her, and she's taken a real shine to
you," Ada said. "Everybody knows that."

Jenny's fingers trembled as she pulled at the strings of her apron, her
mind suddenly back in Charlotte months ago when she'd dialed 911 for
an ambulance for her mother.

Ada was already pushing her out the door. "They'll be taking her to
Craighead. Get a taxi to bring you back. I'll pay for it." She gave Jenny
one more little shove. "Hurry, child, else they'll be away without you."

Jenny sprinted down the street and reached the ambulance while Dr.
Hall talked to the two uniformed attendants. "Hang on a minute," she
said, breathlessly. "Mrs. Malone from the shop said for me to go with
Sarah. Is that OK?"

"Yes, yes," Dr. Hall said. "It'll help a lot if you go. I've rung Sarah's
house but nobody answers. I've already rung the hospital but I'll give
them another ring to tell them you'll be with her. This way you won't
have to do much explaining."

"Come on, love," the chubby ambulance attendant said. "In you
go." He held out his hand and helped Jenny up the steps.

She hesitated in the ambulance doorway as an unexpected feeling of
unease raced through her. She half turned to back out but it was too late.
The attendant gave her a final gentle shove toward one of the seats
alongside the gurney. "Don't forget to buckle up," he said, watching
while she did it, then gave her a thumbs up before slamming the door.

Sarah lay on the stretcher, with a red blanket over her, her eyes half-
closed. "I'm glad you're coming," she wheezed. "I'll be all right now."

"Yes, honey," Jenny said, her mouth suddenly parched. "You'll be
just fine." She held on to Sarah's hand as she felt the ambulance pull
away from the sidewalk. "Do you hurt?" she asked, trying to get her
mind off herself and at least show some sympathy for Sarah.

"I walked a long way," Sarah said. "Got so tired and hot. I was sick
all over Walter."

"It's OK. You couldn't help it. Walter knew that. He was real
concerned and so was Ada."

Sarah s eyelids drooped. "If I go to sleep, don't leave me."

"OK, but hush now. I'm right here."

Sarah closed her eyes and within a couple of minutes, her mouth slackened and her breathing deepened. Jenny gently let go of her hand and leaned back in her seat, eyes focused on the ambulance ceiling while she took deep breaths and tried to ease her own racing heart. There'd been those other rides, the first one four months and three thousand miles away. Instead of Sarah, her dad now lay on the stretcher while Jenny's mother sat beside him clutching the emaciated claw that was his hand. Jenny sat beside her mother, comforting hand on her shoulder, as the ambulance crept through Charlotte's bumper-to-bumper five o'clock traffic. There was no need to hurry, none at all, because her father was already dead. Jenny blinked and the person on the stretcher changed again. Now her mother lay there, and it was she, Jenny, who clung to her hand. Her mother was not breathing, but Jenny begged her not to die, told her over and over she was sorry for the things she'd said. This time the ambulance didn't creep but tore, sirens screaming, through the city's early-morning streets. It had been a hopeless race. As they pulled into the hospital's emergency entrance, and the doors were yanked open, the medic in the ambulance with them shook his head.

The solemn tolling of a bell yanked Jenny back to the present. She unsnapped her seat belt and rose to look out the small window. They were passing St. Mary's and there in the churchyard stood Father Woodleigh, deep in conversation with two nuns. He wore jeans and a shirt as if he were an ordinary person. He looked lean and fit, and Jenny couldn't help but feel a secret knot of pride, couldn't help but wonder how life would have been if things had been different, if he and her mother had married. He looked toward the ambulance and Jenny waved to him through the dark window. Even though he couldn't see her, it felt good to know he was just a few yards away. One of the nuns crossed herself as she looked at the ambulance, then the church disappeared from view as the ambulance turned the corner. Just the sight of the priest made Jenny forget her resolution not to see him again. She would go again to Mass first chance she got. The very thought of it made the ride in the ambulance a tad easier to bear.

Ten minutes later they drove through the hospital gates and pulled up in front of the emergency entrance. The attendant jerked the door open and pulled out the steps. He smiled at Jenny and held onto her hand until she was safely on the asphalt. The hospital was a huge rambling building, probably hundreds of years old. Perhaps the parking lot had once been a courtyard or maybe even a formal garden. The building all but surrounded Jenny, closing her in on three sides. It reminded her of pictures of workhouses she'd seen illustrated in some of Charles Dickens' books. Gargoyles leered down at her, ready to pounce from the gutters above the fourth floor windows. The building was nothing like the multi-storied state-of-the-art hospitals she was used to in Charlotte. A huge black cloud obscured the sun and the first drops of rain began to fall. Fighting the urge to bolt, she stood to one side while the gurney was lifted out of the ambulance. Sarah was awake, even reached for Jenny's hand as she walked alongside.

The attendant pushed the gurney through the open doors. "See, here's Accident and Emergency. You'll probably have a bit of a wait." He gave Jenny a wary look. "You all right? You look a bit off color yourself."

Jenny gave a weak smile and nodded. "I'm OK."

He leaned over Sarah and patted her shoulder. "You comfy, love?"

Sarah nodded. "I'll be all right now. I've got Jenny with me."

The attendant turned and looked at Jenny. She saw his doubtful look and could have sworn he shook his head. Was her unease showing that much? He glanced around the almost empty room. "Looks like a slow day so maybe this won't take long. You just sit tight here." He picked up a magazine from a table close by and handed it to her. "Have a glance at this." He looked again at Sarah. "See, she's drifting off again."

There were other people in the large room but Sarah was the only stretcher case. A man sat in the corner with a little boy on his knee. The boy had a bloody bandage tied around his leg and held onto a soccer ball. In the corner a man had his arm around a woman, her head resting on his shoulder. Jenny stared unseeingly at the magazine's pictures, every minute or so, looking up at Sarah. When she eventually opened her eyes, she reached for Jenny's hand and held on tight.

Within half an hour a woman in a white coat came toward them, clipboard in her hand. She pulled curtains round the gurney, instantly making a cubicle, then began asking Jenny questions. No, she was no kin to Sarah, just an American over here on holiday.

"Was no one else available to come with her?"

The doctor scribbled away while Jenny told her Sarah's parents were dead. There was a live-in housekeeper, a sort of guardian. She's been there for years, since Sarah was little. She cooked meals and things. Jenny hated to add that last part, feeling it put Biddy on a pedestal, yet was suddenly mindful of Andy's words. If the Social Services thought Sarah wasn't being properly cared for, they might whisk her away to a place far away from home. The questions went on. No, she didn't know Sarah's exact age, but she did recall her saying she was Catholic. When the doctor asked why she had accompanied Sarah when she was practically a stranger, Jenny said she did it as a favor because nobody else was available. Also she was under the impression that Dr. Hall had explained all this on the phone, and could she please leave now.

"The information from Dr. Hall was mainly regarding Sarah's condition," the doctor said, her voice suddenly cold at Jenny's seeming indifference. "It would help if you'd stay until we get her settled in a ward." She beckoned to an attendant, then handed him the clipboard, which he slipped in a wire pocket at the front of the gurney. He motioned to Jenny to follow then he was away down the hall.

Jenny pulled a tissue out of her pocket and wiped her sweaty palms. She half-walked, half-ran, in an effort to keep up with the man as he raced along a maze of corridors, farther and farther from the way out. The hospital may have looked different on the outside from Charlotte hospitals, and even inside wasn't quite the same, but still the same old hospital smells were here. Formaldehyde, Lysol or some similar disinfectant, mixed with carbolic soap and Clorox. In there too was the sweet sickening odor of anesthetic as well as a hundred nameless medicines. Food carts were parked at intervals along the corridors filled with the same smell of overcooked food that permeated the halls of hospitals in Charlotte.

The attendant turned to her, his eyebrows drawn together in a deep frown. "Are you all right? You're white as a sheet."

"I guess so," Jenny rasped, one hand to her throat. "I don't like hospitals much and I can't seem to keep up." She undid the top button of her blouse and fanned herself with her hand. "Is it always this hot in here? I'm burning up."

The man slowed his pace to a crawl then took her hand and placed it on the handle bar of the gurney. "You lean on this trolley, love," he said. "We're nearly there. See there it is just ahead. Ward 9A."

It was the largest ward Jenny had ever seen, beds about eight feet apart stretching down each wall. The attendant whispered something to a nurse who pointed to the empty bed near the entrance; they both turned to look at Jenny. The man left the gurney and guided her to a chair just inside the doors. She forced her mouth into some sort of hideous grin then flopped into the chair. "Sit here till you get your sea legs," he said. "Put your elbows on your knees and hang your head forward while I get you a drink." A minute later he was back with a glass of water. "Take a few sips of this. It'll make you feel better." The man was an angel.

Jenny nodded her thanks and waited until the thumping in her chest eased. She returned the attendant's thumbs up and watched him walk out of the ward. A few minutes later, a young nurse handed her a cup of scalding tea.

"Sorry you don't feel well," the nurse said. "There's a waiting room with comfy chairs just outside the ward on the left. Soon as you feel up to it, perhaps you'd wait in there until we call you. Shouldn't be too long."

The waiting room was empty except for a group in the corner, huddled together, some wiping their eyes. From their conversation, Jenny gathered they were grieving over a dying mother. From the table she grabbed a dog-eared copy of *Nature* and flicked through the pages. She sat on the edge of the chair nearest the door and forced herself to concentrate on yet another story about the ozone layer and how the earth was heating up.

Chapter Eleven

Biddy sat on the side of the bed and kneaded her throbbing temples as she stared at the empty gin bottle on its side next to her teeth and glasses. There was a piece of broken glass on the floor by the night table. She must have knocked the glass off the table in her sleep or more than likely it was Sarah. The girl was clumsy as an ox. The last thing Biddy remembered was Sarah whining on about how mummy and daddy would hate to see her drunk like that. The nerve of the girl. But Biddy would make her pay. She put on her glasses, then reached for her slippers at the foot of the bed. Grabbing hold of the bedpost, she pulled herself to her feet, and tottered out of the room.

"Sarah," she called down the stairs. "Bring me a cup of tea and two aspirins. My arthritics are acting up something awful."

No answer. Sarah was down there somewhere, probably sulking in a corner. Biddy made her way down the hall to Sarah's room. The bed was made as usual. Biddy sniffed. Why did the room always smell so much fresher and cleaner than the rest of the house? She held on to the banister as she made her way down the stairs and into the kitchen. The note standing upright between the salt and pepper shakers caught her eye. She ran a shaky hand across her brow as she read the large childish scrawl. Sarah had set off on her own to walk all the way to the village and if anything happened to her, Biddy would get the blame. The headlines in tomorrow's *Daily Courier* flashed in front of her: *Bridget Helen Biggerstaff charged with neglect.*

She put her head in her hands. It wasn't as if Sarah was seriously ill. Waiting another day to see the doctor would not have made a scrap of difference. Biddy pulled her last bottle of Bombay Gin from under the sink and stared at the picture of Queen Victoria on the label. The queen ignored her and stared off into space. Biddy poured herself a large one. The hair of the dog always got her back on track.

More in control now, she yanked open the catch-all drawer and rummaged through until she found the ice pick the Fitzgeralds had used before they'd bought the new fridge with the icemaker. She slipped on her robe and went out to the car. She gave the tire one quick jab but nothing happened. It took ten minutes of pushing and twisting before she heard the hiss of air.

She leaned over the car's boot as her breath came in little uneven gasps. Her back ached from bending over the wheel and her head still throbbed.

There was a soft rustle from behind and Biddy sneaked a look over her shoulder at the tree. She felt a prickle at the back of her neck as the limbs swayed in a nonexistent wind and the rustle of invisible leaves grew louder. She stumbled back to the house and up the steps, slamming the kitchen door behind her. After fumbling with the chain, she scooted through to the dark hallway. It had no windows except for the stained glass in the fanlight and down the sides of the front door. She huddled on the first stair until the phone rang ten minutes later.

"So, you are at home." Ada Malone's self-righteous voice came down the line. "We all wondered. What in the name of heaven, we asked each other, was Biddy Biggerstaff thinking of to let Sarah walk all the way to Dr. Hall's by herself. Even Walter Pudsley commented and you know how diplomatic he is."

Biddy clutched the receiver with both hands, while she listened to Ada Malone go on about Sarah vomiting all over Walter's shoes just as she collapsed into his arms outside the doctor's surgery. Dr. Hall had called for an ambulance to take Sarah to Craighead Hospital.

Biddy pulled out a chair and sat down. "She couldn't have been that bad off," she said into the phone. "All she had was an upset stomach. You know how her kind are. They come down with every ailment under the sun."

"Sarah's been ill for some time, Biddy," Ada said. "I've mentioned it to you before. Maybe now something will be done."

"Something is being done," Biddy snapped back. "Dr. Hall's been up here to see her. I was planning on taking her in today but last night the arthritics started acting up something awful. The painkillers didn't help much so I took a couple of sleeping pills."

She paused, waiting for a comment from Ada, at least a word or two of sympathy.

"Go on," Ada said. "I'm still here."

It was all Biddy could do not to hurl the phone across the room. "When I wake up I find Sarah's gone off on her own. Soon as I saw her note, I looked out the window but there was no sign of her. That's when I looked over at my car and noticed the front tire was—"

"Don't tell me, let me guess. You had a puncture."

Biddy spat into the phone. "You really are a first-class bitch, Ada Malone. Come and take a look at the bloody tire if you don't believe me."

"Yes, well, you needn't worry," Ada said in the same needling tone. "Jenny Robinson went with her. You know Jenny don't you? So capable, not a flibbertigibbet like most girls these days. Sarah will be right as rain with her."

"Yes, but—"

"I have to go," Ada said. "The shop's crowded. I'm swamped and here all by myself until Jenny gets back."

A loud click then the dial tone. Biddy slammed down her receiver. She hated that woman. Always had. But she hated that girl even more. Here she was sweet-talking her way further and further in. Even going with Sarah to the hospital. Biddy lit a cigarette, and took long deep drags as she tapped her lighter on the table while weighing up the situation. What if Sarah had something incurable, maybe even fatal? How would life be without that great big mongoloid albatross hanging round Biddy's neck? Maybe there was a God in heaven after all. Even if Sarah recovered, Biddy could insist, as her, well, as her guardian, that the girl be declared incompetent. Wasn't today's incident proof positive the girl needed to be put away. Leave her alone for more than five minutes, and she's off down the road lickety-split.

Biddy flicked ash onto the floor. Even though Sarah was slow, she was dependable. Sometimes she'd surprise even Biddy. Her room was the neatest in the house and whatever the task, she did it well without complaining, even if it took all day. She kept herself clean, was always washing and ironing her clothes, shampooing her hair every other day. Still, the Social Services didn't know these things, and surely they'd take Biddy's word over a mongoloid's. Biddy would tell them how hard she'd tried until she'd come down with the arthritics. She remembered the paragraph in the will that stated if Sarah predeceased her or some *unforeseen circumstance* arose, everything would go to Biddy. She'd get the house, the money, the whole shebang. Surely if Sarah was committed to an institution, it would be classed as an unforeseen circumstance. Yet Biddy couldn't stop thinking about that girl. If only Biddy had left her alone, she may never have become intrigued, never bothered to find out Biddy used to be a midwife. She may be long gone by now, probably on the continent somewhere, or even on her way back to America. Biddy dropped her cigarette end in the half-empty cup and listened to the hiss.

There had to be a way to get the girl out of Stoney Beck before Angus Thorne came back from France.

***

The grieving family had left the waiting room and Jenny now had it all to herself. Still shaky, she struggled to concentrate on the crossword in yesterday's *Daily Mirror*. What was the capital of Turkey, six letters. Surely it was Istanbul but that had eight letters. She scratched her head with the pencil and moved on to the next clue. A nurse stuck her head in the doorway. "You can see Sarah now. We've given her a sedative but it'll be about twenty minutes before it takes effect."

Sarah was propped up on four or five pillows and wearing a white hospital gown. She looked lost and lonely in that long narrow ward full of sick people she didn't know. She smiled self-consciously as Jenny came near.

"How's it going, pumpkin?" Jenny said softly as she pulled a chair close to the bed.

"OK. Just sleepy." She poked Jenny in the chest and smiled. "You called me a pumpkin." She bit her lip and reached for Jenny s hand. "I've done it this time. Biddy'll go mad when she finds out."

"That's crazy talk, Sarah. It's not your fault you got sick."

"No, but she'll murder me for walking all that way by myself." She looked beyond Jenny to the ward entrance. "Is she out there?"

"Not yet."

"I tried to wake her, but she'd had too much mother's milk."

"Mother's milk? What's that?"

"It's some stuff she drinks."

"Oh?"

Sarah looked down and traced a finger along the pattern of leaves and acorns on the faded bedspread's tree. "When she drinks it, she bumps into things then gets sleepy. Sometimes she sleeps all day and all night, and—"

"And what?"

"I can't tell you. She'll clobber me."

"No she won't because I won't tell."

"Spit on your hand and cross your heart, then hold up your hand like this."

Jenny did as she was told.

"Now say hope to die."

"Hope to die."

"She wanders round the house talking to herself. Really loud sometimes, and then laughs. She laughs at nothing and sometimes she even screams. I always pretend I don't notice."

"Good girl. What else does she do?"

Sarah clasped her hands and held them under her chin. "Sometimes bad things. Really bad."

"Tell me Sarah. What sort of things?"

"She blindfolds me and makes me stand on a stool even when I'm not naughty, and —"

Out of the corner of her eye, Jenny saw the woman in the next bed leaning toward them.

"Do you want to whisper it," she said to Sarah, "or would you rather wait till you get home."

Sarah shook her head as she put a hand round her mouth and whispered in Jenny's ear.

"She makes me stand in the corner in just my knickers. Sometimes she even forgets about me and falls asleep."

Jenny felt a sudden mixture of anger and pity course through her like rain. She put her arms round Sarah's trembling body. "Have you told this to anyone else?"

Sarah shook her head. "I nearly told Ada once, but didn't think she'd believe me. There's nobody else except Andy, but I can't talk about knickers to him."

"I'm glad you told me," Jenny said.

Sarah leaned back on the mountain of pillows. "It's 'cause you're my best friend. My very best friend of all time."

"Now, don't you be saying that. One of these days I'll be gone, back to America. And anyway, you said Ada and Andy were your very best friends."

"I know, but Ada's old. Said she's pushing fifty. Andy's nice, but he's a boy. They're not girls like us." She looked the length of the ward. "I'm safe in here. Biddy can't get me and the ward's full of nice ladies." She smiled at the woman in the next bed as if to prove her point, but the woman, her leg in a cast from hip to ankle, turned away and pretended to read the magazine open on her lap. Jenny felt a jolt. The woman's face was heavily made up and her hair wrapped around big rollers. She didn't acknowledge Sarah's comment even though Jenny knew she'd heard. Jenny remembered Andy's words. Sarah was up against it all right, and yet she strove so hard to fit in. It wasn't only Biddy, bad as she was.

There were others like the woman in the next bed, those who stared out of curiosity or ignored her altogether.

Sarah's bottom lip trembled as she turned back to Jenny. She raised her hand to pick at her face.

The nurse tapped Jenny on the shoulder. "I'm afraid you'll have to leave now."

"But I just got here."

"It's hospital policy, I'm afraid. You were allowed some time because you came with Sarah. Visiting hours are from two to eight. It's just twelve fifteen. Perhaps you could come back later."

Jenny got to her feet. "It's not the same in North Carolina. People pretty much come and go as they please."

"Uhm, yes well, it's different here." The nurse ran an efficient hand over Sarah's bedspread, smoothing out the wrinkles. "Too much disruption for the patient."

Sarah held out her arms, suddenly very frail. As Jenny bent to give her a hug, Sarah whispered in her ear. "That lady in the next bed's very poorly, I can tell. She smiled at me when you weren't looking, and I bet her leg hurts. I think she's nice."

Jenny kissed the top of Sarah's head. "You're the one who's nice, Sarah. You hang in there and we'll have you back in Malone's in no time."

Jenny walked beside the nurse to the ward entrance. "Can you put some cream on her face?" she asked as they moved out of earshot. "It looks sore and she's always picking at it."

The nurse nodded. "We'll take care of it. It's from the eczema she has."

"May I use your phone?" Jenny said. "I need to call for a taxi."

The nurse waved her arm toward the hall. "There's a public phone at the end of the corridor."

From the doorway, Jenny turned to wave, but Sarah's eyes were closed. The medicine was already taking effect. As Jenny faced the miles of hallway, she felt the inner trembling coming back, racing up and down her arms. She wiped the perspiration from her upper lip with the back of her hand, while she tried to focus on remembering what was in the brochure on panic attacks that Dr. Bissell had given her. Rapid heart beat, breaking out in a sweat, dizziness.

Deep breaths helped, the pamphlet had said. Jenny clung to the rail that ran along the walls, and set off at a crawl, her mouth open, not sure whether she was taking deep breaths or gasping her last. As she edged ever nearer to the phone, she tried to quicken her pace but her legs trembled so much, it was all she could do to walk at all.

The double doors at the end of the corridor swung open, and Jenny stopped in surprise as she watched Father Woodleigh breeze through. She leaned against the wall and dabbed at her face with a tissue as she waited for him to reach her.

"Why it's Jenny, our American friend," he said with a surprised smile. "You're the last person I expected to see. What are you doing here?"

She stuck her hands in her pockets and stammered her way through the story of Sarah's collapse. "She's been sick for ages, poor thing," she said, using Sarah's condition as an excuse for her own pathetic behavior.

The little network of lines around the priest's eyes deepened. "Are you all right? You're very pale. Can I walk with you to the entrance?"

Jenny shook her head and forced her mouth into some sort of smile. "No, honestly. I'm OK. It's just that it's like an oven in here. Can't wait to get outside."

"At least let me run you back to Stoney Beck. I have some business there."

"Oh yes please. That'd be great."

He pointed toward the doors. "There's a tearoom in the lobby. Perhaps if you wait there?"

"No, no," she said too loud, too fast. "I'll wait outside near the steps." She looked down the hall. "Is this the way out?"

The priest looked at her even more closely. "Just follow the arrows. But you look pale. Are you sure you're all right?"

She faked a laugh. "Yes, honestly. I'm fine."

"I'll be on my way then. One of my flock is desperately ill. Her family's expecting me."

Jenny watched him walk away, perhaps to perform the last rites on the mother of those people who'd huddled together in the waiting room. And she did feel better, almost normal. Talking to him had broken the back of her fear. No matter how hard she tried to blame the priest, to hate him even, it was impossible. Because of him, her step was surer now, more solid, as she neared that last door. She nodded to the woman in the bathrobe shuffling slowly down the corridor, hanging on to her IV pole, and smiled at the little girl of about ten who had no hair, yet stood at the door of her ward, smiling back and hugging her Barbie doll. A good-looking guy in pajamas and robe, and leaning on a crutch hobbled toward her. "Hello, beautiful," he said and winked as they passed each other. With that final door just yards away, Jenny returned the grin and even winked back. One big push of the doors, and she was in the hospital's lobby. She longed for a soda to slake her thirst, but marched past the tearoom and onto the front terrace. The rain had stopped and a watery sun shone through a break in the clouds. The air smelled of wet grass, new mown, while a pair of swans, the first Jenny had seen in flight, flew low overhead, across the hospital grounds and headed for a lake just visible in the distance. She looked up at the gargoyles, not so scary now she was headed out.

Half an hour later, the priest and Jenny walked across the hospital parking lot to his car.

"Maybe this is a blessing in disguise for your friend," he said as he stuck his key in the lock. "At least it got her in here fast. Now they're bound to run tests."

"I hope so."

"How's the sightseeing coming along?" he asked as he switched on the ignition.

"Haven't done much. Sarah asked me to fill in for her at the shop. They're short-staffed and I hated to say no. Anyway, it'll probably only be for a few days."

"That was extremely generous, especially since you're over here on holiday, and you two have just met."

"Ah, that's OK. I don't have an itinerary. My return ticket's open, and I don't have a job to go back to. Not yet. Besides, I like the Lakes. And the Hare and Hounds is a nice friendly place to stay. Do you know it?"

"Yes, it's fairly well known. People come from all over." He turned to her and smiled. "You for instance."

"It's beautiful here," she said, looking out the window at the everlasting hills. "Have you been at St. Mary's long?"

"Going on five years. I was born in London, but never had a church down south. For years I had a parish in Birmingham, then Liverpool. When I was appointed to St. Mary's, I couldn't believe my luck. I've always liked this part of England."

"Ah, so you'd been here before?"

"A long time ago. I'd come here on holidays to hike."

"I didn't know priests did things like that."

He laughed. "What? Exercise? In the winter I loved to ski. Still do if I ever get the chance. Even the pope John Paul liked to ski when he was younger."

Jenny wanted to ask him how many years it had been since he took his vows, but somehow the words wouldn't come. It was as if she'd lost the opportunity. Perhaps another time.

Charles Woodleigh shifted gears to tackle the steep hill looming in front of them. Even though he kept his eye on the road, he was conscious of Jenny's gaze on him at times, almost as if she were weighing him up. "What do your parents think of you traveling around England all by yourself?" he asked.

"Mom and Dad both passed away this year. I was an only child. There's just my Uncle now."

He didn't turn his head to look at her, but he'd heard the break in her voice. "I'm so sorry. That must have been very hard."

"Yes. Yes, it was."

There was that last hill and Stoney Beck lay below them.

She stretched out her hand to him when he pulled up at Malone's. "Thanks for the lift, Father."

"My pleasure. If you get a chance to come again to St. Mary's, it would be nice to see you. And, well, if you need someone to talk to, about anything at all, you know where to find me. If not, well, good luck, Jenny."

She looked toward the shop then back to him, suddenly reluctant to get out. He was on to her. She could tell by his voice. Oh, not that he was her father, but because of her crazy behavior in the hospital, he'd guessed something was bothering her. Why else would he say things like come to see him if she needed someone to talk to?

Suddenly, afraid she might give herself away, she opened the door. "Thank you, Father, but I'm fine." She stepped out and bent down to the window. "There is one thing. Don't know how long they'll keep Sarah in, and I know you're real busy, but if you're in Craighead again any time soon and you have a few minutes, I bet she'd love it if you stuck your head round the door and said hello."

"I'd already planned to visit even if you hadn't asked. I'm at the hospital at least twice a week. Consider it done."

The priest watched her walk toward the shop and go inside. She was still grieving for her parents, which might explain her strange agitation in the hospital. She had Beverly's same easy loping walk. Funny how he'd remember that after all these years. When he looked into Jenny's eyes, it was as if he was looking at Beverly all over again. Even though the chances of Jenny being any relation were remote, the likeness was uncanny. He had been trying again to think of a way to ask her mother's maiden name, but when Jenny said she had died, he had lost his nerve.

Looking back now to that night all those years ago, when Charles had sat beside Beverly on the bench, love had been the furthest thing from his mind. He had gone to the Lakes to spend a month before entering the seminary. Within days of their meeting, they had made love and for the next couple of weeks, Charles's dreams of becoming a priest had evaporated into the Lake District mist, while dreams of a wife and family had taken their place. How could he have known for her it was just an interlude. A couple of weeks later, he had murmured into her hair how much he loved her and wanted her to go to London to meet his parents. But she had pulled away from him and said something about not meaning to lead him on, then had gone inside the cottage and closed the door. When he rang the inn the next day, the landlord said Beverly had checked out, left on the morning train. He had hurt so much at the time, he thought he'd never get over it. But of course he had. He was only young, they both were. How could he blame her. It had all been too fast.

Before Beverly had gone away, Charles had telephoned his mother and told her he had fallen in love with an American and planned to ask her to marry him. His mother had been livid but she'd had the last laugh when Beverly left him. And when his mother rang three weeks later to say there was a letter addressed to him that had been forwarded from the seminary, he'd asked her to read it to him over the phone. He had been accepted, the letter had said. Straightaway he'd packed his things and arrived in London the next day.

He had been a priest for seven years when he returned home to attend his mother's funeral. He found the newspaper clipping, yellowed with age, while he was going through her things. *Would Charles from London please contact Beverly in the Lakes?* How his mother, who never bothered with the personal column, had come across the item was something Charles would never know. She was not yet in her grave, but the awful hurt at her deception almost destroyed him. She had let her lofty ecclesiastic ambitions for her son take precedence over everything, indeed his very happiness. Even though many years had passed, he had telephoned the Hare and Hounds to see if Beverly had left a forwarding address. By this time the owner had died and a Mr. Pudsley was the landlord. He had apologized because he couldn't help and who was calling please. The pub was crowded, he said, and maybe someone in the bar would know the young lady. Charles had said it was of no consequence, thanked him, and hung up. He had agonized all over again. Had Beverly had second thoughts? Had she missed him and realized she did love him after all? Or was there another reason, the one he could hardly bear to think about? Had she come back to say she was expecting Charles's child?

Eventually he had become reconciled to never knowing why Beverly had placed those couple of lines in the paper. He gazed down Market Street to the hills beyond. Even now, after all these years, and mostly when he was tired at the end of the day, he still thought of her, and knew he would as long as he lived.

Chapter Twelve

A few days later, while Jenny stacked the day's newspapers in the rack, Ada showed her the postcard from the girl who'd flitted off to Paris. She'd fallen in love with the place, she'd written, and could Ada manage without her a while longer. "Looks as if I'll have to," Ada said, studying the photograph of the Eiffel tower. She shoved the card in her pocket and continued placing sprigs of parsley between the pork pies. "I wish Sarah was well enough to come back. She may be slow but makes up for it by being so loyal, so determined." She stuck the last piece of parsley in place and stood back to admire her handiwork. "When you get right down to it, I can rely on Sarah more than I can anybody."

"Will it help if I stay on a while longer?" Jenny asked.

Ada's face lit up. "Ooh, if you would, I'd be ever so grateful. Still, I can't expect you to stay forever. That advert in the window isn't doing any good, so I'll ring the paper this morning and put one in there. That's bound to do the trick, and besides, we can't afford to take any more chances. A couple of people have asked questions about how you, an American, can work in this country."

Jenny looked up as she stuck the various newspapers in their slots. "Uh, oh, what did you say?"

Ada retied the strings on her apron. "Just told them the truth, said you haven't been paid a penny. Don't you worry though, love, I've got it all tallied up. When you leave here, you'll get your full dibbins."

She closed the glass door of the refrigerated case, and wiped it with a paper towel. "You've been a godsend, Jenny, I wish there was something I could do for you."

"You're not beholden to me, Ada. I've loved this job and I'll miss it when I go. Since you ask though, there is something. I bought Sarah one of those paint-by-the-numbers pictures. She said she likes to do them. If you'd give it to her tonight when you go, I sure would appreciate it."

"Yes, OK, but why don't you come with me. I'd be glad of the company."

"No, no, I can't go in there again." Jenny said, so fast and loud Ada stared.

Jenny wadded up the damp paper towel, then twisted it round the back of her hand. "What I mean is, I, well, I'm not good at visiting hospitals. I, well—" She shivered and ran a hand over the goose bumps on her arms.

Ada still stared as if she didn't understand, but patted her shoulder. "Ah, that's OK. It isn't as though you know Sarah very well, hardly at all really."

"Yes, but still—" Jenny gave a little false laugh, not about to tell Ada about her crazy phobia. Had Uncle Tim been right all along? Had she come away too soon? She saw again his worried caring face when he'd given her that big bear hug at the airport, and how his smile seemed glued on when he'd waved that last goodbye.

Ada went to answer the phone. "That was Betty Philmore from the Post Office," she said when she hung up. "Her mother's the one who had the gallstones taken out. When Betty visited her last night, she popped in to see Sarah. Guess what. She's coming home today."

The next day they fixed a gift basket for Sarah, careful to include only the items Dr. Hall had suggested. "Thanks for taking this," Ada said as she added a packet of frosted lemon biscuits. "I'd take it myself but I can't stand that Biddy."

Jenny picked up the cute little teddy bear Andy had sent over and stuck its feet in a bunch of grapes. "I don't mind. If it hadn't been for Sarah, I'd never have gotten to know you. Taking this basket is the least I can do." She cast a sidelong glance at Ada. What if the woman knew the real reason she wanted to take it was to get one last crack at quizzing Biddy before Dr. Thorne came home.

Ada added a couple of packets of jelly beans and four tubes of fruit pastilles. "Molly Duggan lives on down the lane from Biddy, next door really. Knows everybody's business. Tells it an' all. Said the Social Services have been at Glen Ellen again. She recognized the man, said it's his third visit this month."

"You reckon that's because of Sarah?"

"Bound to be. They'll be weighing Biddy up too. Looking back, she's always been a bit different. You know, standoffish, kept to herself. But this last year though she's turned downright spooky. A few weeks before you came, I was here in the shop by myself. At least I thought I was. Didn't hear the bell jangle. I heard a cough and when I looked up, there stood Biddy over by the shampoos and soap. She had her arms folded and stared at me without saying a word. It fair put the wind up me, it did. It sounds silly talking about it now but I went into the back. Didn't come back out till I heard voices of a couple of customers. She'd gone by then. No sign of her anywhere."

Jenny finished tying the big pink bow on the basket's handle. "Has Sarah ever said anything to you about Biddy abusing her?"

"Nothing except how cranky she is. I don't think she'd hurt Sarah physically. Surely she'd be afraid Sarah would tell. You know how she tells everything."

"She's told me some things. That day she was sick and I took her home? She said Biddy would clobber her because she wet her pants. At first I didn't pay her any mind, and then when I went with her to the hospital, she told me something else."

Jenny took off her apron and hung it on the nail behind her, while she told Ada about Biddy blindfolding the half-naked Sarah, making her stand in the corner for hours. "Sarah's no child," Jenny said, "but not quite a grownup either, not in her ways, I mean. Is this child abuse or what?"

"I don't know," Ada said through her teeth. "God only knows what goes on up there. The Social Services need to know about this, but even here we have to be careful. They could decide to leave Biddy where she is and cart Sarah off to some place miles away, where she won't know a soul. If that happened, it would break her heart."

"But surely they'd make Biddy leave," Jenny said. "We know she hasn't got all her eggs in one basket and no way would Sarah make up those things she told me."

Ada reached for the Saran Wrap and began to cover the basket. "It would have to be proven. Maybe that's why the Social Services have been up there so much. You know, trying to catch Biddy out. They won't just throw her into the street, even if she is round the bend. There's people who'd argue it's her home too. And even if she was made to leave, Sarah couldn't handle that big place on her own. Maybe somebody else could be found to live with her or she could manage a little flat. But now, her being sick like this, even that would be dicey. If she just had a couple of relatives to go to bat for her, it would all be a lot more cut and dried."

She stood back and watched while Jenny tied balloons to the basket's handle. "Angus Thorne's coming home tomorrow. He's executor of the estate and believe me, it's the first thing I'll tell him."

Jenny let go of one of the balloon strings, and watched it float toward the ceiling. "I thought you said he wouldn't be home for weeks."

Ada reached and grabbed the string. "I did but Andy rang me after we closed last night. Said Angus had changed his mind. He's on his way."

***

As Jenny turned into Glen Ellen's drive, she saw the empty space where Biddy always parked. She leaned gently on the horn and when Sarah stuck her head out of her bedroom window, Jenny stepped out of the car and held up the basket. "Look what I've got. Is Biddy home?"

"No, and the door's not locked," Sarah said. "Come on up. Can you get my medicine out of the fridge? Two bottles, one blue and one red. Biddy forgot."

While Jenny placed the basket on the table and hooked her shoulder bag over the chair back, she watched a huge roach scuttle across the Welsh dresser. Dirty dishes were on the table and in the sink, and the smell of tobacco hung in the air. After she'd picked up the medicine, washed a glass, and placed the bottles inside, she held the heavy basket with one hand and the glass with the other and climbed the stairs.

Sarah was stretched out on the chaise longue by the window, a half-finished jigsaw puzzle on the card table beside her, along with a couple of books and a Pocahontas video. Her sallow face was puffy, and the whites of her eyes had a jaundiced look. She didn't look any better than the day Jenny had gone with her to the hospital.

"You didn't come to see me," Sarah said. "I thought we were best friends."

"We are. I planned on coming. It's just that I—"

"Hospitals give you the heebie-jeebies don't they?"

"Just a bit. How did you know?"

"Ada told me but don't tell her I said."

"I can't help it, Sarah. I'm nowhere near brave as you."

She put the basket on the table by the chaise and started to remove the Saran Wrap. "The fruit's been washed," she said, as she took out the bear. "Bet you can't guess who sent this?"

"It's from Andy," Sarah said, reaching for it then cradling it in her arms. "He knew I wanted a Paddington bear. See, he's wearing his little wellies and a mac."

Jenny untied the balloons and fastened them to the bedpost. "How are you feeling? Everybody that comes into the shop wants to know."

"I've got something bad, Jenny. Biddy said people like me don't live as long as other people."

Jenny sat beside her, longing to tell her what she thought of the old bitch. "Don't listen to her," she said instead. "She doesn't know what she's talking about."

"I'll bet she does this time. I'm already beginning to die. I can feel it."

Jenny ran a hand over the thin straight hair, feeling a strange unexpected warmth at the closeness. "No, no, you're not. It's going to take some time. That's all."

Sarah clutched her bear. "Are you sure?"

"Sure I'm sure. Everyone who comes in the shop says it's not the same without you. Ada, well, she misses you real bad. I try but I'm nowhere near as good as you."

Sarah almost smiled as she poked Jenny in the chest. "Told you."

Jenny looked out the window at the drive. "By the way, where's Biddy?"

"Shopping."

When Biddy pulled into the driveway and saw the blue Ford, her hands trembled so much the car veered onto the grass and she missed the fishpond by inches. She'd warned that girl if she didn't get out of Stoney Beck, she'd be sorry. Not only was she still here, she'd had the cheek to come to the house, probably using visiting Sarah as an excuse to nose around. Biddy felt as if time was running out and the jig would be up if the girl was still here when Angus Thorne came home in a few weeks. She lugged a couple of plastic bags into the kitchen, and heaved them onto the counter. She looked up at the ceiling and listened. Sarah's bedroom was directly overhead and Biddy heard the muffled voices.

She opened the freezer and shoved the groceries out of one bag inside. Six frozen chicken pies, four packets of fish fingers, two roast beef dinners, four pizzas and a carton of ice cream. In the fridge itself she put two slices of ham, then milk, cheese, cartons of rice pudding. The hospital had given her booklets stating that food high in phosphorous such as dairy products should be avoided, along with most prepared foods which had a high salt content. Non-dairy creamers and milk substitutes were recommended as well as unsaturated facts and mayonnaise-type salad dressings. There was a list of things Sarah could eat such as sugar and sweets, gum drops, marshmallows, plenty of honey and jam, certain canned or frozen fruits and a specific amount of carbohydrates. A note was attached to the brochure to say a renal dietician planned to visit the house within the next view days and would be in constant touch. Biddy though had no intention of listening to whoever they sent out.

The other bag contained gin and cigarettes. She'd driven all the way to Kendal, not about to let the nosey parkers in Stoney Beck know her business. She stuck one of the bottles in the cupboard under the sink. After hanging her coat on the peg behind the door, she picked up the bag

and was headed for the bureau in the lounge when she saw the girl's
shoulder bag slung over the chair back. She'd have known it anywhere.
Soft tan leather, not another like it in the village. She looked up at the
ceiling again, heard the girl laugh. Biddy flipped open the bag's flap and
peered inside. First thing she grabbed was the leather wallet. Visa card,
telephone credit card, driver's license, library card. There were
photographs of Beverly and Jenny, as well as two men. One would be the
husband, Jenny's father. The other man looked a lot like Beverly,
probably some relative, her brother perhaps. Several ten pound notes as
well as dollars were tucked in the side flap. Biddy stuffed the wallet back
inside the bag, pushed aside the small mirror, tube of lipstick, packet of
tissues, then pulled out the little hard-backed book and turned the pages.
Nothing much in here except a few poems. A four-leaf clover and a
forget-me-not were pressed between the pages. She snatched at the note
tucked in the center pages and held it away from her eyes to read the
small, almost illegible writing.

My Dearest Jenny,
*   Even though I've freed you from the Robinson curse, I haven't told you*
everything about your birth. For years I've wanted to tell you the whole story
but it was too hard. After you've read this letter, I pray you won't hate me.
But you have a right to know and I'd give the world—

Biddy gripped the table as she lowered herself onto the chair and
stared at the note. It was unfinished, the last few words trailing down the
page, as if the person who had written it had fallen asleep before
finishing, or maybe even—
    Intuition told Biddy she'd struck the mother lode, that here in her
hand was the very reason the girl had come to the Lake District. The
writer of the note was of course Beverly. Biddy had no idea what the
Robinson curse was, but it didn't take a genius to guess what Beverly
hadn't told her daughter. She looked up at the ceiling again and listened.
The sound of a window being raised, then the muffled voices of Sarah
and Jenny. Her hands shook as she folded the note and shoved it back in
the book. A couple of pages further on was a snapshot. She took it over to
the small window in the kitchen door and held it against the light. A
young couple laughed at her as they stood with their arms around each
other in front of the Hare and Hounds.
    The girl was the Beverly that Biddy remembered. Even the green suit
rang a bell. But it was the boy with his arm around her waist that caused

Biddy to gasp and press a hand to her chest. If it had been the Dalai Lama with his arms locked around the Virgin Mary, it would have been less of a shock. The boy was a priest now, that Father Woodleigh from St. Mary's in Daytonwater. She'd have known him anywhere. He was the one who'd helped her when she'd twisted her ankle getting off the bus. When had that been? Twenty years ago? Twenty-five? What did it matter? It was him all right. He'd visited Sarah in hospital a couple of times and even stopped here at the house to tell Biddy that St. Mary's were remembering Sarah in their prayers. He and Biddy had talked and both recalled that day on the bus all those years ago. He'd also mentioned Jenny Robinson, said she'd been to Mass once, and he'd seen her again in the hospital. He'd even given her a lift back to the village, but from the way he'd talked, it was obvious he had no idea who she was. Just an American tourist passing through. He'd said so himself.

Biddy stuck the snapshot in her pocket and flipped through the book's remaining pages until she came to the back cover. The inscription read. *For Beverly, I'll love you always, Charles.* Biddy had never seen the two of them together, but now, all these years later, she saw it all too clearly, them sneaking into the cottage after dark so they could do it. Beverly had rambled on about her fiancé in America, how he'd lusted after her on that last night before she'd left for England, and how she'd finally given in. But what if she'd lied and gone all the way with the priest? He wasn't a priest then of course. Still, he nearly was, waiting to hear from the seminary. It all carried a lot of weight, especially if he was a father and didn't know it. She bit her lip to keep from laughing out loud. She had the bitch now.

Footsteps overhead as someone walked across the room, then the sound of the bathroom door closing. Biddy thrust the book back in the shoulder bag, still hanging from the chair back, then carried the plastic bag into the lounge and unlocked the scrolled top of the bureau. The bag containing the five bottles of gin and a carton of cigarettes she placed on the right, before pulling open the little drawer at the left. She took one last look at the snapshot then stuck it underneath the few scattered papers. Her hands shook less now as she yanked down the roll top.

Overhead, the flush of the toilet, then footsteps across the bedroom floor. A soft footfall on the stairs and a creak as the girl stepped on that third stair. A few seconds later and she was in the room, her bag slung over her shoulder.

Biddy began to rock as she gave the girl her best smile. She could afford to be cordial now.

"I brought Sarah a get-well basket," the girl said. "It's from Ada, Andy, and me." She turned down her sleeves and buttoned the cuffs. "Sarah's not much better is she. Do you know what the prognosis is?"

"I wouldn't tell you if I did." She stopped rocking and glared at the girl. "What's it going to take to keep you out of this house? A court order?"

The girl fiddled with her bag's clasp. "Sarah saw me from her window, invited me up, asked me to get her medicine."

"Still trying to fool me aren't you. I'm telling you for the last time. Get out of Stoney Beck and don't come back, or else."

Jenny took a step backwards. "Or else what? You can't threaten me. Ada told me Angus Thorne used to be the village doctor here. That's why you want me gone before he gets home, because he's the doctor my mom sent my photograph to." With hands on her hips, she stared down at the woman. "Soon as you laid eyes on me you gave yourself away, and if it's the last thing I do I'll find out what's got you so scared. You can threaten me all you want to but I'm not afraid of you."

Biddy moved toward her, her face twisted with hate. "Don't underestimate me. There's a lot I can do to you, and if you don't get your arse out of here, you'll be sorry. I have an ace up my sleeve the size of Europe."

Jenny backed toward the door. "Why do you always talk in riddles? What do you mean by you've got one big ace up your sleeve?"

"You'll find out." Biddy said, as she pointed to the door. "Now get out and don't come back. If you do, I'll call the police and have you thrown out."

"Don't worry. I won't be back." Jenny slammed the door behind her and bolted down the steps.

Biddy watched through the door's window as the girl scooted to her car then drove away. She took the snapshot out of the bureau and stared at it as she sat back in her chair. She'd found it in the nick of time. A bargaining chip, something to make sure the girl would be long gone before Angus Thorne got back. She rocked faster now. From her nurses' training, she knew compulsive rocking was a sign of madness but she couldn't stop. And anyway, it helped her to think.

On her way back to the shop, Jenny tried to figure out what Biddy had meant when she'd said she had an ace up her sleeve. She shuddered. The woman was getting downright scary, rocking fast in the chair like that, her eyes wild and staring. Something had to be done about Sarah. She was sick and at the mercy of that woman. Thank God Dr. Thorne was on his way home. She jumped at the loud blare from the horn of the car directly behind her. She looked through her rear-view mirror, saw the line of cars trailing behind, and then glanced down at her speedometer. Twenty-five miles an hour. She threw up an apologetic hand and stepped on the gas until the indicator crept up to forty-five. As she stepped out of the car at Malone's, she looked across the common to the doctor's house. Her grip tightened on the door handle. There was a light in the front room.

"There's a light on in Dr. Thorne's house," she said breathlessly to Ada as she lifted her apron off the nail in the wall. "Think he's home yet?"

Ada went to the window. "That'll be Andy checking on things. Getting it ready."

Jenny washed her hands in the tiny sink in the corner and renewed her makeup. Since the day she'd told Andy to back off, he'd been cool, even though he still came into the shop. He acted friendly but distant and she'd wished a hundred times she could take those words back. If she got a chance today, she'd apologize, maybe even take the initiative, and ask him for a date.

As she shoved her lipstick into her purse, her fingers brushed against the book of sonnets. She eased it out of her bag for one quick glance at her picture. She turned to the page where she'd kept it ever since her mother had given it to her. When she didn't find it there or anywhere else in the book, she rummaged through her bag, finally turning it upside down and spilling the contents onto the counter.

A jingle of the bell over the door and Andy sauntered toward her.

"Lost something?" he asked, smiling as he looked at her things scattered in front of her.

She shook her head and gawked at him, the little book clasped to her chest.

"Just cleaning out your bag, ay."

"What do you want, Andy?"

Her voice was unexpectedly sharp and caught him off guard. "Light bulbs," he said. "Seventy-five watt."

"Light bulbs? You want seventy-five watt light bulbs?"

He reached for her arm but she backed away. "Jenny? You OK?"

When she didn't answer, or move, he frowned then crossed over to the light bulbs and ran his hand along the shelf.

She shoved her bag and its contents off to one side and stared down at the bulbs as Andy set them on the counter. She prayed he wouldn't start a conversation, that he'd just take the damn bulbs and go so she could sort through her stuff. The picture had to be there, it just had to be.

He pulled a ten pound note out of his pocket. "What is it, Jenny?" His voice was laced with concern. "Something's wrong. I know it is."

"There's nothing wrong," she said, her mouth dry and gritty. "I'm cleaning out my pocket book. Do you mind?" She looked beyond him and focused on a row of hand-woven baskets displayed on top of the shelves. Please let him go so she could search some more.

"You sure you're OK?"

"Yes I'm sure and why in the name of all that's holy are you always asking me that?"

"Well, for one thing, you've got that Oh-My-God look on your face again." He lowered his eyes. "And for another, you've got a white-knuckle hold on those bulbs. You'll cut yourself if you're not careful."

She pushed them toward him, and then stuck her clenched fists deep in her apron pockets, waiting for him to go. "Now what's wrong?" she asked when he didn't move.

"Well, I don't want to make a fuss, but I'm waiting for my change. You're not going to charge me the whole ten quid for a few light bulbs are you?"

Jenny's face burned, and without a word she spun round to the cash register and rang up his purchase. When the drawer shot open, she pulled out his change and handed it to him. She folded her arms as he glanced at the money in his hands, then back at her.

"Jesus, Andy. What is it now?"

"Well, as much as I hate to say it, I just gave you a tenner and you've only given me change for a five." He stretched his hand towards her, his eyes full of concern. "Please, Jenny. What is it?"

She backed away, at the same time sneaking a sideways glance at her things shoved in a heap under the breath mint display.

The bell jingled over the door and a girl Jenny had never seen before stepped inside. She was tall, almost as tall as Jenny herself. She had straight blonde shoulder-length hair, resting on a kelly green silk suit. Her skirt hardly covered her thighs, and she wore sheer black hose over long slender legs. She glided between the canned fruit and vegetables toward them.

"Ah, so there you are," she said to Andy in a voice that sounded a lot like the woman on the six o'clock news. She slid her arm through his, then reached up and kissed him on the cheek. "You said you'd come to the station to meet me."

"I did come." Andy backed off a couple of steps. "But got the times mixed up. I—"

She laughed a tinkling laugh as she stroked his cheek. "No problem, and don't look so worried. I called a taxi."

Andy introduced Jenny to Priscilla Fortescue-Smythe. Jenny nodded and twisted her mouth into some sort of smile. Never had there been a name so suited to its owner. Priscilla barely gave her a nod, and then tugged on Andy's arm. "Come on, darling, let's go. I've got oodles to tell you. You'll love the sheets and pillowcases I bought. They're the softest shade of yellow you've ever seen."

"Hang on a minute," Andy said, flushed and obviously embarrassed as he turned back to Jenny. "Will you tell Ada that Uncle Angus is coming in tonight on the ten o'clock?"

Jenny nodded and watched as he allowed himself to be pulled out of the shop by Priscilla. They left the door wide open and as Jenny went to close it, she was in time to see Pete, who always waited outside while his master was in Malone's, wag his tail and trot over to Priscilla. When he stuck his nose under her strip of a skirt for a friendly sniff, she backed off and shoved her purse into his face.

"Get him away from me," she said as she grabbed Andy's arm. "Get him away. He's so disgusting."

With one sharp command and a snap of his fingers, Andy ordered the dog to heel on his other side, away from Priscilla. Pete slunk along beside Andy, his usually highflying tail drooping now, almost brushing the sidewalk. As they walked across the common, Jenny saw Andy's hand sneak down and give his dog's ears an understanding rub. In a second the tail rose again and Pete's cocky swagger returned as he trotted along at his master's side.

Ada walked the length of the shop and joined Jenny at the window. "So, Prissy Smith's back again."

"Who is she?"

"A local girl, born and bred on Breckenridge Farm up in the Fells."

"She's beautiful."

"Aye, she knows it an' all. Shallow as a two-foot grave though. She won a beauty contest over in Scarborough a couple of years ago and it went to her head. You'd have thought she'd won Miss Universe."

"She was talking to Andy about sheets and stuff, as if they're getting married or setting up house or something."

Ada sniffed. "She dropped him flat after she won that contest and them almost married too. She got some kind of modeling job in London as part of the prize. That didn't last long so she tried to get a job on the stage. All she got were a couple of bit parts. Now here she is back again. Probably couldn't handle the big city."

"Oh, I don't know," Jenny said. "She sounded citified enough to me."

"That's because she took elocution lessons. She hasn't always talked that posh nor had that posh name. She calls it her stage name. Talk about fifteen minutes of fame."

Jenny walked back to the counter and sorted through her things, still looking for the snapshot. "Have you lost something?" Ada asked.

"Just my pink lipstick. It was my favorite."

"There it is." Ada pointed to the pale blue tube near the bag.

"Why, so it is." Jenny picked up the lipstick and examined the case as if it were the first time she'd seen it in years. She gave the rest of her things one more fast shuffle then stuffed them into the bag, snapped it shut and stuck it under the counter. She'd seen enough to know the picture wasn't there.

"Do you think he's been carrying a torch for her?"

"If he is, he's a bigger fool than I thought."

Jenny looked out the door and across to Andy's place. A double whammy. First, she'd lost her precious snapshot and now, with the arrival of the gorgeous Priscilla, she'd lost her chance of getting Andy back. "He left without his change," she said, her voice hollow, echoing inside her head.

When she told Ada that Dr. Thorne was coming in on the ten o'clock, Ada said wasn't it a blessing she'd had his favorite raspberry creams in stock.

In between stocking shelves and waiting on customers, Jenny tried not to think about her picture or Andy, or how she'd gone to pieces that night and cried all over his shoulder. They'd gone to dinner at the Prince of Wales and he'd been real nice but little did she know he'd been yearning for Priscilla or Prissy or whatever the hell her name was. When she'd dragged him out of the shop, he'd acted so reluctant, but anybody could see it was just an act.

While Jenny re-arranged the spices, putting them in alphabetical order, she tried to remember the last time she'd seen her snapshot. At breakfast in the Hare, she'd lingered over a second cup of coffee as she read "Come, Grow Old with Me," one of the sonnets in the little book. She'd had the picture between her fingers when Walter suddenly appeared beside her. He asked who was in the photo and held out his hand to see it. She'd stuck it back in her bag, smiling as she told him he wouldn't be interested. She hadn't opened her bag again, not until she arrived back at the shop from visiting Sarah—

As if watching a movie in slow motion, she saw herself hook her shoulder bag over the chair back in Glen Ellen's kitchen, then balance Sarah's basket in one hand and the glass with the medicine in the other as she went upstairs. She'd stayed with Sarah in her bedroom at least a half hour; when she'd gone downstairs, Biddy was there. She—

Biddy!

Jenny banged her fist on the counter. Her big tan bag would be hard to miss. That's what Biddy meant. The ace was the snapshot. It had to be.

Ada had gone to the bank when the phone rang. "Good afternoon," Jenny said into the receiver. "Malone's Corner Shop."

"I'm ringing to thank you for Sarah's basket," Biddy said in her scratchy smoker's voice.

Jenny positioned the receiver between her ear and shoulder while she rang up toothpaste, Yardley's lavender soap, and pink tapered candles for Nigel from the Bookworm.

"Yes, well I'll tell Ada you called."

"Oops, nearly forgot," Biddy said. "I found your photo on the kitchen table, the one of your mother with that dandy randy priest."

"You're lying," Jenny said through her teeth as she handed Nigel his change. "You stole it out of my bag."

Biddy's laugh was a cackle. "And you can't tell anyone. Got you this time."

"Don't bet on it."

"Your mother did it with him, didn't she. Now what's he going to say when he finds out he has a bastard daughter."

"Why you bitch." Jenny clutched the phone, at the same time glaring at Nigel who stood with his hand on the counter, leaning forward, blatantly listening.

Biddy snickered again. "Now then, temper, temper. If you don't do like I say, I might take it to Mass, pass it round to the congregation. The scandal could ruin him and guess who he'll blame?" There was a long pause. "But if you're out of Stoney Beck by first thing tomorrow, it'll be our secret. Just yours and mine."

"How do I know you'll keep your word?"

"You don't. That's the best part of it."

There was a click of the phone then the dial tone.

"You in some kind of trouble?" Nigel asked as he stuffed his things in a plastic bag.

"What gave you that idea?" Jenny snapped. "And anyway, you've got one hell of a nerve standing there listening in like that."

"Just trying to help." Nigel gave her a long dark look, yanked his bag off the counter, and stalked out the shop.

She stretched out a hand. "Nigel, wait. I didn't mean—" But he was already gone.

Somehow, she made it through the rest of the day, twice giving the wrong change, then weighing out a pound of flitch bacon for old Mr. Skeldon from the cottages who told her he'd distinctly asked for gammon ham.

"What on earth's got into you, Jenny?" Ada asked when the man had gone. "It's not like you to be all of a do-da. Don't tell me you've got your knickers in a twist over that Prissy Smith."

"I couldn't care less about Prissy Smith," Jenny shot back. Still, when she dropped a large jar of sugar-coated almonds, glass shards flying everywhere, but thank God hitting no one, Ada suggested she'd better call it a day. Jenny ran a hand through her hair. "I'm so sorry, Ada. It's time for my period. Sometimes I get really wild."

"Not to worry," Ada said, as she reached for the broom and shovel.

"At least let me help you clean it up."

Ada leaned on the broom handle and looked at Jenny, then at her watch. "No, honestly. You get along home. It's almost closing time anyway."

Jenny took off her apron. "I'm so sorry, Ada," she said thickly. "I'll pay for the jar and the candy."

"Don't be silly. You're just having a bad day. Go back to the cottage and put your feet up or go for a walk. If you need me, give me a ring. I'll be there before you've hung up the phone."

Jenny backed off a couple of feet, afraid of flinging her arms round the woman's neck and telling her everything. If she ever needed a shoulder, she needed it now. Instead she twisted her mouth into some sort of crazy grimace, muttered a quiet thanks, and before she made a complete fool of herself, grabbed her bag from under the counter and bolted out of the shop.

For the first time since she'd arrived in Stoney Beck, Jenny dreaded going into the cottage. There it stood, all lost and lonely, off by itself at least a good fifty yards from the inn. There were hours of daylight left before bedtime, more than enough time to torture herself about being fool enough to leave her pocketbook in Glen Ellen's kitchen.

She shoved her hands deep in her anorak pockets and headed for the lake. Perhaps if she walked the footpath round it, which Walter said was all of ten miles, she'd be tired enough to fall asleep. Fat rain-filled clouds lumbered up and over the mountaintops. Not a good night for a hike. There might be a downpour any minute. She longed to call Andy, just pick up the phone and with a little laugh ask did he realize he'd walked out of the shop without his change. But what if Prissy Smith was there, leaning all over him, kissing his neck while he tried to be polite to Jenny, say the money didn't matter and he'd pick it up tomorrow.

A heron stood on a lone rock and stared into the water, its eyes focused on some unsuspecting fish. She shivered as a raw wet wind stirred up little white caps on the lake and the first big drops of rain began to fall. With a lightning jab the heron stuck his head in the water and came up with a small silver fish clamped in his bill. He swallowed it, then flew away only to glide further down the lake and land on another rock where he resumed his vigil.

On her way back to the cottage, she saw Andy's car pull into the inn's parking lot. She watched as he and Prissy Smith stepped out, laughing at some secret joke, then strolled, arms around each other toward the inn. Jenny had almost made it back to the cottage without being seen, when Andy looked up and spotted her. He waved and took a step toward her but when Prissy grabbed his arm, he shrugged as if for Jenny's benefit and allowed himself to be pulled along. Prissy saw her too and waved, then laughed and leaned her head on Andy's shoulder as they walked into the inn. Jenny stopped and stared after them, legs suddenly heavy, tired. She took her key out and looked at her watch. Seven o'clock, which would make it two o'clock in North Carolina. Only a slim chance Uncle Tim would be home in the middle of an afternoon, but she was suddenly desperate to hear his voice, even if just on the answering machine. She remembered what he'd said that last day at the airport. All they had in this whole wide world was each other. Well, got that right.

The telephone was ringing even as she stuck the key in the lock and opened the door. She ran to get it and collapsed in the armchair as she picked up the receiver.

"Hello."

"Jenny? Hi. How's it going, honey?"

"Uncle Tim." Her voice was too loud, too excited. "Oh wow, are you psychic or what. Gosh, it's good to hear your voice. I was just about to pick up the phone and call you."

There was a pause, then. "Jenny? You OK? You sound, kinda, well kinda—"

"Kinda like I was missing you? I am Uncle Tim. I really am."

A chuckle from the other end. "Ah, I could have told you. You ready to come home?"

"Almost. Won't be long now. But there is something I have to tell you."

"Uh oh. Don't tell me you've lost your ATM card. You haven't lost your passport have you?"

"No, nothing like that."

"What then?"

"It's about Charles Woodleigh."

"You mean your—"

"Yeah, my real father."

There was another pause, longer this time. "What about him?"

"Are you sitting down?"

"Yeah. Is it that bad?"

"Let's see what you think. He's a priest, Uncle Tim."

A sharp brittle laugh came down the phone. "Can you speak up. I could have sworn you said the man was a priest."

"I did. He has a church and everything."

"Are you telling me your father's an honest to God practicing Roman Catholic priest?"

She nodded into the phone. "I went to Mass at his church. Stayed back with some other folks for refreshments. We even talked some, and well, he's real nice. I like him. You would too." She twisted a strand of hair around her finger at the insipid words. She'd just told her uncle she'd found her true father and all she could think to say was he was real nice. No trumpets blared, no cymbals crashed, just silence on the other end of the line.

"Uncle Tim? You still there?"

"Yeah. Just trying to take it in. Why haven't you mentioned this before?"

"Didn't know how you'd take it."

"Son of a bitch," Uncle Tim finally said. "Son of a bitch."

"See. This is why I didn't tell you. Knew you'd get mad."

Uncle Tim coughed. "I'm not mad, Jenny. Honest. Just surprised as hell."

"I know. I don't know whether he was a priest when he had that affair with Mom. There's never been a real chance to find out. I need your advice though. If you were a priest, what would you do if you suddenly found out you had a—had a twenty-three-year-old daughter?"

"Oh, God, Jenny, how would I know. I'm about as far from the priesthood as anyone can get."

"Uncle Tim, you've got to help me. There's no one else I can ask." She took a deep breath and searched for the right words. "He's got a good life here. If I tell him, it might ruin him. I saw this movie once where a priest had an affair and his bishop banished him to some rundown church in the middle of nowhere. Still, if I don't tell him, maybe someday I'll wish I had, someday when it's too late. Please, Uncle Tim. What do I do?"

Her palms felt sweaty on the receiver while she waited for her uncle's answer, and then:

"Tell him, Jenny. Show him the picture of him with your mom. See how he reacts. If he wasn't already a priest, it won't be so bad. And if he was a priest, well, you've put the ball in his court. Let him decide. You can't take responsibility for something that wasn't your fault."

"Yeah, I guess you're right." She tapped the phone lightly with her index finger. How to explain to her uncle some malicious old bat had stolen the picture and was blackmailing her.

"It must have crossed his mind more than once that there could've been a baby," her uncle said. "And as far as I'm concerned, he's damn lucky to have a daughter like you. Damn lucky."

Tears pricked her eyes. "Thanks, Uncle Tim," she said thickly. "I really needed that."

"You want me to come over? I got my passport renewed just in case. One word from you and I can be on the next plane "

"Not yet. Let me see how things go. There's no need in your spending all that money, not yet anyway."

"It isn't so much the money. It's just that right now I'm in the middle of one of the biggest deals of the century."

Even in the midst of all her problems, she couldn't help but smile. As far back as she could remember, Uncle Tim had been in the middle of one of the biggest deals of the century. She held on tight to the phone. He made it all sound so simple, so right. What good would Biddy's blackmailing be if the priest already knew.

"Have you had any luck finding out anything else?" her uncle asked.

Jenny clutched the receiver. He meant her mother's note. "No but I'm working on it." She told him about Dr. Thorne, said he was probably the doctor her mom had talked about, who at this very moment was on his way home from France.

"Ah. Well, you be sure to call and let me know how it goes," he said. "Just remembered something I read once. It might help. *The truth will set you free.*"

"You bet and, well, thanks for getting the passport just in case. Thanks for everything. Love you, Uncle Tim."

"I love you too, honey."

After she'd hung up, she put the kettle on for a cup of tea then fixed a cheese sandwich. Thank God for her uncle. She didn't have a clue why Biddy wanted her out of the village, but it had to be something crucial and she'd be damned if she'd let the woman get away with it. Come to think of it, she may even be doing Jenny a favor.

Tomorrow she'd go see Dr. Thorne. Here was where she had an edge over Biddy who wasn't expecting him back for at least another month. When Andy told her his uncle was coming in on the ten o'clock, he'd just been on the phone to him in Paris. The only other people who knew were herself and Ada.

She took a slow leisurely bath then put on her terry-cloth robe. She gazed out the bedroom window that overlooked the parking lot. Andy's car was still out there. The soft sounds of the inn's grand piano, one of those old romantic tunes she couldn't quite recall, something from the fifties or sixties, wafted through the window. The inn door suddenly opened and Andy and Prissy came out. They were laughing as they dashed through the rain, a newspaper over their heads. Prissy grabbed his hand and pulled him close, clinging to him like a tentacle. Jenny looked at her watch. Nine thirty. Time for Andy to head for the station to pick up his uncle. Well, let him go. She had more important things on her mind. Still, she slammed the window shut and yanked the drapes closed before stomping into the kitchen to straighten up. After an hour of television she went to bed.

Chapter Thirteen

The next morning, when Jenny entered the shop, Ada stood with a mug of tea in her hand, talking to a man who looked to be in his middle seventies. Except for his outlandish clothes, he was an older version of Anthony Hopkins, one of Jenny's favorite movie stars. The man wore tweeds, with a royal blue vest and cloth cap to match, all topped off with a blue and white striped bow tie. He leaned his back against the counter, a folded newspaper in one hand and a mug of tea in the other.

Ada beckoned Jenny over. "Come and meet Dr. Thorne. I've been telling him about you."

"Nothing bad, I hope. Can't believe you're still speaking to me after yesterday. Boy, was I a klutz."

Dr. Thorne gave a bellow of a laugh as he placed his mug on the counter and stretched out a giant paw. "Not only is she speaking to you, she's been singing your praises to high heaven. Said you deserve a medal."

Jenny's gaze was riveted on the man. Even his voice sounded like Anthony Hopkins. She finally let go of his hand. Was she at long last standing face to face with the man who had brought her into the world?

Ada reached for another mug then picked up the teapot. "What do you say to someone like her, Angus?" she asked as she poured the tea and handed the mug to Jenny. "Over here on holiday from America, and just because Sarah asks her to stay and help me out, she says yes without thinking twice."

Jenny took a sip of the tea, and then set the mug on the counter. "I like being in the shop," she said, surprised at her normal voice. "I've made friends and it'll be something to tell the folks when I get home."

The doctor tilted his head to one side and gave her a quizzical look. "Have you been to the Lakes before? I have this strange feeling I know you from somewhere. "

Jenny shook her head as she leaned against the counter. A solid thump had started deep in her chest.

"You put me in mind of someone," he said, "and I'm dashed if I can think who it is. It'll come to me later. At my age, sometimes I'm lucky if I remember my own name."

"Good grief, Angus," Ada said. "You talk as if you're a hundred. Seventy-five isn't old these days."

He looked at his watch then at Ada. "I'm going up to Glen Ellen later. Jonathon's told me the same thing he told you. Sarah's been diagnosed with nephritis. It could go either way. She's on medication as well as a special diet. If the pills work, she should be able to come back to work in a fortnight."

He pulled a scrap of paper out of his pocket. "Here's a list of things I'll need till Gladys comes home. If you'll load them into a box, then give Andy a ring, he'll pick them up."

Ada scanned the list. "I'll have these ready by lunch time. The pies should be here by then. Do you want me to stick one in with your order?"

"A steak and kidney would be just the ticket, and perhaps a Cornish pasty." He looked at Jenny again as he tipped his cap. "Nice to meet you, young lady." It seemed for a moment he was about to say something else, then changed his mind. "I'll be getting on home. There're a million things to do. Need to get reacquainted with Indigo. That cat's spent so much time at Andy's, she probably thinks I've died."

Jenny watched through the window as the doctor made his way across Hallveck Common then stumped up the brow to Andy's place. "I'm sorry about Sarah," she said as Ada joined her at the window. "What's nephritis and what did he mean, it could go either way?"

"It's something to do with the kidneys. I suppose he means she'll either get better or else—"

"Or else what? You don't mean she could die?"

"A Jonah's the last thing I want to be, Jenny, but, God help her, she could end up on dialysis waiting for a transplant. Let's hope it doesn't come to that. The queue for kidney transplants is probably twice the length of Market Street, and where someone like Sarah would stand on the list is anybody's guess."

"I'm so sorry," Jenny said as she put the tea things on the tray. "Poor Sarah. I knew she was sick but had no idea it was that serious."

Ada put an arm across Jenny's shoulder. "You've been awfully good to her, Jenny, especially since you hardly know her. And look how you've helped me. There must have been places you wanted to go. Well, today you can start planning. I've had a couple of replies to my adverts."

"Oh?"

Ada told Jenny that the two women had telephoned early that very morning. One was a university student looking for a summer job, and the other a writer waiting for her big break. Both were coming in later for an interview. "It never rains but it pours," Ada said as she waved to a couple of women wandering the aisles. "For weeks there's been just you and me and now someone's opened the gates."

Jenny straightened the morning papers on the rack. "Guess this is my last day then." She cursed the quiver in her voice as she looked around the shop. It was as if she'd worked here for years. She forced a smile, suddenly aching to confide. Perhaps she'd tell Ada some of it after she'd talked to Dr. Thorne.

Since Uncle Tim's phone call, and his wise words, Jenny had made up her mind. *The truth will set you free.* No way would she submit to Biddy Biggerstaff's blackmail. The woman was unpredictable, and would probably show the picture to the priest anyway. Jenny would go to Mass again tomorrow. On her way out of church, she would hand him a letter. At least he would know he had a daughter. What he did with the knowledge was up to him.

Ada took Jenny's hands in hers. "I'll be sorry to see you go, love. I honestly don't know how to thank you. You've turned into a good friend, and I feel as if I've known you for ages."

"Same here," Jenny said. "Still I can't stay forever."

Ada went to the back of the shop to wait on a couple of women, while Jenny checked out customers at the cash register. She hurried to the door to hold it open for Spud Murphy who balanced a tray of pies on his head, held steady with his right hand. The mouth-watering smells wafted in with him, all mingled together. There were pork pies, meat and potato, steak and onion, steak and kidney, Cornish pasties. Jenny had tasted them all and never could decide which she liked best.

A couple of hours later, Jenny was stacking tourist guides on a shelf by the cards when Ada walked over. "I'm sorry things didn't work out with you and Andy. I know you think he's got something going with that Prissy Smith, but—"

"It doesn't matter, Ada. I'll never see him again after I leave here." She picked up Dr. Thorne's grocery list. "Why don't you let me get this together. I'll be glad to take it up to his house."

Ada shook her head. "It'll be too heavy for you. Let Andy take it in his car."

"No, it isn't that. You see, I—"

Ada leaned forward. "Yes?"

"It's just that I'm fascinated with the houses up here in the Lakes. They're different from those back home. Yours and Glen Ellen are the only ones I've been in. I'd like to go in a few more before I leave."

This seemed to satisfy Ada. "Well, if you think you can carry the box, get it together while I put the kettle on."

Ada watched through the shop window as Jenny pulled her car up to the curb outside Angus's house. She lugged the huge box out of the boot and balanced it on the garden wall, while she struggled with the gate latch.

"Be with you in a minute, Bertha," Ada shouted over her shoulder. What had got into that girl. Jenny had been all of a twitter ever since Prissy Smith had tromped into the shop and fallen all over Andy. Still, it didn't take a Sigmund Freud to see something else was on Jenny's mind, losing things, breaking jars of sweets. Andy was right. There was something mysterious about her, always biting her lip, staring into space, at times tense as a coiled spring. Why was a pretty American girl hanging round an English village when she could be gallivanting all over Europe? She obviously wasn't short of a bob or two. You only had to look at her clothes to see that. Was it really out of the goodness of her heart that she had offered to fill in for Sarah, or was there more to it? This morning, for instance, when Jenny was introduced to Angus, it looked as if she was never going to let go of his hand. And what about him saying she looked familiar. It was as if he knew her from somewhere. After he'd gone, Jenny was at the window staring up at his house every chance she got. Ada leaned forward to get a better look as she watched Jenny struggled to press the front door bell.

Chapter Fourteen

Jenny grappled with the heavy box, pressing it between her chest and the wall while she stretched out her hand and pressed the bell. She smiled up at Dr. Thorne when he opened the door. "Quick, can you grab one end of this?"

The doctor stepped outside. "Good God, child. I told Ada that Andy would pick it up."

"Ah, don't be mad at her," Jenny said as they maneuvered up the steps into the vestibule. "I wanted to bring it."

"Come on then. The kitchen's through here."

After they'd heaved the box onto the counter, Jenny dusted off her denim jacket and jeans. "Everything's in there," she said. "Ada said the raspberry creams are on her, sort of a welcome home."

He glanced inside the box then turned to Jenny. "Do you have time to stop for a cuppa? I've already got the kettle on."

"That'd be great." Her voice was at least half an octave higher than usual.

He led her into the large front room or lounge as he called it. "Make yourself at home. I'll put a few things on the trolley and be back in a jiffy. There's the kettle whistling now."

The lounge was a startling mishmash of old and new. Danish modern and antique furniture stood side by side on what appeared to be an authentic oriental rug. A cubist Picasso-like painting hung over an ancient upright piano on the inside wall. The coffee table was a slab of slate resting on two stacks of white brick. Built-in bookcases on either side of the fireplace were crammed from floor to ceiling. A couple of Barbara Cartlands were wedged between *The Brothers Karamazov* and *Robinson Crusoe*. *War and Peace* stood next to Carl Sagan's *The Cosmos*. There were poetry books, cookbooks and books on travel, as well as how-to books on almost everything. The bottom shelves were crammed with weighty tomes on medicine, while still more were stacked on the floor. The sofa and three chairs were flowered chintz, all different prints, while wild bizarre wallpaper, some sort of jungle scene, covered the walls. White and pink carnations, freshly picked, lay on a newspaper on the windowsill ready to go into a crystal vase already filled with water. There was a basket near the hearth for Indigo but the huge midnight blue cat was stretched across the back of one of the chairs gazing at Jenny out of half-open somnambulant eyes. She sat on the sofa in front of the coffee table and flicked through an old *National Geographic* until Dr. Thorne wheeled the squeaky trolley into the room.

He pointed to the refreshments. "The cheese is from Provence, and I picked up the pastries yesterday in a bakery in Paris. Those chocolate ones with the cherries on top are out of this world."

"I didn't expect this," she said. "You're very kind."

"Nonsense. It's the least I can do. And besides, I think you'll be interested in this."

When he handed her the dark green folder from the trolley's lower shelf, Jenny gave a loud gasp. She ran her suddenly trembling fingers across the fleur-de-lis embossed in gold on the cover, knowing already what was inside. There were five or six exactly like it at home. It was her graduation picture, the day she'd received her degree in English literature from Queens College.

"It's you, isn't it," Dr. Thorne said softly after she'd opened it. "You're Jennifer, Beverly Pender's daughter."

Jenny nodded without looking up, eyes riveted on the familiar writing on the folder's inside cover. *I thought you'd like to see what a lovely young lady my little Jennifer has turned out to be,* her mother had written.

"Yes, sir," Jenny said, hoarsely. "I'm Jennifer."

Dr. Thorne took a long deep breath, flopped down in the armchair opposite, shaking his head and running a hand across his forehead. "At last. After all these years. A jingle of the bell over Malone's door and in you come."

Jenny sat on the edge of her chair, her back rigid. "It sounds like you've been trying to find me. I don't understand."

He peered at her over his half-frames, picked up the teapot. "Do you take sugar, milk?"

"Just milk, please."

He poured the tea and pushed the cup and saucer toward her. "Why don't you start? For instance, why have you suddenly come? It's been at least twenty-three years."

Jenny looked beyond him, her gaze fixed on the wallpaper. A tiger stalked through the undergrowth, vigilant eyes fixed on her. *Be careful, watch your step,* he seemed to say. *They've been looking for you. Something's up.*

"I came to see where I was born." She squirmed under the doctor's piercing stare as he leaned forward, elbows on the arms of his chair.

"OK," she said as she pulled her mother's note out of her purse and handed it to him. "This is the real reason."

Dr. Thorne read the few lines, his lips moving as he read. "Is this what I think it is?" he asked softly without looking up. "Why it's unfinished?"

Jenny nodded. "It was an accident. Too many pills, and well, she drank some wine. The combination—"

"Ah, that's so sad, a terrible shock." He fingered the note almost tenderly and read it again.

"My mother had been through a very rough time, she—" Jenny stopped herself. Telling this man about her father's long illness would serve no purpose except perhaps to cause the doctor to ask questions, maybe to speculate that she herself was under the gun, a likely candidate to develop Huntington's disease. The issue of course was irrelevant because that dear man was not her father after all. She leaned forward, pointing to a line in the note. "See here where she says she didn't tell me everything about my birth, then here on this last line, she said she'd give the world. Have you any idea what she was trying to tell me?"

"Let's have a shot at it, shall we," the doctor said. "First off, do you have any brothers and sisters?"

She shook her head. "I was an only child."

"I see. Well, how much did your mother tell you about her time here in England? I mean, she must have told you something."

Jenny ran her dry tongue over her lips, then picked up her cup and sipped some tea. "Mom didn't talk about it much. At least not until that last night. She said she'd sent my portrait to her English doctor, but she never did say your name."

Dr. Thorne cut the brie into small pie-shaped wedges and eased a couple of pieces onto a plate. He helped himself to four or five crackers, while Jenny told him of her mother's reunion and subsequent marriage to Michael Robinson.

"And there were no other children?"

"No. I've already said—"

"It's just that, well how else to tell you but to come right out with it. You're not an only child, Jennifer. You have a twin sister."

Twin sister.

Jenny tilted her head and blinked as she tried to bring the doctor back in focus. Suddenly there were two of him, both of his big Anthony Hopkins' faces gawking at her. The two figures got up and crossed the room to the sideboard then fused back into one as he poured two snifters of brandy from the decanter. He handed her a glass.

"You'd better drink this. You look as if you need it."

Jenny took it with both hands, struggling to hold it steady while she raised it to her lips. She closed her eyes as the warm smooth liquid slipped down her parched throat. She leaned her head on the back of the sofa. This was what her mother had tried to say in the note. All those years she'd lived this lie. Was it any wonder it had been so hard to tell?

"Do you know where this twin is?" she asked.

Dr. Thorne's rheumy china blue eyes peered into hers. "You've been taking her place in Malone's."

Jenny gave a bark of a laugh. "Surely you don't mean Sarah. She couldn't be. She's got——"

"You think she couldn't be your twin because she has Down syndrome? It's not as uncommon as you might think. You and Sarah aren't identical twins. You're fraternal."

The cat leapt down from the back of the chair and jumped onto the sofa beside Jenny. She reached out a hand and stroked it, heard the soft purring sound. This was the reason her mother had not wanted anyone in England to know her whereabouts. She couldn't risk someone writing about Sarah, the child she had left behind. Nobody in America knew about her, certainly not Uncle Tim and possibly not even Jenny's father.

Dr. Thorne stared into the snifter as he swished his brandy, and talked of her mother's friendship with the Fitzgeralds, how they'd met in the Bookworm.

"You were a beautiful healthy baby. Little Sarah though wasn't so fortunate."

Jenny ran a hand over her jeans, saw the hole beginning to form at the knee. "Did the Fitzgeralds know? I mean can you tell at birth?"

"This was the reason they wanted her. Fred and Edna knew what to expect. People like Sarah sometimes have this deep, unconditional love. This is what they wanted and they weren't disappointed. You've met her. You know how she is."

He clasped his hands together, making a steeple, his eyes far away as though remembering. Beverly was in a quandary all right, he said, and when the Fitzgeralds befriended her, practically begging her to let them have Sarah, she finally agreed. They had resources and promised Beverly that Sarah would want for nothing. To protect her from village gossip, a pact was made with those involved. They would tell no one. Dr. Thorne told Jenny how hurt the Fitzgeralds were when they realized the address Beverly gave them was fictitious.

"My mother grew up in a strict Southern family," Jenny said. "Maybe she thought taking one baby back was bad enough, but two! Maybe she was too scared to tell her father about Sarah, afraid he'd say she was being punished. You know, the sins of the fathers and all that stuff."

The doctor's eyebrows went up about half an inch. "Surely you don't believe that."

Jenny shook her head then drained her glass. "You'd think the Fitzgeralds would have realized Mom didn't want to be found and let it go at that."

Dr. Thorne told her he was the executor of the will, and that Beverly and Jenny had been named co-beneficiaries along with Sarah. The Fitzgeralds had tried for many years to find Beverly and her daughter. As the years passed, Fred and Edna discussed drawing up a new will, but it was not until a week before their last trip to Lourdes, that they made an appointment to see their solicitors. A new will was to be drafted when they returned home.

"As you know," Dr. Thorne said, "they didn't make it back. That means the original will is still valid. You and Sarah are joint beneficiaries. There are provisos of course. These are mainly to do with making sure Sarah is well cared for." He lifted up the tea cozy and felt the pot. "It's only lukewarm, but let's have half each, shall we?"

While he poured, he told Jenny to bear in mind the will had been drafted twenty-three years ago, just months after her birth. It stated that in the unlikely event of the Fitzgeralds' early deaths, the estate was to be held in abeyance for two years. If Sarah's mother or twin weren't found within the stipulated time, then the housekeeper, Bridget Biggerstaff, was to be named as co-beneficiary with Sarah. If Sarah predeceased her, the housekeeper would get it all.

Indigo crawled onto Jenny's lap, purring loudly as she curled herself into a huge midnight blue ball of fluff. She ran her hand across the cat's back, felt the slight crackle of static.

The doctor leaned forward. "Have you met Biddy Biggerstaff, the housekeeper?"

Jenny could only nod.

"The Social Services rang me in France. They're concerned about Biddy. She's always been eccentric but lately it seems to have manifested. I'm retired now of course so Dr. Hall keeps an eye on her. Still, I am executor of the will, so they want me to get involved. Because of all this, I had planned to contest the will. But now that you're here, it pulls a whole new slant on things."

For Jenny, all the bits and pieces of Biddy's bizarre behavior made sense at last.

"I'm convinced of course that you're Sarah's twin," Dr. Thorne said. "Still, we'll need documentation. You know, copies of your birth certificate, your mother's marriage license, any pertinent information which might be useful, especially your mother's and father's death certificates. This is more a formality than anything else."

Not in the least hungry, but unable to sit still, Jenny busied herself fixing a plate of crackers, a wedge of brie, and a few grapes.

"Does Sarah know she has a twin?" she asked as she struggled, with shaking fingers, to maneuver the cheese onto a cracker. When the cracker snapped between her shaking fingers, she picked up the brie and popped it into her mouth.

The doctor shook his head. "When she was old enough to understand, they told her the same story many adopted children are told. That they'd chosen her over hundreds of others because they loved her best."

Jenny eased the cat off her lap. "What you're saying is if I stay here in England to be a companion for Sarah, I'll come into a good deal of money and if I leave, I get nothing?"

"She is your sister after all," Dr. Thorne said.

"Yes, but until half an hour ago, she was just somebody I was doing a favor for. And now, just like that," she said snapping her fingers, "I find out she's my twin."

Dr. Thorne's face darkened. "What's bothering you? Is it that she's handicapped?"

"No, it isn't that."

"What then? Are you homesick? The estate's substantial, Jennifer. There's more than enough for you to come and go, back to North Carolina, which you're bound to want to do. Surely we could come to some sort of arrangement. Perhaps we can find a couple to live in the house with Sarah. Along with the house, there are stocks and bonds. And there are one or two other properties. There are some of Fred's paintings. Sarah's father was a fairly well-known artist.

"Plans have been made for Biddy, in the event that you were found and agreed to the conditions. There's a house for her near Kendal. She already has a generous stipend. With that and her pension, she'll be better off than most."

Jenny pretended to examine the geometric design of the rug beneath her feet. Dr. Thorne had asked for her father's death certificate. When he saw the cause of death was Huntington's disease, the questions would come. How could she tell the doctor that her and Sarah's biological father was the priest in the next village when the priest himself didn't know? Jenny had mulled over this at least a hundred times. Now she would have to tell him he had two daughters instead of one.

There was something else to take into consideration. If and when this concern could be resolved, then what consideration would be given to Jenny's own welfare? If she went along with this carrot the doctor dangled in front of her, would she be capable of handling it? Not only had she just been told the staggering news that she had a twin sister, but this sister had a prolonged, life-threatening sickness. Was Jenny destined forever to take care of the sick in her family, even those she hadn't known existed until less than an hour ago? What about her own welfare? Did anybody really give a damn?

"I'm sorry Sarah's sick," she said. "I like her a lot. But what about me? I don't even know if I can do this. And after all, you hardly know me."

"This has all been a shock to you," he said. "And all I'm really doing here is presenting you with the facts. I can see you're still grieving for your own parents. You can always decline of course. You and Sarah are more or less alone in the world, and the two of you—"

Jenny got to her feet. "I have to go. Ada's bound to be wondering what's taking me so long. I can at least tell you this much. I will call my uncle when I get back to the Hare. He knows where all our papers are. I'll ask him to send them to me. All I'm thinking about here, mind, is that Biddy doesn't get anything."

"Good girl. Don't worry about the ins and outs of all this. We can work out something. We could probably—"

"Please," she interrupted. "I do have to go." She grabbed her bag and headed down the hall and out the door. She didn't look back, didn't even turn to look at Andy who called to her from across the street. As she stalked down the hill, she was already thinking of ways to explain to Dr. Thorne that the man who'd died of Huntington's disease was not their father. Perhaps Jenny could convince the doctor that she didn't know who their real father was. There was no need to implicate the priest. Yet, she couldn't help but wonder what Biddy's reaction would be when Dr.

Thorne told her he had finally found the lost twin. Biddy would not hesitate to show the doctor the snapshot. Moreover, it wouldn't take the intelligent Dr. Thorne long to guess the truth. Jenny crossed the common toward Malone's, barely able to think of the consequences. One thing Jenny knew for sure. She would do almost anything rather than let Biddy get her hands on the estate.

***

Andy wiped the oil off his hands as he watched Jenny stride down the garden path and out the gate. He put his hands around his mouth and yelled to her, but she kept her head down as she marched down the brow, even though he knew she'd heard. His uncle stood in the doorway with his hands on his hips watching her go, until she finally disappeared into Malone's.

"Keep an eye on things will you, Alf," Andy said to his mechanic. "Won't be long." He patted his dog on the head. "You stay, Pete. Good boy." He waited for the tourist bus to pass then crossed the street to his uncle's house.

Chapter Fifteen

Biddy sat at the kitchen table, waiting for her cup of tea to cool. Her head throbbed and the cigarette dangling from the side of her mouth tasted vile. With the tips of her fingers pressed against her eyelids, she tried to make sense of last night. She remembered Sarah helping her up the stairs, undressing her, even putting her teeth in a glass. Then had come those weird dreams. She took the cigarette out of her mouth and sipped her tea. Even her eyeballs hurt as she turned toward the sink where Sarah stood, selecting fruit from the basket that girl had brought.

Sarah tackled this job the same as she did everything, with a slow, studied thoroughness. She peeled an apple and sliced it into thin wedges, then arranged them on her plate in the form of a crescent moon. After carefully inspecting them and washing a handful of grapes, she placed one on each apple slice. She chose five of the largest strawberries and held them under the tap for at least three minutes, before drying them on a paper towel. After cutting them into halves, she placed them over to the side of the crescent. She wiped her hands and stood back to admire her handiwork, reminding Biddy of a jeweler inspecting a display of precious gems.

Biddy felt the heat from the cigarette on her fingers and gave a little cry as she dropped the end into her teacup. Sarah bustled to her side and reached for her hand.

"Ah, you burned your finger. Does it hurt?"

"*Yes* it hurts," Biddy said, pushing Sarah away. "You spend hours preparing a bowl of fruit. It's enough to drive even a saint up the wall." She stared down at her finger, waiting for the blister to form.

Sarah opened the catch-all drawer and rummaged around until she found the tube of Vaseline. "If you rub this on, it won't hurt as much."

"Yes, it will," Biddy snapped. "Fill a glass with cold water. I'll soak it for an hour. You can make another pot of tea and use fresh tea bags. That last cup tasted worse than a cup of pee."

After Sarah had given Biddy the glass of water and a fresh cup of tea, she brought her bowl of fruit and glass of iced water to the table. In spite of Biddy's bad temper and the awful night they'd had, Sarah felt better than she had in ages. Perhaps the pills were already working.

"If you ask me, I'm a lot sicker than you are," Biddy said. "I can't eat a bite and my head's pounding."

The spoon stopped halfway to Sarah's mouth. "That's because you were in the mother's milk again last night."

Biddy glared at her. "How dare you use that tone with me. Anyway, what's wrong with having the odd nip. You're making a mountain out of a molehill."

"No, I'm not," Sarah said, waving the spoon at her. "You came screaming into my room and pulled me out of bed."

Biddy squirmed. So it hadn't been a dream. "I don't know what you're talking about."

"Don't you remember? You pulled me out of bed and dragged me to the window to look at the tree? You said its big black eyes were staring at the house. I tried to tell you they're not eyes. They're just holes. But you wouldn't listen. That's were the squirrels put their nuts, Biddy. I think they've got their babies in there."

Normally Biddy would have told Sarah to shut up, but this time she wanted to hear the rest of it. All she could remember were snatches of what she had thought was a nightmare. "You're just imagining this. Could be that medicine you're taking. It can do things to you."

Sarah rubbed the back of her neck, still sore from Biddy's rough grip the night before. "You pushed my face up to the window so I could see and said the tree was moving toward the house." She rested her spoon on the side of the bowl as she felt herself getting short of breath. "Everybody in the world knows trees can't move, Biddy. Why are you so frightened of it? It's just an old dead tree."

"If it's just an old dead tree, why do *you* talk to it? And don't say you don't because I've seen you."

"I'm not really talking to it. I'm just thinking out loud. We used to sit under that tree in the summer. We'd eat ice cream and Mummy would laugh at Daddy singing his songs. Remember, Biddy, the way she'd laugh."

Biddy leaned across the table and grabbed Sarah's arm. "Why don't you spit it out. You know as well as I do they're in that tree watching us."

"How could they be?" Sarah said, frightened at the look on Biddy's face. "They died in the car wreck."

"Don't give me that. Are you trying to tell me it was just a wild coincidence that lightning struck the tree the very same time they were killed a thousand miles away."

"No, no. It wasn't like that. You're getting it all mixed up."

Biddy raised her hand for Sarah to hush, and pushed her cup away, sloshing tea over the sides. "I'm having the damn thing cut down and burned, roots and all." She put her hands on the table and pulled herself up, then came around and grabbed hold of Sarah's arm, twisting it behind her back until she cried out. "And if you breathe one word to anybody about last night, you're in deep trouble. The other night in the bath was just a sample. Next time it won't be just ten minutes and I can make the water colder. If you're not careful, you'll be in for half an hour, along with a bucket of ice cubes."

Sarah rubbed her arm as she held back the tears. "I won't tell, honest I won't. Please, Biddy, can't we be nice to each other. I'm so tired of all this squabbling. I'm nearly better now and I'll be back in Malone's soon. Then you can have the house to yourself all day."

"Don't bank on it, Sarah. Once you get kidney trouble you can go just like that." Biddy snapped her fingers in front of Sarah's face. "And we all know your resistance is already rock bottom." She put her hand under Sarah's chin and squeezed until tears rolled down her cheeks. "Still, if the nephritis doesn't grab you, the men in the white coats will. One call from me and they'll be over here fast as quicksilver. They'll come racing up the drive pulling that paddy wagon behind them."

Sarah wiped her eyes on her napkin, and then picked up her spoon with a shaky hand. Her appetite had gone now, but she slowly, deliberately, ate the fruit, chewing every piece. "Jenny said you're just trying to frighten me. She said there's no such things as men in white coats with paddy wagons."

As soon as the words were out, she clapped her hand over her mouth.

Biddy leered, exposing her toothless gums. "So, you've been tattle-taling again. And to that girl of all people. Even after I'd warned you, you still went ahead and told."

"I didn't mean it. Honestly I didn't. It was the day I was poorly. You remember when I wet my knickers and Jenny brought me home."

Biddy cackled. "I'll get you for this, and you can forget all about your friend Jenny. If she hasn't already gone, she soon will be."

Sarah banged on the table with her fist. "That's not true. She wouldn't go without saying goodbye. She's my friend. My very best friend."

"Don't make me laugh. She can't stand the sight of you. You're the very reason she's going. Nobody likes you, you little fool. Not a single soul."

Sarah didn't believe Biddy, even though the words hurt. Lots of people liked her. Andy and Ada for starters. Hadn't Andy got Sarah the job in Malone's and wasn't Ada always telling her what a good help she was? Then there was that nice Walter Pudsley. Even when Sarah had been sick all over him, he had held on to her so she wouldn't fall. And he had come to see her in hospital and brought a lovely bunch of flowers as well as a pink nightie with roses round the collar that he said was from the staff and some customers at the Hare and Hounds.

And what about that nice Lottie Mellville who had been in the hospital bed next to Sarah's. Lottie hadn't liked Sarah at first, which was the way it was with a lot of people when they first met her. But later, they had become best friends. She wore a lot of makeup and curled her hair every morning, as if she expected someone to visit her. But nobody ever came. Not a soul. When Lottie sometimes cried in the night from the pain in her broken leg, Sarah climbed out of her own bed and sat with her. They had held hands and whispered stories to each other until Lottie finally dropped off to sleep.

Then there was Dr. Hall. He had put an arm round Sarah and explained things to her in front of Biddy. He told Sarah she must keep a daily record of how much she drank, how often she went to the toilet, and to always check her urine for blood. He had even got cross with Biddy for not paying attention when he was showing Sarah how to press a thumb against her ankles to check for swelling. If a dent stayed where Sarah's thumb had been, he wanted to know about it. He had arranged for her to go to the village clinic twice a week to have her blood checked. Surely the doctor wouldn't go to all that trouble if he didn't like her. He had even taped a copy to the fridge of good things to eat.

Best of all though was Jenny. When Sarah had asked her if she'd help out in the shop, she had said yes straightaway. And they had only known each other for just such little while. She called Sarah a pumpkin and had even gone with her in the ambulance to hospital. You'd have to think an awful lot of someone to go to all that trouble. Biddy was fibbing again. Jenny would never leave without saying goodbye.

Sarah washed her bowl and placed it in the drainer. While she busied herself in the kitchen, out of the corner of her eye, she watched Biddy try to light another cigarette. Her hand shook and the flame jiggled until she held the lighter steady with two hands. She took a long drag and stared at a snapshot she had propped up against the sugar bowl. Every time Sarah had walked behind her chair to take a peek, Biddy had turned the picture face down on the table.

Something was very wrong with Biddy. Here it was, two o'clock in the afternoon, and she was still in her dirty dressing gown. She hardly ever combed her hair any more or even put her teeth in. When Mummy and Daddy were alive, Biddy had been nicer. Back then, friends came to visit. Daddy had been an artist and some of his paintings sold for a lot of money. All the rooms in the house had their doors open, with the sun streaming through the windows. When Sarah tried hard she could still smell the furniture polish mingling with the scent of flowers from the garden. Now though, every door was closed except for the lounge and kitchen, and even they smelled of Biddy's cigarettes and mother's milk, as well as a funny smell, like old stuff. Worst of all, Sarah was all alone with Biddy, and didn't know what she was going to do.

She pulled out a chair and sat across from Biddy at the table. "Who's on the snapshot?" she asked, trying to make friends as well as see the picture. "Can I see it?"

"No."

Sarah got up and went to the window when she heard the unmistakable sound of tires on the gravel outside. Thank heavens. Somebody was coming to see them.

"It's Andy," she said, her breath coming out in a rush. "And, oh, Biddy, you'll never guess who's with him. It's Dr. Thorne. Good old Dr. Thorne. He's come home."

Biddy stuck the snapshot in her pocket and pushed her chair back with such force it toppled over. She left it there as she joined Sarah at the window. "What the hell is he doing here. He's not due back for another month."

Sarah opened the kitchen door as Dr. Thorne stepped out of the car and headed for the house. Andy stuck his head out of the car window and yelled he'd be back in a few minutes, then circled the drive and drove off.

Biddy looked around for the glass that held her teeth but remembered it was upstairs in her bedroom. Too late now. Dr. Thorne was coming through the door.

Angus's gaze swept the room, not missing the half-empty gin bottle near the sink, and five or six cigarette ends in the ashtray on the kitchen table. Biddy stood in the middle of the floor, toothless, her hair like a bird's nest. Even with the day half gone, she was still in a robe that he'd bet a pound hadn't seen soap and water for a year or more. His heart softened when he looked at Sarah. She wore a spotless long-sleeved pale blue dress, her fine light hair was clean and combed neatly to the side.

But he didn't miss the yellow cast to her skin, the puffiness in the face, her red-rimmed eyes, as if she'd been crying. She beamed up at him in her funny timid way, so obviously happy to see him.

"So, how's my best girl?" he asked. He put his hands on her shoulders and held her away from him. "Let me get a good look at you."

"I'm trying to get better as fast as I can, aren't I, Biddy?" she said, avoiding Biddy's eyes.

"Yes love." Biddy put her arm round Sarah's waist. "We're doing all we can to make this pretty girl good as new."

Dr. Thorne ran his hand along the handle of the fruit basket. "Where did this come from?"

Sarah straightened the huge pink bow tied onto the basket's handle. "It's from Ada, Andy and Jenny. You've got to meet Jenny, Dr. Thorne. She came all the way from America by herself."

"An American, ay," Dr. Thorne said, avoiding Biddy's eyes. "I can't wait to meet her, especially if she's a friend of yours."

Without asking he opened the fridge and looked inside. "So, what's this, Biddy? TV dinners, frozen pizza, hamburgers? You used to be a nurse and should know better." He closed the fridge and rapped the chart with his knuckles. "Check the list, Biddy. Check the list. All the good foods are on the left. See, starches, pasta, rice, bread, and marshmallows, or jelly beans if Sarah craves something sweet. There are fruits too. Strawberries, apples, some tinned fruits. I can't stress too strongly that dairy products are bad for her. No milk, cheese, chocolates, and no junk food."

"We know, we know," Sarah said with a little nervous laugh. "I've just had apples and strawberries out of the basket and I'm taking my medicine."

There was the soft beep of a car horn and Angus looked out the window. "Andy's back. He had a couple of tires to deliver. Sarah, why don't you keep him company outside for a bit. It's a beautiful day. Biddy and I can sit here and natter over a cup of coffee."

Andy stood with his hands on his hips halfway between his car and the house as he watched Sarah open the door and walk toward him. He and his uncle had planned it all beforehand. He was to keep Sarah occupied while his uncle weighed up Biddy. Less than an hour ago, his uncle had told him about the twins born to an unmarried American woman, one healthy and one with Down syndrome. When he'd handed Jenny's portrait to Andy and said she was the long-lost twin, a two hundred-watt bulb switched on in Andy's head. All these years his uncle had never said one word about Sarah being one of the twins born to an American, or the complicated will left by the Fitzgeralds. It was a pact, his uncle told Andy. However, since Jenny now knew the whole story, it wouldn't hurt to tell Andy. It was just a matter of time before the whole village knew.

Andy stared across the fields. Did all this mean he still stood a chance with Jenny? He remembered the day she'd stepped off the train, looking all lost and lonely yet obviously trying to appear worldly. But it wasn't until the day he'd found her on the bench outside the Hare, her eyes full of tears, that he realized he loved her. Now, for what had to be at least the tenth time, he thought about that evening. How he'd held her in his arms and she'd wept on his shoulder as she told him of the recent deaths of her parents. Then later, from their table in the restaurant, they'd watched the sun set behind the fells. They'd strolled by the lake and talked as if they'd known each other for ages. And he hadn't imagined that look she gave him when she told him he was nice. After he'd let her out at the cottage, he thought about her all night long and couldn't wait to be with her again. But the next day she'd stunned him by telling him to back off.

Yesterday, he'd finally convinced himself he was giving up too easily, and gone into Malone's to ask her for a date. She had her things all over the counter, wouldn't even give him the time of day, so he'd pretended he needed light bulbs. Then out of nowhere, and of all people, Prissy Smith comes floating in, acting as if they'd never split, even talking about sheets and things. Was she crazy?

Sarah was tugging at his sleeve. "Andy? Why don't you answer me?"

"Sorry. I was miles away. What did you say?"

"Biddy said Jenny's leaving." She grabbed both his arms and stared up at him. "We've got to stop her, Andy."

"I saw her in the village this morning," he said. "Didn't look like she was leaving to me."

"She's my very best friend. Andy. Please don't let her get away."

"Don't worry. I'll fix it," he said, more to himself than to Sarah. "We'll get her back. Just trust me."

"But you didn't even know she's leaving. I thought you loved her."

"What an imagination you've got. I hardly know her."

She reached for his hand. "But you do love her don't you? Please marry her, Andy. Have some babies. Have five or ten, just to be on the safe side. If you don't do it for yourself, do it for me. Jenny would never be able to leave if she's got you and a houseful of babies. And I can be their nanny."

He smiled down at her. "You paint a pretty picture, Sarah. But a girl like Jenny wouldn't be interested in me."

"Why? What do you mean?"

"I'm just an ordinary guy who fixes clocks and owns a garage tucked up here in the middle of nowhere."

"This isn't the middle of nowhere," Sarah said. "People come from all over just to see it. Daddy told me."

The seat that wrapped around the dead tree was faded now, paint peeling off, but still a nice place to sit, a good spot to remember the old days. They leaned back and stared up at the sky, watched the hawk hovering overhead, wings quivering. Suddenly it folded its wings against its sides and dived straight down, finally disappearing behind a hedge bordering the field beyond.

"Do you think birds and other animals get kidney problems and stuff?"

"Probably," Andy said, having no idea. "They get lots of things we do."

Sarah looked down at her shoes as she scuffed them in the gravel. "Doctors can't do everything. Even if they fix my kidneys, I'll still be different. I'll never be like everybody else."

Andy put an arm across her shoulders. "Ah, be proud, Sarah. Look how far you've come from the little girl I used to push on that swing there."

***

Angus Thorne looked through the window at Andy and Sarah while he waited for Biddy to dress. Eventually she came downstairs, hair combed, teeth in, and wearing a fairly clean dress.

"Beverly Pender's daughter came to see me this morning," he said. "Can you believe it, her turning up after all this time." He folded his arms and leaned against the fridge, pretending not to notice Biddy's face turn the color of old parchment or the muscles in her jaw twitch, as she pulled out a chair and flopped into it. "I could hardly believe it myself," he said, "but in she walks, into Malone's. She said she'd already met you. Told me all about you saying you recognized her from a portrait her mother had sent to a doctor, then later said you'd got mixed up, case of mistaken identity. Why did you say that? You knew damn good and well it was her."

Biddy stared at the floor.

"Ah, but Jennifer Robinson is the very last person you'd want to see," Angus said. "Isn't that right?"

"Easy for you to say." Biddy ground the words out. "You with your paid-up house, God knows how much money in the bank, and that fancy place you've got in France. What do you care about the likes of me, me who's hung on here for years looking after Sarah. Then, at the last minute the long-lost twin turns up. Oh, she acts so bloody innocent, but she's not fooling me. She's here to cheat me out of everything."

Angus shoved his glasses to the top of his head. "Whether you believe it or not, Jenny was flabbergasted when I told her Sarah was her twin. You can fake a lot of things, but not turning white as a sheet. It was as if, as if she didn't want any part of it. Even when I told her about the will, she brushed it off, then said she had to go, couldn't get out of the house fast enough."

Biddy nodded, her mouth opening as if she was about to say something, then she pursed her lips and turned away.

Angus stuck his hands in his pockets as he weighed the woman up, then slowly, deliberately, looked around the kitchen. "I don't want you smoking in this house, Biddy. If you feel you can't live without one, go outside. And get rid of the gin. This place smells like a brewery. Sarah's got nephritis and I don't have to tell you how serious that is."

Biddy thumped the table with her fist. "Sarah, bloody Sarah. That's all I ever hear. Even in the night I hear it. Whispering voices coming from out there."

"Out where?"

She jerked her thumb towards the window. "Out there. That tree may look dead but don't you believe it. If you thought a tree couldn't move, take a good look at that one. It's about six feet closer to the house than it was two years ago. Its branches are longer too and its leaves rustle, even though there are no leaves and the wind isn't blowing."

Angus felt a stiffening in his shoulders as he chose his words carefully. "Perhaps you've been overdoing things. Is there anything you'd like to talk about? We've known each other a long time. Maybe I can help."

"I knew you'd say something like that." She got up close to his face. "But I'm not crazy. Fred and Edna Fitzgerald are in that tree, hell bent and determined to get in here. You don't think the bloody tree can move on its own do you."

She got up and took a cautious step toward the window. "That's why I've got the curtains closed. So they can't see me. I'm even afraid to go outside. The tree, them, they're out there waiting."

"But surely—"

"But surely, nothing. Once they get in here it's God help me."

"But why would they be after you?"

Biddy grabbed hold of his sleeve. "How the hell should I know. I've done nothing but work my fingers to the bone taking care of Sarah, but what do they care? I'll show them though. I'm getting the damn tree chopped down, then burned, roots and all, every last bloody twig of it. I'll get the spot concreted over, then that'll be that."

"Perhaps you're right," Angus said, suddenly deciding to humor her. "It is rather unsightly."

"Sarah isn't going to like it though," Biddy said, "Still, I've got to think about myself."

Angus forced himself to place an arm on her shoulder, even patted it once or twice. "Why not let me handle this. I know someone who'll do it cheaper than anyone else."

"OK but I want it done this week. Every day it creeps an inch or two nearer."

"Tomorrow's Sunday but I'll ring him first thing next week. He's busy and it might take a few days, but I promise you that tree will be gone and the spot paved over as soon as he can get to it."

"Good. I want it carted off and burned."

Angus looked up at the cuckoo clock and checked it with his watch. "I need to be getting back. There's a cleaning crew coming in at three. The house needs a good clean before Gladys gets home." He headed for the door then turned, praying for diplomacy. "How'd it be if I take Sarah with me, just for a few days. What with her being ill, it's bound to have been hard on you. Perhaps you could pack a suitcase?"

He watched Biddy closely, saw the relief, followed by a frown. "Can't you wait until the tree's chopped down? She's company for me, and Fred and Edna wouldn't dare try anything with her in the house. If she goes, I'll have to go too. I'm not staying here by myself until the tree's gone."

Angus nodded, concerned for Sarah's well-being, but what Biddy said eased his mind. As long as the tree was still on the lawn, Sarah was safe. Besides, if Biddy had to leave, where could she go? She didn't have relatives. The whole problem needed to be thought through. Glen Ellen was just three miles outside the village. He'd give Jonathon a ring. See what he said.

"All right," Angus said, his hand on the doorknob. "I'll get in touch with the man about the tree. I'll be back up here tomorrow."

Before Biddy could say another word, he opened the door and walked toward Andy and Sarah who stood talking beside the car.

"I'll find Jenny," Andy said to Sarah when he saw his uncle come out of the house. "Just trust me."

"OK, then you can get married and start on the babies. It's the only way."

"What's the only way?" his uncle asked.

"Never mind." Andy shook his head and smiled. "I may tell you later."

As Sarah watched Andy's car turn the corner, the postman cycled up the drive.

"Got something for you, Sarah," he said as he lifted a brown paper parcel from the wire basket in front of his bike.

She grinned and poked him on his breast pocket. "Don't you be teasing me, Harry Hogan. Nobody's ever sent me a parcel, never once in my whole life."

Harry grinned back, looked at the address then back at her. "Miss Sarah Fitzgerald. That's you isn't it? Still, if you don't want it, I can take it back."

Sarah almost snatched the parcel out of his hand. "Thank you, Harry," she remembered to say, then bustled over to the tree. She sat on the seat and hugged the parcel to her breast. Somebody had thought enough of her to send her a parcel, had even gone to the trouble to wrap it up in brown paper and string, then put stamps on and post it. She ran her fingers over her name and address before she tore off the wrapping. Inside the cigar box were six hair slides, all different colors, and a yellow chiffon scarf, as well as a tiny box containing the prettiest pearl earrings she'd ever seen. She held them in her hand and wondered who in the world would take her to get her ears pierced. The note was from Lottie Mellville, her friend in the next bed at Craighead Hospital. The note said she'd bought the things in the hospital gift shop and hoped Sarah liked them. Lottie was back in hospital for a few days of therapy, some sort of hiccup to her leg was how she put it. This time though there was no Sarah in the next bed to talk to.

Sarah fingered each slide in turn, tried on the scarf and read the note again. Finally she placed the trinkets back in the box and stood for a few minutes, the sun warm on her arms. While she thought of Lottie, she watched Bill Bass and his two dogs round up the sheep in the field across the lane, and then she headed back to the house.

***

As Andy drove toward Stoney Beck, his uncle gave him a rundown on his conversation with Biddy. "I'll ring Jonathon when I get home. He's their doctor here now, but Biddy's headed for a mental collapse, no doubt about it. Maybe he can talk her into committing herself. I can't do it. She doesn't trust me."

"Biddy's been sliding downhill for a long time," Andy said. "But even if we can get her out of there, Sarah can't stay by herself. Maybe she could've handled a small flat in the village, or a small cottage maybe, but even that's out now."

Angus let out a long, deep sigh. "If she gets any worse, we're looking at dialysis, even a transplant if we can get one."

Andy slowed down to avoid a dog that had darted into the lane. "I'm still trying to get used to the idea that Jenny's her twin. It's hard to believe you've known all these years and never said a word about it."

"I was the executor as well as the physician. It was for Sarah's sake, especially since we had no idea where the mother and sister were. No way would Biddy tell because the last thing she'd want is them turning up. What I can't understand is Jenny's reaction when I told her. I know she likes Sarah, so it's not that." He glanced at Andy. "Do you get the feeling something else is on her mind, that there's more to this than finding the answer to her mother's note?"

Andy shifted into second to tackle the hill ahead. "There's a priest at St. Mary's in Daytonwater, a Father Woodleigh. Do you know him?"

"Never heard of him. What's a priest got to do with anything?"

"On that first day, when Jenny rented one of our cars, she said she was going to St. Mary's. Somebody back home had said it was very old and worth a visit. But Walter Pudsley told me she'd asked him on her first day if he knew anybody named Woodleigh. And what with the priest at St. Mary's being called Woodleigh, well, I just thought it odd, that's all."

He crawled behind Herbie Hunt's tractor from up at Marsdon Tarn Farm. "And there's something else. She's got this morbid fear of hospitals. Her father was sick for years before he died, then a couple of weeks later her mother died from an overdose. Maybe it all got too much."

"Did she say what her father died of?"

"No."

"We need to know because of Sarah. Did she tell you herself about her fear of hospitals?"

Andy told him the ambulance driver had stopped at the garage to put air in his tires and when Jenny had walked across the common, the man said he recognized her. She'd gone with Sarah in the ambulance. He said Jenny seemed uneasy when she'd climbed into the ambulance, and later a hospital orderly told him she'd had some sort of panic attack while she was in the hospital. Not screaming or anything, just hot and out of breath. She couldn't keep up with him and told him she hated hospitals.

"Maybe that's part of it," Angus said. "If she's got some sort of hospital phobia, the last thing she'd want to be is Sarah's twin. If Sarah ends up needing a kidney, wouldn't all eyes turn to Jenny?"

Andy saw the clear stretch of road ahead and pulled around the tractor, throwing up his hand to Herbie as they passed. "Ever since she came to the village, I—"

His uncle turned toward him. "You what?"

"Oh, I don't know. Sometimes I wish I'd never laid eyes on her."

"You're not falling for her are you?"

"Wouldn't you? Have you seen anything like her around here lately? I was at the station when she got off the train. Gave her a lift to the Hare. Thought I was really getting somewhere, but then she cooled. Come close, she seems to say, but not too close. Yesterday, in Malone's, I was all set to ask her for a date when in walks Prissy acting like nothing ever happened." He tapped his fingers on the steering wheel. "God, what did I ever see in her."

"So, you're over her at last, ay?"

Andy glanced at him and gave a short laugh. "What do you think? I didn't know it then but she did me favor that day she walked out. Next to Jenny, she just doesn't stack up and what's more, she knows it. Oh, I had a drink with her at the Hare and told her it was over but she didn't believe me until I dropped her off at the farm. She told me then how she'd noticed the way I looked at Jenny. I didn't know I did that but you know how women are. They don't miss much. I drove off then because it was time to pick you up, but she kept ringing me last night until I finally took the phone off the hook. She rang again this morning and said she was going back to London."

His uncle drummed his fingers on the car door. "We've spent half the afternoon talking about Jenny and this is the first time you've said one word about falling for her. What's the big secret?"

"There isn't one. If anything had come of it, I would have told you. Anyway, she's an American. How do I know she hasn't got some guy waiting for her back home. And what would she want with the likes of me anyway? All I've got is a room full of clocks and a garage tucked up here in the hills. Not very exciting is it?"

"It is to you. You do have a degree in marine biology. You're the one who wanted the garage, and you're one of the best damn clock people in the North West of England."

Andy stopped at the post office and waited while two cyclists passed. "I'll pull into Malone's, so you can have a word with her."

When they went inside, Ada Malone told them Jenny had left early, said she was going for a long drive. No, she didn't say where.

***

Biddy lit a cigarette and poured herself a strong one. She propped up the snapshot once more against the sugar bowl and blew smoke on Beverly and the priest as Sarah came into the kitchen. "How about you and me putting on our glad rags tomorrow and going to church."

Sarah clapped her hands. "Do you really mean it? We haven't been since the funeral."

Biddy turned to look at the window, making sure the curtains were closed. She picked up the snapshot and held it out to Sarah. "Take a look at this. Do you recognize anybody on it?"

Sarah sat opposite her and squinted at the picture. "He looks a bit like Father Woodleigh. It's not his son is it?"

"No. It's him when he was young."

"Oh."

"What do you think of the girl with him?"

Sarah held the snapshot at arms length, and then brought it up close again. "She's very pretty. We don't know her do we?"

"No. She's someone the priest was in love with." Biddy put her thumbs in her mouth and pressed them against her upper plate. "How about you and me having some fun while we're in church tomorrow?"

"We can't have fun in church, Biddy. We have to behave."

"Oh, it won't be that bad." Biddy leaned forward, warming to the idea. "We'll wait until halfway through the service. This should be the perfect time."

"Perfect for what?"

"For you to walk down the aisle and show him this snapshot."

Sarah's hand came up to cover her mouth. "I can't do that. Father Woodleigh would get very cross. Why can't we give it to him on the way out?"

"Don't ask stupid questions," Biddy said, her voice high and strange. "We'll do it when I say so."

Sarah lowered her head, uneasy now, feeling Biddy's eyes on her, wild like they were a lot these days. "OK."

"You can wear that red dress with the white polka dots and we'll put a new red ribbon on your white straw hat. Your mother loved you in that getup."

Sarah looked at the snapshot closely. Maybe Father Woodleigh wouldn't be cross after all. He had been so kind to visit her in hospital even though she didn't know him. Lottie had teased her and said that he had taken a shine to her. When he came again, he told Sarah he was a friend of Jenny's. On another day he had stopped here at the house and told Biddy that a prayer would be said for Sarah during Mass. Sarah could hardly believe that part because she hardly ever went to church any more.

"Was Father Woodleigh in love with this girl?" she asked.

"What do you think? Look at his hands. They're all over her."

Sarah nodded, anxious not to upset Biddy. "You're right. He'll be so pleased when I show him."

"Tickled pink more like it," Biddy said.

Sarah leaned on the table, chin in her hands. "If I do this, will we be friends forever and ever? Will you cross your heart and promise?"

"That's right, Sarah," Biddy said, crossing her heart. "We'll be friends forever."

"Can I get my ears pierced?"

"You can get your nose pierced if you want to."

Sarah giggled. Biddy hardly ever tried to be funny. If showing the snapshot to the priest meant so much to her, Sarah would do it. She'd do anything to keep Biddy happy. Perhaps she'd been teasing when she'd said Jenny was leaving. So if Sarah showed the picture to Father Woodleigh, maybe, just maybe, Biddy would be in such a good mood, Sarah could coax her into swinging by Jenny's cottage and inviting her to tea.

"Tomorrow's going to be such a lovely day," she said. "I can hardly wait."

"Neither can I. Now be a good girl and ring Dr. Thorne. Don't mention tomorrow or anything. Just say you were glad to see him today and that you and I are very happy together. If you'll do this, I promise we'll be friends forever."

Biddy gave the phone to Sarah and listened while she talked to Dr. Thorne, making sure there were no slip-ups. Later, when Sarah had gone to her room to listen to her records, Biddy leaned back in her chair thinking about tomorrow. After Sarah had given the snapshot to the priest, this would clinch it for Biddy. Thorne coming home early would make no difference. When Jenny Robinson found out the priest had the snapshot, you wouldn't see her for dust. Biddy would get the whole shebang. Everything was going to be all right after all.

Chapter Sixteen

In the cottage that same evening, Jenny sat by the phone and tapped her international phone card lightly on the desk. Finally she punched in the numbers embossed on the card and added her uncle's home phone number.

"Hello."

"Uncle Tim? How's it going?"

"Jenny? It's so good to hear your voice. Seems like you've been gone forever."

"Is everything OK?"

"I guess so. I was up at the cabin yesterday. Beautiful day. Eighty-five degrees. Carolina blue sky with just a whisper of a breeze. I looked at your skis hanging there, covered in dust. Couldn't help but wonder when you're coming home?"

"Not yet awhile. Got something to tell you, Uncle Tim."

"Oh? You've told the priest? How did he take it?'

"Haven't done that yet. I want to tell you something else. Are you sitting down?"

"Oh, God, Jenny. Every time you say that, you hit me with a two by four."

"I've found out what Mom was trying to tell me in that note."

As calmly and succinctly as she could, Jenny brought her uncle up to date. She told him about her conversation with Dr. Thorne and how the man had broken the news to her that she had a twin sister named Sarah. By the time Jenny had explained the complicated will, at least half an hour had passed. Somewhere in all of this, she told her uncle about Biddy, at the same time trying to paint her as a befuddled old woman rather than the bitch she really was. Finally Jenny asked him to send copies of the documents Dr. Thorne wanted and could he please mail them the fastest way.

"When we talked the other night," Uncle Tim said, "I thought then you might be on to something. But I never dreamed it was anything like this."

"Neither did I and I'm still trying to take it in. You will get those papers off won't you?"

"I'll get them off tomorrow. Thank God we found all these things before you left. But are you OK? Over there by yourself with all this going on?"

Jenny leaned back in her chair, feeling the load lift just a little. "Yes. I'm fine. Especially now, since I've told you all this. Everybody here seems nice and friendly. There's no telling what Dr. Thorne thinks of me after I stalked out of his house. I think he expected me to jump up and down, but all I could think about was the priest. I mean how do I tell him he's got grown-up twins?"

"You have to tell him Jenny. This is as much his problem as it is yours. You can't carry all this on your own shoulders. Don't forget what we said. *The truth will set you free.*"

"I know, I know. I'm so glad I called you. It's as if a load has been lifted off my shoulders. I'll write the letter tonight. Tomorrow I'll go to church and slip it to him when I'm leaving."

Her uncle now knew almost everything except that Biddy had stolen Jenny's snapshot. But what would be the point in telling him that?

They chatted for a few more minutes, long enough for Uncle Tim to tell Jenny he'd met a nice widow. Yes, he knew he'd said one failed marriage was enough but that was before he met Mary Louise.

***

Jenny stuck her hands in her anorak pockets as she trudged toward the lake, mentally composing the letter to the priest. She felt a strange and surprising sense of release. Not only was she about to beat Biddy at her own game, but at last she had plucked up courage to tell the priest. What he did after he'd read the letter was up to him.

She stood at the water's edge and watched a large brown trout glide over the lake's sandy bed and head away from the shore. A couple of mallards preened on the lone rock the heron had fished from the other day.

She jumped as a Frisbee was plopped at her feet, and gave a little surprised laugh as she looked down at Pete. He panted beside her, at least six inches of tongue dangling out the side of his mouth, his friendly, keen eyes begging her to throw his Frisbee.

"Don't throw it," Andy Ferguson said as he strolled toward her. "You'll only encourage him."

There he stood with that crooked smile, his hair flopping across his forehead, the way she'd seen him that first day when she'd stepped off the train.

"Hey, Pete, you good dog, you," she said as she bent down and rubbed his ears before picking up his Frisbee and hurling it across the water. Pete flung himself off the grassy bank into the lake.

"Show off," Andy shouted after his dog as he sliced through the water.

Jenny dug her heels into the ground and clasped her hands behind her back to stop herself from reaching out to him, for a touch of any kind. At the same time, a strange unexpected envy coursed through her veins, a sort of yearning for the friendship these two had for each other, this man and his crazy, wonderful dog.

"What are you doing here?" she asked.

"Looking for you. Thought you might need some company."

"I guess your uncle Angus told you everything. I saw you cross the street to his house."

"You did, ay. I could have sworn you hadn't seen me. When I shouted out, you didn't even look up."

"I know. I was so blown away by what he told me, I just had to get away. You know, to think. I mean it isn't every day—"

"He knows that."

She looked out at Pete slogging back through the water, Frisbee clenched between his teeth.

"Did you know Sarah was adopted?" she asked Andy.

"Yes, but—"

"But you didn't tell me."

"Well, you didn't ask. It just never came up. It's no secret. The whole village knows, even Sarah herself. But I don't think anybody knew about the twin part, except shady old Uncle Angus and Biddy. The Hare's old landlord knew but he's been dead for years. Even I didn't know. The solicitors did of course, but other than that—"

Jenny kicked a loose stone by the water's edge, and then dodged back as Pete leaped out of the water.

"Don't you dare shake all over Jenny," Andy said, as he picked up the Frisbee and tossed it back in. Pete leaped into the air and caught it on the fly before crashing into the lake.

Andy grabbed Jenny's arm. "Watch out, here he comes again."

She jumped at his unexpected touch and felt her face burn. Had he noticed? He still held her arm but his gaze was on Pete who shook where he was, Frisbee still in his mouth.

"Listen," Andy said, "how about us getting a drink in the Hare then you coming home with Pete and me for dinner. I've got some of the world's best Spaghetti Bolognese simmering on the stove. I'm an expert cook, one in a million, and if you don't believe me, ask Pete. He eats everything I cook."

"OK," she said, trying not to sound too eager. Andy Ferguson wasn't the type to beg, and if she refused, he'd probably never ask her again. "I'll come if you promise not to ask questions."

"It's a deal." He took her hands and breathed on them, then rubbed them between his own as a parent would a child's. "You're cold. Come on, let's go in the pub."

Pete trotted beside them until they reached the bar door.

"Stay, boy," Andy said. The dog moved to the side as if he'd done it hundreds of times before. He sat against the wall, set his Frisbee down beside him, then stared sentry-like, straight ahead.

"What have you done with Miss Priscilla Fortescue-Smythe?" Jenny asked as she sipped her chardonnay, looking for something to talk about besides the twin thing.

"I thought you said no questions."

"I did, but—"

"But you didn't mean you couldn't ask me anything, ay." He grinned as he picked up his glass of beer. "Only kidding. What is it you want to know about Miss Priscilla?"

"Are you two serious about each other?"

He smiled as he looked at his watch. "Right about now, I'd say she's probably climbing into her big West End director's bed. That Prissy'll do anything to get her name up in lights."

As Andy stuck the key in his door, he told Jenny that a wealthy spinster aunt had left him the hundred-year-old house. His parents who now lived in Torquay had lent him the money to buy the garage next door. He led her along a passage at the side of the house for a quick look at the garden out back, half an acre he said proudly, big by English standards. There were vegetables growing on one side of the path and a lawn with a border of flowers on the other. A fishpond, complete with miniature waterfall, and which Andy said was full of koi, was in the center of the lawn. Even as they stood there, a mist seemed to literally climb the wall and spread across the garden.

The first floor of the three-story house, or at least the huge room they'd entered, was wall to wall with clocks. Standing side by side against the far wall were three grandfather clocks and a couple of grandmothers, which even Jenny, with her limited knowledge, guessed were worth a great deal of money. There were shelves with wall clocks and mantel clocks of every size and type, some antique, some modern. The two work tables in the center of the room were strewn with clock parts and machinery.

"Oh, man," Jenny said. "I knew you tinkered with clocks, but I can't believe this."

He walked across the room to one of the grandfathers and adjusted its pendulum, then ran a hand down its side, stroking it almost tenderly. "It started out as a hobby. Now though it takes up more of my time than the garage." He stood with his hands in his pockets as he looked around the room. "Sometimes, especially at night, I get down here and start tinkering. Before I know it, it's two in the morning. This friend of mine tells me he forgets what time it is when he's surfing the Web, but with me, it's clocks. I go to all the estate sales, haunt flea markets looking for deals. I buy clocks and sell them. I fix and appraise them for people too." He grinned. "When I get old, all the kids round here will probably call me that crazy old clock guy."

"I bet they don't," Jenny said. "These clocks must be worth a fortune. Aren't you scared you might get robbed?"

He pointed to the locks on the door and the box over it. "I've got as much security in this place as the crown jewels in the Tower. That burglar alarm shoots right through to the police station."

It was one of those old English homes Jenny had seen in magazines. There were nooks and crannies everywhere, with two or three stairs leading to each room, each little separate place. It had exposed oak beams and the windows were leaded glass with small diamond-shaped panes. All the doors had glass knobs which Jenny could have sworn were lead crystal, and there was a huge stone fireplace with thick leather cushions at each end of the wide hearth. The off-white walls were covered with wildlife prints and travel posters, some framed and others stuck on with tape. In the corner was a grandfather clock, its case inlaid with mother-of-pearl, and looking as if it was worth a great deal of money. She wandered over to Andy's bookcase. At least three or four books on clocks, a couple on the history of trains, marine biology, with at least two to do with Greenpeace. There were a couple of novels by Grisham, Clancy, and other men's type books. Piled high next to the bookcase was a stack of *Popular Mechanics* magazines. There was a threadbare carpet on the floor, and deep leather chairs to lose yourself in which Andy said he'd picked up for a song at an estate sale. The worn brown leather chair near the hearth bore the telltale imprint of Pete.

Andy looked toward the French doors at the far end of the room. "There used to be a window there but I had it made into a door, then made a terrace out of the garage's roof. It's a good place to sit and the highest spot in the village. The tourist bureau comes up here and takes pictures of the view." He peered upwards through the mist. "There's a full moon tonight, up there somewhere. Maybe this fog will lift later."

Jenny stood beside him, able to make out lawn chairs, a couple of hanging baskets as well as birdhouses on poles. There were tubs in all four corners filled with begonias and geraniums. She turned back to the room. This was a man's house without the touch of a woman anywhere, unless you counted the huge glass vase of roses and carnations on the sideboard, as well as two brand new pale blue candles in wooden holders were in the center of the table which was already set for two.

"Everything's ready. Were you that sure I'd accept?"

"No, but I used to be a Boy Scout."

She nodded and smiled. "I know. Be prepared."

Andy snapped his fingers and turned to his dog. "I told you she'd twig. Why did I listen to you." Pete ignored him and leaped on to his chair.

Jenny sat in the chair across from Pete while Andy went into the kitchen and came back with a tray laden with glasses of red wine, cheese, and crackers. He placed it on the low table by the hearth and took a match to the laid fire. It caught and the flames leaped up the chimney. He switched on the stereo down low—Nat King Cole and Natalie singing *Unforgettable*. Jenny smiled shyly up at him. A silence had come between them, as if neither knew what to say.

Pete slipped off his chair and sidled towards her, then lowered his head onto her knees and nudged her hand with his nose. Unable to resist his pleading look, slowly she began to rub his ears.

"I need to put the pasta on," Andy said. "I don't want to mess anything up."

"Can I help?"

"If you like. There's lettuce and stuff in the fridge for a salad."

He grinned and the awkward moment was gone.

He fixed a bowl of the same food for his dog, right down to sprinkling it with Parmesan cheese and even adding a dash of salt and pepper. Pete leapt out of his chair.

"I'm glad I came," Jenny said after Andy lit the candles, and she'd taken the first bite of food. "You and Pete have got it made. You're a good cook too. This is delicious."

He passed her the basket of hot French bread. "Ada gave me the recipe. I was worried about making it but she said there was no way I could mess up."

"I thought you said you made the best Spaghetti Bolognese in the world."

"I lied," he said cheerfully. "I've never made it in my life. Ada was right though. It was easy."

For dessert there were strawberries and fresh cream from the local farm, as well as cappuccino coffee.

They stacked the dishes in the kitchen then sat on the sofa and drank Drambuie. Pete, asleep in his chair, whimpered and his legs twitched, probably chasing his Frisbee in some dog dream. Jenny felt a quiet peace. It was this house. Here in front of the fire like this, it was the most natural thing in the world for Andy to put his arm around her while she nestled next to him.

She didn't want to talk any more about Sarah or Biddy, didn't even want to think about the priest. She wanted to tell Andy something of her own life in Charlotte, maybe talk about Uncle Tim. But against her will, and maybe because she'd had three glasses of wine, as well as the Drambuie, she felt her eyes closing.

Andy eased himself off the sofa and very gently placed a pillow under her head. He brought a lap rug from the chest in the corner and draped it over her. He stood, hands on hips looking down at her and fighting an urge to scoop her up in his arms and place her in the middle of his bed. If he did, would she reach for him, eager as he was, or would she jump up and bolt for the door? In the end, he gently smoothed away the hair that had fallen across her left eye, before going into the kitchen and loading the dishwasher. Later he sat opposite to her and flicked through a couple of sports magazines. Every now and then he looked across at her, watching her sleep, with her hands tucked under her cheek.

Pete slipped down from his chair and stretched full length in front of the couch where she lay. Andy smiled at his dog. "You like her too don't you Pete," he whispered. "I never saw you do that with Prissy."

At midnight he knelt beside her and gently shook her shoulder. "I hate to wake you, but it's late. I don't want you clobbering me in the morning if I left you to sleep here all night."

She sat up and rubbed her eyes. "I didn't mean to fall asleep."

"That's OK. You were tired. You don't have to go back to the cottage if you don't want to. I mean, you're welcome to spend the night with me and Pete." He turned to look at his dog standing beside him, head cocked to one side as he stared at Jenny. It was as if he understood every word his master had said and was begging her with his eyes to stay.

"I've got extra pajamas," Andy said. "They'll be a bit big but you could make do, and I've got at least one new toothbrush. There's a spare bedroom upstairs with its own bathroom." He held up his hand in a sort of pledge. "No funny stuff, I swear."

"I believe you," she said softly, unable to resist a big smile at his pitch. "Still, I guess I had better get on back."

He held her face in his hands and kissed her gently on the lips. "Are you sure?"

She swung her legs off the couch and got up. "No, I'm not sure, but yes, I guess I really should go."

He took her hand and led her toward the French doors.

"The mist's lifted. Before you go at least let me show you the view from my terrace."

A full moon shone on the wet rooftops, and Market Street's cobblestones. It cast a mantle of silver on the hushed midnight village and the lake beyond. Stoney Beck was a scene from the middle ages and Jenny could almost see the town crier of hundreds of years ago. He walked down Market Street in his breeches and tri-cornered hat, swinging his lamp in one hand and ringing his bell in the other as he shouted *oyez, oyez, twelve o'clock and all's well.* Or something like that. Lights twinkled here and there in the fells beyond and somewhere far off they heard the call of a night bird.

"What do you think?"

She let out a deep sigh. "It's beautiful."

"Would you like to live here?"

Jenny kept her gaze on the view as she felt his hand tighten its grip.

"I don't necessarily mean here in the house of course," he said quickly. "I mean in the village, in Stoney Beck."

"I don't know. It's—"

"A nice place to visit but you wouldn't want to live here?"

"I didn't say that."

"I know. Just kidding. And anyhow, anybody from a sultry climate like North Carolina would never survive a winter up here in the lakes."

"Are they that bad?"

"It depends who you are, what you like. I love them, but they're not everybody's cup of tea."

He snapped his fingers at Pete. "Come on, boy. This woman's got scruples. Let's walk her home."

Pete gave a little woof then trotted toward the box that held his Frisbee.

"Leave it Pete. It's midnight for God's sake."

The tail drooped a bit but the dog did as he was told.

As they walked down Market Street, Andy put his arm around her and pulled her to him, while Pete walked beside them, his tail swinging from side to side. Lights were still on in a number of houses. People stayed up late in England. The big tabby sat in the dim glow of the Knitting Needles window and eyed them suspiciously as they walked past the shop. Jenny wondered if the cat ever slept. There was laughter from somewhere down the street, then snatches of hushed conversation from a group under a street lamp near the Hare and Hounds.

When they reached the cottage, Jenny pulled out her key and opened the door. "I had a real nice time tonight," she said. "The spaghetti was delicious and you went to so much trouble. You know, the flowers and all. Sorry I fell asleep."

"I told you it was OK."

He moved toward her and reached for her hair, hanging loose on her shoulders. He wound it around his hand and pulled her to him. The kiss made Jenny glad he hadn't done that inside his house, because if he had, she'd have stayed for sure. He smoothed her hair back in place and held her face in his hands then ran a thumb across her lips.

"Are you sure you don't want me to come in?" His voice was hoarse, ragged.

Jenny looked behind her through the open door. She stuck her hands in her pockets.

"Better not," was all she could manage. What would be his reaction if she told him she herself had been conceived in this very cottage. But this of course she couldn't say.

"OK. I'll see you some time tomorrow."

A breeze blew his hair across his forehead. Under the lamp outside the cottage, his blue eyes were the same color as his shirt collar worn outside his navy jersey. Hardly aware she was doing it, she reached out and stroked his face. He brought up his own hand and placed it over hers then kissed her palm.

She kneeled beside his dog and put her face next to his. "Night Pete." Then she went inside.

At five the next morning, already wide awake, she heard a car start up in the parking lot. Somebody getting an early start. She took five or six sheets of stationery off the rack on the table and began the letter she would give to Father Woodleigh after church.

Chapter Seventeen

Jenny walked into the tearoom and picked up the Sunday paper from the rack near the entrance. She nodded or mouthed a good morning to five or six of the guests she recognized as she made her way to the table by the window, the one with the reserved sign placed there especially for her. She returned the waves of the archeologists as they straggled in separately. She knew them now. Dagmar and Nils were from Copenhagen and Peter from Oslo. Hilde came from Vienna and the others were from different parts of the UK. They were in the middle of excavating a site of Viking remains. Jenny had joined them in the bar a few nights and played darts or dominoes. They'd also taught her how to play lawn bowls on the green at the back of the inn.

She slung her bag over the chair back and watched Walter Pudsley walk toward her. He carried a tray with a pot of coffee, toast, jam, some butter.

"Mind if I join you?"

He didn't wait for an answer as he began taking the things off the tray. Even though Walter was friendly, he had never sat with Jenny in the dining room. Surely he hadn't found out about her and Sarah already. News traveled fast in a small town.

"Ada tells me you've finished your job in the shop."

"It was time. She's got plenty of help now."

He picked up the coffee pot, poured two cups, and placed one in front of her. She picked up her spoon and stirred the coffee absently. As much as she liked this man, she wished he would go away. She needed all her concentration on how she could get her letter to the priest, and then leave the church gracefully without explaining.

"I don't know how much longer you plan on staying," Walter said, stroking his beard, "so I have to strike while the iron's hot. The thing is, if you could see your way clear to doing me just this little favor."

She took a slice of toast from the rack. "I will if I can."

"It's all to do with Ada y'see. For instance, on slow days in the shop, when you were having a cuppa and talking about this and that, did she ever say anything about me? You know, maybe ask how I'm doing or anything?" He fiddled with his napkin, rolling it up in the corners, and then straightening it out. "What with you working alongside her and staying here at the inn too, it'd be only natural wouldn't it?"

Jenny spread her toast with butter and reached for the gooseberry jam. "Sometimes we'd get to talking about the inn and all, and well, yes, we talked about you some."

"Ah, but she never comes into the pub. Not the type, too reserved altogether."

Jenny bit into the toast. "She told me her husband was a sot, said he was never out of this pub."

"Aye, that's true enough. Fergel Malone was the village drunk but he's been dead for years. It's time she was getting over it. I've been having a think about all this, and what with you two getting on so well, I've decided nothing ventured, nothing gained."

"You want me to ask her to join me for a drink in here don't you," Jenny said, smiling in spite of herself. "Then you'll sort of wander casually over and say hello."

Walter laughed like a teenager. "Tonight would be perfect if you're not too busy? Sunday is Pub Quiz night. It'll give us something to do besides trying to make conversation."

Jenny reached for the milk. "Ah, the famous quiz game." Hilde had asked her to join them a couple of times, but something else had always come up.

"It's a sheet full of questions," Walter said. "Costs fifty pence. It's popular in a lot of pubs these days, especially on Sunday or Monday nights when things are slow. It attracts a certain type. You take those archeologists," he said, inclining his head toward their table. "That sort knows a lot and they nearly always win."

"I probably wouldn't know a thing on the sheet."

"Ah, I'll bet you're just being modest. Still, it'd be a nice evening. We could ask Andy Ferguson to join us. If we did, it wouldn't look too contrived. And anyway, Andy's brainy. He may look rough and ready in those overalls of his but he could have been just about anything he wanted."

"OK," Jenny said, the idea so much more appealing now that Andy had come into the picture. "I'll call Ada if you'll get in touch with Andy."

After Walter had gone, Jenny poured herself a second cup of coffee and stared out the same window she had on that first day. The place had taken on an air of familiarity, almost as if she had been here for years. She watched the two Canada Geese, Romeo and Juliet to the locals, preening themselves on the lawn in front of the inn. Walter had told her

Romeo had injured his wing years ago and even though the RSPCA had tried to mend it, all he could manage was a sort of chicken flight as far as the lake. Juliet never left his side, and together they'd parented a clutch of goslings every year.

Jenny glanced at her watch. Time to get ready. She'd wear her grey suit and that floppy red velvet beret that had been her mother's. She stood up and headed for the door, returning Walter's knowing wink as she passed him on her way out. Before she left the cottage, she called Ada and asked if she felt like coming to the Hare that night for Pub Quiz.

"Walter and Andy'll be joining us. Sounds as if it might be fun."

Ada gave a tinkle of a laugh. "Did Walter put you up to this?"

"Yes, but don't you dare let on."

"You can trust me. And, yes, of course I'll come. I'll wear my new blue blouse. I remember Walter telling me at a dance in the village hall more than thirty years ago how much he liked me in blue."

Jenny sat in the car in the inn's parking lot and took out the letter to the priest. After she'd read all five pages for what had to be the fifth time, she folded it and placed it in the buff colored envelope with the Hare and Hounds crest. She sealed it before tucking it carefully in her bag, then turned the ignition key and headed slowly out the parking lot toward St. Mary's.

Chapter Eighteen

In the same pew as before, she tucked in beside the stone pillar. After the service, the parishioners would straggle out, and the priest would stand in the doorway shaking hands and saying all the usual things. She'd hand him the envelope face down so he wouldn't see the words *extremely personal* she had written in the corner as a precaution against it being opened by a church secretary. After a smile and breezy wave of her hand, she would stroll to her car, drive out of the parking lot, and out of his life.

He stood before his congregation as he had that other time. When he spotted her, Jenny could have sworn he winked. He walked over to the choirmaster and whispered something. When the boys sang "Ave Maria" for their first hymn, she knew he hadn't forgotten. It was especially for her. She fudged her way through the service as she had the other Sunday. At first she struggled to find her place in the prayer book, then gave up and listened to the priest and the responses from the congregation.

Father Woodleigh finally mounted the steps to the pulpit for his sermon. For a moment he looked at his notes then with the flat of his hands resting on the corners of the lectern, he began. "Somebody once said the word *solitude* was coined for those people who love to be alone, and that the word *lonely* for those people who hate it. For some, a walk alone in the woods is a delight, for others it's a nightmare. There's a world of difference between—"

He stopped and looked down the aisle as a murmur rustled through the congregation at the rear of the church. Heads turned to see the cause of the disturbance.

Jenny also looked over her shoulder, and then clamped a hand over her mouth to stifle the gasp. Sarah, her face flushed and arms pressed stiffly against her sides, plodded down the aisle toward the lectern. She drew level with Jenny's pew and passed without seeing her, eyes focused dead ahead. Jenny looked to the back again. Biddy sat across the aisle, two or three rows from the back, arms folded, watching Sarah with all the concentration of a drill sergeant.

Sarah wished a great big hole would open up in the floor, some place she could fall into and just disappear. Here she was, right in the middle of Mass, walking toward Father Woodleigh to give him a snapshot she could just as easily have given him on her way out, or even posted it to him. Biddy had shoved the snapshot in her hand and booted her out of the pew, hissing it was now or never. Sarah cringed as she clomp-clomped down the aisle in the heavy old-lady shoes Biddy had made her wear. Every step she took bounced off the flagstones and echoed around the church. And even though Sarah kept her eyes straight ahead, she could feel every eye in the church on her, burning through her red and white polka dot dress.

She looked past Father Woodleigh and fastened her gaze on the stained glass window behind him. The Virgin Mary in a bright blue robe sat on a stone bench and bounced baby Jesus on her knee. He had blonde curly hair and laughed up at his mother. A tall man with a long beard and in a cloak stood beside them. This was probably Joseph, baby Jesus' father. He had a halo round his head too, like his wife and little boy.

And suddenly Sarah was standing in front of Father Woodleigh. She had expected him to be frowning, but he wasn't. There was even a trace of a smile on his face that reminded Sarah of the way her Daddy used to look at her when he knew she was afraid. It was as if Father Woodleigh knew she was dying inside, that none of this was her idea.

"What is it, Sarah?" he said, his voice so soft, so gentle, she felt her eyes fill up. He leaned forward, his gaze on the snapshot in her hand.

She reached up and handed it to him, then stretched on tiptoe, hands around her mouth so nobody else could hear. "It's a photo of you when you were younger," she whispered in a shaky, hoarse voice. "It's you and your sweetheart, your young lady."

Father Woodleigh stared at the snapshot for what seemed ages, yet couldn't have been more than a couple of seconds. When he looked back at her, his face had gone a chalky white and it didn't look as if he was going to thank her as Biddy had promised. Instead he gripped the lectern with one hand and the snapshot with his other and just stared as if he couldn't think of a single thing to say.

Suddenly, out of nowhere, and just when she needed her most, Jenny was standing beside her. Her Jenny, her very best friend. Who would have believed it?

Jenny took hold of Sarah's sweaty hand and gave it a little squeeze as she stretched her other hand toward Father Woodleigh. "Please Father," she said in a tight, strained voice. "The picture's mine. I don't know how Sarah got hold of it."

"But where did *you* get it?" he asked, his voice trembling slightly as he stared from her back to the picture.

"My mother gave it to me. That's her in the picture with you."

The murmur rippling through the church grew louder.

Sarah pulled her hand away from Jenny's and wiped her eyes on the sleeve of her dress, then flapped her arms up and down as if trying to take flight.

"I didn't know, I didn't know," she said loudly, turning from the priest to Jenny, then back to the priest.

"Biddy said it would be all right. She said you'd be thrilled." Sarah's lip quivered as she looked wildly round the church before she swung round to return to her place.

Horrified, Jenny watched Sarah, her head lowered as she took quick little clunky steps back down the aisle. Biddy had moved to the entrance and stood, feet apart, arms still folded, waiting for her. Sarah was a bug lurching toward a giant frog ready to swallow her whole. Jenny couldn't bear to watch and turned back to the priest, her mouth in some sort of hideous grimace.

"Sarah didn't mean it, Father. She didn't understand."

The priest's pale face frightened Jenny, even though she raised her hand again for the snapshot, he held on to it. She didn't know if he was too overwhelmed or too reluctant to part with it.

"I'm so sorry," she said, then not knowing what else to do, spun round and followed Sarah down the aisle and out of the church. She was in time to see Biddy, with Sarah in the seat beside her, pull out of the handicapped persons' parking space and screech out of the parking lot toward Stoney Beck. Jenny felt bile rising in her throat. What was the point in chasing after them now? The damage was done.

Charles Woodleigh stuck the photograph in his vestment pocket as he watched Jenny stride down the aisle, head held high, her shoulder-length hair bouncing with every step. Beverly's hair did that. And that walk, it was Beverly's all over again. When she'd looked up at him, it was through Beverly's eyes. He'd noticed those eyes before but wouldn't let himself believe. Now though there was no doubt. Even Jenny's red velvet beret was familiar, so becoming on Beverly all those years ago.

He took long deep breaths while he pretended to peruse his notes, then looked up and gave an almost casual shrug as well as an apologetic smile to his parishioners. No need to explain. Disruptions happened everywhere these days, sometimes even in a church. He leaned heavily on the lectern to ease the weight from his trembling legs. As he struggled to focus on his sermon about loneliness and how to deal with it, he bet not one of those faces gazing up at him was aware of the self-control he had mustered to stay in the pulpit and not go racing down the aisle after the young woman who'd just marched out of his church.

Jenny dragged herself to the rectory and rang the bell. Mrs. Thwaites opened the door wide and wiped the flour off her hands with her apron.

"It's Jenny isn't it?" the woman said, beaming at Jenny, at the same time eyeing the envelope Jenny thrust toward her. "Father Woodleigh's in the middle of Mass. If you'd care to come inside and wait."

"No, no, but thanks anyway. Just please make sure he gets this envelope. It's very important."

Mrs. Thwaites cocked her head to one side, a puzzled smile on her face. "Yes, lass. The very minute he comes in. Perhaps it's just as well if you don't stay. He's not having his tea and biscuit affair today. After lunch he'll be on his way to Liverpool. There's a special Mass at the cathedral tonight, then he's off to a retreat. Won't be back for a month."

"I see. But you will make sure he gets the envelope?"

"Absolutely. I'll set it in the middle of his plate."

***

Biddy was silent as she drove back to Glen Ellen, her mind still back in the church. She could tell by the look on Sarah's face, the girl thought she'd made a cock-up of the job. Biddy, though, had relished every minute of it. Jenny Robinson being there was an unexpected bonus and when she'd scuttled along her pew and dashed to the front, Biddy had almost wet herself with the thrill of it all. The best part had been when the girl had reached her hand toward the priest, obviously expecting him to hand over the snapshot. But all she'd got was a long astonished stare. The poor sod was in shock and the American girl had finally turned away from the pulpit empty handed.

Biddy tapped her index finger on the steering wheel as she drove a steady thirty-five miles an hour. It didn't matter any more that Dr. Thorne had come back early and told that girl everything. And it didn't matter much either that she hadn't left Stoney Beck. The incident in the church made up for everything. There were still a few bits and pieces to the puzzle that Biddy hadn't figured out but was convinced now that the priest was the father. You only had to look at his dead white face to realize that the news had come as a colossal shock.

As if from far away, Biddy heard Sarah's whining voice.

"You lied to me, Biddy. You said Father Woodleigh would be tickled pink to see the snapshot. But his face went all white and funny. And you never said Jenny would be there. I could have just died. That lady in the picture was her mother. I didn't know that." She beat her fists on the dashboard. "Jenny thinks I stole it. I know she does."

Biddy drove without saying a word, a big smile on her face to aggravate Sarah even more. Sarah grabbed her arm. "You stole it didn't you, Biddy? That was very wicked and I hate you, Biddy. I hate you more than anybody in the whole world."

Without taking her eyes off the road, Biddy flung out her arm and hit Sarah hard on the mouth with the back of her hand, then turned on the radio, loud. Crazy rock music she hated but at least it blocked out Sarah's sniveling. There was a bottle of gin waiting for her in the sideboard back at Glen Ellen, and after she'd let Sarah know who was boss, she'd have a few drinks and sleep for the afternoon. If the priest came asking questions, she'd think of something. What else could you expect from someone like Sarah, she'd say. She'd get the devil himself in trouble if she could.

***

Jenny pulled out of St. Mary's parking lot and drove in the opposite direction from Stoney Beck. She stopped to check the signpost at the fork in the road, and then headed toward Bowness on Lake Windermere. The day was warm, shirtsleeve weather. She peeled off her suit jacket as she watched a hoard of people board the ferry for the two-hour sail on the lake. After it pulled away from the landing, she walked beside the lake, her guidebook open as she pretended to read items of interest. She aimed her camera at scenery that was nothing more than a blur. When a young American couple offered to take her picture because she was obviously on her own, she handed over her camera, then stood with the lake behind her and smiled into the lens.

Later she wandered through the Steamboat Museum, her brain still hammering with unanswered questions. What had the priest thought of the letter? Jenny could see him now, his eyes growing ever wider as he turned the pages. Weak in the knees he would flop into the nearest chair and stare off into space, repeating *Oh my God* over and over, then cover his face with his hands. And it wasn't only him. What was Jenny going to do about Sarah, who was sick and at the mercy of a spiteful, half-crazy woman? What if Sarah's nephritis worsened? Leaving her with Biddy was as bad as a death sentence. Jenny would sign every paper they put in front of her as long as it got Biddy out of Glen Ellen and away from Sarah forever. Finally, after an hour in Windermere, Jenny headed for her car.

After the Mass, Charles stood as he always did at the top of the church steps. With a glued-on smile, he shook hands and struggled through the usual give and take of after-Mass small talk with parishioners whose names had suddenly escaped him. Some of them held on to his hand, stood in front of him longer than usual as if they longed to ask what the commotion had been about, but were either too polite or didn't have the nerve. When the last person had gone, he wiped the perspiration from his brow and strode toward the rectory.

"Lunch is on the table, Father," Mrs. Thwaites said as she met him in the hallway. "You need to be on the road by four. On a day like this, everybody and his brother will be out. It'll be choc-a-bloc all the way to Liverpool."

"Be down in a minute," he said as he whipped past her and took the stairs two at a time to his bedroom. He pulled out the snapshot and placed it on the dresser. From under his bed, he yanked the old battered suitcase he'd carried with him since his schooldays, adding memorabilia as his life unfolded. He took out the old shoebox, full of precious snapshots, all the way from his baby pictures through school. Some were of his trips to Rome, a couple of a holiday he took once in the Isle of Man. There were others of his family, his mother and father, both dead now. Three or four were of his sister who lived in South Africa with her husband and family and hadn't written to him in years.

Ah, here it was, in the middle of the box. Charles plucked it out and reached for the snapshot Sarah had handed to him. The two pictures were almost identical. Perhaps his head was a little closer to Beverly's, and yes, she was smiling a little more on this one. He remembered as if it were no more than a few weeks ago, even days. They had asked a passing stranger to take their pictures, the last two on the roll, then gone, arms around each other, that very afternoon to get them developed.

The very night Charles had shown Beverly the snapshots, and told her to take the one she liked best, they had made love. For the last time, it turned out. The next night, when he told her yet again he was in love with her and wanted to marry her, she had laughed and told him not to be so serious. By the following morning she was gone. And now, after all these years, the snapshot she had taken was given back to him. Jenny had said the picture was hers and that Beverly was her mother. Did this mean there was the remotest possibility—

But where did Sarah fit into this? Her housekeeper or companion had been with her, that Biggerstaff woman. Charles tried his best not to think ill of anybody but something about the woman disturbed him. She had forced Sarah to walk down the aisle with that snapshot, he was sure of it. She would never have thought to do this on her own, especially in the middle of Mass. Why and how had the woman got hold of the picture in the first place? What was her motive and why was she living with the gentle, defenseless Sarah? Most of all, was today's incident some sort of vendetta against Jenny and if so, why?

He looked at his watch as he pushed the suitcase back under the bed with his foot. The Mass at Liverpool's Christ the King Cathedral was at seven o'clock followed by a month's retreat at a village in Cheshire. As much as he longed to see Jenny, ask her questions, a phone call would have to do. He changed from his vestments into his street clothes and went downstairs to lunch. He picked up the envelope in the center of his plate and slit it open. The letter was long, five pages of neat script. Quickly he turned to the signature. It was from Jenny.

He read slowly, letting every incredible word sink in. When he came to the part about Beverly putting a note in the personal column of a newspaper trying to find him, he went to the sideboard and poured himself a scotch, agonizing all over again at his mother's treachery. Beverly, all alone, had stayed on in England to have not one baby, but two, concocting some wild story about a boy back home being the father. Jenny had written she and Sarah were born on a Good Friday. Charles walked to the window, thinking back. My God, the very day Beverly had given birth to twins, he had been in Rome.

With the letter still clutched in his hand, Charles went outside and headed for his rose garden. He stood on the red brick path inhaling the scents, watching a thrush splash about in the birdbath. In the shed, he picked up the pruning shears, and wandered among his flowers, snipping off the dead blooms, keeping his restless hands busy while he struggled to bring some sort of order to his jigsaw puzzle of a mind. At last, after all these years, he knew. Beverly was dead. No need to wonder any more what sort of life she was living, or if she ever thought of him as he thought of her. No need now to look for her among the tourists passing through the Lakes. No more speculating how he should act if she ever came into his life again. No need to wonder whether he would be able to smile a welcome as she offered her hand, then perhaps introduced him to her husband and children, before explaining this was the first leg of their European tour. Would Charles have given an easy-going laugh at her light-hearted remark about him being a priest, and how surprised she was to see him wearing a dog collar?

There was closure at last, another page to be turned. But the story wasn't over yet, just the ending to the chapter headed "Beverly." He sat on the bench at the bottom of his garden, leaned his head back, and closed his eyes, seeing Sarah, all nervous and afraid, walking down the aisle toward him, then Jenny dashing out to stand beside her. Jenny had written that the Biggerstaff woman had stolen her snapshot and was blackmailing her. This was the sole reason for the letter. Otherwise, Jenny would probably never have told him. She had finally written the letter because he was a priest and she wanted him to beware, to save him, if she could, from any ugly surprises. That first time he'd seen her at Mass, little had he known then what she was going through, snapshot in her hand, waiting for him to stand in front of the congregation. How she must have struggled for composure when she had recognized him and realized her father was a priest. Still, she had stayed for refreshments after Mass, even seemed to enjoy the companionship and easy chatter of the others.

All of this had to be a sort of closure for Jenny too. It wasn't until yesterday she herself had found out Sarah was her twin sister. It was obvious from the way Jenny wrote, as well as strangely puzzling to Charles, that the news had come as a bombshell. But she was still grieving for her parents. Perhaps time was all that was needed. She had written about the strange will. With the second anniversary of the Fitzgeralds' death only weeks away, and no contenders in sight, at least not until Jenny turned up, the Biggerstaff woman, along with the vulnerable Sarah, stood to inherit a windfall.

Mrs. Thwaites was at the back door as he approached the house. "What is it, Father?" she said, her voice all concern. "You're white as a sheet. Have you had bad news?"

"Some of it was," he said, as he slowly folded the letter, "not all of it though."

She gave him a worried, curious look when he apologized for not being hungry and that he couldn't eat her casserole. He suggested that perhaps Father Doyle, the substitute priest, would be hungry when he arrived around five. After Charles assured her he was fine, she loaded her tray and ten minutes later was on her way to catch the next bus to her sister's.

He poured himself another scotch, unable to remember the last time he'd had two drinks in the middle of the day. He leaned against the mantelpiece while he pondered how he would break this incredible news to his new bishop. Vincent Fitzpatrick had been assigned to the diocese just three months ago. He had replaced Richard Delaney, Charles's friend for more than twenty-five years, who had dropped dead of a heart attack a few seconds after throwing a coin into Rome's Trevi Fountain. Richard had known all about Beverly, and Charles knew if his friend were still alive, he would have given a sympathetic ear. But Vincent Fitzpatrick, cast from a different mold, was a deep believer in the old ways of the church. He told Charles on their first meeting it was a sad day for him indeed when it was decided the Catholic Mass should no more be conducted in Latin.

Charles dialed the bishop's number and felt a stab of relief when a male voice told him Father Fitzpatrick was in Dublin but planned to be at the retreat by Tuesday. Charles replaced the phone in the cradle. He should probably tell his bishop first but with a matter of this kind, perhaps it was better to send a letter to the parish, which he knew he would be expected to do anyway. Both had to be told. While Charles was away at the month-long retreat, his parish could talk amongst themselves, have meetings, then decide if they wished to talk to their bishop.

Charles took his empty glass into the kitchen. Then he rang Mrs. Kendale, the church secretary. Something had come up, he said, and if she could come in and do a couple of hours work, he would be forever grateful. He'd have the letter typed by the time she arrived. It was to everyone on the church register. He had never learned how to set the computer to do the tricky things, like putting different addresses on each sheet, or to set the printer. It would be easy for her to pull up the list of names and addresses they had compiled the other week, then print out the labels. Yes, he had envelopes and stamps.

He then rang the Hare and Hounds and asked to be put through to Jenny. After a minute the voice came back to say Miss Robinson didn't answer and was there any message. No, no message, Charles said, thanked him, and hung up.

Mrs. Kendale completed the job in just over an hour. The woman was a treasure, who, although surely staggered by the news, didn't bat an eye. There was concern in her face, perhaps because it was obvious from Charles's jerky manner and shaky voice, he was close to coming unglued. Instead she chatted of other things. What in the world did they do before computers and did Father Woodleigh remember the time when a job like this would have taken all day.

"I'll be glad to drop these in the post box," she said. "It's on my way home."

"I'd be very grateful," he said, "and thank you for being so understanding."

"Not at all." She turned and headed out the door.

Mrs. Kendale had been gone about ten minutes when there was a knock at the door. As he strode down the hall, he caught a glimpse of red through the beveled patterned glass. Jenny's beret. Charles's suddenly wooden fingers fumbled with the lock until at last he yanked the door open wide.

"I saw your car in the drive," she said as she stepped inside. "May I come in for a minute?"

They stood in the hall staring at each other, weighing each other up, until Charles remembered to close the door.

"I rang the Hare and Hounds but you weren't there," he said. "You'll have to bear with me, Jenny. Your letter, well, it's hard to know where to begin. Still, I don't know how to put it except—"

Jenny bit her lip, then pounded her fist into the palm of her other hand. "I shouldn't have told you. I shouldn't."

Charles took hold of her arm. "No, Jenny, please. I haven't finished. I was going to say I don't know how to put it except I'm glad."

He snapped his fingers as the realization slammed into him. "Yes, that's it exactly. I've just realized you've made me a very happy man."

Her eyes grew wide and her hands went up to her mouth. "Happy? You mean you want us?" The tears spilled out of her eyes. "I didn't know. I honestly didn't know."

"Ah, there now," he mumbled, reaching for her hand. "Do you think we could start by being friends? Come on into the lounge. I'll make us some coffee."

After they struggled through an awkward beginning, neither knowing where to begin, Charles told her how he had waited weeks for Beverly to come back, but when he heard he'd been accepted at the seminary, he returned to London. Oh, he didn't blame her for leaving. What had started out as a light romance grew too serious for her, especially when he had pushed her for a commitment. They were so young, so foolish. Still, he would blame himself forever for not waiting just a few weeks longer.

"It wasn't your fault," Jenny said. "I realize that you didn't know. I'm glad now I told you, that you know at last. You won't believe how I worried, afraid what it would do to you, what with you being a priest and all."

"I can well understand how you felt. This isn't supposed to happen to priests is it? But I'm not the first and won't be the last. And I can't help the way I feel. I mean it isn't every day a man in his fifties finds out he's the father of grown-up twins." Charles suddenly longed for a cigarette but had given them up two years ago. "I could tell from your letter that finding out Sarah is your twin came as a shock. That's understandable I suppose. Still, she's very sick, Jenny, and in many ways desperately alone. She needs family, someone to care. Now that you've told me, it won't all be on your shoulders. Even if you go home to America, it isn't as far as it used to be. We can visit each other."

Jenny couldn't believe how easily he had accepted it all, how he was suddenly standing on the edge of God knows what, yet was determined to do the right thing. The swelling inside her filled her chest. She wanted to fling her arms round his neck and tell him how proud she was of him, to let him know she herself would try harder to be kinder, more compassionate. It wasn't that she didn't like Sarah. She was very fond of her. Of course she was. It was just the sister thing, the twin thing. It would have been a shock to anyone. Now, because the priest was looking into his own tunnel of uncertainty, she, Jenny, would try harder to overcome her fear of Sarah's sickness looming dead ahead.

Within an hour, they had it all worked out. Charles would go to the retreat, at least for a few days. With him out of the way, the parishioners would have time to digest his letter, while it gave him the opportunity to tell his bishop. Sarah would be told the story in two stages, because hadn't Dr. Thorne already warned that keeping her blood pressure on an even keel was vital. Jenny would tell her tomorrow that they were sisters, then perhaps a few days later, Sarah would be told the news that her father was the priest in the next village.

Jenny assured him that when she left the rectory, she would head straight for Dr. Thorne's house and ask him to go with her to Glen Ellen to get Sarah. "Dr. Thorne has known Sarah all her life," Jenny said. "He was the doctor who delivered us. He has this way about him, this air of authority. I think he knows how to handle Biddy. And there's no way I'll let Sarah spend another night in that house."

"Be sure Dr. Thorne goes with you," he said. "It wouldn't be wise to go alone."

Jenny nodded. "Dr. Thorne and the Social Services have told Biddy she must leave the house. She's getting more unstable and might have to be hospitalized."

Charles wrote on the pad by the phone. "This is the number of the retreat," he said, tearing off the sheet. "Let me know how it goes. My bishop won't be at the retreat until Tuesday, so I hope you can bear with me."

Jenny glanced at the number and stuck it in her handbag. "There is one thing. So far, nobody else knows about us. Not even Dr. Thorne or Andy. I haven't told a living soul."

"It's all right," he said, almost shyly patting her shoulder. "We'll tell them in good time."

Eventually, while Jenny made for Stoney Beck, Charles headed for the M-6 and Liverpool.

Chapter Nineteen

Biddy drove up to Glen Ellen's kitchen door, and then eased the car onto the grass and round to the back of the house, away from the prying eyes of Fred and Edna. Sarah had fallen asleep for the last couple of miles and as Biddy shook her awake, she noticed a trickle of dried blood coming from the swollen lip. Once inside, Biddy stuck a frozen macaroni and cheese in the microwave for herself and plonked an apple on Sarah's plate.

Sarah pulled out a chair and sat at the table, shoulders hunched, her bluster gone now. She was back in the house, alone with Biddy who had that look on her face Sarah had seen before, the one that filled her with dread. For twenty minutes, while they sat at the table, Biddy demanded total silence.

"Did I do all right, Biddy?" Sarah finally said, her hand reaching across the table for Biddy's arm. "I tried to get it right, honestly I did."

Biddy knocked her hand away. "Maybe you did and maybe you didn't. But you made a big mistake accusing me of stealing that snapshot. On top of that, you said you hated me. That was a bad thing to say, Sarah. A very bad thing."

"I didn't mean it. Walking down that aisle was so scary. Then when Father Woodleigh looked at me like that, I felt like a—"

With a deliberate sneer dallying around her mouth, Biddy folded her arms and peered at Sarah. "You felt like a what?"

"I don't know. Like a—"

"You felt like a great big fat mongoloid didn't you?"

"No, I didn't mean that."

"Yes you did. Come on, Sarah. Say it. Say 'I felt like a great big fat mongoloid.'"

Sarah leaned forward, her forehead touching the table, the cramps in her calves tightening. "I felt like a great big fat mongoloid," she muttered.

Biddy stuck a cigarette in her mouth and lit it. "I can't hear you. Get your head off the table and sit up straight. Now shout it as loud as you can. Do it three times."

Sarah leaned back in her chair, her gaze fixed on the ceiling. "I felt like a great big fat mongoloid," she shouted in her wheezy voice. "I felt like a great big fat—" She took off her glasses and wiped her eyes as a

great shuddering sob rattled her body. "I can't say it again. I just can't."
She folded her arms on the tabletop and rested her head.

Biddy silently puffed on her cigarette.

"What are you thinking about?" Sarah finally asked without lifting
her head.

"Your punishment. Which one to give you."

Sarah rose and reached a hand toward her. "Please, Biddy, don't.
I'm sorry I said those wicked things. Didn't I do my best? I gave Father
Woodleigh the snapshot like you said."

"That's not the point."

"What then?"

"You, Sarah. You're the point. I can't stand the sight of you and you
have to be punished."

"But I tried so hard."

"Just shut up, take everything off but your knickers, and get on the
stool."

"Biddy, please. It's cold in here and I'm not well. You know I'm
not."

Biddy stuck her cigarette end into the leftover macaroni and cheese
still on her plate.

"Oh, all right. You don't have to stand on the stool. I don't want you
falling off and getting bruises that'll show. You still have to stand in the
corner in just your knickers. You're uppity and insolent, Sarah, and you
need to know once and for all who's the boss in this house. It isn't cold in
here. That's just your imagination. And if you don't get a move on, I'll
make you put on the blindfold and stand there stark naked."

A few minutes later, Sarah was in the corner facing the kitchen wall
while Biddy sat at the table behind her, drink in her hand, leaning her
back against her chair. After the first ten minutes, Sarah leaned against
the wall trying to ease the pains in her legs.

Biddy watched through a haze as she felt herself nodding off. "Keep
your eye on the clock," she said "When the cuckoo shoots out at four you
can get dressed, but not a minute sooner. If you try to trick me and I
wake up, there's other games. You don't want to spend the rest of the day
in a cold water bath would you?"

Sarah shook her head.

Biddy let out a shout and swung round as the back door suddenly
crashed open and slammed against the wall. Andy Ferguson stalked into
the room followed by Angus Thorne. For a split second they stood by the
table, eyes flicking from Sarah standing in the corner half-naked, then to

Biddy leaning back in her chair, feet on the table, cigarette dangling from one hand and a half-empty bottle of gin in the other.

Andy took a couple of steps toward her. "Why, you crazy, spiteful bitch—"

His uncle grabbed his arm. "Hold it, Andy. Just get Sarah."

Sarah had turned around, her head bowed, arms covering her breasts. Andy was already taking off his jacket as he strode across the room toward her. "Come on, love," he said, as he draped it around her shoulders. "Let's get your clothes on."

"You leave her where she is," Biddy said. "She's got to stand there until four o'clock. You can't come barging in here right when she's being punished."

"Take Andy up to your room, Sarah," Dr. Thorne said, his voice dangerously quiet, as he picked up her clothes off the back of a chair and handed them to her. "He'll help you pack a suitcase."

Biddy grabbed hold of the table and pulled herself to her feet. "That door was locked and you almost yanked it off its hinges. I'll report you for breaking and entering as well as kidnapping. Sarah's under my care. You can't take her away just like that."

"Just you watch us," Dr. Thorne said, as he picked up the phone and held it out to her. "Here, go ahead and report us. In the name of God, what were you thinking? And what about her swollen lip? Did you do that?"

Biddy stared at the phone but made no attempt to take it. "So self-righteous, aren't we? It's enough to piss off a saint. I'll bet if you had her, you'd have done a bloody sight more than make her stand in the corner."

Dr. Thorne took a step backward. Biddy had always been something of an oddity, which he and everybody in the village had looked upon as more of an eccentricity than anything else. But this woman standing before him had a wildness about her, her dead white face twisted with hate. "Go on, stand there and gawk," she said. "But I'll tell you once and for all. Glen Ellen's mine, not Sarah's. I deserve it and I'll never give it up. Never."

"You know the terms of the will," Angus said, in the same calm voice. "You'll be taken care of. There's nothing to worry about."

"I don't care what the lousy will says. And you can forget about your precious Jenny. When Sarah gave the snapshot to the priest, that girl shot out of her pew and went up to the front to try to get it back. But the priest hung on to it. You should have seen his face, white as a dead man's."

Angus's forehead creased in a puzzled frown. "What in the name of God are you talking about?"

"The snapshot. The priest's got it now."

"You mean the priest at St. Mary's, don't you? But what snapshot?"

Biddy slapped the flat of her hand on the table and snorted. "That's right. You didn't know. Well, let me tell you, your precious Jenny flew out of there as if her arse was on fire, and I'll bet a fan dancer's fart we've seen the last of her."

"We're taking Sarah back to the village with us," Angus said. "There's nothing more to be said."

He turned away from her, and walked out the door. In the hall, he paced up and down at the foot of the stairs. Every now and then he peeked in the kitchen to see Biddy, arms folded, glazed eyes staring at the Welsh dresser.

Andy had mentioned the priest, a Father Woodleigh, before, and Biddy had babbled something about Sarah giving him a snapshot. He'd ask Sarah. She'd know. At last he heard her and Andy walking along the landing above.

"Have you got your medicine?" he asked as Sarah came down the stairs holding onto Andy with one hand and clutching her Paddington bear close to her chest with the other.

She nodded, then let Andy, carrying her suitcase, lead her out the front door.

Angus stuck his head in the kitchen doorway. "Somebody will be in touch with you in a day or two. Until then, you can stay here."

"What do you mean, *until then?*" Biddy ground out. "I'm not leaving here, not ever."

He looked around the room, and then back to Biddy, who hadn't looked at him but kept her gaze on the dresser. He was reluctant to leave her here alone, but in the end he walked back into the hall and out the front door. He'd get in touch with the Social Services. They'd know how to handle it.

As soon as Biddy heard the car doors slam, she was at the kitchen door watching the three of them drive away. She pressed her face against the glass. Thorne really was insane if he thought he could get away with kidnapping Sarah. Wasn't she, Biddy, not just the housekeeper, but also the legal guardian? She examined the door to assess the damage done by Andy Ferguson's heavy shoes. Even though he had kicked it open, it hadn't suffered much, and after she'd fiddled with the lock, she managed to get it closed. Next week she would have it repaired and tell the locksmith to send the bill to Ferguson's Garage. She took out her teeth and put them in the glass, then rubbed her sore gums. The nerve of Angus Thorne telling her she'd have to get out of Glen Ellen. Over her dead body.

***

When Jenny arrived back in Stoney Beck she pulled into Andy's and waited while he studied a map with a couple who looked like tourists, then pointed down Market Street toward the fells beyond.

As he walked toward her, and before she could say anything, he told her he and his uncle had gone to Glen Ellen a couple of hours ago and come back with Sarah. He inclined his head toward the house across the road. "She's asleep right now. Uncle Angus called Jonathon in and they decided that for the time being she's better off staying with Uncle Angus. They've explained all this to her, and told her she won't have to live with Biddy ever again. Uncle Angus is a doctor, even if he is retired, and Jonathon will drop in every day. Your cottage is nice but maybe not so good for Sarah, at least until she's been to Manchester Royal. They've got a big kidney unit there, one of the best in Europe."

Jenny let out a big sigh. "I guess you're right. I'll go see her tomorrow. Your uncle and I can talk. Tell him I came will you?"

Andy nodded. "See you tonight," he said.

Back in the cottage, she called the number of the retreat, and left a carefully worded message for the priest. Sarah was staying with Dr. Thorne. Jenny hadn't broken the news to her yet but would do so tomorrow.

Chapter Twenty

At eight o'clock Jenny walked into the crowded tearoom. The sign at the entrance read *Whether or not you went to college, come in here and test your knowledge. Pub Quiz begins promptly at 8:30 - First prize thirty pounds.*

Tables were pulled together to accommodate the larger groups. Ada and Walter were at one of them, both standing up and waving Jenny over. The archeologists' table was close by and Jenny stopped to say she'd heard they won most times but could forget about it tonight. They teased her back and said they always won. Her table didn't stand a chance.

While Walter flirted with Ada, telling her she got prettier all the time and she giggling like a sixteen-year-old, Jenny examined the beer mat in front of her. A picture of Wordsworth on one side and the first half of his sonnet, "Upon Westminster Bridge" on the other. She picked up another beer mat. Coleridge's picture on this one and a few lines from "The Rime of the Ancient Mariner" on the flip side.

A light tap on her shoulder and Andy was by her side. "I've got Sarah with me," he said. "She's in the loo and won't come out. She wants to talk to you."

Andy focused on the tiny gold flecks in Jenny's grey eyes. "Uncle Angus and Jon checked all her vitals and decided if she rested all afternoon, she'd be OK to come out tonight. Jon said a night out with friends, having some fun for a change, would be good for her. She goes to Manchester Royal in a few days. Jon said they'll probably put her on dialysis."

Jenny pushed open the rest room door and went inside. Sarah stood by the mirror, her face pale, anxious, arms clutching a huge canvas bag. "I didn't know Biddy stole the picture from you. Honor bright I didn't. Please don't be angry."

Jenny put her arms round Sarah and found herself locked in a bear hug. "It's OK, Sarah. I know it wasn't your fault." Her words came out muffled, buried as she was in Sarah's neck. "We'll be friends forever if you promise me one thing."

Sarah slowly let go. "Anything. I'll do anything."

"Just don't say a word about any of this at the table. Please Sarah, let's keep it our secret, at least for tonight. OK?"

"You can trust me, Jenny. I won't breathe a word."

"Spit on your hand, cross your heart, then say hope to die."

She waited while Sarah carried out the sacred ritual, and then reached for her hand. "OK, let's go. We don't want to hold them up."

"Am I still your pumpkin?"

Jenny gave her that little push on the shoulder Sarah liked. "What do you think?"

Andy stood up, beaming at them as they walked to the table holding hands. He pulled out a chair for Sarah who insisted on sitting between him and Jenny.

Ada reached across the table and took Sarah's hand in her own. "It's good to see you, Sarah. Andy said you're staying with Dr. Thorne for a few days."

Sarah looked anxious as she held on to Ada's hand. "I'm trying hard to get well. Please, Ada, don't give my job away."

"I wouldn't dream of it."

Walter handed out pencils and sheets of paper filled with questions. "Press hard when you write your answers," he said. "Otherwise it won't go through to the yellow sheet. That's our copy."

"What do we do?" Sarah asked.

"It's easy," Andy said. "Jim, that guy behind the bar, the one with the pony tail, sits at the table in the corner and calls out the questions. We write the answers on these sheets. Our table's a team so when you know an answer don't blurt it out loud so the other tables can hear."

"Got yer," Sarah said with a little giggle.

At eight thirty, Jim rapped on the table with a small gavel.

"OK, everybody. Pick up your pencils and let's get started. Question number one. What was the name of the only horse ever to win the Grand National three times?"

Jenny looked round the tearoom as almost everybody laughed and wrote something down. Walter leaned across the table.

"That one's dead easy for an Englishman," he whispered to her. "Red Rum. Smashing horse he was."

"Question number two," Jim shouted. "What was the very last spoken sentence in *Gone with the Wind*?"

Andy and Jenny both opted for *Frankly my dear, I don't give a damn.*

"No, that isn't it," Ada whispered excitedly, her hand over her mouth. "After Rhett said that and walked away, Scarlet closed the door, then went and sat on the stairs. She was crying. *I'll go home to Tara*, she said. *I'll think of some way to get him back*, or something like that. But the last sentence was definitely *After all, tomorrow is another day.* If you'd seen that picture as often as I have, you'd know. I've even got it on video. It's my favorite film."

"I've never seen it," Walter said. "If it's that good, maybe I could come over to your place one night and we could watch it together."

Ada smiled coyly and patted her new hairdo. "We'll see."

Sarah dug her elbows into Jenny and Andy, smiled, then rolled her eyes.

Jenny knew a couple of the answers nobody else at the table knew. One was the name of the tallest building in the world before nineteen hundred.

"It's the Eiffel Tower," she whispered. "I don't remember where I read it but it's true."

She got the next one too. "What is the slogan for America's Kentucky Fried Chicken?"

All four at the table turned to her. "Finger lickin' good," she whispered loudly. Sarah put a finger to her lips to warn Jenny she was talking too loud. Then she looked around to make sure nobody had heard.

Andy and Walter both remembered Roger Bannister was the first to break the record for the four-minute mile way back in 1954, and it was also Andy who knew it was Alexander Graham Bell who called out *Mr. Watson, come here. I want you.* He knew too it was the god Artemis for whom the Greeks had built a temple in Ephesus in Turkey, and judging from the buzz at the archeologists' table, so did they.

"Well, they would wouldn't they," Ada said. "It's their business to know. That's what they get paid for, poking around looking for old buried temples and stuff nobody else cares tuppence about."

"And now for the last one," Jim said thirty minutes later. "In Rudyard Kipling's poem, 'The Road to Mandalay,' what was the name of the road?"

A little murmur went around the room. Jenny sneaked a glance at the archeologists. They leaned toward the middle of the table whispering, heads shaking. Even they didn't seem to know the answer to this one.

Walter tapped the pencil against his teeth and rolled his eyes. "Is that a trick question?"

Andy laughed. "Come on, Walter. Don't they give you the answers ahead of time?"

"Are you kidding? It's just that I know the poem all the way through but the name of the road isn't mentioned."

Most of the time, Sarah had copied her answers from Andy or Jenny, but now, while the others stared blankly at each other, she had her head down, her tongue curling out the side of her mouth as she pressed hard on her stub of a pencil.

Andy leaned over and looked at her sheet. "What are you writing?"

She pushed her glasses up on her nose and looked guardedly at the tables close by. "I know it, I know it," she whispered, squirming in her seat, her face flushed, fists gently pounding the table. "I know the answer, but I can't spell it."

He gave her a playful push. "Come on then, little miss know-it-all, how about letting us in on it."

She pulled his head down, and with her hand over her mouth, whispered in his ear, then turned and gave the others a shy knowing smile.

Jenny had her elbows on the table, chin resting in her hands. "Well?"

"She said it's the Irrawaddi, the Irrawaddi River."

"Ah."

"How did you know that?" Ada asked, her tone skeptical.

Sarah sneaked another furtive look around the room, then crooked her finger, beckoning the others to come in closer. She put her arms across Andy's and Jenny's shoulders. "Daddy told me. We used to sing it marching up and down the path."

She began the poem, in a tuneless hoarse style, hardly above a whisper. "*On the road to Mandalay, where the flyin' fishes play, And the dawn comes up like thunder outa China 'cross the Bay*. I laughed and laughed at Daddy and said he had it all wrong. How could fishes fly and play on a road. They couldn't fly. They swam so how could they swim on a road. Daddy laughed and said it wasn't a road. They just called it that. It was this river, the Irrawaddi."

Andy patted her cheek and turned to the others with a shrug. "Well, the Irrawaddi is in Burma, or Myanmar, whatever they call it now."

"Well, I'll be jiggered," Ada said. "That was the hardest question in the whole bunch. Well done, Sarah."

When Andy collected the sheets and took them to Jim, Sarah scooted over and sat next to Jenny and stuck her arm through hers. Jim called out the answers, and when he said Irrawaddi River for the last one, Sarah giggled.

"Told you."

Nobody in the room had all thirty questions correct, or twenty-nine, or twenty-eight. When Jim called out the number twenty-seven, everybody at Jenny's table raised a hand, everybody except Sarah who got to her feet and raised both arms over her head.

"We've got twenty-seven," she shouted. "Twenty-seven at this table."

The archeologists were next with twenty-six. Jenny's table had won by only one point.

"You won it for us, Sarah," Walter said. "Without you knowing about those flying fishes, we'd have tied with the archeologists. You're a very clever girl."

"Will someone from the winning table come up for the prize," Jim said into the microphone. "Sarah, how about you? Andy Ferguson just whispered to me it was you who knew the answer to that last very tricky question."

Sarah's usually sallow face turned bright pink and a self-conscious smile spread across her face as she got to her feet then threaded her way between the tables to Jim who handed her thirty pounds and a certificate.

"Come on, everybody," he said. "Let's give Sarah a big hand."

From out of nowhere the feeling came as Jenny watched Sarah raise the certificate above her head for all to see. When everybody got to their feet and clapped and cheered, even whistled, Sarah gave a funny awkward curtsey. A standing ovation. Unsophisticated astonishment and happiness shone from her face with all the loveliness of a sunflower.

The sudden unexpected rush of love washed over Jenny, saturating her, flowing through her like rain. The smile froze on her face and her ears started to ring. She felt dizzy, out of place, as she raised a hand and pressed it against her chest as something almost akin to pain settled deep inside her. This brave, wonderful, beautiful Sarah was her twin sister. Who in the name of heaven would have thought it?

As Sarah walked back to the table, her face still flushed with delighted amazement, Jenny took a couple of steps toward her. Big tears slipped down Jenny's cheeks as she stretched out her arms. "I'm so proud of you, Sarah," she said, her voice trembling. "I honestly didn't know until just now how much I really cared."

Sarah was the first to back away, her smile glued on, eyes wide with innocent surprise.

Jenny gave a little embarrassed laugh as she turned to look at Ada and Walter, both of them wide-eyed and staring, mouths hanging open. Andy was suddenly beside her, a hand on her shoulder. She turned to him as he handed her a tissue. She wiped her eyes but still held on to Sarah's hand.

"I feel like such a fool," she said. "Guess I just got so excited for Sarah."

Ada's eyebrows were raised almost to her hairline as she looked from Jenny, Sarah, and Andy, then to Walter and back again to the other three who stood close together by the table.

"Is something going on here Walter and I don't know about?"

Jenny held on to the back of the chair while she waited for the dizziness and tightness in her chest to ease. She half opened her mouth to answer Ada's question, had a sudden urge to stand on her chair and tell everybody in the room. But when she looked at Sarah, with that puzzled look of happy surprise still on her face, Jenny knew she owed it to her sister to tell her first.

When Sarah placed the certificate and money in the middle of the table, Walter handed them back.

"You keep them, love," he said. "We couldn't have done it without you."

She beamed. "OK. I'll get my ears pierced so I can wear Lottie's earrings."

"Why don't you get the certificate framed," Ada said. "That way you'll always remember the fun we had tonight."

Jenny didn't like the beads of perspiration glistening on Sarah's forehead, but still couldn't trust herself to speak.

"I'd better take her home," Andy said as if he'd read Jenny's mind. "She's had enough excitement for one night."

"How'd your uncle Angus get her away from Biddy?" Ada asked. "I'll bet that wasn't easy."

"It was for him," Andy said as he took hold of Sarah's hand and pulled her arm through his. "He told Biddy he wanted to do an around-the-clock check on her for a few days. You know how he is when he makes up his mind. Jon's her doctor now of course, and Uncle Angus did call him in to get his consent."

He stretched his other hand out to Jenny. "Will you walk with us to the car?"

Jenny picked up her purse, tears at last under control. "I had a real nice time," she was able to say to Ada and Walter, even managed a smile and sly wink for Walter to let him know he now had Ada all to himself.

Sarah walked between the two of them, linking arms, while Andy hung on to the precious certificate and envelope with the money.

At the car, Jenny kissed Sarah on the cheek. "We had a lot of fun tonight, didn't we."

Sarah nodded sleepily and put her arms round Jenny's neck. "I wish you were my sister instead of my best friend," she said, then climbed into the car.

Andy smiled at Jenny. "Boy, is she in for a nice surprise."

"I'm glad, Andy. So glad," Jenny said in a hoarse, almost choking voice.

He put his hands on her shoulders and held her at arm's length, then pulled her to him and kissed her gently on the mouth as the first big drops of rain began to fall.

"Run inside before you get soaked," he said. "We'll see you tomorrow."

***

Jenny washed off her makeup and put on her nightgown and robe. The rain had stopped, just a summer shower that happened almost every other day or night in the Lake District. She sat in the rocker with her feet propped up on the ottoman while she relived the evening all over again, closed her eyes as she watched the transformed Sarah walk to the front to collect the prize. Jenny had sneaked a look at Andy, mainly because he was whistling and applauding louder than anybody. He had been as proud as she was. Still, even though tonight had been a three-hour break from the real world, and Jenny had realized at last how much she loved her sister, Sarah was still desperately sick and might not live if she didn't get a kidney.

Jenny thought about Debbie who lived three doors down on her street in Charlotte. Fifteen years ago, she had been near death, when her brother had donated one of his kidneys. Since then the brother had become a lawyer and Debbie had given birth to two healthy children, traveled through Europe and every Saturday played a pretty good game of golf. She lived a normal life and without the gift of her brother's kidney she would either be dead or fastened to a machine three or four days a week.

It would be harder for Sarah of course because she had other health problems besides kidney failure. She wasn't sturdy, not physically, but so courageous. If anybody deserved a break, she did. Jenny closed her eyes and leaned her head against the back of the rocker.

"I'll make her well, Mom," she said to the empty room. "Everything will be all right. You'll see."

Chapter Twenty-one

Next morning, when Jenny stopped at the desk, Uncle Tim's envelope had just arrived by overnight express. She checked the contents, glanced quickly through the attached note, then stuffed the envelope in her pocket book and headed for the door. Walter, out front, dead heading his geraniums, straightened up and began kneading the small of his back as she walked toward him.

"I've been thinking about last night," he said. "I can't remember when I had such a good time, thanks to you."

"Thanks to me? I didn't do anything."

"You invited Ada didn't you? I'd never have had the nerve. After you three left, we got to talking, and guess what? All this time she's had her eye on me. She's even invited me to her house to watch *Gone With the Wind*."

Jenny grinned. "Congratulations. I hope everything works out for you both."

"Thank you, Jenny, and thanks again for your help."

"I told you I didn't do anything."

Walter dropped the wilted flower in the box at his feet. "You've done a lot more than you realize. There's a new sparkle in Andy Ferguson's eyes. And what about Sarah? I hate to see her so sick, but it didn't seem to bother her last night. I haven't seen her have such a good time in ages. She'll miss you when you go. We all will."

Jenny cleared her throat. "Sarah loves working in the shop and can't wait to get back."

"By the look of her, it's going to take a miracle. A miracle or a brand new kidney." He picked up the box. "Still, maybe if she gets on dialysis, it won't be so bad. Will you be seeing her today?"

"I'm on my way there now. She called me at six thirty. Wants to get her ears pierced."

"There, see what I mean? Don't forget to tell her about Ada and me. Tell Andy too if you see him."

Jenny sauntered along Market Street, and threw up her hand to Harry, the postman, who returned the wave as he pedaled toward the inn.

The doctor was sitting on a box painting the bench against the wall of his house. "Sarah's upstairs," he said as he struggled to his feet. "Said she was getting in the shower, and then wanted to sort out her clothes. You go on in while I stick this brush in a jar of water. Won't be a tick."

Jenny went into the lounge and a few minutes later the doctor pushed the squeaky tea trolley into the room. He positioned it in front of her and eased himself into the chair opposite. Jenny studied the royal blue and pink knitted tea cozy pulled over the teapot like a woolly hat. There were holes for the spout and handle, and on the top was a cluster of crocheted petals in the form of a flower. There were two cups and saucers, sugar and milk, a plate of chocolate biscuits and the ever-present raspberry creams. Did the English ever stop making tea? Did anybody go inside a house anywhere in all of the country and not be offered a cup of tea as soon as they stepped over the doorstep? Even the window cleaner at Malone's was given a mugful before he wet his chamois.

Jenny pulled the envelope out of her bag and placed it on the slab of slate. "This came by Overnight Express. Here are my birth certificate, Mom's marriage license, her death certificate. Uncle Tim threw in other things like photos of us through the years. There's a letter from him stating I'm Beverly Pender Robinson's daughter. Our minister witnessed it, as well as a lawyer who lives next door. Uncle Tim had it notarized, just to make sure."

"We won't worry about that now," Dr. Thorne said as he poured the tea. "I'll get them over to the solicitors this afternoon. While you're here, I want you to tell Sarah that you're twins."

"You mean right now? Today?"

"Let's have a cuppa first."

He pushed a cup of tea in front of her and placed the biscuits in the middle of the trolley. Funny how she was already calling the cookies biscuits.

"Tell me about your home," he said. "You know, what life is like in Charlotte. Anything that comes to mind."

Jenny reached for the milk pitcher, and while she sipped her tea, told the doctor how Charlotte had trebled in size over the last fifty years. It had turned from a sleepy Southern town into one of the largest banking centers in the United States, how it was impossible to go more than a couple of miles without seeing some sort of construction, how whole subdivisions sprang up almost overnight.

"It's not all brand new of course," Jenny said. "Some of the houses in our section of town are sixty or more years old. I've just sold our house and I know I'm going to miss it. There are willow oaks that form a canopy of shade over the whole road. I wish you could see Charlotte in April, Dr. Thorne. That's when the azaleas and dogwoods bloom. There's no place in the world any prettier."

"It sounds a lovely place," Dr. Thorne said.

Jenny noticed the doctor's wry smile as he picked up his cup. Had he thought she was bragging? "Ah, I only told about the good parts. Charlotte's got the crack houses and the homeless like big cities everywhere. Not only that, we've torn down so many old and lovely buildings, just to make way for new stuff. We've got developers everywhere and it's God help anyone who stands in the way of a bulldozer."

She looked out the window and from where she sat could just see the roof of Stoney Beck's village hall, at least a couple of hundred years old.

"Nothing like living here, ay," Dr. Thorne said. "If someone who's been in the village churchyard for the last couple of hundred years rose out of his grave and walked down Market Street, he'd recognize almost everything. He could probably find his same old stool he sat on in the Hare and Hounds. Nothing much changes here."

"I think Stoney Beck is a little bit of heaven. If I could change just one thing here, I honestly don't know what it would be. Apart from the scenery, there's this sense of time standing still that we don't get at home. I feel as if I've been ferried back to the middle ages. Yet the neat thing is the people are so up to date."

Like a schoolboy, Dr. Thorne pushed a couple of chocolate biscuits aside and went for a raspberry cream. "Andy told me your father was ill for a long time before he died. I don't mean to pry, Jenny, but need to know because of Sarah. What did he die of?"

Jenny put her hands around her knees to stop the sudden shaking, while at the same time looking around the room for something to latch on to. The same tiger stared back at her from his wallpaper jungle. This time his face was a mask as if he had more important things on his mind. She looked along the wallpaper and watched the back of him slink into the undergrowth.

"My dad had Huntington's disease," she said. "His mother and all three siblings died of it." She patted the top of the envelope. "His death certificate's in here too."

The very air in the room felt charged as she reached for the top button of her blouse to undo it, give herself space to breathe, only to discover she had on her green cotton turtleneck.

"That must have been very hard," Dr. Thorne said at last, a deep frown creasing his forehead. "Have you been tested?"

When she didn't answer, he repeated the question. "You do know there's a foolproof way to determine if you're carrying the gene don't you? Sarah will need to be tested too."

Jenny took a deep breath and let it out in a long slow sigh. "I don't need to be tested and neither will Sarah. You see, Dad, well he wasn't my, I mean he wasn't our *real* father, not our biological one. I didn't know until the very night my mother died. That's when she told me."

The doctor set his cup back on the saucer with a clatter.

"Did she tell you who your real father was?"

Jenny nodded without looking at him, her gaze on the trolley. Her tea was getting cold, biscuit untouched. Dr. Thorne leaned forward. "I'm not trying to meddle, and if this didn't involve Sarah, I wouldn't dream of asking. But if Michael Robinson wasn't your father, who was?"

"Can we talk about this later? I just don't feel like getting into it now."

The look on Dr. Thorne's face let Jenny know he was aware of her discomfort, but in his obvious need to get at the truth he shoved the blade in further. "Sarah told Andy and me what happened at St. Mary's. She said you told Father Woodleigh the girl in the picture with him was your mother."

He held out his hands, palms upwards. "What's his role in this, Jenny? Sarah said the picture was taken in front of the Hare but I'm dashed if I can remember him. I may be out of line here but have to know. Is it he? Is Father Woodleigh your father?"

"Yes." Jenny leaned back in her chair and let her gaze wander around the room as she related the full story, starting with the night her mother told her Michael Robinson was not her father and ending with the letter she'd given to the priest yesterday.

"I had no idea what he'd do when I told him. But the news made him happy. Can you believe it? I was just blown away by the look on his face. We still don't know how his bishop or his parish will take this. They probably know by now. Someone's bound to say that their priest's the father of twin bastards? He could lose everything."

"Everything but you and Sarah." Dr. Thorne brushed a few biscuit crumbs from his lap then got up and stood in front of her. "I'm sorry you had to tell me this. I know it was hard, but what with Biddy going off the rails, I needed to know."

"Yes and even though I dreaded telling you, I'm glad now. You had to know sometime and you weren't shocked like I thought you'd be."

"Who am I to judge? Who is anyone?" He went to the sideboard and picked up a file folder. "If you'll just read through these papers, then sign them, I can get them over to the solicitors."

***

Jenny sat beside Sarah on the white wicker bench in the back garden, and as simply and gently as she could, told her about Beverly, the young American who stayed in the Lake District to have her baby.

"It wasn't just one baby," Jenny said. "Beverly had twins. Twin girls. And she could only take one back to her home in America."

Sarah leaned forward, lips slightly apart. "Ah, two teeny babies. Why could she only take one?"

"She didn't have a lot of money, and you know how much babies cost."

"Ah, poor Beverly, and poor baby left behind."

"Yes, but the baby didn't mind. You see two very special people adopted her and she was very happy."

Sarah straightened her skirt with her hands. "That's exactly what happened to me. Mummy and Daddy picked me out of zillions of babies."

"This baby's name was Sarah too and she grew up right here in Stoney Beck."

"She did? Whereabouts?"

"In Glen Ellen."

Sarah's brow puckered as she slowly shook her head. "I think I'm the only Sarah who's ever lived at Glen Ellen, but it couldn't—"

"Yes it could," Jenny whispered, clutching Sarah's wrist. "That baby girl was you. Beverly was your mother as well as mine. Those babies were you and me. We're sisters, Sarah. You and I are twins."

Sarah giggled and gave Jenny a little push. "Somebody's pulling your leg. Twins look the same, not different like us. Look at your hair, thick as anything." She held out her hand and stroked Jenny's face. "And just feel your skin. It's soft and creamy while mine's all splotchy. You're so nice and tall and thin and everything."

"No, no, listen to me," Jenny said, her hands on Sarah's shoulders. "We really are twins. I was the twin Beverly took back, and you were adopted by the two people who wanted you more than anything in the world."

Sarah lowered her head and for at least a minute she fiddled with a loose piece of wicker, trying to stick it back in place. Finally she looked up at Jenny, her eyes full of hurt. "Beverly didn't want me did she?" Her voice was soft, sad. "Biddy was right. Nobody wants mongoloid babies if they can get a better one."

"That's not true. Mom loved us both the same, but she was desperate. With two tiny babies and no husband, she just didn't know what to do. She was only young, even younger than we are now. The two wonderful people who adopted you couldn't have children of their own so they begged Beverly to let them have you. Not me, Sarah. You. They especially wanted you." She reached for Sarah's hand, ran her fingers across the bitten, stubby nails. "People like me are a dime a dozen. But you, you're special. You're one in a thousand."

"One in a thousand?"

"That's right. A thousand to one. I've been reading up on this. God doesn't make very many of you because you're sort of special and there never are enough to go round. Whenever one turns up, there're a whole lot of people waiting to adopt the baby."

Sarah shook her head. "Someone's been telling you the biggest whoppers. There's gobs of people like me in a home near Carlisle. I saw it on the telly. The doctors told the mothers their babies would be better off in a home."

"I know all about that," Jenny said. "It was the same in America. Things are changing though. Those people who gave their babies away will never know what they missed."

Sarah gave a hint of a smile. "Daddy used to say things like that. He said people like me have got an extra chromosome. It's a teeny-weeny little tadpole thing." She screwed up her eyes as she held up her hand and stared at the tip of her index finger. "Even if it was on the tip of this finger, we couldn't see it."

"I wish I could have known your parents," Jenny said. "They sound so special."

Sarah fiddled with the buttons on her blouse cuffs. "They were the most specialist people God ever made. They sent me to school and I learned to read and play the piano. I love Elvis and Elton John and look how I knew the hardest answer last night. You couldn't have won without me."

"I know. I'll never forget last night. Let's take the certificate to Malone's and get it framed. There're brass and wood frames on that shelf at the back by the fishing rods."

Sarah ran her hand back and forth along the arm of the chair. "I can't go out of the house, Jenny. Biddy might grab me." She picked at the flaky skin on her face.

"Not as long as I'm with you she won't. You don't have to worry about her anymore."

Sarah poked Jenny in the chest. "You're not going to let anything happen to your little pumpkin, are you."

"No ma'am. And just to prove it, I'm going with you to the hospital. They can take some of my blood. Being twins, we're bound to be a match. You'll have to hold my hand though 'cause I'm nowhere near as brave as you."

Jenny bit her lip till it hurt. There, she'd said it. There was no going back now.

"You don't think you've caught what I've got do you?"

"No, it's not catching. It'll be just in case you need a kidney." She spread her arms wide and laughed, making light of it. "If you do, you can have one of mine."

"Have you got an extra one?"

"Just two, same as everybody else. I've got this friend back home who— Well, anyway, we can both get by on one."

Sarah put an arm round Jenny. "I'm glad you told me about Beverly and I'm glad she had you as well as me. Will you take me to see your house in America when you go?"

"Let's get you well first," Jenny said, "then we'll go."

When Sarah went to her bedroom to get her sweater, Jenny watched her go then turned to Dr. Thorne. "The pills aren't working are they? Her face is puffy and a funny color, almost yellow. And she's tired all the time."

Dr. Thorne said dialysis wasn't just a probability any more, more a question of when it would start. They'd know more after she had her tests at Manchester Royal.

"I acted badly the other day when you told me about us," Jenny said, "and I'm sorry. I guess it was the shock. But I'm over that now. Sarah's sick, Dr. Thorne, and if she doesn't get a kidney soon, we could lose her." Jenny twisted her fingers around the strap of her shoulder bag. "I guess what I'm trying to say is I want to give her one of my kidneys."

Dr. Thorne put a hand on her shoulder. "That's very admirable, Jenny, especially since you've known Sarah such a short time. But how do you know you're compatible?"

"What do you mean? We're twins aren't we?"

"Yes, but that doesn't mean you're automatically a match. If you'd been identical twins, a match would have been almost a certainty. But you and Sarah are fraternal. Do you know your blood type?"

"O-positive."

"Sarah's A-negative. You couldn't be further apart."

The possibility their blood wouldn't match had never occurred to Jenny. "But, I want to do this for her."

"I know but there you have it. Still, it's early days. Soon as we get Biddy out of the house, it can be rigged for home dialysis."

Jenny cleared her throat. "If Sarah were well, I'd take her to Charlotte for a visit, but with her sick like this, there's no way. No health insurance company in America would come within a hundred miles of her. Will she be put on the list for a transplant?"

"Soon as she has the tests. Still, she may have to wait a long time, perhaps years. Maybe she'll never get one. You must try not to worry too much. Even though a transplant is the best solution, people on dialysis these days can lead fairly normal lives."

Jenny went to the window and stared across the common. "Nigel from the Bookworm helped me find a book on kidneys. There was a chapter on long-term dialysis. It takes its toll, especially on people like Sarah." She turned back to Dr. Thorne. "I wish Biddy was already out of that house. I mean what does it take?"

"The Social Services are handling this," he said. "I don't know about America, but here things like this crawl along at a snail's pace. We'll get Biddy out though. I give her two weeks max."

"The woman scares me, Dr. Thorne. I can't help feeling if something isn't done soon, something awful is going to happen."

The doctor's bushy brows came together. "There's no need to be so apprehensive. Sarah won't be going near the place till we've got Biddy out."

After Jenny left Dr. Thorne's, she pulled into Andy's to fill up.

"You look worried," he said, resting his arms on the open window. "What's Uncle Angus been telling you."

She ran a hand across her brow, looking at him while an idea formed in her mind. "It's not him. It's— Do you think you can get away for an hour so we can drive somewhere?"

Andy looked over his shoulder into the garage then back at her. "Give me a minute while I tell Alf."

She watched him walk toward the office, a confident, easy stride, swinging from the waist down. He said a few words to Alf, who turned and looked at her. Andy laughed as Alf made some remark she couldn't hear, while Pete, listening in, wagged his tail. When Andy turned and headed for the car, Pete padded along behind him obviously ready to go.

"Not this time, Pete," Andy said raising his hand. "Just Jenny and me."

"Ah, let him come. He looks so sad."

"That's his hangdog look. He's a master of it." Still, Andy opened the back door and clicked his fingers. Pete, Frisbee in his mouth, bounded into the back seat. "I'll drive," he said, smiling down at Jenny. "Move over."

A few miles out of town, he pulled the car into a lay-by. "There's a footpath beyond that stile. Let's walk a bit."

He held her hand as they strolled. "You're worried sick, I can tell. What is it?"

"It's just that all of a sudden I don't know where to turn." She kicked at last year's dead leaves strewn along the footpath.

He stopped in mid-stride. "What is it?"

"It's Sarah. Well, Sarah and me. It's hard to explain but in the pub last night, when Sarah went to the front to get the prize, something came over me. I mean something happened. I was suddenly so proud of her. And now I can't get her out of my mind. I'm worried about her too. I can't give her a kidney. Our blood doesn't match. But I want to take care of her. She's my sister and my responsibility. Your uncle was real kind to take her in, but he's old and his wife's still away. I've thought about her coming to stay at the cottage, but need a place where I can cook the things she's supposed to have. I can't trust the pub food. I guess what I mean is, as much as I hate to ask, can we stay with you? Sarah and me in your house? I mean do you have any room? Would we be a bother?"

He put a hand under her chin and raised her face. His eyes bore into hers. "You ask me do I have any room? Would you be a bother? Jenny, are you kidding?"

"I know it's an imposition," she went on, her voice beginning to break, "but soon as Biddy's gone, we can move into Glen Ellen. Maybe by then, the kidney specialists will have told us something. You know, how we ought to be looking at things. What to do next."

Andy pulled her to him and put his arms around her. He closed his eyes as he buried his face in her hair, drinking in the fresh clean smell of her, pulling her ever closer, feeling the outline of her body against his. "Of course you can stay. If you hadn't asked me, I was going to ask you."

He brushed his lips across hers. "God knows, the last thing in the world I want is for Sarah to be sick like this, but at least it's stopping you from leaving. I want to help, Jenny. I'll do anything."

"Ah, you say that now, but there's still a lot about me you don't know."

"What? That your father's a priest. Is that it?"

She looked out across the fields, listened to the bleats from the sheep in the meadow beyond. "Guess it's all over the village by now. I'm no prude, Andy, but my mother and father, right here in this town, in the very cottage I'm in now. That's where Sarah and I were conceived. Can't you just hear the local gossip when we move in with you? *Just like her mother that one. Jump into bed with anything in pants.*"

They walked on, arms around each other, while she told him about Biddy stealing her snapshot. "Can you believe the old bitch actually did me a favor," she said, and then explained about her letter to the priest and its outcome. "I still can't believe how thrilled he is. He really wants us. He's taken his lap top with him to the retreat. He said he's already had some e-mails from his parish, and most are positive. Oh, he'd tell me that anyway, just so I wouldn't worry. But I can't help it. I mean what if someone tells the pope?"

Andy loosened his hold, a hint of a smile on his lips. "As serious as all this is to you, I honestly don't think it'll be important enough to tell the Pope."

"Well, I don't know. I'm not Catholic. I know he's planning to tell his bishop. This man could fire him or send him to God knows where. And there're bound to be some people in his church who'll want to humiliate him."

"Ah, it's probably nowhere near as bad as you think. He wasn't even a priest when all this happened."

"No, but just as good as. He had already applied to the seminary. His trip to the Lake District was a sort of last holiday."

Andy picked up the Frisbee Pete had dropped at his feet and flung it across the grass.

"I've got two bedrooms upstairs with a bathroom in between. They're all fixed up except for sheets and things and they're in the closet. You can move in tonight if you like." He clicked his fingers. "I just remembered. I'm supposed to be in Penrith tomorrow. There's an estate sale and they need an appraisal on some clocks. I can cancel if you want."

"Don't you dare. We can move some stuff tonight. It'll probably suit Sarah to settle in with just her and me. You know, girl talk and stuff."

Andy climbed the steps over the stile and reached for her hand to steady her. Suddenly very aware of him and the way he was looking at her, she lowered her gaze, pretending to concentrate on the steps, then let go of his hand and jumped to the ground.

"I'm glad you're coming," he said, his voice growing softer, full of meaning. "You can stay forever if you want to."

Her heart banged against her ribs. "It's just that I've got a lot on me, finding out things I knew nothing about."

With arms around each other, they looked up and watched the lengthening jet contrail, a widening white scratch in an otherwise cloudless sky. The plane was heading west, probably for America, maybe even Charlotte. They retraced their steps back to the car, then drove for miles, Pete in the back seat with his head stuck out the window. They stopped at a tea shop and ate their meal at one of the outside tables, both of them giving Pete half of their sandwich.

That night, Jenny told Walter Pudsley she'd be checking out of the cottage the following morning, and that she and Sarah planned to stay at Andy's until Biddy was gone from Glen Ellen. Jenny half expected, and at the same time dreaded, a knowing look from Walter, perhaps a wink of some sort.

"Andy's a good man" Walter said instead. "One of the best. He'll take care of you and do his best for Sarah.'

Chapter Twenty-two

The next day, an hour after Andy left for Penrith, Jenny and Sarah moved in with their things, and then went together to Malone's. Ada helped them pick out their groceries. They bought olive oil and mayonnaise for the vegetables, as well as pasta, bread, rice, a couple of chicken breasts to be used sparingly. For treats, they picked marshmallows, a jar of honey, one of strawberry jam, a bag of apples, and two custard tarts which Sarah loved. All labels were checked for no-sodium.

At Andy's house, Sarah sat on her bed and pulled a notebook from her canvas bag and held it open for Jenny to see. "Dr. Hall gave me this. It's special for people like me. On this side I write how much I drink, and on this side, how much I go to the loo. I can't eat ice creams or jellies 'cause they turn to water. I don't mind as long as it'll make me better, but I'll miss my glass of milk at night and especially chocolate. I love chocolate." She brought out a large plastic container and pointed to the notches on the side. "This is to measure my water. I write it down and except for a little bit, swill most of it down the loo." She took off her glasses and rubbed her eyes. "I have to put dates and times and check for blood too. It's very hard."

"I'll help you keep tabs," Jenny said, putting an arm across Sarah's sagging shoulders. "Thursday we go to the big hospital in Manchester. Not long now."

That same afternoon, Jenny asked Dr. Thorne if Sarah was well enough to get her ears pierced and then visit Lottie Mellville, the woman she had made friends with in the hospital.

"You mean she's still there?" Dr. Thorne said. "What's she got?"

"A broken leg. Fell down some steps. She went home then had to go back. Some small thing. She told Sarah on the phone that she's going home tomorrow."

"Well we can't keep Sarah in a cocoon, and Craighead Hospital's not far. If she gets tired, come on home." He gave a half-teasing smile. "But what about you? Seems I heard a rumor you don't like hospitals all that much."

"It's true. I hang on by a thread," Jenny said, looking down at her arms. "Just thinking about it gives me goose bumps. Back home, I was seeing a therapist. He said to face it head on. That's why I asked Sarah if she wanted to go see her friend. It's more for me, really. I'll probably do OK, Sarah being with me and all."

They found a jewelry shop near the hospital, the sign in the window saying they pierced ears. Sarah dangled her earrings in front of the store clerk. "After you've made the holes, will you put these in, please?"

The woman looked at them as if they were contaminated, then produced a pair of tiny gold studs fastened to a card. "She'll have to wear these for three weeks," she said, ignoring Sarah and speaking directly to Jenny. "And it's always better to wear gold. You don't want her to get an infection do you?"

Something inside Jenny rattled, but the unconcerned look on Sarah's face told her this had happened before. "My sister isn't hard of hearing, and understands perfectly. Perhaps if you spoke directly to her."

The woman's face reddened and she pouted her bright red lips. "Well, my goodness. I certainly didn't mean to insinuate anything."

Jenny turned to Sarah. "What do you think? We can get little gold posts made for yours like Ada did with hers."

"OK."

The woman dabbed some solution on Sarah's ears, gave two quick clicks, and the little gold studs were in place.

Sarah laughed. "That was easy."

"Come and take a look," Jenny said, standing by the oval mirror on the counter. Sarah looked first at one ear, and then the other, and then backed off to see both ears. She straightened her yellow hairclip and made sure her chiffon scarf was still tossed over her left shoulder the way Jenny had fixed it.

As they crossed the hospital parking lot, Jenny kept her gaze lowered so she wouldn't see the gargoyles. When she faltered at the entrance, feeling as if she were about to enter the bowels of hell, Sarah pulled her sister's arm through hers and almost dragged her across the parquet floor of the lobby.

"You hold on tight to me, love," Sarah said, her tone almost motherly. "And whistle if you can. Do you know 'Roll out the Barrel'?"

While Jenny puckered her lips, struggling but making no sound, Sarah stopped at a painting on the wall, the first of about ten spaced at intervals on both sides. "All the pictures on these walls were painted by someone very special," she said. "And they're all of the Lake District. See, look, this one's Windermere. There's the ferry."

Jenny held on to Sarah, eyes focused on the painting. "I've been there," she said. "It's real nice."

"Now look down in the corner and see the name."

"Why, it says Fred Fitzgerald. You don't mean— Oh, wow, Sarah. I knew your daddy was an artist but didn't know he was this good."

Sarah brushed her fingers along the signature, then waved a hand to encompass the hall. "He painted all these." She pulled Jenny to the next one. "See this one. It's Ullswater."

Jenny loosened her tight grip. "Oh, Sarah. You must be very proud."

"I am," Sarah said thickly. "Now, the next one's extra special, so close your eyes and don't open them till you've guessed what's on it."

Jenny screwed her eyes tight and let Sarah lead her a few yards further. "Wordsworth's house," she guessed. "Dove Cottage?"

Sarah giggled. "No. You can look now."

It was the same view of Stoney Beck that Jenny had seen from Andy's terrace. But this was a Christmas scene, with snow covering the town and the hills beyond. There were skaters on the frozen lake and Christmas trees sparkled in some of the cottage windows, the little houses seemingly huddled even closer together for warmth. The Salvation Army was in a circle on Hallveck Common and a border collie with a Frisbee between his teeth sat watching them. At the other end of Market Street was the Hare and Hounds, its lights from inside shining golden on the snow. The painting was for all the world a Dickens Christmas card.

"Oh," Jenny said. "It's beautiful. And see, it's even got Pete in it."

Sarah blinked and two big tears rolled down her cheeks. She was so thrilled Jenny liked the painting that she hardly felt the ache in her legs any more. "That's how Daddy made his money, painting pictures." She ran her hand gently along the frame. "This was his very last one."

They went from painting to painting, Sarah having something to say about each one, until they reached the last one at the end of the corridor. Before they turned that last corner, Jenny looked back. She'd made that long, long trek with hardly a qualm. Thank God for Sarah and her daddy's paintings. Just a few more yards and they were inside the ward.

The woman who had turned away from Sarah so unkindly was still there, in the same place, sitting by her made-up bed. When she saw Sarah, her tight-lipped mouth broke into a smile. She got to her feet and stretched out her arms. Sarah, suddenly stronger, tramped across the floor and held the woman in one of her gentler hugs.

"I've come at last, Lottie," she said, handing her the box of chocolates they'd bought in Malone's. She pointed to her ears. "Just got them done. I can't put yours in for three weeks." She fingered her hair clip and flipped her scarf. "Jenny tied it." She reached for Jenny's hand and pulled her forward. "You remember her don't you?"

Lottie turned to Jenny. "When Sarah came in, I was feeling so low. The way I acted. It was inexcusable."

"Ah, that's OK," Jenny said. "I understand."

Lottie cleared her throat. "That first night, when she heard me sniffling, feeling sorry for myself as usual, she got out of bed, pulled her chair over and sat with me. She talked a lot about you, said you'd come all the way from America by yourself."

Sarah nudged Jenny. "Tell Lottie about us being twins."

Lottie's eyes widened as she looked at Jenny. "But you're an American. How——"

Jenny gave a little nervous laugh wishing she'd cautioned Sarah not to mention the twin thing. "It's a long story."

"She's prettier than me because we were in different eggs," Sarah said. "That's why she couldn't give me a kidney, but she did try."

Lottie looked from Sarah to Jenny and back again, some intuition obviously warning her not to pursue the subject.

Sarah prodded Jenny's arm. "Will you talk to Lottie while I go and say hello to the nurses."

They watched as Sarah stopped to pat the hand of the old lady in the bed nearest the door, then disappeared into the nurses' room.

"What's the latest on Biddy?" Lottie asked. The way she said it, her mouth tight, hardly moving, and the sudden flash in her eyes, told Jenny that Lottie knew all about the paddy wagon men, Biddy making Sarah stand half-naked in the corner, and maybe other things Jenny herself didn't even know. Reluctant to discuss Biddy, yet feeling some explanation was needed, Jenny said she and Sarah were staying with a friend in the village until Biddy found another place to live.

"Sarah said you live alone," Jenny said. "Is it near here?"

"Bowness. I rent the flat over the shop that my husband and I used to own. When we divorced, we had to sell it. He's remarried and moved away. I still work in the shop."

"That must be hard," Jenny said.

"Yes, but it's OK. They're nice and I needed the money."

"Do you have any other family?"

"There's a daughter in Australia who comes home about every five years."

"It's good you have her," Jenny said, seeing Sarah in the doorway. "There's nothing like real family."

Because Sarah and Lottie asked her to, Jenny talked about Charlotte and the rest of North Carolina. While she was in the middle of telling them all about the hot summers and how she loved to go to Uncle Tim's place on the lake, she glanced at her watch. It was five o'clock and a cart stacked with trays was being maneuvered into the ward. It was time for the evening meal.

"We'll keep in touch," Jenny said, picking up her purse and waiting while Sarah gave Lottie another hug.

Lottie kissed Sarah's cheek. "Don't you forget about me. I've got a car and can visit you when this leg of mine mends."

Back in Stoney Beck, they went into Malone's. As Sarah made for the greeting card section, Jenny found Ada halfway down the middle aisle arranging a pyramid of homemade black-currant jams.

"Walter's just left," Ada said. "He's been here most of the afternoon and talked a lot about you. He said if you hadn't come to Stoney Beck, the two of us might never have got together."

Jenny smiled. "He said that to me but I told him I had nothing to do with it."

"Where are the girls?" Sarah whispered loudly, hand cupped around her mouth, as she walked toward them.

"They're in the back having a cuppa."

"Well, they've mixed up all the cards. Weddings were in with the happy birthdays and a couple of sympathies and get wells were stuck in with the new born babies." She glanced again over her shoulder. "But don't let on I said. I've sorted them so you don't have to worry."

Ada folded her arms and gave Jenny an I-told-you-so look. "There now. Doesn't that just tell you how much I miss this child. You never got them mixed up did you?"

Sarah shook her head. "Please don't give my job away, Ada. I'm nearly well."

"Yes, love." Ada's voice was suddenly hoarse. "I'll wait for you. You're the best help I've ever had."

Chapter Twenty-three

Jenny sat across the table from Sarah, and watched her push a piece of broiled fish around on her plate. "You feeling OK?" she asked.

Sarah shrugged. "Just a bit tired."

"Maybe we did too much today. We'll take it easy tomorrow."

"I have to get back to Malone's, Jenny. If Ada gives my job away, I don't know what I'll do."

"But you'll have to wait until you're well."

Sarah slapped the flat of her hand on the table so hard it rattled the dishes. "I am well," she rasped. "I know I am. I know I am."

Pete stuck his head round the door and gave a little woof.

"OK, OK. I didn't mean anything." Jenny was anxious because hadn't Dr. Hall warned her mood swings might be a sign of high blood pressure. Sarah's face was flushed and Jenny had never seen her this mad.

Sarah slapped the table again. "I don't want to take it easy. You said yourself God gives us two kidneys in case anyone needs a spare. Well, he'll find a spare for me. Just you watch him."

"Sarah, will you please calm down," Jenny said, looking from her to the dog. "Why don't we leave the dishes and take Pete to the lake. We'll go in the car and just stay ten minutes."

As if he understood every word, the dog raced from the room to his box of toys. In a couple of seconds he was back, Frisbee clamped between his jaws, tail wagging like a black and white fringed fan. Jenny and Sarah burst out laughing.

Later that evening, when Sarah had gone to bed, Jenny flipped through a magazine and wondered why Andy had not returned from Penrith. He had said he'd be around nine, and when the phone rang at ten, she knew it was he.

"Remember when I told you about the mists up here?" he said. "Well, there's one hanging over this town like a veil. Looks as if I'll have to wait it out. Can you live without me for one night?"

"Oh, I guess so, but it's gonna be tough."

"Is there any mist in Stoney Beck?"

She looked out the window. "No. It's clear. I can see lights way up in the fells."

"Is Pete being any trouble?"

"He's an angel." She reached down and ran her hand along the dog's back as he stretched out in front of her, his chin on her feet.

"But I think he's missing you. I catch him staring off some, then looking at the door, as if he's expecting you to come through it."

There was a pause, then, "How about you, Jenny? Are you staring off some, waiting for me to come through the door?"

Her hand tightened on the receiver.

"Jenny? You OK?"

"Yes, I'm OK and really do appreciate you letting us stay here. I know Sarah's safe, tucked up in bed and fast asleep. It's just that—"

"You're worried about her aren't you?"

"I sure am. Think they'll put her on dialysis soon. I'm not superstitious, Andy, and not very religious. Sometimes, though, I get this feeling my coming over here is all some kind of wild destiny, and that I got here just in time." She gave a little laugh. "Bet you think I'm crazy talking like this."

"No, and I don't know much about destiny. I'm just so damn glad you came. I want you and Sarah to stay with me, even after they get Biddy out of Glen Ellen. You'll need some help with this dialysis. You can't do it by yourself, especially in that barn of a place."

"You say that now, but it'd mean a huge commitment. There's probably a lot more to dialysis than either of us realize."

"We can't discuss this over the phone," Andy said. "Let's save it till I get back."

***

Jenny flicked through magazines, at the same time thinking of a thousand and one things that had nothing at all to do with her just a few short months ago. She fixed a cup of cocoa and after checking on the sleeping Sarah, and with Andy's terry cloth robe draped around her shoulders, she headed for the terrace, Pete trailing behind. The night was chilly but she couldn't resist just ten minutes looking out across the little town. Pete sat erect at her feet while she settled herself on the bench up close to the railing. The sky teemed with stars, a sight not seen these days in Charlotte or any big city full of lights. Up in the fells, lights blinked here and there, and far off a night bird called. At this late hour, few cars were on the street, but goose bumps popped out on Jenny's arms as she recognized the green Toyota creeping up Market Street. Biddy's car inched its way up the brow and stopped directly opposite the house. She watched as Biddy rolled down the window, leaned her arms on the door and stared up at her. Jenny stared back. Nothing could harm her, safe as she was up here with the dog. And yet, there was something frightening about the woman. Her hair hung loose, wild and uncombed, while a crazy grin played around her toothless mouth.

Jenny's heart thumped while she tried to get to her feet but the chair held her, wouldn't let her go. "Here, boy," she whispered to Pete through her teeth. "Here boy." The dog gave a worried little whine, leaped onto the bench, and licked the side of her face. Her heart slowed and the shaking eased as she rubbed the dog's head and felt his body bristle as he too stared at the woman in the car. A low deep growl rumbled from the back of his throat.

At the sight of Pete, the grin on Biddy's face disappeared and within a few seconds, she had rolled up her window and driven away. Jenny saw the car turn right on Vallhellyn Lane and disappear.

"Good dog, Pete. You scared her off." Jenny sprang to her feet and headed for the French doors, the dog at her heels. Safe inside, she stood at the window and listened while the village hall clock tolled out the hour, its mellow Westminster chime coincided almost note for note with the golden tones of Andy's grandfather's clock in the hall. Midnight. A shiver ran the length of her body. Sarah had said Biddy never went out after five, but here the woman was in Stoney Beck in the middle of the night. Who could say what was going on in Biddy's deranged mind. Jenny knelt beside Pete, her arm across his back, while he drank from his bowl. She'd never owned a pet, never understood the closeness that could exist between a dog and his owner. Not until now. "Good dog," she said. "You can sleep on my bed tonight?"

***

Biddy Biggerstaff had rung the Hare and Hounds earlier in the evening and asked to speak to Jenny Robinson, only to be told the young lady had checked out yesterday. Hardly daring to hope the bitch had gone at last, Biddy rang Angus Thorne. If anybody knew, he would. But all he did was to tell Biddy yet again she could no longer stay at Glen Ellen. She need not worry, he said in some sort of wheedling tone, because arrangements were being made for alternative accommodation where she would be safe and perhaps receive some counseling. Biddy slammed down the phone, cutting him off. As a last resort, she rang Andy Ferguson's garage. The mechanic told her Andy wouldn't be back until tomorrow morning. Ah, but yes he knew where Jenny Robinson was. She and Sarah were staying with Andy for a few days and who was calling please? Biddy said it didn't matter and hung up. Afraid as she was of the tree, she hated to leave the house after dark, but this time she had to take a chance. Sarah and Jenny Robinson were in the Ferguson house alone. Biddy still had this last chance to coax Sarah into coming back to Glen Ellen where she belonged.

Biddy couldn't believe her luck as she approached the house and saw the girl sitting on the terrace. She parked the car across the street, rolled down the window and stared up at the girl. This was all it took. Even from this distance, it was obvious the girl was frightened. But Biddy hadn't counted on the dog. Suddenly he appeared on the bench beside the girl and returned Biddy's stare, his eyes red like two hot coals, with blood drooling from his bared fangs. He was a devil dog poised to leap over the railings and onto the car. With lifeless fingers, Biddy rolled up the window. She fumbled with the key until at last it turned and she scratched away from the curb. She'd seen that dog umpteen times before but never knew its power until now.

Even at this late hour a few people wandered about, but Biddy recognized no one. Probably tourists, taking one last stroll before turning in. The street lamps on the brow caught her eye. A haze swirled around them and even as she stared, they began to move, to sway and bend as though to music only they could hear. Their lighted heads took on hideous leering faces, with huge almond shaped golden eyes, and every one of them gawking at her. Perhaps if she rolled down her window and screamed at them, they would stop their crazy dance or maybe even disappear the way those worms had. But it was too iffy. If they stuck their heads inside her car, they'd strangle her for sure. She watched a young couple stroll along the pavement, laughing and unaware, even mad enough to kiss under one of the lamps, without noticing it wrap itself around them. Biddy tried to stop the shaking in her leg as she stepped on the accelerator, and headed out of Stoney Beck toward Glen Ellen.

***

Next morning, after spending the night clinging to Pete's collar, even sleeping cheek to jowl, Jenny came downstairs to the smell of burnt toast. Sarah was in the kitchen singing "Blue Suede Shoes" along with Elvis while she scraped the toast. She kissed Jenny's cheek and placed a glass of orange juice next to a bowl of cornflakes and fresh strawberries. Sun streamed through the bay window onto the kitchen table.

Jenny looked across the living room. The French windows leading to the terrace were flung wide with the smell of new mown hay and good fresh Lake District air filling the room. Biddy and last night were far away.

"I'm planning our day today," Sarah said, as she poured herself two ounces of apple juice and another two ounces of milk for her cornflakes. "Let's go for a drive later and see if we can find your digging friends."

Jenny poured milk on her cereal. "Sounds like a winner to me."

"It's going to be a lovely day, Jenny. I'm so glad we're sisters."

"So am I, pumpkin. And we're going to make up for lost time. How about you taking Pete onto the terrace while I straighten up here. Just have these few dishes." She waved a hand. "No, Sarah. You fixed it. I'll clean up."

Sarah leaned against the terrace railing. She could see over the rooftops and up beyond the houses into the fells. She couldn't see Glen Ellen but knew it was up there somewhere. Biddy was in there smoking and drinking. When Mummy and Daddy were alive, Sarah had loved Glen Ellen, but now she didn't want to go near it. Even the tree had died as if its very heart was broken.

The weariness came suddenly from out of nowhere, dropping over her like a heavy blanket. Even as she watched, the scene in front of her blurred. The chimneys lifted off from the rooftops and did a sort of bunny hop across the lake. As if from far away, she heard Pete whimper, felt him paw at her dress. She tried to raise an arm to pat his head, to tell him everything was all right, but it was just too hard. The whimper turned into a funny sounding bark, as if Pete was in a tunnel. At last Sarah managed to grab his collar and held on as he struggled toward the French door. It was as if they were on one of those things she'd seen on the telly, the sort where you walk on it but don't get anywhere. She saw Jenny come to the doorway and call to her, but her voice sounded worse than Pete's, far away and tinny. Through a dark haze filled with big black spots, Sarah saw five or six Jennies with arms outstretched run toward her, but she crumpled to the floor before any of them could reach her.

Chapter Twenty-four

Jenny sat in the cafeteria of Manchester Royal Infirmary while she waited for Sarah to finish her first dialysis treatment. She pulled Andy's cell phone out of her bag to call the priest, then shoved it back. Wouldn't it be wiser to wait for the doctor's report. Two hours ago, she had forced herself to watch as the plastic tube they had stuck in Sarah's neck, of all places, gushed with blood. A smell of formaldehyde hung in the air, reminding Jenny of death. When she felt the bile rise in her own throat she had run gagging from the room, only to crash into a nurse, knocking the tray of medicines out of her hands. Jenny gaped as the tiny paper containers and pills flew all over the place, then with a hand pressed over her mouth she had zipped into the toilet across the hall.

Filled now with self-hate, she sipped on ginger ale and considered the possibility, even hoped, that she would never be allowed anywhere near the dialysis unit again. A man in a white coat appeared in the cafeteria doorway and looked round the room. It was the same man who had hovered over Sarah while her dialysis was being set up. Jenny leaned on the table as she pulled herself to her feet and walked toward him.

"Excuse me? Are you Sarah Fitzgerald's doctor?"

"One of them. I'm Mr. Sidney, the renal specialist."

"Mr.? I'm sorry. I thought you were my sister's doctor."

The man was tall and angular, his pale skin stretched across his pinched face like tissue paper. Jenny could see his pulse beating in his temple. His dark wispy hair was straggly as if he'd cut it himself. It was below his ears and he looked more like a hippie, straight out of the sixties.

"I am your sister's surgeon," he said in a stiff, superior voice as he straightened the papers on his clipboard. "In England, surgeons revert back to Mr." He seemed to look Jenny up and down. "You're an American aren't you?"

Jenny nodded.

"But your twin sister's English. How did that come about?"

"Have you got a couple of hours," she said, forcing a shaky smile.

When he didn't return the smile, she looked down at her shoes, for the first time noticing she had on one white tennis shoe while the other was beige. She looked up quickly but knew the man had seen.

"I'm real sorry I crashed into that nurse. Is she all right?"

"More or less. A slight bruise on her shoulder. An orderly swept up the pills." He flipped a couple of pages on his clipboard. "If you really want to help Sarah, it's important that you stay calm and focused."

Jenny ran a hand across her brow. "I know, I know. I'm working on it. Can you tell me what made her pass out like that? She was doing so great. She was singing and even fixed breakfast."

"It was her blood pressure," Mr. Sidney said. "It shot up so fast, she lost consciousness. It happens sometimes."

"How bad is it?"

"We'll know more after she's been assessed. If we can get her stabilized, she should be able to go home in a few days. We'll make arrangements for her to have dialysis at a nearer hospital." He turned to the next page. "Probably Craighead. If there's a problem with transportation, it can be arranged for an ambulance to take her."

"I have a car," Jenny said. "I'll take her."

"Does she live with you?"

"She didn't used to but she does now. We're sort of between houses." Jenny put her hands on her burning face while the doctor scribbled away on his damn clipboard.

"Do you have other family? Parents? Other siblings?"

She shook her head. "There're just the two of us."

"It's quite a distance from here to the Lakes. Are you staying here in the city?"

"I'm at the Astor."

"Good. Leave your phone number with the staff nurse. Someone will be in touch with you. We need to know more about Sarah's background, her living accommodation. She'll need a stable environment."

"Oh, she'll get that. Everything sounds a bit up in the air, but we're getting it all straightened out."

"So you have others helping you, people you can call on if need be?"

She nodded. "We have dear, close friends in the village. I can give you names."

The doctor gave her a long penetrating look. "We'll be in touch as soon as we've reached a decision on Sarah's dialysis."

He stuck the pen in his pocket and looked at Jenny through narrowed eyes that said it all. What was going on here? What was all this confusion about where they lived? Didn't they have a proper home? And no way would he trust this crazy American with such a sensitive procedure as assisting with dialysis.

All Jenny wanted now was to get out of there. She despised this arrogant man and wondered how he'd feel if she said, "I'm trying real hard to get a handle on this, *Mister* Sidney, and by the way, your hair looks like shit."

Instead, she forced her mouth into some sort of smile, at the same time unable to stop the ache in her throat, or her eyes filling up. "Sarah isn't strong to start with, what with her Down syndrome and all. And now this. It's been uphill for her all the way. She's so brave, though, much braver than I could ever be. I lost my cool in that dialysis room but I'm working real hard on doing better. The truth is if swimming the English Channel would make her well, I'd try it. I wanted to give her a kidney but our blood doesn't match. Can you believe it, and us being twins?" She sniffed and felt in her pockets for a tissue.

Mr. Sidney walked to the counter and came back with a couple of tissues. He handed them to her, along with three or four booklets he pulled out of his pocket. "Read through these," he said, his tone suddenly less brusque. "They'll give you more insight into dialysis. There's information in there for those who know nothing about renal dysfunction. There's also a support group I can put you in touch with, get you started, help you over the rough spots."

He looked at his watch and stuck his clipboard under his arm. "I have to get to a meeting, but we'll be in touch." Without another word he was off down the hall.

Jenny stared after him as he marched away. What a stupid fool she must have seemed to him. Still, when he reached the end of the hall, he looked back and threw up his hand in a sort of wave before he disappeared round the corner.

She stuck her hands in her pockets and kept her head down as she headed for Sarah's room, at the same time trying to think if there was anything she'd forgotten to do. She called Alf and asked him if he would see to Pete and also to let Andy know that Sarah was in the dialysis section of the hospital. Alf told her that the priest, that Father Woodleigh from St. Mary's had rung the garage. He had been ringing the house and got no answer. "I told him about Sarah," Alf said. "Hope I did the right thing. Wasn't sure after he sounded so concerned."

"No, no. It's OK," Jenny said. "I was going to call him anyway. He, well, he's my and Sarah's father. Thought you would have found out by now. Everybody else has." She hung up before Alf had a chance to reply.

Chapter Twenty-five

Charles had waited three days for his bishop to fit him into his schedule. He knocked now on the study door, at the same time thinking of Richard Delaney. Charles had never missed his old friend and bishop more than he did this minute. Richard had known all about Beverly and if he had been alive today, Charles knew he would have received a very sympathetic ear.

Vincent Fitzpatrick swung round from the window as Charles entered. There was no smile of welcome as there would have been on Richard's face, not even an outstretched hand. If this bishop ever smiled, Charles had never seen it. There was an air of self-importance about the man, while at the same time a certain guardedness. The chilly room matched his frigid air, and Charles wondered why the man hadn't lit the gas logs in the hearth.

"I realize you wanted to see me urgently," he said as Charles approached. "This though is the first opportunity I've had." He sat down on a maroon leather sofa, indicating with a wave of his hand that Charles should sit on the chair by the unlit fire.

"Yes, I have been anxious to see you," Charles said. "I've received some news that, as my bishop, you need to know." He reached in his pocket for Jenny's letter. "This is from my daughter. I'd like you to read it."

The bishop's eyes were suddenly alert, attentive. "You have a daughter? I don't understand."

"I didn't know myself until just four days ago." Charles held out the envelope. "Please, just read it. It'll all come clear."

As the bishop unfolded the letter and began to read, Charles made a pretense of studying the painting on the wall over the mantelpiece. It was HMS *Victory*, Nelson's flagship, in full sail, battling a stiff breeze. He turned back to the bishop and watched his eyes move along the lines. His brows had come together in a frown, and every now and then, he glanced up at Charles. At last, he folded the letter and replaced it in the envelope.

"Don't you think you're being a bit naive, taking all this on face value? How do you know this Jenny isn't making this up, that it's not some mischief on her part?"

Charles felt a prick of irritation. "She isn't lying. If you met her you'd know. And anyway, what would be the point? She's making no demands on me and stands to gain nothing. It took courage for her to write this letter. She's still grieving for her mother and the man she thought was her father."

The bishop made no comment but leaned back in his chair, arms folded, waiting for Charles to continue.

"Jenny came to England looking for answers to her mother's suicide note, and almost as soon as she arrives, she discovers that Sarah who has Down syndrome is her twin sister. Sarah is also very sick."

Charles ran a hand across his brow as his voice started to tremble. The last thing he wanted was to lose his cool in front of this man. He wanted to tell him instead how proud he was of Jenny and how already he cared so much for her and Sarah. But he didn't trust himself to say it. He drummed his fingers on the arm of the chair, as he saw again Sarah's tortured face when she'd stood on tiptoe and stretched out her hand to give him the snapshot, then Jenny racing out to stand beside her, her arm reaching across her sister's shoulders.

"Tell me something about this Beverly," the bishop said, his tone belittling her, making her sound cheap.

Resisting the urge to tell his pompous bishop to go to hell, Charles bit his lip till it hurt. He took a couple of deep breaths and even though his voice trembled, managed to give the bishop a rundown of his short romance with Beverly, and how falling in love with her or any woman had been the last thing on his mind. Finally, he told the bishop he'd asked Beverly to marry him, but she'd turned him down.

Charles looked out the window, at the rain beginning to fall, thinking about the newspaper clipping he had found in his mother's things. He had never told another living soul about this and probably never would. What good would it do? It was all so long ago.

"You do understand your parish will have to be told," his bishop finally said.

Charles replaced the letter in his jacket pocket. "I've already done that. I realize I should have discussed it with you first but you were in Dublin, and not due here for three days. I decided to handle my parish first. I sent a letter to everyone on the roster."

"You're right," the bishop said. "You should have discussed it with me first. It's put me in a very difficult position."

Charles wanted to ask what was this difficult position but changed his mind. He felt no shame for the love he had felt for Beverly and wasn't going to let this man make him feel otherwise. All he wanted was to get out of the study as fast as possible.

"I'm sorry if I haven't handled this correctly," he said. "And I realize that as my bishop, you have the right to fire me, send me to Timbuktu, Siberia, or God knows where. I leave it in your hands."

Vincent Fitzpatrick had deep-set dark eyes, slightly bloodshot, as though he drank too much. He looked like a man who had never been young, had never enjoyed a sunset, or climbed a mountain just to see what was on the other side. What had happened in his life to make him so sour?

"What would you propose?" the bishop asked. "That I allow you to stay on at St. Mary's, with a couple of daughters in the next village? Do you think you could cope with a parish sniggering behind your back? Do you think the church could or should tolerate it?"

Charles stuck two fingers under his clerical collar which had been digging into his neck ever since he'd entered the study. "I don't know. In my letter I suggested they discuss it. I haven't heard anything so far."

"You realize that most of them will feel let down," the bishop said. "There are bound to be those who want to know the titillating bits, and then there are others who'll want to see you drawn and quartered. You have to see this through their eyes. Suddenly their priest, their paragon of virtue, tells them he's the father of grown-up twins. And not ordinary twins either."

"Not ordinary?"

"Well, one's English with Down's syndrome and the other is an obviously healthy American. Don't tell me you wouldn't be intrigued if the pope sent us a letter saying he's just found out he's the father of twins from an old love affair. One of the twins is Russian and the other lives in Paris. The Russian twin came all the way from Vladivostok to tell the poor unsuspecting pope. Bound to raise a few eyebrows don't you think?" There was a long pause while the bishop examined his nails and the silence whined around them. "For what it's worth after all these years, I'm assuming you went to confession?"

"I honestly don't remember," Charles said, "I took Beverly's leaving hard. Nothing else seemed to matter."

The bishop's eyebrows shot up another quarter inch. "Nothing else mattered? While you were having this affair, you were waiting to hear from the seminary. Surely the priesthood mattered?"

"Of course it did," Charles's nervousness evaporated and he was unable to keep the edge from creeping into his own voice. "I'm not making excuses. What I did was wrong, I realize that. In the old days, it was thought priests were perfect, even those like me waiting to be priests. Now though, with the media the way it is, it's common knowledge we're not saints. We fumble our way through life just like everyone else."

The bishop acted as if Charles hadn't said a word. "These twins, are they Catholic?"

"Sarah is, but Jenny's Protestant."

Vincent Fitzpatrick looked at his watch and got to his feet. "I have to give you fair warning here and now. I don't look upon this favorably. You'll be hearing from me."

"I understand," Charles said, his hand outstretched. As they shook hands, and in spite of his bishop's sharp words, Charles could have sworn he saw a wistful look in the man's eyes. Had he imagined it or was the man envious?

When he got back to his room, there was a message slipped under his door. Jenny had rung him from the Astor in Manchester, the note said, and would he please ring her as soon as possible. Within the half hour, and knowing his bishop had gone to Mass, Charles scribbled him a note and left it in a sealed envelope in his mailbox. Then lugging his suitcase, he headed out to his car.

Chapter Twenty-six

At the deli next door to the Astor, Jenny bought a smoked turkey on rye and a bottle of sparkly water, before walking to the hospital about a mile away. The priest had come three days ago to visit Sarah. He said he had made arrangements to stay at the rectory of St. Ann's Catholic and would be back in touch with Jenny. But she hadn't seen him since. When she asked him how his bishop as well as his parish had taken the news, he had skirted the question. Was this the reason he had not come back to see Sarah, or even called. She had looked in the phone book for St. Ann's Catholic but never made the call. The priest knew where she was.

Andy had come every day and yesterday afternoon had been accompanied by his uncle. Dr. Thorne said the Social Services had given Biddy an ultimatum. If she didn't leave Glen Ellen voluntarily within the next two weeks, she would be issued a court order. She had become reclusive and refused to open the door to anyone, screaming at the Social Services through the door, that court order or no court order, the only way they would get her out was head first in her coffin.

Jenny checked her watch as she entered the hospital grounds and made for the last of the benches spaced at intervals along the path. Fifteen minutes to go before she made that long, long walk through the labyrinth of halls to Sarah's room. Jenny settled herself on the seat and pulled out the water and sandwich, for the first time thinking about money. She saw again her Uncle Tim, his face worried, anxious, telling her to stay in good safe places because she could afford it. That was true then but how long could she keep it up? The doctors had hinted Sarah was making progress and could be sent home any day. Still, if she wasn't discharged by tomorrow, perhaps Jenny should call the bed and breakfast Andy had recommended. Why shell out seventy quid a night, he had wanted to know, when Walter Pudsley's sister ran a perfectly good bed and breakfast less than half a mile from the hospital?

A couple of pigeons pecked around near Jenny's feet, not once looking at her. They acted as if they hadn't noticed she was eating, but were moving in closer just the same. She broke off a piece of her sandwich and tossed it to them, then looked toward the hospital entrance. She half rose from the bench at the sight of the now familiar figure striding toward her, his hand raised in a sort of wave. With the sun directly behind him, she shaded her eyes with her hand as he reached her.

"Father," she whispered feeling her face burn at the still strangeness of the name, at the way it could be taken two different ways.

"Hello, Jenny," he said, with that gentle smile, the mesh of fine lines fanning out from the corners of his eyes. She shoved her half-eaten sandwich back into the paper bag as he sat beside her. "How's our girl?"

"Being discharged soon, maybe even tomorrow. They're fixing it so she can get dialysis at Craighead two or three times a week." Jenny gave a half-smile, wishing she knew how to address him, how to ask him why he hadn't gotten in touch. "I've been worried about you. I wondered if you'd heard from your parish and what your bishop said."

"Nothing much yet. Think I ought to warn you there'll be some who expected a saint for a priest but instead just got me. Still, we'll cross one bridge at a time. Our main concern is Sarah."

Jenny wanted to hug him, guilty now at her doubts. How to tell him she prayed he'd be all right, but there was this shyness that kept them both apart.

"I wish I could have given Sarah a kidney," she said. "There isn't anybody else except Uncle Tim, but his blood's O-positive, same as mine."

Her father placed his hand on hers, his eyes incandescent. "Aren't you forgetting someone? Someone even closer than your Uncle Tim. Her father for instance?"

Jenny's hand went to her mouth. "But you can't do that. You, well, you're a priest."

"Yes, and a priest with A-negative blood. That's where I've been these last few days. Getting tested. I asked the doctors not to tell you. Didn't want to put the cart before the horse. Even though our blood matches, there were other tests. They've checked heart, lungs, and almost every organ in my body. I'm having a psychological test this afternoon, and afterward there'll be transfusions from me to Sarah. Don't think they're anticipating any snags. Otherwise they wouldn't have given me the OK to tell you."

"Oh," Jenny's voice was soft, her gaze locked with his. "Oh, man. I never expected this. Never in a hundred years."

"I don't know why not," he said with a smile, sounding as if he did this sort of thing every other day. "What father wouldn't do this for his own daughter."

Jenny ached to fling her arms round his neck and by the look on his face, he felt the same, but they both sat there, frozen. "I love that you said that," she said. "It's just that—" She felt the goose bumps pop out on her skin, as she tried to push the apprehension to the back of her mind. What if something went wrong?

Charles saw the fear in her eyes, the way she bit her lip. "There's no need for you to be apprehensive. These operations are done every day. They're practically routine. But just to make sure, I've been praying hard. I rang Father Doyle last night, he's my replacement, and asked for prayers from the congregation. Sarah's the one who'll need them the most. If her body rejects the kidney, she'll be right back where she is now."

Jenny looked down at the same two pigeons, still pecking around at their feet, interested only in a handout and insensible to the dramatic conversation between her and her father.

"What did the doctors say about you being a priest with two grownup kids?"

He shrugged. "Not much. Doctors seem to be a bit like priests themselves, unshockable. There's nothing they haven't seen or heard. I stressed Sarah still doesn't know I'm her father and that I wanted her to hear it from either you or me. They agreed of course. Keeping her blood pressure down is critical."

Jenny still couldn't reach out, still didn't have the courage or whatever it took to give him that first embrace like an ordinary daughter would her father, or tell him how proud she was of him. Instead she pulled the sandwich out of the bag, tore it into bits, and threw it to the pigeons. "Perhaps I should be the one to tell her. What do you think?"

"Oh, would you. It'll sound better coming from you. Less of a shock."

She looked at her watch as she got to her feet. "Come on up to the waiting room in about twenty minutes."

***

Sarah clutched her Paddington bear to her chest as she eyed the spot under the sheet where a hollow plastic tube had been stuck in her tummy. Mr. Sidney had laughed when she'd said it looked like a little hose right there next to her belly button. It was called a cannula, he said, and after a few weeks, when it had settled itself, it would make dialysis much easier.

In this great big hospital she had a room all to herself, with a telly and everything. Still, she missed the ward at Craighead, with Lottie in the next bed. Not that Sarah felt much like talking. Mr. Sidney had promised she would feel better after dialysis, even spit on his hand and crossed his heart, then said hope to die. What a big fibber he was. She'd already had two treatments but they hadn't helped one little bit. Then, just yesterday, he had said she was doing so well, she would be discharged soon. Easy for him to say. He didn't have her legs. When she tried to move them to get comfy, they felt like five-pound bags of sugar. Her back ached and her head throbbed. She glanced at the bedside table to make sure the pan was there in case she had to be sick.

When she had asked a nurse if they'd found her a kidney, the woman said they weren't that easy to get. Sometimes it took years. *Years!* Sarah had half opened her mouth to tell the nurse she didn't have years because hadn't Biddy said mongoloids didn't live as long as ordinary people. If there was no new kidney soon, Sarah might not live to see next Christmas. But she just smiled and told the nurse to have a nice day like Jenny often said.

They didn't have a kidney for her and now were sending her home. Mr. Sidney had said she was getting better just so they could get her out of the hospital without a big fuss. She had heard Ada talking with customers about this very thing. When you were very poorly and the doctors couldn't make you better, they sent you home to die. Sarah closed her eyes. What home? Oh, she and Jenny were in Andy's house, but it wasn't her real home. Maybe Jenny wanted to go back to Charlotte and if she did, who could Sarah turn to then? And what about that Biddy? What if they never got her out of Glen Ellen? What did any of it matter anyway? God already knew all this and was probably making plans to call her up to heaven. Mummy and Daddy were bound to be missing her.

With her arms round her Paddington bear, she must have drifted off to sleep because when she opened her eyes, on the dresser opposite her bed were some pretty yellow chrysanthemums. They were the little kind, baby mums, mixed in with Baby's breath and looked so pretty in a green plastic vase. She picked up the seven or eight envelopes somebody had placed on the night table, then let them slip through her fingers. She would read them later when she wasn't so sleepy.

She looked toward the door as it slowly opened. Someone tall and golden glided toward her along the shaft of sunlight coming through the open door. She rose off the pillows. "Are you an angel?" she whispered, squinting her eyes, looking for the wings.

"Sarah, honey, it's me." Jenny's American voice was shaky but it was Jenny all right. "Here, let me put your glasses on."

Sarah saw Jenny more clearly now, enough to see the tears. "You glowed all over. I thought you'd come for me."

Jenny blew her nose with one hand and pulled over a chair with the other. "It was probably the light from the hall shining on this yellow outfit." After she'd settled herself in the chair, she leaned forward and took Sarah's hand. "There won't be any angels coming for you for a very long time."

"Were you frightened coming in? Did you whistle?"

"Yeah. Did 'Roll out the Barrel' twice, then got halfway through 'You Are My Sunshine.'" She plumped up Sarah's pillows and pulled the chair closer to the bed. "How's it going, pumpkin?"

"OK. I can't seem to stay awake. I keep nodding off."

"How about if I tell you a story? A very special story?"

"Is it true?"

"Yes, but it's not finished. What it needs is a real good ending."

Sarah tried to give a big brave smile. "I'm extra special at doing good endings."

"OK but I don't want you getting excited. Mr. Sidney said if you do, your blood pressure will shoot way up."

There was something about Jenny's face. "I knew it. I just knew it," Sarah said, her voice beginning to rise, as she pulled herself up on her elbows. "They've found me a kidney."

Jenny jumped up and closed the door. "Sarah, please, for cryin' out loud. Are you trying to get me thrown out?" She flopped back in the chair. "Now I'll count to ten real slow while you take deep breaths. Then I'll tell you a story about us. You, me, and our family."

Sarah leaned back on her pillows and took big deep breaths while Jenny counted. "Perhaps if you tell it like a fairy story. You know, once upon a time."

"If you like. Let's see now. Once upon a time, there was a young American girl who came to Stoney Beck. She was feeling kinda lonely and homesick until this real cute guy comes walking up."

"You should say American princess," Sarah said, already settling into the story. "And the boy is always handsome. He's called a Prince Charming. Did they fall in love?"

"They were crazy about each other, went everywhere together. One day they asked someone to take their picture, right outside the Hare and Hounds."

Sarah clutched Paddy to her chest. Something special was coming here. Jenny's voice had gone all breathless, as if she'd just run up the stairs.

"It was the same picture you showed to Father Woodleigh."

"You mean the one of him and Beverly?"

Jenny nodded. "She was the American princess and Father Woodleigh was her Prince Charming, except he wasn't a priest yet. Beverly called him Charles. They were in love but poor Beverly couldn't stay and when she went away, Charles was broken hearted. They never saw each other again. But Beverly never forgot Charles, her handsome Prince Charming, and he never forgot his beautiful American princess. Then one day—"

***

After Jenny had gone, Sarah sat the bear on her propped-up knees. She knew he wasn't real or anything but just had to tell someone. "Everything'll be all right now, Paddy. I've got a brand new daddy who loves me. There aren't many priest fathers. His kidney's bound to be blessed, sort of like a gift from God. I'm a very lucky girl."

When Jenny reached the waiting room, her father stood with his back to her, hands in his pockets, staring out the window. She put a hand on his arm. "You can go see her now."

That night when they left the hospital, Charles told Jenny he was driving back to St. Mary's and could he drop her off at her hotel. He pulled out his keys as they walked across the parking lot, rummaging through them, looking for the right one.

"Sarah said because I'm a priest, my kidneys are bound to be holy." He smiled as he rolled his eyes toward the heavens. "Her words, not mine."

"She's really something else isn't she," Jenny said, as they stood beside his car. "Can you believe someone like her could be so brave. I only wish I had her nerve."

Charles stopped and put his hands on her shoulders, his gaze locking with hers. "Yes, Sarah is something else as you put it, but courage takes many forms, Jenny. You helped take care of the only father you'd ever known, then watched him die in one of the worst ways. When you lost your mother so soon afterwards, your heart must have been close to breaking. Yet look what *you* did. You boarded a plane and came thousands of miles to a strange place with nothing but a half-finished note."

"It was my therapist's idea," Jenny said. "Uncle Tim was worried and to tell you the truth, I was too. But not now. I'm glad I came."

"So am I," Charles said. "So is Sarah. You've saved her life, you know." He waved his arm as Jenny opened her mouth to protest. "Oh, I'm giving her the kidney, but without you none of this was possible. Can you see that? Can you see how proud I am of you?"

And Jenny could see. His eyes shone and for the first time she saw a resemblance between him and herself. Her mouth was his mouth, the same full lips, the same square teeth. And there was that one dimple in the right cheek. Why hadn't she noticed it before? Without taking her gaze away from his face, she opened her bag and felt around for the book of sonnets. "You'll remember this," she said handing it to him. "Mom kept it hidden all those years and gave it to me right before—well, you know."

He stared at it as if it were a priceless volume, then ran a hand gently across the cover. "We read every poem in this book," he whispered thickly as he slowly turned the pages. "And to think she kept it all those years."

"She never forgot you any more than you forgot her," Jenny said.

He put a hand on her wrist. "Everything's going to be all right. You must believe that." He looked up at the sky. "Don't forget the Man upstairs. This is all part of His plan?"

A few minutes later, they pulled up outside her hotel.

"Goodnight, Father," she said as they shyly gave each other that longed for hug. "You be careful driving home now. It's a long way."

Chapter Twenty-seven

Since Sarah's first dialysis, Jenny's relationship with Mr. Sidney had improved. What impressed her most was his kindness toward her sister. Everybody loved a hero, the surgeon said, and it was well-nigh impossible not to wish Sarah well. He'd never known anyone try harder. And now, as Jenny reached the top of the hospital stairs, he was in the hall talking to a nurse. When he spotted Jenny, he motioned for her to stop, then excused himself from the nurse.

"We tried to contact you but you'd already left," he said. "We've brought the transplant forward to next Wednesday." He stood with his back to the window, the sun filtering through his pale wispy hair. Jenny wondered why she hadn't liked him before. He was strange looking all right but somehow, when you got to know him, it only added to his charm.

"Your father's a perfect match, an excellent donor. We've got Sarah stabilized, as good as she'll ever be. This is why we need to get on with it. There's an element of risk if we wait. Don't want to take a chance on her regressing." He gave a self-satisfied smile as he stuck his clipboard under his arm. "It took a bit of finagling to jump the queue for the operating theater but because a transplant is more cost-effective than dialysis, we finally got the go-ahead."

Jenny leaned against the wall and closed her eyes. "Does my father know? He didn't tell me."

"We didn't get in touch with him until just an hour ago. He probably tried to get you but you were probably already on your way."

Jenny called Walter's sister who ran the bed and breakfast, and asked for a room starting tomorrow. Gertrude Tillman said she had a nice en suite for thirty pounds a night, her best room with a lovely view of the park behind her house. Jenny said she'd take it and gave the woman her credit card number. It was half the price of the hotel and just one block further away. Not only that, with this one you got breakfast. She then drove to Stoney Beck making her first stop the Hare and Hounds. Walter rubbed his hands in that special way when she told him she'd reserved a room at his sister's place. Over a beer, she brought him up to date on the transplant. He said he'd put it on the notice board in the hall. The archeologists, especially, were always asking for the latest on Sarah.

After she left the inn, she pulled into Andy's garage. He put a finger under her chin and raised her face. "You look exhausted. If you don't give yourself a day off, you're not going to be any help to Sarah or your father." He looked up at the sky. "It's a nice day. How about putting your feet up for a few hours on the terrace. I'll make you a sandwich and get you something to drink."

He fixed a pillow at her back while Pete trotted over and stretched out beside her. She stroked his back, then rested her hand on his head.

When Andy came out with her snack, she was fast asleep. He stood holding the tray, looking down at her. Did she love him as much as he loved her? He had to admit his chances of her staying were looking better since Sarah and her father had come on the scene. He went inside and came back with a light blanket. "What are we going to do about her, Pete?" he whispered to his dog as he spread the blanket over her. "We can't let her get away."

When Jenny woke up, Ada and Walter were on the terrace, holding hands and talking softly to each other like a couple of love birds. At the same moment, Dr. Thorne came out of the house with Andy.

"Take a look at this," Dr. Thorne said to Jenny as he handed her the *Lakes Chronicle*.

"We've all seen it. Such a good human-interest story. It might even be picked up by the national papers. You're famous, Jenny."

She stared at the front page.

> *Father Charles Woodleigh, the priest at St. Mary's in Daytonwater, who discovered only recently he is the father of twin girls, one American and one English, has offered to donate a kidney to his English daughter who is suffering from kidney failure. The operation will take place in Manchester Royal Infirmary.*

On page six was the gist of the story, American girl looking for her roots, discovers she has English twin with Down syndrome and a father who is now a priest. Father Woodleigh had no idea he was the father of twins from a romance he had twenty-three years ago until his American daughter came to Mass at his church.

Jenny had held her breath so long, it came out in a rush. There were pictures of the priest, one of Sarah outside Malone's and another of Jenny on the bench outside the Hare and Hounds.

"I don't remember anybody taking this," she said.

"That's the media for you," Ada said, "but what are you worried about. You look like a million dollars."

Jenny laughed, looking at the picture again. "It isn't bad, is it."

"I'll scan it," Andy said, "and e-mail it to your Uncle Tim. Then I'll call Trudy's B&B and ask her to book me in for the night of the transplant. After that we'll see how it goes."

Chapter Twenty-eight

Sarah had her eyes on the ceiling as the trolley was wheeled through the double doors into the operating theater. She had the funniest feeling in her tummy, like little mice scurrying around in there. From the operating table, she looked around for her brand new father. She'd expected him to be right next to her, so they could lift the kidney out of him and put it into her. But he was nowhere to be seen. Mr. Sidney was there, came over, and smiled down at her.

When she told him about the mice, he gave her shoulder a nice comfy squeeze. "You're my little trooper, Sarah. When you wake up, those little devils will have packed their bags and scooted away." After he patted her hand, he turned to talk to one of the nurses. The room was just like he said it would be. Everybody had shower caps on their heads and masks hanging round their necks. They would put these over their mouths when the operation started so they wouldn't be breathing all their germs on the good kidney. A nice chubby nurse smiled at Sarah as she fiddled with the bag of clear fluid already dripping into her arm. A doctor leaned over her. It was Dr. Stardust, the man who had come into her room last night and told her he'd be here today to sprinkle stardust in her eyes and send her to dreamland.

"How's it going, Sarah? We don't see many people in here with a smile as big as yours."

She gave him an even bigger one. "It's just a pretend smile. I'm not very nervous though. Mr. Sidney said I'll be a million dollar baby when I wake up. Think he means because my father's a priest, his kidney's as good as gold."

"I'm sure you're right," Dr. Stardust said. "It'll be one of the best kidneys anyone could possibly get."

She glanced again around the room then back at him. "Where is my father? I thought you'd have put him here next to me. Wouldn't it be easier? You know, less steps when you take his kidney out and put it in me?"

"You've got a good point there. I'll discuss it with the others after you go to sleep."

"Please take care of him, Dr. Stardust," she said, a sudden unexpected tremble coming into her voice. "He's a very extra special sort of man."

Dr. Stardust had lovely kind eyes and one of the sweetest smiles she'd ever seen. She felt very safe with this man. He gave her hand a little comforting squeeze.

"And you're a very extra special sort of woman, Sarah."

She felt her eyes fill up and there was a thick feeling in her throat. He'd called her an extra special sort of *woman*. A *woman*, mind you. Nobody had ever called her that, not once in her whole life.

He leaned toward her left arm, ran his hand over the veins in the middle. "God Bless, Sarah. Sweet dreams."

"God Bless, Dr. Stardust. And the same to you."

***

In the half full waiting room, Andy and Jenny sat side by side on the sofa in the corner. He was getting a cramp in his shoulder but didn't dare move for fear of waking Jenny as she leaned against him. He looked down at her fingers, interlaced with his, and rubbed his chin gently across her silken hair while he let his mind wander. Just a few months ago she'd been thousands of miles away, without him even knowing she existed. As soon as she had stepped off that train and looked around, he knew. How had his life been before Jenny entered? He could hardly remember. Amazing.

Every now and then a doctor or nurse came to the waiting room doorway and beckoned to somebody or called out a name. The medical staff was always poker faced and it was hard to tell what the news was. Slowly the room emptied until Andy and Jenny were the only two left. Eventually, Mr. Sidney in a wrinkled hospital gown appeared in the doorway.

"Is it over?" Jenny asked.

He nodded and smiled a weary smile as he flopped down opposite to them, then scanned the sheets on his clipboard. The kidney had started kicking in right away and was already producing urine. Sarah was hooked up to a drip with an anti-rejection drug. If that one didn't work, there were others they could try. She'd have the catheter for a couple of days and then, if she continued to improve, it would be removed.

Jenny held on tight to Andy's hand and let out her breath in a long slow sigh. Maybe everything was going to be all right after all. "You mean she came through OK? No hitches?"

"None so far." He looked down at his notes, ran his pen along the lines. "Remember though, it's early days. Our main concern is will the body accept the kidney or reject it. So far it looks like a perfect match. The next few days are crucial though. If we can make it past the first fortnight, I'll have a better feel."

When the surgeon stood up to go, Andy and Jenny got up too.

"What about our father? How is he?"

"Somebody will be along soon to give you a report on him. As far as I know, everything went according to plan."

After he'd left the room, Jenny flung her arms round Andy's neck. "Can you believe it? Can you honestly believe it."

He nodded. "The success rate for kidney transplants these days is high. These guys know what they're doing."

When Mr. Valseaton, the priest's surgeon, arrived ten minutes later and said her father was also in recovery and doing well, relief slammed into Jenny and raced down her body, even to her toes.

"They'll both be in recovery for some time," the surgeon said. "I'd suggest you stretch your legs and come back in a couple of hours."

They thanked him and watched him march off down the hall. Jenny felt Andy's arms go round her, holding her tight like he never wanted to let her go.

"Come on," he said, "let's give Uncle Angus a ring. Then we'll ring your Uncle Tim. After that, well there's a deli round the corner where we can probably get a beer and a decent sandwich."

***

Sarah opened her eyes and looked at the drip going into her arm. She ran a hand gently over the bandages across her tummy. They'd gone ahead and done it all right.

She didn't know how long she slept but when a couple of nurses came into the room, it was already dark outside. One was tall and blonde, the other short with red hair. They each went to opposite sides of her bed and put their hands gently behind her back. "Sit up for us Sarah, there's a good girl."

"Did everything go OK?" Sarah asked as they eased her to a sitting position.

"Did it ever." The blonde nurse pointed to a bottle of liquid the color of apple juice on the little table. "That's all from you. A couple of liters already, and that's just for starters." She lifted up the plastic bag. "This is a catheter and it's inserted in your bladder. As long as you have this, all your urine goes into here. We'll probably be able to take it out in a couple of days. Then you can go to the toilet on your own."

The red-haired nurse reached for one of Sarah's pillows. "Do you think you could hold this against your stomach for us? Ah, that's a good girl. Now, could you cough?"

Sarah winced as the cough shot right down to the spot where her new kidney was. "Do it again, love," the nurse said. "We know it hurts but your lungs have to be kept clear. You don't want to get pneumonia do you?"

"No, but I don't want to hurt the kidney either."

"You won't. Now, just a couple more coughs, then you can go back to sleep."

After Sarah coughed twice, both the nurses fluffed her two pillows.

"How's my father?" she asked.

"Somebody will be here to speak to you. They'll tell you. Your father's on the floor above. His room's just about over this one."

"I hope they make him cough too. Don't want him getting pneumonia."

The red-headed one straightened the bedspread. "He's in good hands, same as you. We're very pleased with you, Sarah. You're a wonderful patient, a good brave girl. If you keep this up, you'll be on solid food in a day or two, probably soup and crackers."

The blonde nurse winked. "Maybe even some ice cream."

***

After Jenny had left a message for Bishop Vincent Fitzpatrick at the retreat giving him the good news, and after a visit to the hospital to see Sarah and Charles, she and Andy went back to Trudy's bed and breakfast. Walter had told Andy that his sister Trudy was as straight-laced as they come. But she didn't seem that way to Andy. She had given him and Jenny rooms next door to each other, with a connecting door between them. It was locked for sure, but the keys were in the locks. But Trudy was a talker and she cornered Andy, bombarding him with questions. What did he think about Walter planning to marry Ada Malone and was Andy going to their wedding? Trudy had heard they were going on their honeymoon to Provence, where that doctor friend of theirs had a house. Oh, the doctor was Andy's uncle. Well, fancy that.

By the time Andy got a chance to look around, Jenny had disappeared. Half an hour later, when he entered his own room, he immediately looked toward the connecting door but it was locked. He stood against it, knuckles poised to knock, then lowered his arm. She was worn out and needed the sleep. But it wasn't only that. Jenny was not the sort who took sex lightly. She was under enormous pressure and his heart ached for her. Even though she tried to hide it, sometimes he felt the tension radiating from her. When this was all over and things finally settled down, he would let her know he had loved her since that first moment he'd set eyes on her, looking all lost and worried at the railway station.

The next day, Andy went with Jenny to the hospital. When he saw that Sarah's second floor room looked down on the hospital's loading dock, he asked and was given permission for Jenny to come and go that way. Because their father's room was almost directly over Sarah's, all Jenny had to do was enter the back door, go up one flight of stairs, without having to navigate what to her was still a scary maze of corridors.

She went with him to his car. "I'll miss you, Andy," she said. "I don't know what I'd have done if you hadn't been with me."

"I'll come when I can," he said. "They're both doing great. This will all be behind you before you know it. Still, if there's the slightest hitch, I'm just as close as the phone. I can be here in a couple of hours."

The first person Jenny called was the bishop. "The prayers worked," she said, hesitating on her form of address. Was a bishop called *Father* or perhaps something more exalted? To be on the safe side and trying hard not to offend, she called him Reverend. He asked her if she'd called Father Doyle at St. Mary's and when she said she hadn't, he said he would do it.

Ten days after the operation, as Jenny headed up the back stairs, she remembered Andy's words. And he had been so right. There had not been one single hitch. Their father was already walking up and down the halls. He was in and out of Sarah's room, and had even taught Jenny how to play chess. Andy said it was as though they had taken out his appendix instead of something as vital as his kidney. Andy had stayed at Trudy's a couple of nights. Unable to get the room next to Jenny's, he'd stayed in the floor above.

Mr. Sidney told Jenny, in the presence of Sarah, that Sarah's body had accepted the transplanted kidney like a welcome relative come to stay. And why shouldn't it, Sarah had said. Wasn't her father's kidney just about the best relative you could have. Mr. Sidney agreed and said you couldn't get much closer than that. Her temperature was normal, she ate everything on her plate, and the yellow pallor had almost gone from her face. If she kept this up, Mr. Sidney said, she would be discharged any day.

Jenny spent less time at the hospital and once had even gone for lunch and a movie with Andy. Sometimes she wandered around Manchester's shopping district. On the day she bought Sarah a new blouse, she carried it into the hospital, longing to show it to her. She took the stairs two at a time to the second floor, which the English insisted was the first. She fingered Sarah's earrings in her pocket. She'd had a jeweler change the metal inserts for 14-carat gold as a safeguard against infection. Lottie need never know and Sarah was sure to be pleased.

Jenny peeped around Sarah's half-open door and saw she was asleep, Paddy clutched to her chest. Jenny placed the blouse on the chair in the corner, and then scampered up the stairs to her father's room. She came to a full stop outside his door and stared at the sign hanging there. In big bold three-inch letters, it read *NO VISITORS*.

Chapter Twenty-nine

Jenny dug her nails into her palms, as she stared at the two words. At the starched swish of a nurse's uniform, she whirled around. It was Nurse Ramirez from Jamaica whom Jenny thought beautiful and the friendliest of all the staff.

She tapped the sign with the knuckle of her index finger. "What does this mean? No visitors. Is everything OK?"

The usual twinkle wasn't in the nurse's eyes and Jenny didn't like the serious set of her mouth. "We phoned you but nobody answered," she said in her Calypso accent, usually so upbeat, but saturated now with apprehension. "Mr. Valseaton's on his way." She looked toward the lift as the door slid open. "Here he comes now."

Jenny and the nurse stood back as the surgeon, with barely a look at them, swept past and strode to the nurses' station.

"If you'll take a seat in the waiting room, we'll get back with you," the nurse said before hurrying after him.

But Jenny leaned against the wall outside her father's door and stared as the nurse and surgeon talked in hushed whispers just a few yards away. Had her father had a heart attack? A stroke? As the surgeon stuck his pen in his breast pocket, he marched toward her. She opened her mouth to speak, but his raised hand stopped her.

"Not now," he said, in a voice used to being obeyed.

He pushed the door open and went in, followed by the nurse. Jenny craned her neck to catch a glimpse of her father, but the door swished closed behind them. She tottered into the waiting room and flopped in a chair nearest the door. About ten other people sat around the room. One man, asleep in the corner, snored softly, some read magazines, others stared at the walls or the floor. A man and woman in the corner talked in whispers. The woman was crying.

When the dizziness finally eased, Jenny folded her arms and stared through the open door, desperate to talk to the doctor, yet dreading what he might say. There was a clock on the wall opposite and she stared at the second hand as it jerked itself around. One minute, five, fifteen, then half an hour. People left the waiting room and others came, some looked as worried as she obviously did, while others seemed ready to drop from fatigue. Then there were the lucky few with big smiles all over their faces.

Jenny pulled out a tissue and wiped the perspiration from her upper lip as she looked back over the last couple of weeks. Even with all the euphoria, somewhere deep down inside her, there'd always been a trace of unease. And now she knew why. It had all been too easy, just too damn easy. As pins and needles raced up and down her arms, she got to her feet and walked to the window. There was the blue Ford just below, ready for a fast retreat. She went into the hall, walked to the top of the stairs, hand on the rail, looking down to the door, to the way out. How easy it would be to tear down the stairs, jump in the car and drive away. She paced up and down the hall, until Mr. Valseaton finally came out of her father's room and beckoned to her.

He opened a door across the hall and ushered her in. It was a small conference room, with a table in the center and eight or ten chairs around. On the wall opposite was a picture at least forty years old of the queen and Prince Phillip. The queen was young and pretty, and Phillip, good-looking and knowing it in his naval officer's uniform, stood beside her chair. Both were smiling, so sure of themselves, so plainly unaware of the hard road up ahead.

The surgeon motioned to her to sit as he pulled out a chair for himself on the opposite side of the table. He opened the file in front of him, put on his glasses, and scratched the side of his nose. "During the night your father developed an infection." He didn't meet her eyes. Instead he stared at the notes in the file.

A thud started deep in Jenny's chest. "An infection?"

"His temperature's risen to thirty-seven."

"I don't know centigrade. What's that in Fahrenheit?"

The doctor didn't even have to work it out. "One hundred and four."

Jenny kept her hands clasped together under the table to keep herself from grabbing hold of the man's sleeve, or maybe even his throat. "How could he have gotten an infection?" she said, in a strange high-pitched voice, not like her own voice at all. "He passed all the tests and his health was good. He told me so himself, said he's never had a sick day in his life."

The man doodled rectangles and circles on the file's inside cover, then looked up, his nervous fingers clicking away at his pen. "Even though every precaution is taken during an operation, there's always the danger something can go wrong. We're moving him into intensive care."

All he had to offer was the usual stuff. Everything possible was being done. But Jenny wasn't fooled. Intensive care was for the critically ill.

The surgeon closed the file, checking his watch as he got to his feet. He was saying as little as possible, the same as the doctors in Charlotte, probably the world over. She could almost hear Uncle Tim's voice. This man was covering his ass.

Jenny held onto the banister as she made her way down the stairs, past Sarah's floor, down to the floor below, to the way out. Forty-five minutes ago, she had bounced up these same stairs. Hard to believe. In less than an hour she had aged twenty years. She pushed open the exit door and leaned against the outside wall before heading for her car. She opened the door and collapsed on the seat, her car keys in her hand, then leaned her head on the steering wheel. Finally she fastened her seat belt, put the car in gear, and was about to back out when she looked up at Sarah's window. Her sister's stricken face looked down at her, while she motioned for Jenny to come back. Jenny wanted to stick her head out the window and scream *no way*. Instead she looked behind her as she backed out and headed for the street.

She drove for a half hour before pulling into a tea shop. The waitress led her to a seat by the window. Coffee, just coffee, Jenny said, then watched the dowdy people bundled up in the chill late summer rain as they hurried along the dreary Manchester Street. Just a couple of days ago, she and Sarah had sat in their father's room, playing Snap, a children's card game which Sarah loved, and because she was having fun, Jenny and their father enjoyed it too. From all his get-well cards, he had singled out Uncle Tim's and shown it to them. Sarah had laughed and said she'd got one too. All those who came to visit said wasn't it amazing how smoothly everything had gone without a single hitch.

How quickly the breeze had shifted. Sarah had a new kidney all right, but at what expense? Her father's life? And where was the guarantee Sarah would make it? She hadn't rejected the kidney yet but what about next week, next month, next year even? What if they both died?

If Jenny hadn't come to England, the priest would be contented and unaware, the way she'd seen him that first Sunday in St. Mary's. Sarah could probably have lived for years on dialysis. And it was a sure bet Biddy would have been made to leave Glen Ellen. Surely a couple, a perfect man and wife team, could have been found to live with Sarah. They'd have all gotten along just fine without Jenny. Why had she ever thought they wouldn't?

She was finishing her third cup of coffee when she heard the small voice inside her head. What good would running away do? Wouldn't it break her sister's heart? What if her father woke up and called for her? What if he was lucid right to the very end and she wasn't there? She picked up the check the waitress had left on the table, and now, suddenly so anxious to be gone there was no time to give the waitress the money, Jenny placed a five pound note on the bill and almost ran out the door. Back at the hospital, she parked in her usual place, jumped out of the car, and dashed up the stairs to Sarah's room. A nurse met her at the door. Mr. Sidney had told Sarah about her father's condition and ordered her a mild tranquilizer. She wasn't asleep but the nurse made it clear there was to be no excitement.

When Jenny pushed open the door, Sarah rose and stretched out her arms. They clung to each other, each murmuring comforting words, patting each other's back.

Sarah was the first to pull away and wipe her eyes. "We'd better not let him see us cry," she said. "We'll have to put on big smiley faces. And anyway, 'tensive care doesn't always mean you die. Dr. Thorne was in there and he didn't die."

"I didn't know that," Jenny said, picking up some of Sarah's caring yet calm tone. "What was wrong with him?"

"His heart. The doctors took it out and held it in their hands." Sarah cupped her hands and stared down at them, as if seeing the very heart. "They did something to it then stuck it back in."

Jenny shuddered. "Oh, wow. How long ago was that?"

"Donkey's years. But look at him now. He's got one of the kindest, biggest hearts in all of England."

Jenny rang Andy on his cell phone. Until that moment she hadn't known for sure how much she really cared for him, but knew now she wanted him near her more than anybody else in the whole world.

"Please come, Andy," she said. "I know Alf's not there, but I need you."

"Hang on, love," Andy said. "I'll be there soon as I can. See if you can get me in at Trudy's."

"Yes, OK. But please hurry."

The next person she called was the bishop. Even as she listened to the ringing, waiting for him to pick up, it hit her why he hadn't visited her father, why there'd been just that one call. Bishop Fitzpatrick didn't approve and this had to be the reason why her father hadn't said much about the man. He hadn't wanted to worry her. Any ordinary good bishop would have been there already. Her father had made a great sacrifice for a daughter he hardly knew. Who did this bishop think he was to pass judgment?

"Bishop Fitzpatrick," came the stern voice down the line.

"This is Jenny, Father Woodleigh's daughter. My father's been moved into intensive care. There's an infection of some sort and he's listed as critical. Perhaps you could come." She felt herself beginning to babble, and before the bishop could even answer, she hung up, then closed her eyes, and leaned against the wall. What he would think of her, she didn't know and didn't care. But if he didn't come soon, she could call her father's friend, that priest at St. Anne's here in Manchester, or maybe Father Doyle in Daytonwater.

She returned to Sarah's room and found her asleep holding onto her Paddington bear. The tranquilizer had taken effect. Jenny put her hand on her sister's forehead. It felt cool, but she asked the nurse to check her temperature to be sure. It was normal, the nurse said, no sign of fever or rejection, and yes, she should be discharged any day now.

Jenny went into intensive care twice while she waited for Andy. Her father looked pale and gaunt, his eyes closed. He had an IV in his arm and an oxygen tube in his nose. She sat in the waiting room alone until Andy walked through the door. He opened his arms wide and she walked into them. "I'd have been here sooner," he said, "but there was a holdup on the M-6."

Late that night, while Sarah was asleep, Mr. Valseaton came into the waiting room and whispered to them it might be wise to call another priest or perhaps a bishop to perform the last rites. As the surgeon got to his feet, Bishop Fitzpatrick walked into the room.

Charles had been drifting in and out of sleep. Sometimes he'd wake while they were taking his temperature, checking his IV drip. His brain was fuzzy, probably from the medication, but he was alert enough to know he was in intensive care. He was in no pain, just a sense of slipping, of the bed moving around as if it were one of those waterbeds.

Through a haze, he saw Jenny and Sarah walk toward him. Sarah leaned on Jenny's arm and he watched Jenny ease her into a chair then pull up the other chair for herself. They held hands and spoke to each other in hushed whispers, turned to look at him from time to time, then back to each other to whisper again. He longed to tell Sarah how proud he was she'd been so brave, but he was just too tired.

The next time he opened his eyes, his bishop, Vincent Fitzpatrick, was in the room, stole already across his shoulders. When he leaned over him, Charles nodded to let him know he was aware he was dying. His bishop pressed his hand gently and turned to the girls. While they talked, Charles closed his eyes and delved into the ragbag of the years, searching for something new to cling to. All he could dredge up were the same well-worn but priceless memories. He stood now on the wall that spanned the brook, poetry book in front of him, hamming it up as he read "How Do I Love Thee?" Beverly laughed up at him, then he watched her rise into the air and fly away, still laughing. He called for her to come down, but she disappeared into the mist.

The scene shifted to St. Mary's. He was at the lectern staring down at the largest congregation he'd ever had. The boys choir was singing "I Wanna Hold your Hand," while Jenny and Sarah, dressed all in white, carried bouquets of pink tea roses and danced down the aisle toward him. When they reached him, they raised their hands toward him and the congregation clapped.

He opened his eyes and was once more back in hospital. The bishop was telling his girls something, moving his arms, explaining. Something inside Charles swelled. The bishop liked them, Charles could tell. These girls were his own flesh and blood, his very own family. The tall, beautiful Jenny, so like her mother, and the gentle, vulnerable, yet so brave Sarah. He'd known them hardly more than a few weeks yet there was this great love. He blinked and felt tears slide out of the corners of his eyes across his temples onto the pillow.

"Come closer," he whispered, "so I can see you."

Together they stood beside his bed. "We both love you so much," Jenny said. "We're so glad we found each other."

"At the rectory, a suitcase, odds and ends. The poetry book and snapshot." He wanted to tell her there were two photos, almost identical, and to give one to Sarah, but he couldn't get the words out.

"I wish I could give you your kidney back," Sarah said, banging her fist on her knee. "That dialing machine wasn't so bad."

Even now he felt his lips curl in a semblance of a smile. Sarah had never been able to say dialysis. "For you—all my love," he murmured, his voice dry and cracked.

He watched as his bishop made preparations for the Sacrament, whispered something to the girls. They moved to the bottom of the bed, while he adjusted his stole with one hand and held the Ritual in his other. Jenny closed her eyes and bowed her head, while Sarah put the palms of her hands together under her chin, squeezed her eyes shut and raised her head.

Charles had delivered his share of the Sacrament over the years and now it was his turn. While Vincent Fitzpatrick read from the Ritual, Charles closed his eyes and prayed harder than he'd ever prayed before. Not for himself but for his girls. He prayed for them to be happy, to find solace in each other. He already knew them so well, enough to know they both had absurd guilt feelings. Sarah because she would blame his death on the transplant, and Jenny who would blame everything on herself for coming to England in the first place.

After the Sacrament, Charles opened his eyes and blinked his thanks to the bishop. Vincent Fitzpatrick nodded, a gentle, sad smile hovering round his mouth. Sarah and Jenny moved back to the side of Charles's bed and he stretched a hand toward them. As they both held on, he took a deep breath and let it out in a long slow sigh. The very act surprised him. It was a good breath without the drag he'd needed before. It was as if he could have done it on his own without the oxygen. And it hadn't hurt. Cautiously, he took another, and it didn't hurt either.

He saw his bishop bend forward, look into his eyes, then turn to whisper something to Jenny and Sarah. Charles tried to smile and didn't know if he'd made it. His eyelids grew heavier as he felt himself being pulled toward sleep.

Jenny watched her father take those breaths before he fell asleep. Without taking her gaze away from him, she spoke softly to the bishop. "Did he—does he sound to you as if he's breathing just a tad easier?"

"I'm not sure," Vincent Fitzpatrick said, his voice tight. "Perhaps it does seem so. Yes, I do believe you're right." He turned again to Jenny and reached for her hand.

They watched while a nurse came in and took his temperature, then looked at her watch as she checked his pulse.

"I need to get the doctor," she said. "Excuse me."

Within five minutes, a woman doctor Jenny had never seen before came in and asked them to wait outside the intensive care unit. Andy was there and when Jenny and Sarah went to him, he opened his arms wide and held them close.

Five minutes later the doctor came out, a cautious smile on her face. "His temperature's dropped. Down almost a degree. Let's not be too optimistic, yet it does seem—" She had an Irish brogue, which sounded suddenly to Jenny's ears, like tinkling bells.

Hours later, long after Sarah had gone to sleep, and Bishop Fitzpatrick had returned to his hotel, a weary Mr. Valseaton told Jenny and Andy the priest's temperature had dropped another half a degree.

"Sometimes these things are false alarms," he said. "So we have to view them with caution. We have him on a brand new antibiotic and there is a slight improvement. His breathing's not so labored. He should sleep now and it might be a good time for you to catch a few hours yourselves. You're close to the hospital and we have your phone number."

There was something about his face, something in his eyes. Jenny clung to Andy's arm to stop herself from reaching for the surgeon and hugging the life out of him, the very same doctor she had been ready to throttle a couple of days ago.

Back in the bed and breakfast, they sat in the little sitting room. "He's going to make it, Andy," she said as they drank hot chocolate Andy had made with ingredients on the tray in his room. "I've never been more sure of anything in my life."

Andy took the cup out of her hand and placed it on the table beside his own. "I think you're right," he said, as he traced a finger across her lips and then took her in his arms.

When they pulled away, Jenny saw the look of desire showing plainly in his eyes. "Andy, I can't. Not now. Not like this."

He kissed her on her forehead. "It's OK. Don't worry about it."

At six o'clock the next morning, Jenny called the hospital. Father Woodleigh had spent a comfortable night, the nurse said. Jenny closed her eyes and sent up a prayer, then put the phone back in its cradle. Even though information from the nurses' desk was usually non-committal, the word *comfortable* jumped right out. A comfortable night, mind you, not a restless one.

When she and Andy arrived at the hospital an hour later, the doctor told them Father Woodleigh had turned the corner. The crisis was over. They called Bishop Fitzpatrick who said God had answered their prayers and he would come to visit Father Woodleigh within a couple of days. That very afternoon, the priest was moved out of intensive care back to the room he'd had before.

Two days later, while Sarah read by the window and Jenny and their father were back to playing chess, Mr. Sidney walked in and said Sarah was to be discharged tomorrow. He shook hands with Charles, called him *Father*, and wished all of them the best of luck.

After the surgeon had gone, Jenny turned to her father. "I couldn't stand that man at first. Guess a lot of it was me being worried. He's real nice when you get to know him."

Like a physical thing, Jenny felt the load rise from her shoulders. Her father and sister were going to be all right and she, all of a sudden, had this urge to be with Andy, to feel his arms around her. She phoned Trudy to say she was returning to Stoney Beck that night and would be back tomorrow to settle her bill.

Chapter Thirty

Biddy sat at the kitchen table, a glass of neat gin in her hand, while she listened to the rain pelt against the window. She thought back to the night she'd stopped outside Ferguson's garage and put the fear of God in that girl. That was ages ago and she hadn't been out of the house since. Even though Angus Thorne had told her he'd have someone chop the tree down, nothing had been done. The milkman came every day as usual and left bread, milk, eggs, cheese, so Biddy wasn't hungry. Desperate for cigarettes, she had called to one of the young boys passing the house and offered him a pound if he would bring her a couple of cartons. Now though, she was down to her last pack, as well as her last half-bottle of gin.

The Social Services had come to the house a couple of times, but Biddy hadn't answered the door. Instead she had shook her fist and yelled at them to go away. She wasn't letting them in the house ever again. No telling what they had in mind. That old bugger Thorne had come too, shouted through the letterbox that Sarah was about to be discharged and if Biddy didn't at least open the door to discuss the matter, the authorities would have no alternative but to break the door down. Biddy hadn't answered, just hoped he'd stand there long enough for the tree to grab him. It could move around more now and sometimes was so close to the house, Biddy could hear its branches scraping against the windows. It had made her a prisoner in her own home.

She couldn't keep up with time any more and sometimes night blended into day. She placed the cigarette ends around the edge of the huge ashtray to form a circle, then ran her finger through the ash, making a face, using the leftover cigarette butts for the mouth and nose.

She peered at the closed curtains, checking for chinks. Even though Fred and Edna were spirits, it didn't mean they had the power to see through the house's brick wall or even the kitchen curtain. Biddy knew all about spirits. Most of them were confined to one place, a house perhaps, or a bend in the road where a car had skidded out of control. Or maybe a moor, where someone had fallen off a horse. Then there were the other kind, the spirits that returned to their home, even though they'd died somewhere else. Edna and Fred Fitzgerald belonged to this group.

Ever since Biddy had first suspected they were in the tree, she had been baffled as to how they'd had the power to make that incredible leap from a mountain road in the Pyrenees, to Stoney Beck, and yet land twenty-five feet short of their goal, in a tree of all places. Then one day it hit her. They'd done it deliberately, afraid if lightning hit the house, it would have started a fire, perhaps even killed their precious Sarah. Biddy once thought Fred and Edna were doomed to dwell in the tree for eternity. Then came the day when she'd noticed the tree was at least a foot closer to the house than it used to be. She'd almost wet her pants, and shaking all over, she'd dragged Sarah outside to show her. But Sarah had just gaped at Biddy, and even had the nerve to say Biddy was seeing things. Biddy could have explained about cosmic energy in the spirit world but Sarah would never have understood. Biddy understood though and it was only a matter of time before Fred and Edna moved the tree close enough to poke a limb through a window. Then they would come zooming in.

Biddy now knew it was Fred and Edna who had sent the worms to torment her. Sometimes the slimy things came in droves, even slithering up close and eyeballing her with their little beady pink eyes. She'd clap her hands and the worms would vanish. But they always came back, crawling all over her pillow or squirming around inside the toilet.

She lit a cigarette and leaned back in her chair as she watched a cockroach crawl across the floor and disappear behind the can of petrol she'd brought into the house. All day, she'd been trying to get up the nerve to go outside and soak the tree with petrol, and then set it alight. Surely even spirits couldn't survive that. But Biddy hadn't counted on the rain. It had started about an hour ago, lightly at first then turning into a downpour, ruining any hope of setting the tree on fire. She leaned against the kitchen counter and pounded her fists into the Formica. If only she could drum up the courage to go outside, walk through the rain to the tree, and explain things, surely they'd be grateful. Perhaps they would even show themselves. If they did, Biddy would tell them that Sarah's real father wasn't Beverly's American boyfriend as they had always thought. Instead he was a randy English priest from the next village. Confined as they were up there in that tree, they had no way of knowing that this girl who had come to the house those few times was Sarah's long-lost twin. But the Fitzgeralds had surely seen Angus Thorne and his toffee-nosed nephew drag Sarah out of the house, shove her in the car then drive off with her. And now, with their x-ray eyes, they were watching, waiting for her to come back. Surely if Biddy braved the thunder and lightning and all the soaking rain, they would appreciate her efforts. All she had to do was gain their confidence. Then maybe in a couple of days, when the tree had dried, and they were least expecting it, she'd go outside again but this time she'd take the can of petrol with her.

She got to her feet and tried to ignore the undulation of the kitchen walls, in and out, in and out, keeping time with her thumping heart. It grew louder, stronger, until it throbbed in her ears. She picked up the portable phone on her way to the fridge, then ran her finger down the list of phone numbers on the scrap of paper Sarah had shoved under the magnet. Here it was, Angus Thorne. She punched in the numbers.

"Hello," came the sleepy voice which told Biddy the doctor had already retired for the night.

"Did I wake you?"

"What is it, Biddy?"

"I'm wondering what you think Fred and Edna will say when I tell them Beverly was screwing around with an honest-to-God practicing Roman Catholic priest. What are they going to think when I tell them he's Sarah's father?"

Angus Thorne sat up straight in his bed clutching the phone. "You've said this sort of thing before, Biddy, so let me spell it out again. Fred and Edna are not living in that tree. They died two years ago, so why don't you do them a favor and let them rest in peace."

"You think I'm losing my mind don't you, but it's you. You're the crazy one."

Angus stared into the mouthpiece as he heard Biddy slam down the phone, then came the dial tone. Just before she'd hung up, she'd laughed, a mad bray of a laugh.

He replaced the receiver in its cradle. First thing tomorrow he'd get on the phone to Jonathon and the Social Services. This had all dragged on far too long. Biddy Biggerstaff was plainly deranged and if something wasn't done immediately, she might be capable of doing herself harm, or, God forbid, harming Sarah or Jenny. He thumped his pillow and turned out the light.

***

Biddy couldn't stop giggling as she dropped the phone on the counter. Suddenly she felt in control, the way she used to before that girl came to the village. Even the walls had stopped their pulsating. Still, she began to shiver. The scariest part still lay ahead. It was time to tell Fred and Edna. She had never actually seen them in the tree. They were too shrewd for that. But sometimes, mostly at night, when she opened the kitchen door, she heard the jangle of the charm bracelet Edna always wore. Sarah stood beside her and when Biddy asked if she heard the clink of her mother's bracelet, the girl gave Biddy a wide-eyed look as if she was the loony one instead of the other way round. Even though Biddy had heard the sound many times since, she had never mentioned it to Sarah again.

Now, with one quick tug, she opened the curtains and stared at the rain lashing sideways against the windows. For the first time in ages, she forced herself to look at the tree. Not sure how Fred and Edna would react, Biddy picked up a tea towel and smiled as she waved it over her head. There was no answering sign from the tree, but they were there all right, probably peeping through those holes that Sarah said were squirrels' nests. Biddy opened the pantry door wide so Fred could see her lift his old yellow mackintosh off the nail behind the door. He'd always thought a lot of the tattered old thing and would appreciate her taking care of it. She put it on slowly, looked toward the window, and gave another wave. Then she laughed for Fred's benefit as she looked down at the mac nearly touching the floor. Far too long for her, the laugh said, but not to worry. She lifted her walking stick off its hook, then opened the back door and stepped out into the teeming rain.

Once outside, Biddy was glad of the stick. In between the forked lightning flashes it was pitch black and the grass was slippery underfoot. She half turned to go back and switch on the outside lights, or at least get a torch, but if she did, she'd give herself away. Edna and Fred would know she was terrified. Rain lashed against her and the wind whipped the mac as lightning zigzagged across the sky followed by roll after roll of thunder. The tree, with its bleached dead bark, leaned toward her. Its huge limbs, at least fifteen of them, all had small dead branches at the end, sticking out like skeleton's fingers, flexing like real hands.

Leaning on her stick, she stumbled along on jelly legs, her heart banging against her ribs, until she stood about twelve feet from the tree's massive trunk. For the first time, even in all this wind and rain, she got a whiff of Edna's favorite perfume, a sickly smell of flowers that had always reminded Biddy of a funeral. She tried to look up but the rain beat down on her glasses blurring her vision, plastering her hair against her head.

"Beverly told us a pack of lies," she screamed into the wind. "There was no American fiancé. Sarah's father's a priest."

Over the din of the storm, Biddy heard the sighing. *Sarah, Sarah.* That's all. Just Sarah over and over. The dead branches swayed from side to side. Those unseen leaves rustled about Biddy, behind as well as in front, the fingered limbs stretching toward her, swiping across her face.

She wanted to brush them away but the howling wind was so strong, if she took even one hand off her walking stick she'd lose her balance and fall.

Her quaking wet hands pressed on the stick as she struggled to stand upright, and strove to raise her head. She saw him then, standing in the fork of the tree. If it hadn't been for his green anorak she would never have recognized him. A cold awful dread clutched at Biddy's vitals. She had expected the handsome, laughing Fred, as he was before the wreck. But this hideous apparition had half his face torn away, with one eye hanging out of its socket on his blood soaked cheek. His head leaned crazily to one side as he pointed a finger at her. And suddenly Edna was there too, perched on a lower branch. At least Biddy thought it was Edna because she recognized the pale blue suit. Otherwise she wouldn't have known because the disgusting thing had no head. Biddy had heard Edna was decapitated in the wreck but had almost forgotten it until now.

Biddy's chest felt as if a huge bird was in there, banging its wings against her ribcage. She bent her head and pressed all her weight on her stick. Yet the harder she tried to get away, back to the safety of the house, the more she felt herself being dragged down, as if the very ground was sucking her in.

The lightning forked again, and this time there was the same sort of splintering crack she'd heard when the tree was struck two years ago. She pressed hard on her stick, trying to get a foothold. And now another sound, a crunching, accompanied by a chattering. The grisly things had come down from the tree and were walking on the gravel very close to her, carrying a light of their own. She saw them then. At least she saw Fred's feet. She closed her eyes as his horrible dead hands grabbed hold of her, pulling her from each side, tearing her to pieces.

***

As Jenny drove north on the M-6, she switched on the radio and flipped from station to station, searching for something light. When she heard Glen Campbell singing "Southern Nights," she took her hand off the dial, remembering other summers in Charlotte. How, as children, she and her friends watched for the first lightning bugs and how they'd run with their jars trying to catch them. Before her Dad had gotten sick and her Mother knew what a bad nerve was, they would pile in the car and drive to Uncle Tim's place on the lake. Jenny, as a teenager, spent hours water skiing with her friends while Dad or Uncle Tim pulled the boat. Then after sunset, before night set in, there was that deep purple of the sky, when the grownups would each have a beer while she and her friends drank Pepsi. The grill was fired up for hot dogs and hamburgers, while Mom tossed a salad or made slaw. Those were the good times.

As the song ended, and the first drops of rain began to fall, Jenny switched on the windshield wipers. Within minutes, she was in the middle of a violent late summer storm.

She came off the motor way and slowed her speed to twenty. Driving conditions were bad enough on the highway but especially hazardous as she maneuvered the narrow, inky country lane.

She looked to the left as she passed Glen Ellen. The blinding quicksilver flash lit up the house and the massive dead tree out front. She glanced in the rear view mirror before slowing the car to a crawl. She wasn't imagining it. Somebody was actually standing under the tree. She turned into the drive and eased the car toward the house, the tree directly in her headlights. She came to a stop close to the tree, left her lights on high beam, then bent her head into the wind and rain as she dashed across the gravel.

"Why are you out here?" she shouted at Biddy.

Her words were blown away by the howling wind.

She grabbed Biddy's arm. "It's dangerous under this tree. You could get struck."

Biddy beat her fists against Jenny's chest, at the same time screaming at her to stop pulling her into the ground, that she didn't want to be buried alive. Jenny saw the problem straightaway. Biddy's cane was caught in the hem of her raincoat and the more she leaned on the cane to pull herself up, the deeper she shoved the coat into the sodden ground. Jenny yanked on the cane and pulled it free, causing Biddy to lose her balance and fall against her.

Biddy's hair had come loose from its bun and hung in wet strands on her shoulders. Her face was ashen, her eyes wide with terror, telling Jenny the woman wasn't seeing her but someone or something else. Still shrieking and flailing her arms, her claw of a hand came within an inch of Jenny's eyes. Biddy was a small woman compared to Jenny but shoved with the strength of a big man, sending Jenny sprawling onto the bench under the tree.

She watched Biddy lurch toward the house, scramble up the back steps on her hands and knees, then stagger inside and slam the door.

For a couple of minutes, Jenny leaned her back against the bench, shivering. Then, suddenly petrified Biddy might open the door and come after her with God knows what, she made a run for the car. She fell onto the front seat, locked the doors, and picked up the cellular phone. With a trembling finger poised over that first button, she hesitated. Bad as all this was, did it really warrant dragging Andy, or his uncle, or Dr. Hall out of bed in the middle of a night such as this? In North Carolina it would be unheard of. Surely the woman was safe in the house from whatever terror she thought was in the yard. Jenny would call Dr. Thorne in the morning. He would then call Dr. Hall and between them they could decide what to do. She lowered the phone onto the car seat and turned the key, then drove slowly round Glen Ellen's circular drive and headed down Vallhellyn Lane toward Stoney Beck.

At the intersection of Market Street, she turned left toward Andy's house. The lights were on and all she wanted was for him to take her in his arms and hold her until she stopped shaking. She parked her car next to his van then dashed through the pouring rain up the path. Although she had a key, she banged on the door until he opened it.

She wasn't prepared for his open-mouthed look of surprise. "Jenny, what in the hell— You're wet through."

She looked down at her soaking clothes, ran her hand through her sopping hair. Then, like a child she let him take her hand and lead her upstairs. While she shivered and stuttered her way through her skirmish with Biddy in the storm, Andy gently removed her wet clothes, wrapped his terry cloth robe around her, and ushered her into the bathroom to take a hot shower. When she came out, he rubbed her dry with a huge warm towel, even blow-dried her hair. Finally, he carried her to his bed, the covers already turned down. He climbed in beside her, and pulled her to him, shushing her with his mouth on hers when she tried to tell him the rest of the story. She was safe now, he said, nothing mattered at this moment, nothing but the two of them all alone.

***

Biddy came round and found herself on the kitchen floor, her back propped up against the door. She couldn't see the cuckoo clock, had no idea what time it was or how long she'd been out. As if it read her thoughts, the damn bird shot out and cuckooed once. It had been eleven o'clock when she'd gone out in the storm. Two hours ago. She cowered down lower. If she lived to be a thousand she'd never forget the sight of Fred and Edna in that tree. She could still feel Fred's awful dead hands as they grabbed her. God alone knew what he would have done if she hadn't broken free and beat him to the house.

But a small thing like a locked door wasn't going to keep those two out now. Could they already be inside, hiding, watching her lying there? She raised her head and looked across the kitchen into the hall. Was that scratching, chattering sound coming from the lounge? She stretched her stiff arms above her head, grabbed hold of the doorknob, and cried out from the pain that shot through her legs as she struggled to stand.

On her feet at last, her chest heaving, she slung off Fred's mac and hobbled to the table. She seized a book of matches and shoved them into her pocket before reaching for the can of petrol she'd placed near the table leg. With the heavy can weighing her down, she stumbled out of the kitchen and across the hall to the lounge.

The strange sound was louder now and coming from the fireplace. She squinched her eyes almost shut and with all the concentration she could muster, stared at the wall over the mantelpiece. The bricks became glass and Biddy screamed at the sight of Fred struggling in the chimney breast, a foot or two below the headless Edna, holding onto her hand, guiding her as they made their way down the chimney. If they had heard Biddy's screams, they weren't letting on.

Because of her trembling hands, it took her ages to unscrew the cap on the petrol can, but at last it gave. She tossed the cap away and weaved across the tilting room, her gaze lowered, too terrified to glance again at the fireplace or the wall over it. Just a few steps away from the hearth, she slung half the can's contents on the chimney wall and the surrounding carpet, then as she backed out of the study, sloshed the rest on the furniture, the floor in the hall, then halfway up the stairs until the can was empty.

Panting from the effort, she leaned against the kitchen doorpost. The worst was over. Surely not even Fred and Edna could survive what Biddy was about to do. Ever since they'd died she'd practically worked herself to death taking care of this house. She'd done her best for Sarah too. But in spite of everything, nobody cared, and none of it mattered any more. She'd make them pay though and at the same time make sure the American bitch didn't get her hands on this house. Biddy smiled as she reached in her pocket for the matches. In another second or two, Glen Ellen would go up in smoke.

Chapter Thirty-one

When Jenny opened her eyes, Andy stood beside the bed looking down at her, a mug of tea in his hand. He placed the mug on the night table, then sat on the side of the bed and pulled her to him, while she struggled to keep the sheet up over her naked breasts, blushing as she leaned against his shirt, thinking of last night.

"It's only five thirty, but I had to wake you," he said as he rubbed his hands across her back. "Uncle Angus rang about twenty minutes ago."

Jenny pulled away, pulling the covers up to her neck at the sudden chill. For the first time, she noticed Andy's grave face and somber tone.

"Something's happened," she said. "Did they call? The hospital?"

"No, no. I rang soon as Uncle Angus hung up. Your dad is fine and Sarah is still coming home today." He held her face in his hands. "It's about Glen Ellen, Jenny. There was a fire up there last night."

She dug her fingers into his arms. Biddy under the tree in the storm flooded back. "How bad?"

"Half of the front of the house is gone, and—"

The early morning call of a bird close by was interrupted by the roar of a motorcycle tearing up Market Street.

Andy reached for the blanket at the foot of the bed and put it around her. "Biddy's dead."

Jenny's mouth opened and closed but no words came.

He picked up the mug and handed it to her. "Here, drink this else it'll get cold. Uncle Angus is coming over. Your clothes are on the chair there, all dried out. Can you eat something? A piece of toast?"

She shook her head almost gagging at the thought. Then, after gulping some tea, she snatched up her clothes and with the blanket around her ran into the bathroom.

She was at the table with Andy when Dr. Thorne arrived. His usual debonair appearance was gone. He had on a V-necked maroon sweater fraying at the cuffs, pulled over a shirt, unbuttoned at the neck. He hadn't combed his hair and it was the first time Jenny had seen him without one of his wild bow ties.

He scratched the bristle on his chin, making a scraping sound, then pulled out a chair. "Molly Duggan couldn't sleep," he said for Jenny's benefit. "She saw the flames and called the fire department. Half the downstairs is gutted as well as the room over the lounge, and the main staircase is gone altogether. Biddy kept most of the rooms closed. Good thing too. It helped contain the fire. By four o'clock they had it under control."

He picked up his mug of coffee. "Couldn't save Biddy though. They found her up against the kitchen door, petrol can clutched in her hand. It was the smoke."

While Andy made toast and poured coffee, Jenny told Dr. Thorne all that happened last night at Glen Ellen. The doctor buttered his toast while he listened, then scooped a spoonful of marmalade out of the jar. The man was made of iron. How could he eat with all this going on?

"God only knows what she was doing out there in the first place," Andy said. "It was a hell of a night."

His uncle wiped his hands on his napkin. "She finally went over the edge. It's a damn good thing Sarah wasn't there."

"I had the phone in my hand to call someone," Jenny said, her voice beginning to tremble. "Maybe if I had, we could have stopped her."

"I wouldn't start going down that road if I were you, Jenny. Who knows what she would have done." Dr. Thorne placed a piece of toast on her plate and pushed across the butter and the marmalade. "Eat this. Andy, give her a bowl of cereal and a banana if you've got one."

Jenny took a bite of the toast and swallowed hard trying to get it down. She finally made it when Andy poured her a glass of orange juice.

"Sarah doesn't need to know any of this yet," Andy said. "I'll go with you to bring her home. We'll get off the M-6 one exit earlier onto a back road, and we won't have to go past Glen Ellen."

Chapter Thirty-two

Bishop Fitzpatrick called at the hospital to see Charles, and at the same time brought a picture of the Madonna and Child for Sarah. Father Woodleigh was wan and pale but it was clear to the bishop that the priest was on the mend.

"Please, Charles," Vincent Fitzpatrick said, with a half-smile, "don't try to get up. I've come to wish you well and to deliver some news, something for you to mull over."

The bishop told him that even though most of St. Mary's parishioners wanted Father Woodleigh to remain as their priest, he himself had something else in mind. He had decided for Charles's own sake, as well as for the sake of his girls and the church, he was recommending that Father Woodleigh be moved to a church at the southern tip of Cornwall. "Seems a long way, I know," he said, "but I think you'll come to realize this is a fair proposition. The church I have in mind is near St. Ives, and I don't think I have to tell you how beautiful it is down there. In fact, I'm a Cornish boy myself, grew up not far from St. Ives. You aren't known there and if the question comes up, especially when the girls come to visit, which I hope and pray they will, people will be discreet enough not to question." He rubbed his hands and nodded as if to himself. "All in all, I think it's the best solution."

He got to his feet. "I hope you're not too disappointed."

Charles smiled. "I don't think I am. I think it's a wonderful idea, a perfect solution."

"Ah, I'm so glad. Now how'd it be if I get us a cup of coffee. There's a snack bar of sorts on the floor below. You take it black?"

"Yes, but let me go with you," Charles said. "The exercise will be good."

"You can lean on me," the bishop said. "We'll take the lift."

Jenny had bought Sarah a pale pink sweater with black skirt, black panty hose, and black suede sandals. Her hair had been washed that morning and Jenny clipped it with one of Lottie's barrettes, the pink one to match her sweater.

Sarah handed her the earrings. "Can you put these in for me, and can I have some of your lipstick? Will you put it on?"

Jenny inserted the earrings, and pulled out her pale lipstick. "OK," she said, "do like this with your lips."

Ever the diplomat, Andy came armed with two huge boxes of chocolates, one for Sarah's nurses and the other for those taking care of the priest. He told Jenny he'd get himself a cup of coffee in the cafeteria and join them in about ten minutes in their father's room. While Sarah said her goodbyes to everyone on her floor, Jenny bounded up the stairs. Back now in the room he'd had before, the priest sat by the window, his head down while he scribbled on a yellow legal pad propped on his knees.

She knocked softly on the open door, then walked toward him. "Writing your sermon?"

"This is the second one I've written today. Being a patient instead of a priest coming to visit has given me more compassion and insight into situations I could only imagine before." He tapped his temple with his fingers. "There are at least ten more sermons up here waiting to be written. Being in a new church, I want to make a good impression."

She pulled a chair up close to his. "After all you've gone through, it just doesn't seem fair that you have to move all the way to Cornwall. You won't know a soul down there."

He reached for her hand. "Meeting new people has never been a problem with me, Jenny, and Cornwall really isn't that far. This isn't the end for us, you know. It's just the beginning. Cornwall is one of England's loveliest counties. Wait'll you see it, and St. Ives is a little bit of heaven. You'll fall in love with it as much as you have with the Lakes."

Jenny studied his face. "You really mean that don't you?"

"Yes, I do. I'm not being thrown to the lions, Jenny. St. Peter's is a very beautiful church. Vincent brought six or seven pictures that I'll show you later. He and I, well, we've become friends since I first told him of my two beautiful daughters. He wants me to stay at St. Mary's at least another month, until I get my strength back. Father Doyle will assist me. I'm not leaving in disgrace. Most priests move on sooner or later."

"I know. I just want you to be happy." She glanced down at his notebook. "These sermons. Are we in any of them? Sarah and me?"

"You're all over them, although sometimes only I will know. You'll probably both drift in and out of my sermons as long as I'm a priest. I won't be hammering it home, but you'll be there."

She edged her chair closer, and as gently as she could, she told him about the fire and Biddy's death. "I still can't believe it," she said. "The Social Services wanted her out. We all did. But not like this."

Her father set his pad and ballpoint pen on the windowsill, then got to his feet. "I'm very, very sorry." He thrust his hands in the pockets of his paisley robe, as he paced, head down across the room. "Does Sarah know?"

"Not yet. Do you think we should wait a bit?"

Charles stood near the window and folded his arms. Jenny was giving him a chance to make fatherly decisions. "Feel her out on the way home. See how she reacts. You'll know what to do."

"I guess so," Jenny said. "She'll probably take it like she does everything else. Right on the shoulder. One good thing, the house is insured to the hilt and Dr. Thorne says it'll look good as new after the workmen get through. Sarah told me ages ago she doesn't want to live there any more, thinks it's too big. And it is. She said she's got her pictures to remind her of the good days with her parents."

"What will you do now?"

"Andy wants us to stay with him. His house is big. We talked about this way back when Sarah first went on dialysis."

Her father put his glasses back on. "Andy came to see me one afternoon, when he knew you'd gone shopping. We talked about you. He's a good man, Jenny."

Jenny leaned forward. "What did he say? Can you tell me?"

"Oh, I think it'll be better coming from him. But sitting there, listening to him, I couldn't help but be struck by the coincidence. You know, both of us being English, and both falling in love with American women."

"I've thought of that too," she said. "He's really been there for me. For us. I honestly don't know what I'd have done without him. He's downstairs now getting a cup of coffee, wanted to give us some time alone."

"Ada and Walter came yesterday," her father said. "Walter's talked Ada into selling Malone's. Said it'll be too much for her once they're married. It's going on the market soon. Sarah knows this. She talks about the shop a lot, said she wished it was hers."

Jenny whacked the arm of the chair. "Of course. Malone's." She got to her feet, and kissed his cheek. "What would we ever do without you."

His raised his hand and touched his face where she'd placed the kiss. "What did I do?"

Jenny laughed. "As if you didn't know. It's the answer to everything. Sarah's going to jump at this, and I think I know someone who'll jump at the chance to live there with her."

When Sarah came into the room, Jenny let their father tell Sarah the good news about Malone's while Jenny went into the hall to call Ada. Right there over the phone, the deal was struck. As she put the receiver back in its cradle, she patted it, and looked down the hospital hallway. She waved at the old lady shuffling along, and then smiled at Nurse Ramirez, the one she liked so much. Hospitals weren't so bad after all. Miracles were performed inside these walls.

When Andy arrived and they told him the news about Malone's, they talked about making renovations to the living quarters over the shop. All it needed was a kitchen upstairs as well as another bathroom to make it a self-contained flat. The kitchen and bathroom downstairs could use some fixing up too. And yes, they'd get in touch with Lottie, ask her over for tea, discuss things.

"Oh man," Sarah said in her best Jenny voice when they told her. "Oh man."

Charles watched from his window as Andy eased the car to the door while Jenny helped Sarah out of the obligatory wheelchair. They both stood beside the car and looked up at his window. Jenny waved and Sarah blew kisses, then while Andy placed Sarah's suitcase in the boot, Jenny fussed over her as she helped her into the car. Tears filled Charles's eyes. What had he done to deserve all this happiness at this time of his life? After the blue car disappeared in the throng of traffic, he closed his door and reached for his rosary, then got down on his knees beside his bed.

Sarah sat in the back while Andy drove a steady forty-five, chatting softly to Jenny in the seat beside him. He was careful, said he was watching out for potholes or bumps that might jar Sarah's incision. She leaned back in the seat and ran her hand across her abdomen to feel her father's sacred kidney. The pains in her legs were gone at last and except for a spell of sleepiness in the afternoon, she felt better than she had in a long time.

***

People came to visit at Andy's. Walter came with Ada, and Dr. Thorne came with his wife, Gladys, who'd at last returned from Provence. When it was quiet, with all the visitors gone, and even Andy in his garage, Jenny told her that Biddy had died in the fire at Glen Ellen.

Jenny sat beside her on the sofa. "Biddy was real sick, Sarah," she said. "Her mind was all mixed up."

"I know," Sarah said, as she measured Jenny's long fingers against her own.

"Those days are behind you now. Try to think only about the good days when you were happy with your folks. And don't worry, we won't go near the place until it's restored."

"You mean they can mend it?"

"Uh, huh. Thanks to Molly Duggan's insomnia, the fire crew got there fast. The house is insured to the hilt. We'll get someone to cut down the tree, and then maybe hire a gardener. After we get rid of all those weeds and get the grass mowed, it should look real nice."

"What about my cuckoo clock? And my photos. I've got hundreds. Have I lost them?"

"Your room was untouched," Jenny said. "The kitchen was filled with smoke and your poor old cuckoo took a beating. He's black as the ace of spades and doesn't pop out any more. But Andy says he can fix it. You know how good he is with clocks."

***

Not many people attended Biddy's funeral. Her body was cremated and Molly Duggan said the ashes were to be scattered over the hills. She told Jenny she'd wanted to flush them down the loo but if she did, wouldn't she forever be afraid to sit on it? Finally, her son promised to take them to the very north of the Lakes and not to breathe a word to anyone where he'd scattered them.

Chapter Thirty-three

The bell over Malone's door jingled as Andy pushed it open. He stood in the doorway, Pete at his side with a brand new psychedelic Frisbee in his mouth.

Hammering and banging were going on upstairs as well as at the back of the shop. Sarah sat on a chair by the cards, sorting through a new box, giggling as she read some of them before adding them to the rack. Lottie, who had moved into the shop a week ago, sat behind the counter, half-frames perched on the end of her nose, ledger open in front of her, a calculator beside it. One of the girls chatted up Spud Murphy whose pie van was parked outside, while the other sliced bacon for Nigel from the Bookworm.

For Andy it was now or never. Just that morning Jenny had surprised him when she'd said she and Sarah would move into the shop at the end of the week. Even though they had stayed at his house for over a month, he could count on one hand the minutes he'd spent alone with Jenny. She and Sarah had separate bedrooms, with the bathroom between them. Sarah though had insisted on leaving the doors open. He finally said as much to Sarah just yesterday, who rolled her eyes and said if he'd wanted to cuddle Jenny, he should have said something sooner. She could take a hint. It was while Jenny was in the shower, Sarah told him of the surprise she had for her sister.

Jenny appeared from behind the cake mixes and biscuits and joined Andy at the door. She bent down and held her face against Pete's. "How's it goin' boy? You been behaving yourself?"

Pete's answer was a low ecstatic rumble from the back of his throat.

She straightened up and smiled at Andy. "Aren't you coming in? We've got the kettle on."

Sarah's loud whisper from the card rack reached them. "Andy, for cryin' out loud," she said in her new American accent.

Jenny looked from him to Sarah and back again. "Am I missing something?"

"It's nothing," Andy said, giving Sarah one of those don't-you-dare-let-the-cat-out-of-the-bag looks.

"Can you get away?" he said to Jenny. "For a drive up into the hills?"

"Sure. Just give me a minute to change my shoes."

They walked for miles along one of the footpaths which were everywhere in the Lake District, Pete racing on ahead, then waiting for them to catch up. The highest peaks were now covered in snow and the slopes were shades of grey blending into purple. From the meadows came the familiar bleating of sheep, coats grown thick and woolly ready for the coming winter. As usual, Andy had brought his binoculars and as they sat on his rubber-backed blanket, they took turns watching a pair of peregrine falcons dart about while Pete chased after rabbits. When one dived down a hole, he stuck his nose in, his behind high in the air.

Jenny told Andy the rabbits in North Carolina didn't dig tunnels, but just froze and hoped for the best.

Andy lay on the grass while she stretched beside him, her face turned to his. "American rabbits aren't educated like the English ones," he said as he traced her jaw line with a piece of grass. "Our rabbits have warrens and little rooms and things under the ground where almost nothing can get them."

"So safe," Jenny said. "What a neat life, out of harm's way."

"Well, most of the time," Andy said. "Except for the ferret. He can wriggle down there but the rabbits always have more than one way out."

Jenny shuddered.

"What is it? Are you cold?"

"Some. Hope the weather picks up for Uncle Tim and Mary Louise. Can you believe it, Andy? After all that's happened, Uncle Tim coming here on his honeymoon, staying in the cottage?"

She looked up at the mountains, at the early snow on the highest peaks. It was the middle of October, time for the leaves in North Carolina to be turning red and gold, bringing tourists from all over flocking to the Smokies and the Blue Ridge. Those Indian Summer days in the South were hard to beat. Cool nights and soft golden days, so welcome after the stifling summer heat and so different from this wild, cold scene. Yet there was something exhilarating about this place that sharpened the senses, something about facing into the wind that cleared the brain and lifted the spirit.

"What are you going to do now, Jenny?" Andy asked. "That CIA look has gone from your face at last. You've found all your answers. Sarah's got the shop, your father's happier than he's ever been in his life, and there're already a couple of people interested in buying Glen Ellen."

"You mean am I staying here or going back to North Carolina?"

He put a hand over her mouth as if scared of her answer. "Not now," he said as he stood up, reached for her hand, and pulled her to her feet. "Come on, let's go to my house. Sarah's left something for you, a thank you she said."

At his front door, he made her cover her eyes with her hands then with an arm across her shoulders, he led her into the living room. "OK, you can open them now."

Propped up on the couch was the winter scene of Stoney Beck that had hung in the corridor at Craighead Hospital. Jenny ran her hand along the frame. "Oh man, Fred Fitzgerald's painting. How did Sarah get the hospital to part with it?"

"They only have a print. This is the original. Sarah said you liked it so she got it out of storage. She wants you to have it."

Jenny looked from him to Pete, who'd placed his Frisbee on the floor, cocked his head to one side, his face as expectant as Andy's. These two were obviously in cahoots.

"What's wrong, Andy? You look so serious."

"I am serious. I've given you more rain checks than you can stuff in your pocket but you still haven't given me a straight answer. Please, Jenny, I have to know. Are you going back home to Charlotte or are you going to marry me and stay here?"

She placed her hands on either side of his face. "I've been dropping hints all morning and if you hadn't said something, I would have. I thought you knew, that it showed. Yes, I'm going back to Charlotte. One day. But not without you. I'd like Sarah and Dad to come too. I want you all to see North Carolina. It's a beautiful place, Andy, and I guess I'll always love it. It's where my roots are. Still, when you get right down to it, it's people that count, and outside of Uncle Tim, all my family's here. This is my home now."

"You mean—"

"She means she wants you to kiss her," Sarah said suddenly appearing in the hall. "Kiss her, Andy. Go on and kiss her."

Andy laughed. "Well, OK, but only to please you."

His face grew serious as he opened his arms and Jenny walked into them

After the kiss Jenny held on tight, almost afraid to let go in case somehow he would disappear. But Andy only laughed and with one arm still around her, he held out his other to encompass Sarah.

Later, when they'd untangled themselves, Jenny ran her hand along the gilt carved frame, studied the painting of the little village in the grip of a white Christmas, then turned to Andy and studied the landscape of his face.

"How about grabbing one end of this," she said to him. "Let's see how it looks over the mantel."

END

CPSIA information can be obtained at www.ICGtesting.com
Printed in the USA
BVOW02s0852240713

326732BV00001B/4/P